PRAISE FOR *TOM HARRIS*

"An unusual, compelling, thought-provoking, remarkable novel."
—*Library Journal*

"Ingeniously and imaginatively perverse."
—Kenneth Burke, *American Scholar*

"Stefan Themerson has an absolutely elegant sense of humor."
—Albert Goldman, *New York Times*

"This book is not only a mystery and an entertainment—it is a fascinating puzzle."
—*Christian Science Monitor*

OTHER WORKS BY STEFAN THEMERSON IN ENGLISH

NOVELS
Bayamus
Cardinal Pölätüo
General Piesc
Hobson's Island
The Mystery of the Sardine
Professor Mmaa's Lecture
Special Branch
Wooff Wooff, or Who Killed Richard Wagner?

CHILDREN'S BOOKS
The Adventures of Peddy Bottom
Mr. Rouse Builds His House

POETRY
Collected Poems

OTHER PROSE
Aesop, the Eagle & the Fox & the Fox & the Eagle
Apollinaire's Lyrical Ideograms
The Chair of Decency
factor T
Jankel Adler
Kurt Schwitters in England
Logic, Labels & Flesh
On Semantic Poetry
Semantic Divertissements
St. Francis and the Wolf of Gubbio
The Urge to Create Visions

Tom Harris

a novel by
Stefan Themerson

Introduction by Nicholas Wadley

Dalkey Archive Press
Normal · London

First published in the UK by Gaberbocchus Press Ltd., 1967
First American edition published by Knopf, 1968

Library of Congress Cataloging-in-Publication Data

Themerson, Stefan, 1910-1988.
 Tom Harris / by Stefan Themerson ; introduction by Nicholas Wadley.— 1st
Dalkey Archive ed.
  p. cm.
 ISBN 1-56478-371-5 (alk. paper)
 1. Identity (Psychology)—Fiction. 2. London (England)—Fiction. 3. Criminals—
Fiction. I. Title.

PR6039.H37T66 2004
823'.914—dc22

2004052733

Partially funded by grants from the Lannan Foundation, the Illinois Arts Council,
a state agency, and the National Endowment for the Arts, a federal agency.

Dalkey Archive Press is a nonprofit organization located in Milner Library at
Illinois State University and distributed in the UK by
Turnaround Publisher Services Ltd. (London).

www.centerforbookculture.org

CONTENTS

PART / TWO

INTRODUCTION:
ON STEFAN THEMERSON

There cannot be many philosopher-novelists who started their careers as visual artists. But it was part of Stefan Themerson's philosophy to defy categories. He made films; he ran a publishing house. As well as his nine novels, he wrote stories for children, poems, a play, an opera and essays on philosophy, language, logic, literature, science, art, film, and typography. Until his death in September 1988, he also spent spare moments making drawings: abstract, coloured configurations in which lines, points and planes are bent into paradox, satirising their own logic. The sum of this prodigal diet of interrelated activities reveals itself now as concentration, justifying his fundamental belief that the effect of respecting boundaries or classifications—whether cultural, professional or political—is at least inhibiting, and usually negative.

The first experience to fire his imagination was discovering the magic of the camera. Drifting out of his studies in physics and architecture in the late 1920s in Warsaw, he started to improvise with photograms, collages, and various combinations of the two. Subsequently, he made seven experimental films—five in Warsaw and two in London—in collaboration with his wife, the painter Franciszka Themerson (who also died in 1988, two months before him).

Themerson later wrote that these films were a form of collage, free of symbolism. He recalled Moholy Nagy's reaction to the most ambitious of them, *Europa*, when he saw it in London in 1936. Nagy called it 'a sophisticated film,' about which Themerson said:

> I was too young then to tell him that he was wrong. That the film was primitive . . . Primitive people would have taken it as it was meant to be taken. Would have seen it as it was shown. Without further inter-polation.[1]

He referred to his first films as 'photograms in motion' and he likened their syntax both to the concentration of poems and to the rhythmical patterns of music. He insisted on their autonomy:

> It is something unique.
> It is a photogram.
> It doesn't represent anything.
> It doesn't abstract from anything.
> It is just what it is.
> It is reality itself.[2]

Four of the five Warsaw films did not survive the war. And none of those that did survive allows us close enough to the free, lyrical attributes that he prized so much in the medium, to properly evaluate his achievement as a filmmaker. *Adventures of a Good Citizen* (1937, Warsaw), while it is a shrewd satirical fantasy, full of autograph poetic qualities and morals, is nevertheless uncharacteristic of his Polish films as he described them. Unlike the lost films, it has a clear narrative sequence and it has a spoken soundtrack.

Of the two films that the Themersons made together in London, *Calling Mr Smith* (1943) is an explicit protest—moral, not nationalistic—against the systematic destruction of Polish culture by the Nazis (outspoken enough to be refused by the British censor). *The Eye and the Ear* (1944) is an imaginative improvisation with abstract forms, representing the interaction of musical sounds.

Of all their films, Themerson saw *Europa* (1932) as their major achievement. It was a visualisation of Anatol Stern's futurist poem and was highly praised by Stern himself. The few frames that survive can only hint at the fluid visual sequences that he described. However, the qualities that he valued in film as a medium, especially the free association of images that refer to nothing outside themselves, are clearly recognisable in most of his work as a writer. The initiative behind his concern with semantics was to free words of confusing sentimental or literary references, and, as with the photograms, to expose their own incontrovertible identity. The autograph character of his later novels is of several simultaneous currents of narrative and thought that may appear only obliquely related and that, together, create their own cumulative reality and sense. His whole œuvre as a writer is like that: a continuous collage, its parts distinct but full of allusive echoes and repetitions.

*   *   *

In the winter of 1937–38, the Themersons moved from Warsaw to Paris, intending to live and work there. 'There was no sense of escaping from Warsaw,' Stefan told me, 'I simply knew I had to be in Paris.' It was 'a sort of Mecca'; one which realised all of his expectations. But his plans were disrupted by the course of the war and by 1942 he found himself in London, where he and Franciszka spent the rest of their lives.

Themerson wrote in the three languages of the countries in which he successively found himself. That the majority of his writing was in English is a matter of the vagaries of history.

When asked why he chose to write in English, he replied that the language chose him.[3] During the war he experienced the loss, disorientation and cultural negation that was the lot of his generation. As well as his first four films, the (Polish) manuscript of his first novel also disappeared. But his reaction to the force of events was more positive than simply stoical. He upheld unequivocally a concept of the writer carrying his culture with him and he believed creeds of nationalism and patriotism to be actively dangerous:

> Writers are never, writers are nowhere in exile, for they carry within themselves their own kingdom, or republic, or city of refuge, or whatever it is that they carry within themselves.
>
> And at the same time, every writer, ever, everywhere, is in exile, because he is squeezed out of the kingdom, or republic, or city, or whatever it is that squeezes itself dry.[4]

As a teenager in his native town of Plock, he already saw English and French literature as major elements of his indigenous cultural world. Nevertheless, up to a point, his writing in each of the three languages—Polish, French, English—appears to have different characteristics or points of focus. Apart from articles, principally about film, most of his pre-war Polish writing consists of stories for children. In France he wrote poems and the prose-poems, *Croquis dans les ténèbres,* and he mused to me once about how different his writing might have been had he stayed in Paris: might it have remained as lyrical as the *Croquis?* There is no doubt that much of the imagery of the *Croquis* appears quite distinct from his English writing, more oblique and submerged. In Barbara Wright's translation, the poetic mirror-image of poet and angel on each side of the window-pane, with its evocative inversions of interior and exterior, of the emptiness of matter and the 'hardness' of abstraction, is a case in point. The angel looks 'outside from

the exterior,' a paradox he emphasised typographically. Both
the poet and the angel lose their sense of balance as they approach the world of the other. Even in the poems written in
England, we seldom find this sort of imagery, and the poems
are only a small part of his English *œuvre*. It was in London
that he embarked upon his theoretical writings on philosophy
and language.

In other respects, these apparent differences of place are mis-
leading. The early 'English' novels (*Bayamus, Professor Mmaa,
Cardinal Pölätüo*) were written originally in Polish, and *Bayamus*
was first published in instalments in *Nowa Polska*, 1946. They
read now as the bedrock of his English writing and there is a remarkable homogeneity—in means as well as content—through-
out his *œuvre*, whatever the medium or language.

He was absorbed by language, fastidious as well as idiosyn-
cratic in its usage. His meticulous and sometimes eccentric use
of punctuation, for instance, often plays an important role in
the repetitive structures of his writing. He wrote extensively on
aesthetics, semantics and typography. His writing on the art of
Kurt Schwitters is essentially about meaning contained in the
uses of language, as is his revealing essay *Apollinaire's Lyrical
Ideograms* (1968). Set beside such concerns, the question of
the language in which he wrote appears a secondary issue. And
he almost never pursued his interests in language for their own
sake. The short novel *Wooff Wooff, or Who Killed Richard
Wagner?* (1951) might appear at first reading like a semantic
diversion, but in reality is as cautionary a tale as anything he
wrote. Elsewhere, in discussing the value of linguistic philosophy, he went out of his way to dissociate himself from those
obsessed with language *per se*. He wrote, of 'the academic
Goddess of Ethics,' that

> she is only interested in herself. I am interested in ethical be-
> haviour, but she is interested in ethical terminology. For the last

eighty years she's been sharpening her linguistic tools, but she thinks it would be unladylike to use them.[5]

He came to feel at home with the English language remarkably quickly. He took English lessons while stranded in France, 1940–42, and again when he arrived in London, and in 1946 he published his first article in English, in *Polemic*. He often spoke of the dual properties peculiar to English: its exactness and its crystalline shades of meaning—the latter a quality that he alternately relished and mistrusted.

Feeling at home with England and reading its social codes was another matter. He once talked to me about cultural differences between Poland, France and England:

> In Poland when you met someone, their instinct was to doubt your values or worth. You had to prove them. Friendships were hard-won. In Paris, you were accepted as a friend until and unless you did something to lose that status. In London, of course, it's different, neither one nor the other. There's this objectivity and you sometimes don't find out if you are a friend until long afterwards.

He was to remain as detached from the British literary establishment as when he arrived. He did not fit into established groups; he was not even an *emigré* academic. As Anthony Burgess once complained, 'there's a strange idea in this country that you can't be both a composer and a writer,' and Themerson was both of these things and others besides. But these were circumstances he observed with sardonic amusement. He valued his independence and anyway, in art as in life, he despised synthetic categories. During the 1950s and 1960s, he submitted a number of poems to the *Times Literary Supplement* but none were accepted. To prove a hunch to himself, he sent to the editor yet another poem, '*My childhood . . .* ,' as a translation, over the signature Tomasz Woydyslawski. It was published (on 5 March 1964)—and identified as Themerson's work by friends.

*   *   *

It was a wish for independence as much as anything else that motivated the Themersons' decision in 1948 to found their own publishing house in Maida Vale, the Gaberbocchus Press: to be free to publish what they wanted and in what form they wanted. The earlier Gaberbocchus books were printed at their home in Randolph Avenue. Subsequently, they acquired premises in Formosa Street and at that point, the Themersons were joined by two other directors, Barbara Wright and Gwen Barnard. The full list of Gaberbocchus titles demonstrates the imaginative character of their publications, including Barbara Wright's first English translations of Jarry, Queneau, Pol-Dives and others. What a list cannot do is express the originality of format, typography and design that rapidly became a Gaberbocchus hallmark. Franciszka Themerson was the art director and she illustrated many of the books, but they worked together in the same close collaboration as on their films, to produce what they described as 'best-lookers' rather than best-sellers. Asked in a questionnaire what were the Press's main strength and weakness, Themerson gave the same answer to each question: 'refusal to conform.'[6] The 'unclassifiability' of Gaberbocchus Press expresses the essential Stefan Themerson.

As an offshoot of the Press, the Gaberbocchus Common Room was opened in Formosa Street, to provide 'a congenial place where artists and scientists and people interested in science and art can meet and exchange thoughts.' Themerson's concern was again with the dissolution of obsolete boundaries. In 1946, he had edited five issues of *Nowa Polska* on 'Literature, Art and Science in England' and by the later 1950s, had become increasingly interested in exposing the common philosophies of art and science. He corresponded at the time with C. P. Snow. For two years, from 1957 to 1959, the Common Room was a vital, informal weekly forum with a membership of more than a hundred. The members were addressed by writers, painters, poets, actors, scientists, musicians, film-makers, philosophers. There were talks on physics, metaphysics and pataphysics; readings of Jarry, Shakespeare, Beckett, Strindberg, Queneau and Schwitters; performances of modern music and scientific film. Among other contributors, Sean Connery and Bernard Bresslaw read O'Neill; Dudley Moore accompanied Michael Horovitz's poetry reading; Konni Zilliacus spoke on the immorality of nuclear weapons. The project was only reluctantly abandoned because it consumed too much working time. In such a catalogue lies at least part of the reason why, as a writer and publisher, Themerson was not embraced by the establishment.[7]

In the 1940s and 1950s, his circle of significant friends included writers, artists, scientists and philosophers, some of whom he had known in Warsaw or Paris. He enjoyed close friendships with Kurt Schwitters and Jankel Adler, both of whom he published. In 1950 Bertrand Russell wrote in warm praise of *Bayamus* (1949), 'nearly as mad as the world'. Their long correspondence and exchange of manuscripts, bantering criticism and thoughts on philosophy and the world at large began early in 1952 and continued until Russell's death. The original draft of *factor T* (1956) was written as a long letter to Russell. Russell wrote the preface to *Professor Mmaa's Lecture* (1953) and Gaberbocchus published Russell's *Good Citizen's Alphabet* (1953) and *History of the World in Epitome* (1962), both with Franciszka Themerson's illustrations which, Russell said, 'heighten all the points I most wanted made.'[8]

As well as becoming deeply involved in Russell's principles and methods as a philosopher, Themerson appears to have drawn strength from his scale of human values. Although he later felt reservations about Russell's total commitment to CND—it was too much like one of the burning 'aims' by which Themerson felt the native instincts of individuals were led astray—he shared Russell's doubts about faith in a good society. 'A good *society*' inspired less hope for the future than 'good people.'

* * *

Russell's supportive appreciation also seems to have encouraged Themerson's pursuit of semantics as a major interest. But, if any single factor bore significant influence upon this area of his activity as a writer, it was the earlier encounter with Kurt Schwitters, in wartime London. Themerson heard Schwitters perform his sound-poems on several occasions and was the first to publish Schwitters' English writing. He gave many talks on Schwitters—the earliest in the Gaberbocchus Common Room in the 1950s—and his notes for these talks include his most sensitive and eloquent thoughts on anyone else's work. As well as his justly celebrated essay *Kurt Schwitters in England* (1958), he published 'Kurt Schwitters on a Time-Chart' (1967) and *Pin* (1962), the polemical manifesto of new poetry that Schwitters was compiling with Raoul Hausmann shortly before his death in 1947. The choice of title for Themerson's 'Semantic Sonata' (written 1949–50; published in *factor T*, 1956) may be seen as some sort of homage to Schwitters' *Ursonata*. Furthermore, the initiative behind his concept of 'Semantic Poetry' sprang from a polemical wish to purify language that strikes very comparable attitudes to those advanced in *Pin*. In *Bayamus*, the narrator explains to the audience at the Theatre of Semantic Poetry, 'each of the S.P. words should have one and only one meaning.'[9] In a radio talk in Warsaw, 1964, Themerson elaborated:

> Semantic Poetry doesn't arrange verses into bunches of flowers. It bares a poem and shows the reality behind it. There is no room for hypnosis in a semantic poem.[10]

And finally, in introductory notes for a reading of the 1970s, which are themselves full of bravura verbal bouquets, he wrote more on his rebellion against 'linguistic harmonics.'

> I wanted to strip words of their associations, to cut their links with the past. This rebellion was anti-romantic and anti-ecstatic. It was directed both against political rhetoricians and against Joycean avant-coureurs. Against associational thickets of Eliot and the verboidal surrealisms of History. I wanted to disinfect words, scrub them right to the very bone of their dictionary definitions. That was how—somewhat ferociously and sardonically—I invented Semantic Poetry. It was meant to be funny. Both serious & funny. It became the subject of my novel Bayamus.[11]

* * *

In some respects it is inappropriate to consider Themerson's novels separately, so closely is all of his writing interrelated. There are several instances in which Themerson brought together plots and structures from very different writings to create a new work. The opera *St Francis and the Wolf of Gubbio* (1972, written 1954–60) was born from the text of *Semantic Divertissements* (1962, written 1949–50) and a paragraph in *factor T* (1956).

He viewed the novel as one of several vehicles available for his current concerns. In 1952, having read the manuscript of *Cardinal Pölätüo* (1961), Russell wrote to Themerson suggesting alterations, because 'I think you have tried to combine into one book things which do not readily fit together.'[12] But Themerson never saw this as a problem, and in any case he saw most of his novels as each having its own distinct philosophical or linguistic subject. He deliberately chose to treat philosophical subjects in novels because of the freedom that the genre offers:

> Fiction allows you to do things that history or treatises can't—especially in the sense that you can rescue or retrieve meanings that are lost from generation to generation. These time barriers are harder to cross than geographical barriers.

He was genuinely concerned that the ideas of any one time should not be lost to another generation of readers. (He discussed the publishing policy of Gaberbocchus in these terms.) Themerson's natural ability to treat matters of gravity with apparent levity comes to the fore in the allusive style of his novels. (As one reviewer saw it, 'Death and philosophy have rarely been so much fun.'[13])

Of the longer novels, *Professor Mmaa's Lecture* (1953) is the earliest. The original Polish version was mostly written at the same time as *Croquis dans les ténèbres*, from 1941 to 1942 during the eighteen months or so that he was stranded in Voiron, in the 'free zone' of France, and then finished in Scotland in 1943. In his preface to the book, Russell likens its form of satirical allegory to Swift. The follies of human conduct are observed with guileless candour by a society of sightless termites. They observe by their highly developed sense of smell and they learn through their digestive systems. It is an exposé of human conformism in face of 'progress' and absolute government.

Themerson wrote *Bayamus* (the first novel to be published, in 1949) to launch his invention of Semantic Poetry. The poet-narrator is aided and abetted in propagating his new art by the mercurial, three-legged Bayamus, with all the fugitive wisdom of a Shakespearian fool.

In the later long novels like *Tom Harris* (1967), *The Mystery of the Sardine* (1986) and *Hobson's Island* (1988), he approached the genre differently, flirting openly with the form of the modern thriller. (He read a lot of detective fiction and had particular respect for Chandler.) Within that seductive idiom, he played many concurrent games. Usually there is a large cast of characters:

Sometimes it is like a party. Many people meet each other there. No special reason why they should meet, but just to give a picture of life. Otherwise, it seems somehow—provincial.[14]

The characters bring with them an equally large cast of ideas, arguing and discussing, as at a party, whatever concerns them (him). Burning political issues mingle with discussions of social mores, realities with dreams, the dramatic with the mundane. There is a lot of sensible pragmatism. 'If a young man becomes depressed by reading Samuel Beckett,' one character declares, 'that very fact proves that he's perfectly sane.'[15] Faced with the implausibly spectacular circumstances of the early plot of *Hobson's Island*, a perplexed secretary at the Vatican asks over the phone, 'please tell me straight: is this meant to be a parable or is it on the level?'[16]

The Mystery of the Sardine (1986) and *Hobson's Island* (1988) form, with *Cardinal Pölätüo* and *General Piesc* (1976), a sort of family saga, their plots enacted by successive generations, with several characters reappearing. In the cast of *The Mystery of the Sardine*, General Piesc—who does not in person appear in the novel because he is dead—is listed as 'absent.'

Themerson wrote *Hobson's Island* with the knowledge that it would be his last book and it is not difficult to read it as a final work. In turn, it is the most spectacularly dramatic and the most introspective of all of his novels. The isolated simplicity of life of the Hobson's islanders is set on collision course with the overwrought values and conduct of the outside world. The conclusion is a *tour de force*, both tragic and contemplative. At the end, the narrator (Scan D'Earth) levitates above the island, surveying those actors that survive from the theatre of a life's work.

For all the diverse riches of their discourse in mortal and immortal values, there is nothing in these later novels without a calculated role in their elaborate jigsaws of logic, paradox and morality. Extravagant and comic images always refresh meaning and are crafted into the structure as meticulously as the elegant clarity of the language. The lurking love of paradox is only allowed to run loose in an occasional 'wild card' character. One of the things Themerson enjoyed in detective stories of the 1930s and 1940s was their characteristically irrational element, the character from nowhere. The surreal role of the man from Mars in *The Mystery of the Sardine* or the enigma of Nemo in *Hobson's Island* are comparable devices.

*　　*　　*

The moral principles that underlie all of Themerson's work were first clearly set out in the essay *factor T* (1956). This essay exposes the 'Tragic factor'—a fatal flaw in the human condition. It is the product of a discrepancy between man's Dislikes (D) and his Needs (N). Themerson's first analogy is about members of a tribe and their Need and Dislike for tomatoes. They have a vital, biological Need of tomatoes as their only local source of vitamin C. However, since the eating of tomatoes is forbidden by their religion, the tribesmen have developed an equally vital Dislike of the taste. Hence, 'factor T.'

Later on, he examines the example of 'killing':

> I do not know about weasels, but it is difficult to imagine two anthropoid apes that would kill each other, or steal from each other, unless they happened to be unanimous. They have to be unanimous in their desire for one and the same female, or for one and the same coconut, if they are to fight. And even then their dislike for killing and stealing must be great if they feel compelled (as soon as they develop a language) to invent some lofty reasons for this unpleasant behaviour, and thus build philosophical systems, religions and police forces.

xix

We invent our god to exculpate us when we find it necessary to perform the unpleasant act of killing those who invent their god when they find it necessary to perform the unpleasant task of killing us. And we invented the police force, not only to *prevent* others from killing us when they find it necessary, but also to *force* ourselves to kill the others whenever this act, which we dislike, is found necessary for us.

There is a tragic discrepancy between our dislike of killing and the necessity of doing so. I call that discrepancy *factor T*, and it seems to me neither virtuous nor wise to ignore it.[17]

And again:

Certain vital needs of our guts (N) cannot be satisfied without affecting our nervous system in a certain way (D). The resulting state of perplexity (T) is basically unavoidable.[18]

He successively investigates the inability of philosophy, religion and science to deal with the problem, suggesting at one point:

It seems to me a pity that rational ethics underestimates our need to know that our original Tragedy is at least recognised. Rational ethics concentrates either on Dislike or on Necessity, but refuses to face the Tragedy that is imbedded in the situation. And this is why we are compelled to think rational speculation utopian or sentimental when it emphasises Dislike; materialistic or fascist when it emphasises Necessity; opportunist when it switches from one to the other; hypocritical when it preaches D and kills for its N, and donnish when it studies our N and leaves D to believers.[19]

Just as elsewhere he suggests that the novelist may have more to say on morality than the computer scientist,[20] so here he proposes literature as the only fruitful field of research into the tragic dilemma, because without it 'we shall never know what it is that has been built up . . . in our brains.'[21]

He concludes:

> I propose to call 'Man' anything (a beast, a plant, or a machine) whose nervous system is split into two parts so that one part prompts it to perform actions leading to the satisfaction of its primary needs while the other part restrains it from performing such actions whenever they are (as they invariably are) to the detriment of other organisms—thus producing a neural tension which results in its building gothic cathedrals, chinese pagodas, houses of parliament, bull rings, Royal Societies, revolutions, counter-revolutions, heavenly kingdoms, Stratford-on-Avons, in short, anything uneatable and uninhabitable, even if it doesn't amount to more than an aspirin tablet of hypocrisy.

> I propose not to call 'Man' things (whatever their anatomy) whose nervous systems, free of the split, allows them to do without hesitation the necessary pillage in the woods of the world.

> The study of the split is a pleasure. Yet, if our scientific research goes so far as to make us able to meddle with it, the pleasure will become a danger. Because, if the split is what makes a thing a 'Man,' then mending it would be synonymous with the extinction of human kind.[22]

Towards the end of his life, Themerson returned to the subject in another essay, *The Chair of Decency*, given as the Huizinga Lecture at the University of Leyden, 1981. Using a generous repertoire of allegory and fable, he set out a sustained argument for a return to basic human values. He suggests that the self-conscious aims and missions of the modern world have deluded us into losing sight of the intuitive decent values in our behaviour towards each other that we are born with. Aims are cultural, he says, but the proper Means are biological. The highest of our natural human instincts have been discarded in the misguided and blinkered pursuit of beliefs and causes:

> no Aim is so exalted that it be worth a heartbeat more than Decency of Means. Because, when all is said and done, Decency of Means is the Aim of aims.[23]

Looking backwards from this declamatory manifesto of his philosophy, we may see different faces of the same thought in almost everything else he wrote. The Polish stories for children address themselves to questioning the real world—the practical experience of daily life, human values, the ambiguities of language—with no suspicion of condescension or cultural improvement. The lyrical parable of the film *Adventures of a Good Citizen* champions the liberating experience of walking backwards, in face of conventional prejudice.

The ironic meaning of Themerson's 1949 version of Aesop's *The Eagle and the Fox* was so coolly stated that it went unobserved by any reviewer. After the original rendering, he repeats the whole fable, word for word, except that the two protagonists exchange roles. At the end, he appended this moral, tongue scarcely moving in cheek:

> These two fables are a warning to us not to deal hardly or injuriously by somebody who can defend himself by dealing hardly or injuriously with us. There are many less subtle and imperious creatures which we can eat in peace, and to the Glory of God.[24]

Quite apart from the stories for children, there are several instances of a fable-like use of non-human characters. There are the termites in *Professor Mmaa's Lecture*, and in the tragi-comic opera *St Francis and the Wolf of Gubbio* (1972), the hero is confronted with the modern dilemma of survival by the wolf, who runs a factory canning lamb chops. ('God gave me a carnivorous stomach,' the wolf argues, 'God must help me fill it.')[25]

Time and again, we see characters in Themerson's novels possessed by and then growing out of the consuming ambitions of their time. The accumulated wisdom of these characters in their old age reflects Themerson's own growing certainty about the relative value of Means and Aims. Dame Victoria, surrounded by young political zealots in *The Mystery of the Sardine*, says in her dying speech:

> I'm so thankful that I don't understand about Ideas. I'm thankful that when I was a young girl I wasn't educated to have Ideas.[26]

The sub-title of *General Piesc* (1976) is 'The Case of the Forgotten Mission.' When the ageing general is at last in a position to realise his lifelong mission, its reality dissolves and he no longer remembers what it is. Instead, he spends his last days in a tender relationship with a fellow-being (from which union is born Ian Prentice, the prodigious critic of Euclid in *The Mystery of the Sardine*). And all of this without trace of sentiment. It is another child of General Piesc, the ubiquitous Princess Zuppa, who voices one of the final statements on the theme of decency, towards the end of *Hobson's Island*:

> 'Beware of love. Love is cruel, and decency is gentle. Love is ugly and decency is beautiful. Love is easy and decency is difficult. Love creates hate.'

'But what does decency create?' she is asked.

> 'Alas Mrs Shepherd, decency creates love, and that's our human vicious circle.'[27]

Stefan Themerson's writings methodically expose religion, politics, patriotism, power, success and love as equally unerring paths towards inhuman behaviour. Stated so baldly, this seems an unreasonably bleak account of his work, against the grain of his own affirmative openness and belying his wit, humour and lightness of touch. Nevertheless, the stark events at the conclusion of his last novel appear to hold out little hope for the struggle between Means and Aims. When I told him of my reaction to this tragic finale, he expressed genuine surprise. For him, the same tragedy is present in most of his writing. 'It just brings us back to square one', he said. 'It simply reminds us that the choice is ours.'

Nicholas Wadley
1990, 2004

NOTES

Any uncredited quotations of Stefan Themerson are from his conversations with the author.

1 Stefan Themerson, *The Urge to Create Visions* (London and Amsterdam: Gaberbocchus and De Harmonie, 1983), p. 61.
2 *Ibid.*, p. 57.
3 C. H. Sisson, 'News & Notes', *P.N. Review* 15:3 (1988), p. 4.
4 Unpublished letter to the 'Committee for Writers in Exile' of *Pen International*, London, 29 January 1951.
5 Stefan Themerson, *The Chair of Decency* (Amsterdam: Athenaeum and Polak & Van Gennep, 1982), pp. 21–2.
6 Audrey and Philip Ward, *The Small Publisher* (Cambridge: Oleander Press, 1979), p. 187.
7 In 1962, Gwen Barnard ordered three Gaberbocchus books (Héafod's *Gimani*, a Themerson novel and *Kurt Schwitters in England*) at Hampstead Public Libraries. The Chief Librarian wrote back to

her: 'I have had an opportunity of examining these books and they are, in my view, of such bizarre nature that they are likely to add little to the Library's resources. I do not, therefore, propose to add these volumes to stock' (letter, 17 December 1962).

8 *Autobiography of Bertrand Russell*, 1944–1967 (London: Allen & Unwin, 1969) p. 38.

9 Stefan Themerson, *Bayamus* (London: Poetry London, 1949), p. 64.

10 'Before publication', Polskie Radio, Warsaw, 2 April 1964.

11 Unpublished notes.

12 Unpublished letter, 18 July 1952.

13 Will Blythe, *New York Times Book Review*, 29 December 1986.

14 Quoted in Hugh Hebert, 'As Mad as the World', *The Guardian*, 7 February 1987.

15 Stefan Themerson, *Hobson's Island* (London: Faber & Faber, 1988), p. 56.

16 *Ibid.*, p. 77.

17 Stefan Themerson, *factor T* (London: Gaberbocchus, 1956), pp. 6–7.

18 *Ibid.*, p. 27.

19 *Ibid.*, pp. 11–12.

20 In 'Oh God' (autobiographical fragment III, 1988). See p. 250.

21 *factor T*, p. 27.

22 *Ibid.*, p. 28.

23 *The Chair of Decency*, p. 15.

24 Aesop, *the Eagle & the Fox & the Fox & the Eagle* (London: Gaberbocchus, 1949), p. 33.

25 Stefan Themerson, *St Francis and the Wolf of Gubbio* (London: Gaberbocchus, 1972), p. 69.

26 Stefan Themerson, *The Mystery of the Sardine* (London: Faber & Faber, 1986), p. 39.

27 *Hobson's Island*, p. 153.

Tom Harris

PART ONE

He was to be interrogated at ten o'clock in the morning. I knew that. And so at 10.30 I stood on the pavement, opposite Paddington police station, and waited. A circus elephant was passing slowly from Paddington Green towards Bishops Bridge. Yet, to me at least, it seemed that a man who stands idly in Harrow Road, as I did, becomes after a few minutes more conspicuous than an elephant and a clown and a trumpeter parading through the traffic. Not knowing what to do with myself, I tried to read the few square feet of the portrait of Queen Victoria, displayed in the printer's window, just opposite the police station. I was literally reading it, as the Queen's features in it were composed not of lines but of engraved words, 173,000 words describing the history of her reign; it had taken a Mr D. Israel, the author, four years and seven months to execute the portrait. The time seemed to me as long. It was five minutes past twelve when Tom Harris appeared in the doorway.

For a moment he looked like a man who has just woken up and doesn't yet know very well where he is. He looked to the right and left, he hesitated, turned, took a few steps, stopped, and then crossed on to my side of the road. He glanced at a theatrical poster displayed in the window of a glass-cutter's shop, turned left and started walking in the direction of Edgware Road. In the meantime, two men in civilian clothes came out of the door under the blue lamp, turned, and went the same way. That was how our strange dance across London began. The weather was fine, the country was free. Tom Harris was free to go wherever he wanted. They were free to walk behind him. And I was free to follow them as I pleased.

At the corner of Edgware Road, I thought he would turn to the left and go towards Bell Street, where I knew he lived. Yet he went straight on, till, in the middle of the road, the traffic lights arrested us all; when we set off again we crossed the other half of the road amicably all together—but then resumed our marching in a file. In Seymour Street he hesitated, turned back, retraced his steps as if he had changed his plans, then turned back again, and we all four had to pass each other twice as if in a strange silent ballet. I didn't know if he knew that he was being followed, or if he cared. Neither did I know if the two policemen were aware of my being there behind them, or if they would care if they did. It didn't occur to me either that there might be still somebody else there, following me as well.

When we came to Trafalgar Square, I felt sure that I could guess what he was going to do. And as we arrived at Charing Cross station, I had no more doubts. I knew the name of the little place for which he would buy a ticket.

We still had some twenty minutes till the departure of the train. He went to the buffet and bought himself a glass of beer and a sausage roll. So did the two policemen. And so did I. Two skinny, sombre-looking men were standing at the entrance eating some sort of snacks which they had taken out of their pockets. There was something sinister about them. But, it may be that in their eyes there was something sinister about us.

When the train arrived at C. and we found ourselves in the square in front of the little station, it became obvious

4

that the place was not at all familiar to him. I could have told him that he ought to cross under the railway bridge first, and then go all around the village green where white clothed people were playing a slow-motion game of cricket,—but it wasn't my business to precipitate the course of events. Especially as I didn't know what sort of instructions the detectives had received. Was their task to follow him and see what he would do? Had they been told to let him go where he wanted but to keep an eye on him so that he couldn't bolt? or—were they waiting for a trumped-up excuse to arrest him, so that they could keep him in custody without actually charging him with murder? What else were they there for? Plain routine work? Or, perhaps, to protect him. From whom? I looked round but saw nobody in particular. Not a trace of the two men who had been eating their snacks at Charing Cross station. But, of course, the negative evidence of our senses proves nothing.

And then something extraordinary occurred. The cricket ball crossed the sky in a perfect parabola and hit a pigeon. It was so unexpected, so incongruous, that the whole world halted for a moment and people gasped, their mouths wide open. Let some freudians make such conjectures as may please them. I don't care. The inexplicable fact remains: At that precise moment it occurred to me that *I* was the one from whom the police were trying to protect Tom Harris. The thought seemed to me so funny that I laughed. And mine was the only laughter to be heard in the awesome silence of the field. Those who thought I was laughing at the poor, heroic and dead pigeon, or at them?, seemed to be shocked and looked at me with contempt. I was glad when we resumed our journey and were out of their sight.

The house felt secluded though there were no more than a few trees by the road and only a very short path among the flower-beds between the front door and the gate in the fence.

The garden and orchard were on the other side of the house stretching away towards the greenhouses and the fields beyond. People say at times that the picture of somebody they used to know is engraved on their memory. That is not a very happy expression. An engraving may get old and yellow but it does not alter, while the face in the picture we remember changes as time passes. So does the face of the model. And the two faces change not in the same way. The face that lives in one's memory loses a number of traces, its surface becomes smooth as if a Cranach or a photographer were retouching it patiently over and over again. The real face, on the contrary, gains, grows more and more details, each passing year adds to it a little wrinkle, a fold, a grey hair, a new, unpredicted expression. When Tom Harris had pressed the button, a woman's face appeared in the window and, seeing who it was, withdrew with a sudden jerk and disappeared. At that short moment, the smooth picture of her face which I had kept in my memory suddenly became all distorted and wrinkling like a reflection on the surface of a lake when somewhere far away a paddle-steamer shoves off.

Tom Harris stood at the front door, the two policemen at the gate, I behind a tree. He pressed the button once more and, when nothing in the house seemed to have moved, he did it again and again till the bell kept ringing continuously; in the still air it sounded as if a number of alarm clocks had suddenly gone off among the flower-beds, on the tree tops, in the swallow's nest under the slates. The ground floor window half opened and the woman's head appeared in it.

"Please, go away," she said, and I didn't like the cold expression on her face.

"I will not have it," she said, and I didn't like the calm tone of her voice.

I had known the terms of their agreement, or, well, perhaps not so much an agreement as the promise she had made. She had promised him, maybe for the sake of being slightly melodramatic, maybe without thinking he would take it seriously, anyway she did promise him that she would let him see her once again, and would let him see the children, if something "ultimate" happened, war, blindness, death. For him, obviously, the "ultimate" moment had come now. All the way from Paddington police station he must have been feeling the coil of the rope getting tighter and tighter around his neck and this journey must have been a sort of race against time: would he be able to win for himself that precious minute he needed before they laid their hands on his shoulder and shut him away from the outside world,— but whether he wanted to see the children or to see her, I did not know. Maybe he wanted to ask for help? I did not know, but, as I was watching him, I suddenly saw, in a new sort of light, what must have been happening in him, and with him; a sort of acute feeling of awareness gripped my throat, as sometimes, on rare occasions, happens in the theatre,—it is strange, I thought, that in real life we are still less frequently inclined to notice and accept and respect a drama, or a tragedy, than in literature; is it because we are afraid we might become involved or, on the contrary, because we see only the differences that divide us and not the similarities we have in common, and so don't identify ourselves with what we see; is it because there are too many dramatic events all around us, or, on the contrary, because we see them all as exceptional cases that do not concern us and, without the help of the spotlights and without the comfort of the seat we have paid for, we fail to discern their universal pattern?

He pressed the button again and kept his thumb on it. Now a window on the first floor opened, and a man's head stuck out of it.

"Pamela," the man said. "Call the police!"

*

I had often wondered what sort of man he would be. And now, these few words classified him for me at once. "Oh dear," I said to myself, "there have been hundreds of situations like this one, set in prose and in verse, from Shakespeare down to cheap novels romantic kitchen maids find on the bookstalls on both sides of the Seine, but I bet no character in them has ever asked the heroine to call the police." I looked at the two detectives by the fence, they didn't budge. They had obviously heard what the man had said, and they must have found something offensive in his words, or in the tone of his voice, because they now looked like two spiky hedgehogs. They had had their orders, but I felt their sympathies were with Tom Harris.

The door opened.

The man set his foot on the threshold. They were facing each other closely. The man said something, and Tom Harris's face winced as if a gust of bad breath had puffed into his nostrils from the man's mouth. The man tried to push him down the few front-door stone steps but Harris turned round him, so that he was now between the man and the doorway. The man tried to pull.

Harris hooked his left leg on the door-post while his hand grasped the woody stems of vine climbing up the wall around the door.

The man went on trying to pull him down.

The woman's face disappeared from the ground floor window. Was she not interested in what was going on, or did she really go to telephone the police?

Tom Harris jerked his body with a sudden half-pull half-twist and found himself inside the house.

The man jumped after him.

The door shut.

There was no sign of anybody else in the house or around it. The children must have been at their boarding school at

8

this time of year. Did he want to get the address of the school from her? And if so, what for? I did not know. Now, I know that he never seemed to be doing things *for* something, in order to *achieve* something. His acts always seemed to be not the Means leading to achieving Results, but Results themselves, the Results of what had built up in him, the expression of what he felt, or of what he thought, about—what?

One of the detectives walked along the fence, and round the corner, to keep an eye on the back entrance perhaps.

Some five minutes later the door opened again and Tom Harris walked out and down the few stone steps, and then along the path to the gate. There was no definite change in him, apparently. Though his features looked as if they had been re-designed. As if a publicity chief had called a "commercial artist" and said: "—see the drawing of a man on this packet of cornflakes? Well, from now on we intend to sell not cornflakes but pickled snails in sauce tartare in the same packets. Re-design the face of the man so that it suits our new product."

Fortunately, it didn't rain. When, on our way back, we were passing by the village cricket ground again, I looked around wondering what they would have done with the pigeon, and didn't notice when and how it happened that the two detectives were now on both sides of Tom Harris, marching in step towards the railway station. The train hadn't come yet. I found a telephone box and made a call.

We were sitting in the same compartment, all four of us, and when the train emerged from the sooty darkness of a tunnel, I turned to them with perhaps somewhat premeditated courtesy and said: "Excuse me, gentlemen, but I feel like taking a nap. I am telling you this, because it so happens that when I doze off, I start talking to myself, an old habit, you know, very embarrassing, but one can't help any of those things, can one? So, please, if I start talking to myself, do not think that I am addressing you, you may listen, if you wish, but don't tell me then, please, that I am talking to you, because I am not. I am talking to myself. I am telling myself that it is sometimes fortunate if it so happens that there are two medical certificates, two and not one, it gives some freedom to all people concerned, because one medical certificate may be saying, for instance, that the wound was caused by hitting the head with an instrument of such and such a weight, while the other may be saying that it might have been caused by hitting the instrument with the head, as the wound is not inconsistent with the fall that occurred at the moment of the heart attack, which, after all, the post mortem says was the direct cause of the death. It's not so bad to have two certificates. Especially when the body happens to belong to a gentleman who used to sell small arms by hundredweights, to whom?, to some hot-blooded people who haven't yet learned how to promote, or demote, tyranny by more peaceful and rational democratic methods. At some historical moments, a little event, such as finding a corpse, may be welcome: at some other historical moments, such a thing may be a damn nuisance. Therefore, well . . . assuming the legal circumstances to be equal, and they are equal, firstly, one certificate is as good as the other, secondly, the will has already been examined, it seems that the gentleman left the person concerned fifty pounds, fifty; that isn't good enough as a motive for murder, is it? Now if he had had time to open the attaché-case while Sir Francis was peeing, he would have known there was no more than fifty pounds in his legacy, and that wouldn't have been enough for him to be tempted, would it? On the other hand, if he didn't open it, there is no evidence that he knew what was in the attaché-case, or that he was interested to know—and so, oh dear, another tunnel, it seems the less fuss is made the better, most embarrassing, all those international journalists, I'm sure some top people are praying at this very moment that the two police officers won't show too much zeal in executing the instructions they received somewhat prematurely earlier in the morning. If I were one of them, I would, at least, try to telephone my superiors before doing anything decisive. It's very fortunate that I'm not, oh, here is some light, the end of the tunnel, did I talk in my sleep, gentlemen? I hope I wasn't being a nuisance?"

"You didn't say a word, sir," one of the detectives said coolly.

I glanced at Tom Harris. He was looking at me as if he had just noticed me for the first time in his life.

On our way back from Charing Cross station, we arranged ourselves in the same *ensemble* as before: he first, apparently free, the two officers behind him, I—hanging on to their rear, and the rest of the street—a *corps de ballet* around us. In one of the streets in Marylebone, he suddenly stopped in front of a pet shop. There was a little monkey in the window there who, as soon as he appeared, greeted him frantically as if he had known him and been waiting for him all his life. He jumped up, tapped the glass with his little fists, he ran along and gesticulated like a mime actor who is trying to convey the idea that the person he loves cannot possibly leave him alone in the cruel world of an incredible void, he turned his eyeballs up, showing that he'd die if he were left unheard, he pushed his hand forward and showed a little peanut between the tips of his black fingers, as if he wanted to bribe him. Tom Harris stood in front of the window as if the whole of the rest of the world had fallen into oblivion. The two detectives, still behind his back, smiled.

He took two steps to the right, entered the shop, and we glued our noses to the window-pane. A minute later, a girl appeared on the other side and removed the monkey. We looked round and lighted our pipes and cigarettes. Ten minutes later Tom Harris appeared, a cheque-book in his hand.

"Would you be so kind," he said to one of the detectives, "as to tell these people my name and address. You know it, don't you? They won't accept my cheque otherwise."

"What's that?" said the detective.

But the other detective giggled.

"Please," said Tom Harris.

"There's nothing like that in the regulations," the detective said. He actually pushed his hat back and scratched his head. "Perhaps this gentleman will do it for you," he jerked the thumb of his left hand at me.

But the other detective was still giggling:

"There's nothing in the regulations that says you mustn't do it."

The detective bit off the end of his cigarette and spat it on to the pavement. "O.K.," he said, and went with Tom Harris into the shop.

The situation was entirely changed now. All four, plus the little monkey on Tom Harris' shoulder, we moved off together and marched almost gaily through the streets of London. We all knew that no English policeman would arrest a man with a monkey until he had found a good, safe lodging for the animal first.

Spring 1963 / M I L A N

WWhen I cross the Channel, I know I'll meet some people who know some people I know. These coincidences are sometimes complicated and of consequence. But let me not jump ahead of the events. Their chronology is jerky enough as it is. I had no doubt that my train was going to Venice: the couple at the opposite window were like so many couples one sees in the Piazza San Marco. She was, I thought, just over thirty, white arms, black hair, I don't know the name of the cherry-coloured lipstick. He looked as some men over sixty look when they look like men over sixty who look just over fifty. It was his greying hair, well groomed, and his complexion, not military, but Turkish bath and massage at the barber's or, perhaps, high blood pressure? I couldn't decide. But sympathised. To me, they looked refreshing. Especially as just a day before, a young Italian poet, whose father owned a cinema and whose sister was a teacher, had sighed and said his grandfather was the happiest of us all: a peasant in Calabria. This remark whetted my appetite for any human being that looked happy; all in vain; there was no face that did not carry some sort of twist acquired recently, or complicated wrinkles from the past;—till I saw *them* and felt enormously pleased when, from the steward's basket full of bottles, they chose the "Oransoda," not champagne, and drank it with bravado. "God," I thought, "this train *does* go to Venice." Her right hand was now again—I say "again" because I had noticed it before—on his left thigh. Caressing it. Now, I do not wish to be obscene, it wouldn't amuse me; yet, we are not children, and any tailor if you ask him'll tell you the difference between the left thigh and the right.

In front of me, a lady dressed in black, black gloves, black hat, black eyes, and obviously a widow, sat motionless; yet I read her thoughts and knew she was aware (and disapproving) of what she actually couldn't see on the other bench, where the girl's hand was stroking the man's thigh, not playfully now; there was something dramatic in that persistence, yet what? I did not know. It wasn't exactly love, it wasn't lust; but it was evident that only a thing of great importance could make that faithful obstinacy so oblivious of the outside world that when the train ("rapido") stopped, and he stood up and looked out of the window at Verona, the hand continued. For my own sake, I tried to see the comic side of the whole picture, but I could not. Never did forwardness command such respect.

At Vicenza they disappeared; I got up to stretch my legs and saw her through the window, on the platform. So, after all, she wasn't going to Venice. There, by the door, she stood, her face all smiles, waiting for our train to depart, but the back of her head, and her black hair, and shoulders— were already somewhere else, in Vicenza or, perhaps, miles away.

It wasn't till the *rapido* recovered its full speed that he came back and took his former place. His face expressionless, his eyes wide open. But big round tears were running down his cheeks. He ignored them. A minute later he took up one of the glossy magazines and tried to read. So it wasn't exactly love; it wasn't lust either; it was goodbye.

The widow opposite me was still. I didn't notice her glance at him, not once, yet I knew that nothing had escaped her. Her thoughts were written in her eyes. And her eyes

14

panicked. They saw a picture of reality so different from those they must have been dreamingly painting during the long centuries of her marital life. Not a muscle stirred. But her face changed. Like that of a portrait when you take it down from its faded wall, reframe, and hang it somewhere else, on a different background, facing a different window, behind which a new landscape reflects the light of the sky.

The train stopped at Padova, and the man got up and off. So he wasn't going on to Venice either. Neither was I. I changed trains at Venezia Mestre (Venezia Mestre is not *the* Venezia), and went to a little town up North, which however has nothing to do with this story. A few days later I went back to Milan where, half an hour after my arrival, in the Piazza Duca d'Aosta, I was knocked down by a tram. For a fraction of a second, when my body was falling to the ground, my mind thought (mark the trichotomy: body+ mind+ I!): "Oh, well, so that's how it all ends, my mission unaccomplished." I don't know what I meant by "my mission" this time. I am quite certain it had nothing to do with what had taken place years before, at a time which didn't exist any more, when I had told myself that my mission was to find out more about Tom Harris. Nevertheless, all these coincidences and encounters led me straight in his direction.

The nurse at the emergency ward was all in white, and the little red cross on the big cornetta emphasised still more this sun-bleached whiteness which only in Italy stays pure and spotless all day long. Yet, in spite of that prim starchiness, she looked so casual when she leaned over the operating table: her blue eyes could have been scrutinising a tray of pastries, and her blond hair, showing under the cornet, could have been tussled by a breeze, or a cat, or just negligence. Watching her hesitant fingers as they peppered the wound with penicillin, cut some gauze, put a wet pad on the abrasion, I asked myself if they were just clumsy, or if they were trying to be gentle and not hurt. "Would you dine with me tonight?" I asked, half-jokingly.

Her name was Maria. She lived in a two-roomed flatlet on the fourth floor of one of those modern houses in Corso Europa, and deeply believed that the world is basically perfect, therefore, if something went wrong anywhere, it must have been because somebody was either stupid or wicked, or both. And as both stupidity and wickedness are curable, the betterment of the world is possible. She would vehemently deny that conflicts and contradictions may be present at the very basis of life, in the chemistry of a living cell, and accuse me of believing in original sin, though under a different (biological) name; this I found rather amusing, as I was entirely innocent of any religion, and it was she who would kneel by the bed to say her prayers, and cross herself after having fixed with some professional dexterity her Dutch cap which she had imported from Switzerland.

On the fifth of the seven days of rest prescribed by the doctor, at about ten o'clock in the morning, I heard the bell and a knock. Maria was out. I put down a copy of a Milanese newspaper with a story about a rubber company in Malaya which had ordered 200 bicycles from a British firm and received 20 cases of rusty small arms instead—and opened the door. I said I opened the door but it felt as if it didn't open but closed with something more bulky than the rectangle of wooden planks on iron hinges. His head touched the upper beam of the door-frame, and his broad shoulders, somewhere high above my eyes, seemed to be blocking it entirely. He looked to me like a fusion of two animals. I felt quite certain that I knew what the animals were, but somehow, as in a dream, could not see them clearly. A lamb's head on an elephant's body is still the nearest approximation I can think of. And the colour of a bear.

"What are you doing here?" he asked.

"And who are you?" I riposted.

He looked at me as if he were wondering if it was my concern.

"I came to see Maria," he said, reluctantly.

"You can't," I said. "She is at the hospital."

He shrugged his shoulders.

"Today is Thursday, isn't it?" he said.

"Yes," I said, "does it make any difference?"

"Well," he said. "Thursday is her day off."

He definitely had outflanked me.

"Are you quite sure?" I asked.

He was so enormous that the room felt like a cage.

He didn't answer. He opened the bottle of Conegliano dry "champagne" which he had brought with him, and filled two glasses.

I liked him. As for him, it seemed to me that he was looking for an ally and thought I might be one.

"Really," he said, "I am interested in Silvia."

"Who is she?" I asked.

My question surprised him.

"Did Maria never tell you? She is her sister."

He paused for a moment and then said simply:

"Silvia is a kept woman, and I love her."

He used the word *mantenuta*. Judging only by his tone of voice, one could have thought that he had said nothing more important than for instance: "It's raining, and I'm going for a walk."

He took out his wallet. It was a thick, big old-fashioned leather affair. He opened it and produced a white envelope. An aperture was cut in it showing a bit of a photograph.

"Silvia," he said.

I held it in my hands and tried not to look at him.

17

"What's the matter?" he asked.

"She has dark hair. She doesn't look like Maria's sister," I said evasively.

"She *is* her sister," he said.

I held the envelope in my hands and had no doubts whatever. It was a photograph of the woman I had seen in the *rapido* train going to Venice.

"She looks lovely," I said. "And I'm sure she must be nice."

"She is," he said. "She is soft like a precious stone."

I didn't so much as utter a syllable.

He watched me intently. I have no idea what my face looked like in his eyes, but he must have found in it something that encouraged him.

"Will you do me a favour?" he said. "Will you talk to Maria?"

"Good Lord!" I said. "How do you think I could do that? Six days ago I didn't even know about her existence. And sixty minutes ago you and I were perfect strangers."

"Time!" he said. He paused for a second and then unstrapped his wrist-watch. Without looking at its face, he took it between his gigantic thumb and two fingers, like a beetle, and slowly squeezed it. I thought I could still hear it ticking away when the glass cracked, the metal case gave way, and the little bits of its mechanism fell out and rolled on the table. Unconcernedly, he threw it into the ashtray.

I didn't know what he did it for. To illustrate what he meant by "Time"? Or to intimidate me? To show that he was rich enough to throw Swiss watches away? Or to demonstrate that what he had in mind was not just another love affair but something final, a swan song, for which he was prepared to pay any price? I didn't know.

Not without some impatience, I asked:

"Well, what do you want me to tell her? Do you want me

18

to tell her that you don't love her, that you are in love with Silvia?"

"No," he said. "That she knows very well. What I want you to do is to find out if she thinks the operation is advisable."

I didn't need to ask him what operation. On his neck, just above the collar, there was a pinkish-violet, one-inch thick, four-inches long fold of flesh.

"Look," I tried to reason with him. "Maria is very nice, and intelligent, and good. Still, she is only a nurse. I suppose you have consulted a surgeon?"

His arms were too big to gesticulate with. So he put his elbows on the table and accentuated what he was going to say by stretching his fingers, one after another, as if he were counting or explaining some arithmetic to a child.

"Yes, I have seen a specialist. I have just been to London to see one. This, I was told, isn't going to be a cosmetic operation. It's serious. And I am an old man. It is not absolutely necessary from the medical point of view. That is why I must know what Silvia's feeling about it is. If she doesn't mind, I'll let the thing stay where it is. But if she can't look at it I shall have it removed. What I want you to find out is if this thing is distasteful to Silvia. Maria will not tell me. But there is no reason why she shouldn't tell *you* the truth." He put his hand into his hip pocket, took out a bundle of huge Italian bank-notes, and transferred it to his breast pocket. "And you, of course, may have some reason for conveying it to me."

It was as simple as that. No allusion in the gesture. Just a subtle association of ideas. A kind of film-scenario poetry. Very refined.

The church clock struck eleven, and then three, times. It took it two minutes to achieve this. In another thirteen it would strike twelve. These prolonged quarter-hourly reverberations were amusing the first day, annoying the second, and almost natural the third. No, there was no reason why Maria shouldn't tell *me* the truth. As a matter of fact, she had already told me quite a lot, in an anecdotal sort of chatter, without my realising that the girl she was talking about was Silvia, and that Silvia was her sister.

"I can't promise anything now," I said. "I know so little about the whole set-up. Why, I don't even know your name."

"My name is Bruno X,"—here he pronounced a name very well known in Italian politics. It surprised me so much that I forgot to tell him mine and he didn't ask for it.

"No, I'm not *the* X," he explained. "Not even a relation. Unless *à rebours*."

"How do you mean?" I asked.

"I mean, I have no common ancestors with *the* X. But may have common progeny, I hope. My son is marrying his daughter."

I congratulated him, but he insisted on coming back to the subject. Putting his giant palm on his left breast pocket, he said:

"If you consent to do what I am asking . . ."

I interrupted him. The bloody thing on his big neck looked so vulnerable. And he wanted to have it cut out to please Silvia, the girl who was stroking another man's thigh in the train going to Venice.

"Tell me," I said. "Where does it come from? Seems to me that you must have spent some time in the tropics."

"Forty years. In Malaya. That's where I got it. Came back a couple of months ago. I was born in Florence." His sentences were very short now. The strong man was watching his step. "Do you remember 'Pirelli'?" he asked. "Automobile tyres. They were made of real rubber in those days. I went to Malaya when I was eighteen. Agriculturalist. Rubber plantations. Now it's synthetic rubber. But it still goes on.

New processes, you know. Plastics. Over six hundred thousand tons. Latex. Oil. It isn't Pirelli any more. A British firm. Everything's British. Fighting? Fighting there's not what you imagine here. Fighting goes on, British firms remain. Rubber plantation. Agricultural engineering. Home every two years. This time for good. Retired. Should have retired long ago. Beautiful country, Malaya."

I pushed the newspaper across the table.

"Have you seen this?"

It was the story about the 200 bicycles and 20 cases of small arms.

He didn't so much as glance at the paper.

"Of course I have," he said. "My son wrote it."

"O," I said. "Your son is a journalist?"

"A journalist!" he repeated the word scornfully. "A little baby, that's what he is. A little sort of reporter reviewing second class hits in third class night-clubs." Now, as he changed the subject, he became more eloquent. "My son is nothing, nothing, nothing. A . . . sissy! At his age I . . . Santa Madonna! Well, he's my worry." He folded the newspaper in two, then in four, and refolded it again. "He's a little monkey that apes the American way of life, but he doesn't believe in anything. Pretending to be tough, but it's only on the surface. *Atteggiamento.* Let a little bird in real life be caught by a real cat and he'll be practically crying, the tough journalist! *Atteggiamento,*" he repeated.

"Well," I said. "It can't be as bad as that. This story is well written."

"Thank you," he said. Sardonically. "I wrote it for him, just to show him what he could do if he wanted to be a man. The next story will be a scoop. My wedding present to him."

"A scoop?" I repeated.

"Yes."

"What sort of—? The same subject?"

He watched me thoughtfully.

"You'll see," he said at length.

I had a vague, and silly, feeling that I had been somehow outflanked by him again.

"Look," I said. "There are two things in this newspaper story that puzzle me."

"For instance?" he said.

"For instance: Why were the small arms rusty?"

"Because they had been stuck away in Southampton docks for twenty-four years."

"How do you know that?"

"I went there myself to investigate. On my way to London to see the English surgeon. I told you that."

"And what did you find?"

"I found my 200 bicycles stuck in the place where the cases had been."

"You mean, they made a mistake in Southampton? They put the bicycles next to the twenty abandoned cases and then shipped the cases?"

"Apparently, yes."

I looked at him and decided not to press the point.

"Another thing that puzzles me," I said, "is: Why did you order 200 bicycles? You are a Rubber Plantation, not a Bicycle Shop."

"O," the tone of his voice and its rhythm had suddenly changed. "You don't know Malaya. Labour is the trouble. The Chinese work. The Indians work. But the Malayans are nice people. They don't like working. What for? Money? They don't need money. There is nothing there they could buy for money. So what do you do? You show a Malayan boy a bicycle. You let him have a ride. He loves it. His eyes shine. Can he have one? Yes, of course he can, you tell him. But bicycles don't grow on trees, you tell him. Somebody has made them. People like him. And they must be paid for. Paid for with

22

what? Paid for with money. But he hasn't got any money. Well, he can easily get some. If he works. You may say, we ordered 200 bicycles to introduce civilization." He said that not without a sort of double-edged irony.

"And your 200 bicycles got swopped for twenty cases of small arms?"

"Precisely."

"I suppose they were produced by the same company?"

His soft brown eyes looked at me sharply.

"What makes you say that?" he asked.

"It occurred to me that the same markings on the cases would account for the mistake."

"You are much nearer the truth than you know," he said. "Or perhaps you *do* know?" he added.

"Don't be silly," I said. "Of course I don't. All this is not my province. Though, I think, I know a man who once upon a time was a secretary to the chairman of a company manufacturing both invalid chairs and small arms. I wouldn't know if they produced bicycles."

"What happened to him?"

"To whom?" I asked.

"The chairman."

"He died," I said.

"Some twenty-four years ago?"

"How clever!" I said. "Yes."

"Killed?" he asked.

"No," I said. "It was a heart attack, I think."

"You think so?"

"Yes. Don't you?"

"No," he said.

"I think it was," I said. "And, anyway, it was so long ago. Everybody concerned must be dead by now."

"Not everybody."

"No?"

"No. Some people may be old now but they are still alive."

"Who, for instance?" I asked.

"For instance the chap they called his 'secretary.' Maybe it's the same one you say you know. The name is Harris."

"Oh," I said. "What about him?"

"Doesn't he live comfortably, respectably, in Genoa?"

"Why shouldn't he?"

"Well, look here, you are not going to tell me that he earns all the money he gets."

"I don't care what he earns, I don't care what he gets and spends. It is none of my business, and I don't see how it can be any of yours."

"It is," he said.

There was a silence. An uncomfortable one. We both watched a fly walking along the edge of the ashtray. He blew at it, and it flew away.

"Ever heard of a man called Giuseppe?" he asked. "Big fish. The one who kidnapped your Mr Harris in London and brought him to Genoa."

"He didn't kidnap him," I said.

"All right. He invited him. Provided him with a beautiful apartment, money, good advice . . . and he's been doing it all these years, hasn't he? Why?"

"All right, why?" I asked.

"Yes, I'll tell you why," he said. "Because they were both in it."

His big, brown eyes looked at me disapprovingly, as if I were a little boy, who had been naughtily non-co-operative.

"Look here," he said, "it is unusual for a consignment of twenty cases to get stuck in some warehouse, is it not? Unless . . ." he continued, "unless somebody *wants* them to get stuck." One of his eyes focussed on me mischievously. "What you think? I think that the best way to stop it at Southampton was to stop the person who was to give further

24

instructions and the best way to stop him was to help him to have his heart attack, no? Small arms business isn't exactly politics, you know? It's like any other business. Catch as catch can."

"And who, do you think, helped him to have his heart attack?" I asked.

Now his voice was perfectly clear and precise:

"Baron Reinach von Reinacherhof, who is dead; Giuseppe, who is well alive; and Harris, who must be kept in comfort if one wants him to keep his mouth shut."

The man was mad.

"Utter nonsense!" I exclaimed. "Utter nonsense!"

He smiled at me patiently, benevolently.

"Let me tell you something," I started.

"Go on," he said.

"Two things . . ." I said.

"Well, tell me the first thing first," he said.

"The first thing is," I said, "that in the spring of 1938 when Sir Francis died, Tom Harris and Giuseppe didn't even know of each other's existence. They didn't meet till several months later, by chance, as complete strangers, in a Black and White milk bar in Soho. Harris told me about it himself. And this is a fact."

This was a fact, but it left him unimpressed.

"And the second thing?" he asked.

"The second thing is," I said, "that when Sir Francis died, there was a full police enquiry, and they decided that he died a natural death."

"If it was a natural death, why the police enquiry?" he grinned.

"Oh, don't be such a bore," I said. "The fact is that they didn't find anything to charge him with, and they let him go."

"O yes," he said. "How typically British! It was expedient

that no fuss should be made at the time so they let him go. Only to pinch him again some eighteen months later and send him to jail for four years, for what? For being a little rude to a barber!"

I jumped up.

"Bruno," I said. "Show me that photograph again, will you?"

He did. He took out his old-fashioned wallet and produced the white envelope with an aperture showing Silvia. Before he had time to stop me, I tore open the envelope and saw a man standing behind her. It was the man of the *rapido*. I read a few words written in the corner, and now I knew who he was.

"Look here," I said. "What was it you said about that next installment of your story; the scoop? Are you fabricating it to make a wedding present for your son, or to spite Giuseppe?"

He was so big that he must have smashed a number of table-tops during his lifetime, simply by letting his heavy fist fall on to them. That was probably how he had developed this strange technique which consisted in arresting the movement suddenly, a fraction of a inch above the surface. The effect was unexpected and somewhat comic.

He stood up. Then he turned round heavily and walked out.

The strange thing was that I still liked him. The big man with a nasty thing on his neck which he wanted to have cut out for the sake of a woman; the sex-besotten maniac from Malaya unearthing a quarter of a century old plot that had never existed. Ha ha. Ha ha ha. But it was not funny. Should I go to Genoa and warn Tom Harris? Why should I? All that was none of my business. None whatever. The church bells went on ringing. I wrote a note to Maria. Not without effort, I managed to lace my shoes and went out. To the hospital first (it *was* her day off, they told me), and then to the Stazione Centrale. All the time telling myself that I was nobody's keeper, and all that was absolutely none of my business.

/ GENOA

They say Columbus was born there. Perhaps in one of those little streets, too narrow to let you open an umbrella when God decides to sprinkle with His rain the fish, the prawn, the betrothal ring, the silk, the brassière, the dead fowl, the glitter, the smell, and the taste, displayed, as you stroll down or up, on both sides of you, in front of the coffin-sized shops. Or, perhaps in one of those streets that don't rise and fall up and down the slope but flow parallel to the smelt but not seen sea, in the canyons at the bottom of which, as you wander and then retrace your steps, you come upon the same, it seems, centuries-old females, fat and motionless, and bump into the same sailors, drifted back here through time and ocean, one-eyed, or limbless. That's the terraqueous anthill the man who discovered America came from. What America sent it back is just round the corner: sky-scrapers.

It was in Genoa, of all places, that I got lost in a sky-scraper.

"Signor Harris?" I asked.

"Twenty-first floor, Lift D," they said.

Six people in a shiny, aluminium packaging, each pressing a button, and the electronic brain of the lift sorting out the floors. I pressed my number twenty-one, and the lift, after having stopped at eighteen, went straight to twenty-three. I wanted to climb down these two miserable floors but they said you were not allowed to use the staircase. Back in the aluminium, I pressed my twenty-one button, and the lift went down to the ground floor. They said: try Lift B. I tried Lift B and went to floor thirty-six, and then down, stopping at each *piano*, except the twenty-first, which I wanted. The electronic brain of the lift was bored with me. I didn't fit it. I played with it in each of the six lifts, A, B, C, D, E, F, for half an hour, and finally, defeated, walked out. And there I saw him, in the hall, as he was approaching the door on his way out.

"Harris!" I shouted.

He turned round, saw me, and smiled.

I was immediately struck by the change that had taken place in his appearance; he now looked ten years younger than he had when I last saw him, which was in 1945 (or was it '46?), at the Green Man. It was his shoulders and the way he carried his head on his neck that made me notice him here, now, in the hall of this Genoese sky-scraper. Had I seen his face first, I wonder if I would have recognised the Old (old?) Man with the Monkey. His shabby grey beard was gone; his long grey hair that used to cover the collar of his dirty mackintosh was cut short, close to the skin. He wore an Italian-made black suit, an immaculate white shirt and a dark tie with a silver clasp. The last time I saw him, I talked to him as one does to somebody who is much older, and accepted as an old man, once and for all. Now he seemed to be the younger of the two.

I said I was lucky I hadn't missed him and I mentioned the story of the lifts.

"They should have told you to go to *piano* twenty," he said. "The twentieth floor is Conference Rooms. Twice as high as the others. There you would have found an inner staircase leading to the entresol where I live. Between the twentieth and the twenty-second, say, twenty-one and a half. Typical. Just as it used to be in Old England."

29

This puzzled me. Why should he think it typical? And what in it reminded him of England, I was asking myself, when, with graceful ease, he added:

"Well, I suppose, lifts never stop between floors, you can't expect them to stop between floors, not anywhere. Which, in a way, is a pity."

And then, quite abruptly, he changed the subject:

"Pamela is staying not far from here," he said, "at Nervi."

"O," I said.

"It's just a coincidence," he said. Then he glanced at his watch. "What are you doing tonight?"

"I want to talk to you," I said.

"Good," he said.

I was looking forward to seeing the blue Golfo da Genoa from the window on that mythical twenty-first and a half floor of his sky-scraper. My eyes were wearied of having all the time something not farther than a few feet or a few yards before them,—a chair, a wall, a lamp-post, a taxi-cab, a hurried passer-by. They longed for an empty space through which they could look towards the distant horizon, as one's arms and legs may long to stretch. To my disappointment, he didn't invite me to his elevated entresol. Instead, later on in the evening, he sent a car with a chauffeur who took me to a restaurant, a few miles down, along the coast, where he was already waiting for me. The place, he said, was known to nobody, except the local inhabitants and high class connoisseurs.

They called him *il marchese*. That was at least how the word sounded in my ears, and my ears, I notice, have more and more often the tendency to hear what I imagine fits the situation rather than what actually comes to them from the outside world. And the word *il marchese* fitted the situation fairly. Il marchese Harris of Paddington!

By now, three men in black were encircling our table and

asking the marchese some questions about me. They asked him where I had come from, how long he had known me, whether I was married, what my "line in life" was. All that, apparently, to compose a menu that would suit me. They decided to start with a basketful of big dark-green runner beans, which we split with our fingers to get at the pale-green capsules, so fresh and aromatic, as if they had just been picked by a vegetarian monk somewhere far away from fertilizers and frigidaires.

"Do you know a man called Bruno X?" I asked, at length.

He watched the hand of the waiter who was refilling our glasses.

"The politician?"

"No," I said. "The man I mean has just come back from Malaya. Lived there for forty years."

"Malaya . . ." he repeated, meditatively. "There's a butterfly there, *Papillio Broodiana Albensens Rothschild*. The thing about it is that its female is a rarity. One female to a thousand males. Hum . . . That's about all I know about Malaya."

His sudden encyclopaedic bit of information about the butterfly didn't surprise me. He always used to be like that. But the fact remained that he didn't tell me whether he knew Bruno.

"I only met him yesterday," I went on. "He seemed to know Giuseppe. That's what made me think you might have heard of him."

"Oh, everybody knows Giuseppe," he said, as if to dismiss the subject. But then he looked at me and added: "The thing is that I've got the female."

Now, I'm ashamed to say, a sort of a rather silly, music-hall dialogue followed. I thought he meant Giuseppe's Silvia, and what he had in mind was a female *Papillio Broodiana Albensens Rothschild*.

"I didn't know you collected butterflies," I said, when we

31

had somehow, at last, extricated ourselves from the confusion.

"O yes, yes," he said querulously. "It is enough to pinch a book to become a thief. And it's enough to have one specimen of a butterfly from Malaya to be called a collector."

He must have meant much more than he actually said. He lit a cigarette. Impatiently but as slowly as if the match would burn for ever. He inhaled. Just one puff. The little bird on our plates, at least I think it was a bird, was as black as if the bishop had set his foot in the charcoal on which it must have been cremated, but each of its ruined cells was like a flask of perfume, a burnt down distillery of all the herbs and all the roots the spring and autumn forests can produce. He put the cigarette away and stubbed it out.

"I don't collect butterflies," he said distinctly. "I build them."

And then he told me what he was up to. He was busy constructing artificial electronic analogues of neural nets and he called them "butterflies" because of their grub-pupa-imago metamorphosis. What he actually built was artificial electronic assemblies representing the first (grub) stage. The other two stages (pupa and imago) developed by themselves (electronically of course), without anybody's help.

No, his butterflies didn't possess colourful wings and they didn't fly. All their activities consisted in drawing a considerable number of graphs on a roll of paper.

There was one curious thing in what he said (curious, perhaps, because it was new to me). But it will take more than one sentence to explain it. The assemblies he had built reacted to things coming to them from the outside world and from the inside of themselves (including their own electronic "noise," reverberations, etc.). They reacted by registering the stimulations doing some sort of work (as the result of the stimulation), and registering the fact that the work had been done. So far the thing was simple. But then, there existed, apparently, some stimulations which were too weak to get registered yet strong enough to trigger the assembly to do the work and to register the fact that the work had been done. Now, all that referred to the first (grub and pupa) two stages. But it seemed that on the third (imago) stage a sort of electronic top level would form itself. It would have nothing to do with stimulations and work (anyway not directly). It would deal only with the registrations supplied by the lower levels. In the case of strong stimulations, it was comparatively simple, the top correlated the registration of stimulations with the subsequent registration of the work done and it registered the event in its "memory" for future reference. In the case of a weak stimulation, the thing wasn't simple at all. The top would have found the registration of the work done but wouldn't be able to find the registration of the relevant stimulation, and—as Harris said—it was puzzled. The curves drawn on the roll of paper showed, apparently, how puzzled it was. Not finding the direct "cause" (which could "tell" it why the work had been done), and ignorant of the existence of weak stimulations (which hadn't been registered), it looked for possible causes among all the other registrations memorized in it. Some of them being less improbable than others, it accepted them as registrations of the true causes, which fact, consequently, led it to committing all kinds of "irrational" fallacies, which could be deciphered from the graphs drawn on the roll of paper. He called that part of its activity RAAB—the Religious Activity of the Analogue of a Butterfly.

I looked at him, fascinated.

"It's all on the level, you know," he said.

"Of course," I said.

"And the pretty thing about it is that if you transfer the graphs from the roll of paper to magnetic tape and run the tape at the right speed through the tape recorder, you will hear the assemblies sing, and you will be able to learn to understand their polyphonous soliloquies. What I hope to do is to teach them to listen. Then they will be able to preach their respective RAAB prejudices to each other."

He looked at me and stopped, rather abruptly.

"I didn't know," I said quickly, "I didn't know that that sort of thing is being done at your University . . ."

"Oh no," he interrupted me. "It isn't. I'm not doing it there. I'm not my own boss there. I am a junior. Routine work, you know. What I've been telling you is my private research. My entresol activity. Between the two floors. You know. You must come one day and see."

"I'd like that," I said. And then I looked at him and saw that he had second thoughts and would not invite me.

The red sun was shivering on the brink, hesitating to plunge into the sea behind the window by which we were sitting, and the shadows of some minute objects, the legs of a fly, which was slowly walking across the table-cloth, were as long as the tentacles of an octopus, such as the one the bits of which were floating in the dish we had been served.

"You may be wondering how I can afford to do all that by myself. Well, first, I have some assistance. And then, Giuseppe is most generous. His factory produces all the gear I need. And he sends me everything I ask for, down to bits of wire and solder, gratis, by air."

"Have you seen him recently?" I asked.

He looked like a man who has just woken up.

"Whom?" he asked. "Giuseppe?"

"Yes," I said.

"No," he said. "I never go to London, and he seldom has time to see me when he comes to Italy. He is too busy. Silvia, you know."

"Well," I said, "if that is the reason, then he'll probably have more time now. I think that I was an accidental witness to their parting scene." And I told him what I had seen in

34

the Venice *rapido*. "Of course," I added, "at that time I didn't know they were Giuseppe and Silvia."

He looked at me, surprised.

"Surely," he said, "you would have recognised Giuseppe!"

"No," I said. "Not necessarily. I had never seen him before."

He was taken aback.

"How can that be?" he asked, dropping his napkin on to the floor. "It was you who told Giuseppe where to find me, wasn't it? It was you who gave him the address of the Green Man. Don't you remember?"

"I do," I said. "But it wasn't Giuseppe, it was Mrs Holcman I told I'd seen you there."

They switched the lights on, and the pupils of his eyes shrank to pin-point. The waiter came to recommend a big chunk of a simple parmigiano. It was sharp on the tongue, and had the welcome power of changing your thoughts while you masticated its hardness.

"Mrs Holcman . . ." Harris repeated. He emptied his glass of wine and filled it again. I had a strange feeling that he wanted to keep me more sober than he himself intended to be.

"I only saw her once," he said. "The night she and Giuseppe came to the Green Man. They didn't fit there, you can imagine! Them, offering to stand drinks all round and trying to persuade me to go with them. It was quite a picture. I bet people remember it still."

He beckoned to the waiter and showed him the napkin he had dropped on the floor. Then he looked at me, and asked:

"Where did *you* meet her first?"

"At a party," I said.

"A party," he repeated.

He filled our glasses again.

"But why?" he asked.

I didn't understand what he was asking.

"Why did you tell her?" he explained.

"Because she asked me," I said.

"I imagine so," he said. "But how did she know you knew me?"

"She didn't," I said. "It was one of those coincidences," I added.

"Well, never mind," he said.

I looked at him, curiously.

"It's rather a long story," I said. "Would you care to hear it?"

"Very much," he said. "The night is young, and there is plenty of wine."

I felt slightly foolish and a little bit old-fashioned as I stretched my legs comfortably under the table, took a sip of wine and began to tell him the story of Mrs Holcman. Trying to show a side of the picture which he certainly had had no chance of seeing.

"Well," I said. "At that time, she was already living where she lives now. A two-roomed modern flatlet on the third floor between those old odd houses that form a maze of narrow streets between Park Lane and Grosvenor Square. I've been there a hundred times since, used to visit her as often as I could, especially on Sunday afternoons. These were, I think, the only times when Mrs Holcman knitted. It was always the same piece of white angora wool, after each visit just an inch longer. As soon as I arrived, she would take it out of the drawer, where—I had no doubt—it had been kept undisturbed since my last visit. I felt very much honoured by that distinction but I never ventured to ask her what sort of garment the white angora knitting was meant to become; I somehow knew I shouldn't. It was pleasant to sit there, in 'my' armchair, whisky and a syphon of soda water on a little table beside it. At times it seemed as if the room were really, physically, filled with peace and warmth, as if abstract peace and warmth were liquids which it is possible to spray round and saturate the air with. It was due, of course, to her personality alone. It was her personality that was warm and, infectiously, at peace with itself. She didn't need to laugh, as people do to show that they are not hostile,—as if the world were naturally full of enemies; on one occasion she could be a little gayer, on another—a little sadder, but she was always friendly, she emanated friendliness, and she was a marvelous story-teller.

"Her stories seldom contained anything that she hadn't experienced herself, they were always about events from her own life or the life of people she knew, yet she would tell them in such a quiet and almost impersonal sort of voice, and with such cool compassion, even towards herself, which is one of the rarest things on earth, that it fascinated me. Though, at the same time, I must confess, I wondered, somewhat perplexed, about what a different person she must be in her office, where I had never seen her, to have earned the reputation of being somebody whose drive, cleverness, and ruthless efficiency were indispensable to Giuseppe. That evening I had for the first time an opportunity of seeing the other Mrs Holcman, Mrs Holcman in action.

"It began as usual. I was sitting relaxedly in my armchair, she—on the sofa opposite, knitting, and in her soft, detached voice telling me how it was, or rather what she felt, when she first met Giuseppe. It was he who approached her, at the His Master's Voice gramophone shop at Oxford Street, and then asked her to come and see him the next day in his office. She didn't know exactly what for. Was it to be a rendezvous or an interview? At that time (it was in the middle of the war and she hadn't been more than a fortnight in London) she was billeted in a little room in one of those terraced houses in Ealing.

"An interview or a rendezvous? She didn't know. She

37

looked at herself in the wardrobe mirror, and her eyes were cool and merciless. They could find nothing to excuse the green jumper, mended and clinging to her fat breasts, or the black skirt that emphasised her stomach. But there was no alternative. The wardrobe was empty. The only thing she could improve was her own body.

"She lifted her head, straightened her back, and her reflection in the wardrobe mirror became some two inches taller. The new posture changed her; it was as if a Worth or Paquin had conjured up one of their tricks by adding some inexplicable magic touch to the jersey that fitted her too closely and the black skirt that didn't fit her at all.

"She moved half a step back. There was still no self-forgiveness in her gaze. She put a hat on; she held it for a moment in both hands, then jerked it down. Hats were important. It was a dark blue ribbon hat and it had a short veil hanging from it. Yes, a hat was important. It would soften the impact when something heavy fell on your head; it would give some protection against lice; and, also, when a Christian tried to get hold of your black hair to bend you down as, for some reason of State, he had to kick you in the shins, it would somehow tend to delay the action.

"She went to the door and locked it. Then she came back to the wardrobe. The blue ribbon hat, green jersey, grey gloves (she was wearing gloves), black skirt, beige stockings, nondescript shoes. Only the shoes hadn't belonged to someone* else at one time or another. She opened the wardrobe, pushed aside the empty coat-hangers, removed the bottom shelf, and went in. The floor of the wardrobe creaked under her weight. No, it was a shockingly bad wardrobe. Most uncomfortable. She tried to shut its door from the inside and the hinges squealed, like an informer. The wardrobe was useless. She crossed herself. She said 'Credo.' And 'Hail Mary.' Twice. The wood of the wardrobe cracked impatiently and with anger. The wardrobe was no good at all. It wouldn't save a child. She stepped out of it, and the wardrobe gave a sigh of relief.

"She looked in the mirror again. Her posture had corrected the imperfection of her clothes. Now the poise of her mind must correct the folds and wrinkles that gave that special expression to her face. She knew that was something no face-lift could remove. There were some thoughts imprinted in her mind, and she had to get rid of them. For ever. It was a tragic necessity. Tragic, because she knew that by banishing them from her mind she was being disloyal to something, perhaps to that part of herself which had suffered most and longed most to be freed, and deserved to be freed one day. And now, when the day had come, she had to betray it by refusing it the shelter of her thoughts. Nevertheless, that was what she had to do. She was starting a new life, and the slave that dwelt in her mind, waiting for the day to come, had to go precisely when the day came. It was necessary to empty her mind of things past.

"The air-raid sirens sounded another alarm. Somebody knocked on her door. 'Mrs Holcman, don't you want to go down to the basement?' No, she would not go down to the basement. The sound of the sirens pleased her. The landlady wouldn't understand that. The landlady wouldn't understand that the sound of their boots on the pavement, that the sound of their Aryan-Christian fists knocking on the door, was more horrifying than the sound of a bomb. On the contrary. The sound of a bursting bomb was reassuring. It proved that they were still far away in the air, not on the earth. And so long as their feet were not here, down on the pavement, the risk of being killed, the risk of being burned, was just an ordinary, almost peace-time, risk. There have always been accidents and fires in a big town, so it was only as if our usual, daily chance of death had become incomprehensibly greater, as if a curve had suddenly jumped up in statistics ten times, a hundred times above the norm. But it was still the same ordinary, human thing, and not like the other, which was extraordinary and inhuman. Because what matters is not that you die, everybody must, sooner or later,—but how. A bomb, or a lorry, kills only your body and your mind. A man who jeers at you as he kills you, kills also your person. And it is not the body and the mind, it is the person in us that suffers most.

"She stood in front of the mirror and looked at that unnecessary expression on her face. She didn't try to smile. She knew that to smile would make it still worse. A forced smile would change it into a Greek mask, and that was the last thing she wanted to carry on her face among these people who were still free. And it was the last thing she would care to show to that incredible Italian she had met the day before, Giuseppe.

"An interview, or a rendezvous? She didn't know. An interview would mean: work. And that was what she needed. Not only to earn her living, but to live. A rendezvous could only mean a conversation. And perhaps an invitation to dinner? What was his wife like? She was certainly tall, slim, blond, in silks, and with a string of pearls. Mrs Holcman's nose sniffed at that picture. Houbigant? Guerlain? And, of course, there are some chorus girls in the background. Or young actresses. He was certainly the man for whom the word pied-à-terre was invented. Mrs Holcman liked to gaze at people who liked each other. As for herself, she was, of course, hors de combat. She married during the First World War, in Warsaw, and in November 1918 gave birth to her older son, Henry. All that had occurred without passion, in a state of semi-lethargy. But then, a few days after the confinement she suddenly woke up and ran wild. Henry was given a wet-nurse, and night after night Mrs Holcman went off to tango and to fox-trot or to shimmy in the big hotels' 'dancings,' or in 'cabarets,' with a bunch of young country squires and army officers. This had lasted for four years. She wouldn't be able to tell how many lovers she had had during that period and knew only one thing, that there was not a single Jew among them. Except her husband. Her husband? After all, perhaps he didn't love her. Perhaps he just didn't want to lose her to that set of smart Christian males who would have humiliated him if he had tried to seek their company. One cannot know that now. But, whatever his feelings might have been, one day he decided that they must have another child. Almost by force, he took her to a small place in the country where she would have no chance of meeting anybody, and stayed with her there till she got pregnant. That was how Joseph, the violinist, was engendered. Though he didn't show any wish to come into this world. Her body had to be cut once to get him out, and then again, for some messy surgical reasons, and when she recovered she found that the passion in her was spent, and there was no desire to rekindle it.

"An interview, or a rendezvous? Perhaps neither? Perhaps something else? O no, Good God, please, not that, not this time, anything but that! Her face in the mirror turns white. She isn't frightened of the wheezing sound that comes from the sky above, she hasn't even noticed it. It is what has come to her mind, just now, that frightens her. The thought that when she comes to his office to see him, he'll say: 'Dear Mrs Holcman, will you permit me . . . &c, &c, &c,' and will try to give her his wife's old coat, or a cheque for one pound one shilling. She must prevent this from happening.

"She is in complete control of herself. She has unbuttoned the green jersey and taken out a minute linen bag that has been hidden under the brassière between her breasts. She opens it and carefully takes out two diamond earrings. Once upon a time she bartered a string of pearls for a hiding place in a Christian wardrobe. That was wise, because otherwise, if she had been found, she would have been killed. She bartered a gold watch for a pair of catholic sandals. That was wise, because she had had to walk a very long way. Then she bartered her wedding ring for a real lutheran steak garnished with potatoes. That was stupid, because on the morrow she was as hungry as she had been the day before. But the two earrings were her castle, she would not have bartered them. When on the move, she hid them under a bit of dirty elastoplast, in the deep scar she had on her belly. She knew that the day would come when she would need them, and really. She felt now that the day had come. She attached one earring to her left ear. Then the other to her right ear, and looked in the mirror. The picture reassured her. No man will ever offer his wife's old clothes to a woman who has diamonds hanging from the lobes of her ears.

"She looked in the mirror and for the first time approved of the expression in her eyes. She was now ready to go. To her interview, or the rendezvous, whichever it was to be.

"The first thing she noticed in Giuseppe's office was a row of four photographs above his desk, and a picture on the opposite wall. The photographs were those of Churchill, Roosevelt, Stalin, and Chiang Kai-shek. The picture was by Chirico. That was very clever, she thought, the visitors looked at the official photographs while Giuseppe could fix his eyes on the sepia and blue and white, Mediterranean, yet unreal, landscape. At first she thought he was going to hypnotise her. 'I want you to listen carefully to what I say,' he said. 'Are you comfortable in that armchair? Relax, please, and think of nothing, nothing but what I say.' And then, as she said, within a quarter of an hour she had learned more about those visible and invisible English social divisions than she could otherwise have done in a lifetime. 'It is precisely because you don't belong that I need you,' he said. 'In my business I deal with all sorts of people and I don't wish to have a secretary who has been indoctrinated into seeing the world as something where everybody has his superiors and his inferiors, classified according to some peculiar system of values. Where would I myself be in the eyes of such a secretary? No, don't let yourself be trapped between the various layers of that pyramid. They will crush you. Be outside. Be different. Cultivate your foreign accent, dress simply, but with foreign elegance.' He looked at her. 'Well, I'm very pleased,' he said, and left her in the hands of one of his female assistants whom he had instructed to take her to the shops and hairdressers. But when he was already at the door, he turned round abruptly and said: 'There is one thing still, Mrs Holkman' (that was, apparently, how he pronounced her name), 'if you ever come upon the name *Tom Harris*, or any indication that would help us to find him, let me know instantly. This is Top Priority, remember.'

"At that moment I put down my glass of whisky, and asked:

" 'Did you say: *Tom Harris?*'

"She looked at me, and her eyes changed. It would be difficult to describe what had actually happened to them, but they were different eyes now. She looked ten years younger. Even her hair revived with some strange, electric lustre. As she was getting up, it seemed that it was her head that rose first, drawing with it the straight, unbent neck and shoulders; the white angora knitting fell limply on the floor. An utterly new Mrs Holcman was standing in front of me.

" 'Do you know him?' she asked.

" '*Tom Harris* is not such an uncommon name,' I said, a trifle disconcerted.

" 'I mean Tom Harris, the Man with the Monkey,' she insisted.

"I said nothing.

" 'Do you know him?' she repeated.

" 'I do, yes,' I said.

43

" 'Where does he live?'

" 'I say, I wonder if you'd mind telling me what it is all about?' I hazarded.

"She was actually standing between me and the door now. As if she wanted to bar the way, in case I tried to leave. Without taking her eyes off me, she reached for the receiver and started dialling a number. A few seconds passed in silence, then she asked for Giuseppe. 'Yes, I know he is busy; yes, it *is* very urgent. Tell him please, it is top priority.' She waited. After a minute, 'Giuseppe,' she said into the receiver. 'A friend of mine seems to know Tom Harris. No. He is disinclined to . . . He wants to know what it is all about. You want to speak to him? Here he is!' And, without asking me if I wanted to speak to Giuseppe, she put the receiver into my hand.

" 'Are you there?' the voice asked. A moment later, I was convinced that his mind had already examined all the possibilities as to what sort of person I might have been, rejected all but one, and modulated his voice accordingly. 'Thank you for listening to me,' the voice said. 'I don't know if you are Tom's friend or his enemy. But even if you feel hostile towards him, I trust this will not have any effect on your decision. Will you tell me where he lives? I want to see him.'

" 'Does he want to see you?' I asked.

" 'He very probably doesn't even remember me,' he said. 'It is I who am indebted to him and want to repay it. Do you have any reason for disbelieving me?'

" 'No,' I said. 'You can find Tom Harris most evenings at the Green Man, on the corner of Edgware Road and Bell Street.'

" 'I am most obliged to you,' he said. 'May I speak to Mrs Holkman again?'

" 'Yes, Giuseppe,' she said into the telephone. 'Seven twenty, I shall be ready. Ring the bell and I shall come down. What?' She looked at me. 'No, it isn't necessary,' she went

44

on, looking at me, 'I wouldn't make any suggestion of the sort, if I were you, definitely not.'

"She put the receiver down. Without saying a word, she crossed the room back to the sofa, picked up the white angora knitting, folded it and put it into the drawer.

"I was standing in front of her.

" 'Reggie,' I said. 'I understand that you are going with Giuseppe to the Green Man tonight.'

" 'Yes,' she said. 'I am.'

"I still couldn't believe that was possible.

" 'Are you not going to the concert?' I asked, flabbergasted.

"I didn't tell you that the previous day her son, Joseph, whom she had saved from the Nazis and hadn't seen since the first year of the war, had come to London from South America to give a concert. She had met him for a moment at the airport, but he was surrounded there by a crowd of journalists and musicians who at once took him to his hotel and then to a rehearsal with the orchestra.

" 'Reggie,' I repeated. 'Are you not going to see Joseph?'

"She opened her mouth, and I stared at her, not believing my ears.

" 'What did you say?' I asked.

" 'I said: f . . . Joseph,' she repeated.

"I had no idea she would even know the word. Perhaps she didn't, after all. She pronounced it as if it were spelled *fark*."

Tom Harris had just taken a sip of wine, and now he burst out laughing. The physical effect of this was a trifle embarrassing. We had both stood up and were trying to make use of our red check napkins, when a group of seven men came in.

/ THE SEVEN DOCKERS

They were so strangely assorted that somebody might have specially chosen them so as not to have two pairs of eyes to see the world from the same height, or two spines curved alike, or two belts hooked on the same eyelet. If they had been put into uniforms, there wouldn't have been two of them who could have exchanged their cap, their tunic, or their boots.

And yet there was something between them which seemed to unite them, as if the very bit of space they were surrounding existed as an entity in itself, changing its shape as they moved, shrinking and stretching, yet never losing its identity. They seemed to be always around that space, with none of them ever in its centre, as if none of them wanted to be in the centre. They ordered their meal first and then sat round the long table behind me, but turning my head slightly to the right, I could still see one of them, the one who was sitting at the corner and playing a guitar.

They called him Arturo. He was not deformed. He was just too short for his thick bones and broad shoulders, on which he carried an enormous round head. He looked as if, at one time or another, when he was a child, somebody had put some great weight on his shoulders, so that he wouldn't grow upwards, but that he had nevertheless managed to do so, just up to the height that might already be considered "normal,"

—and then given up. He was under thirty, yet his head was perfectly bald, except for the black, curly hair behind the ears. The baldness of his head made his face look still larger. It was a good, ugly, big face, with a pair of bright coal-black, sparkling eyes, a sensitive, thick nose, and a perpetual smile, always on the verge of breaking into laughter. He ate, drank, played the guitar, sang, joked, laughed, wrinkled his forehead, and peered into your eyes, all at the same time.

Now I knew that my talk with Tom Harris had come to an end. He was no longer with me. His eyes were fixed on Arturo's guitar, and his fingers were playing the tune on the table-top. And indeed, five minutes later, Arturo was sitting next to him, and a bottle of Johnny Walker, brought by the waiter with the compliments of Tom Harris, stood on the other table. I turned my chair sideways, and at once we became one single company. Tom Harris on my left, Arturo in front of me, and Luciano on my right. The adolescent waiter came again, bent over Tom's ear, and said scornfully:

"Nine men! You can't really enjoy yourself without a woman."

Arturo grinned, stopped in the middle of a bar, struck a chord, and started a new song.

"Do not think we enjoy ourselves like this every night. It is only tonight. Because we are on strike," Luciano said.

His head nodded slightly but not in time with the tune. He would not laugh. When he opened his mouth his cheeks drooped. There were no muscles in his face to lift them up. There was a sort of wrinkled sadness around his grey eyes, which looked simultaneously both outside, towards you, and inside, into his own head.

"I used to be a sailor," he said. "Now I am a docker. But don't think we eat, and drink, and sing here, as now, every night. It's only because we are on strike. Till Monday."

What the strike was about, I didn't know. The day was Saturday; it started in the morning, and was to end on Mon-

day. Eduardo would have told me more about it, but I didn't
ask him. They were a group, a gang of seven, who always
worked together, drank together, and now were on strike together, and Eduardo was their political spokesman.

He was heavily built, tall, had a fat belly, dark hair, black,
sparkless eyes, blown up by the thick lenses of his black-
framed spectacles, and extremely white, swollen, puffy
hands in which he was now holding a miniature notebook
and a tiny, thin pencil, no bigger than a match-stick. He was
now standing in the far corner of the room, saying something
to a boy they called Guido, who looked more like a clerk in a
post-office than a navvy in the Genoese docks. Guido listened, and nodded. It was not only with his head that he
nodded, he nodded with his eyelids, then with his nostrils,
and then it was his thin neck that nodded. And now he was
coming towards me with a cunning effort to give himself a
casual air. First he walked half-way towards the door, then
towards the window, and round the table. Then he stopped,
lit a cigarette, and squatted down in the narrow space between Luciano's chair and mine.

"Which company is your friend with?" he asked me.

"I don't think he is with any company," I said.

Guido didn't believe me. For him Genoa was shipyards
and shipping companies. Nothing else was Genoa.

"We are not like this every night," Luciano said again.
"But today we are on strike. That's why."

"Well, then, what does your friend do?" Guido insisted.

Well, what did he do? I looked at Harris. At present he
was drunk. That much was certain. The whole world seemed
to have shrunk for him to the few square inches of Arturo's
guitar, and to the few words and notes of the song, and he
was happily enjoying its narrowness and sensuality. He tried
to sing in chorus with Arturo. His voice was high pitched and
vulgar. Either he wasn't aware of being horribly out of tune,
or he was out of tune with premeditation, in that sort of

reckless way people are when, at closing time at the Green Man in Edgware Road, they try to make it quite clear that they are singing because they are enjoying themselves and not because they enjoy singing.

"He lectures at the university," I said, but Guido still didn't believe me. Perhaps he was right. Because, after all, with all that money sticking out of Tom Harris' pockets, how did I know that he was not with one of the shipping companies? How did I know that he wasn't importing comic-strip cartoons from Canada, or selling oranges to Poland?

"He *is* with a shipping company," Guido repeated, and there was just a trifle too much self-assurance in his voice. "He *is*, I tell you . . ." He broke off suddenly. Without turning his head, he knew that Umberto had approached us and was now standing behind him. He lifted himself from his crouching position between the two chairs and walked away.

Because of his strength, Umberto had to keep a constant, friendly smile on his face. Otherwise no one would dare to venture within the reach of his limbs. His was not a heavyweight boxer's, or weight-lifter's, type of musculature. It wasn't a Tarzan type either. Just as Arturo could have walked out from between the carved stones of a mediaeval Notre Dame, Umberto could have walked out of an anatomical atlas. He was a perfectly well-drawn, standard model of the human male, better than perfectly well-drawn, as every feature of his anatomy was just slightly exaggerated, every bone, every muscle, just a little bigger, but in proportion, so that you couldn't even say where in particular his exceptional strength resided; it was everywhere.

"My wife has baked a pie. All of you come and try it," he said.

"No, we can't," Carlo said. "It's two in the morning. Your kids will wake up."

"That's true," Umberto said. "Hadn't thought about

49

that." He looked with admiration at Carlo. "We can't wake the kids up," he repeated.

Tom Harris lifted his head.

"Whose kids?" he asked. His voice was hoarse now. He coughed.

"Umberto's," Carlo said.

"How many kids have you got, Umberto?" Tom asked.

"Two," Umberto said.

"And how old are they?"

"One is four, and one is five," Umberto said.

But Tom's eyes didn't look like the eyes of people who talk about children.

"And your . . ."

I knew he was going to say something nasty. About Umberto's wife, probably.

"Shut up, Tom," I said in English.

His gaze moved slowly from Umberto's face to mine.

"And who are you to tell me to shut up?" he said.

"You are drunk, and you know it," I said.

"Sure I know it," he said. "You don't need to tell me that I know it. But this is *my* night, and . . ." he stood up and repeated in Italian: "This is my night, and I invite you all to . . ."

Till this moment he had been half drunk and half acting as if he were drunk. Now the acting half had disappeared. With both his hands, he started rubbing his forehead and his eyes. "To . . ." he repeated several times. And then, with a sudden gleam in his eyes, he said: "To the Green Man."

"Where?" Eduardo asked.

" 'The Green Man,' " Tom Harris repeated. And he translated it: " 'Uomo Verde.' "

"Where is it?" they asked.

"How do you mean where is it?" he said. "It is in Via Edgware. Let's go."

50

They looked at him, baffled.

"Tom," I said. "You can't do that. You simply can't."

"And why not, if you please?" he asked. "Why can't we go to the Green Man?"

"Because of the English licensing hours," I said. "You haven't noticed, it is past closing time."

He hadn't been in England for some eighteen years now and it took him a good part of a minute to understand what I said. He took the cigarette out of his mouth and squashed it.

"Bloody English licensing hours," he said. "Bloody English closing time. Why don't they take the whole bloody Island and haul it somewhere else? The bloody thing is still much too near. I hate it. I'll never go back. Never, never, never. I hate all the bloody English Attlees and all the bloody English Churchills, and all the bloody English Gaitskells and all the bloody English Macmillans and all the bloody English zoo-keepers and all the bloody English cops and all the bloody English Jewesses and all the bloody English Italians. I hate them all, I hate Sir Francis and Lady Celia, I hate my father and my mother, I hate my brother and my sister, I hate my wife and all her lovers . . ." he took a deep breath and pointed his finger at me.

"What is he saying?" Umberto asked.

"Nothing," I said. "He is getting things out of his system."

But Umberto didn't understand, and I didn't know how to say it in Italian.

They sat and stood around, not knowing what it was all about, and yet, each in his own individual way, they succeeded somehow in silently, and yet actively, respecting his outburst.

The young waiter came in and grinned:

"Didn't I tell you? Nine men! You really can't enjoy yourselves without a woman!"

"I invite you all to 'Il Paradiso,' " Tom Harris said.

Arturo struck a chord on his guitar, silenced it with the palm of his hand, and stood up. He was impressed.

" 'Il Paradiso'?" Alfredo repeated incredulously, and rubbed his unshaven chin with the back of his hand. Alfredo was nondescript. There was nothing special about him—nothing, except the sort of greyishness that made him disappear unnoticed wherever he was. He would be the average man in the street to whose ways of seeing the things of this world philosophers refer, when it is their wish to describe what they mean by "naive reality." Which only shows how little they know what reality is to the average man in the street, or in the bush, or in the docks of Genoa.

Umberto had a large, black, shiny Ford Anglia, Alfredo had a Fiat Saloon. It was past two a.m. and the roads were empty. We swished on along the bay of Genoa like two gangster cars in an American movie. But it turned out that at "Il Paradiso" they wouldn't let us in. We had only four ties for the nine of us. And so, as "our" night-club didn't want us, they decided to take us to theirs. It was situated at the very bottom of the slope, among the dockyards, and its bright, red neon spelled "Zanzi-bar" into the calm darkness of the night. An officer of the merchant navy was sitting alone at a small table in the first room by the entrance, a white cap on his head, and a bottle of gin in front of him. In the second room, the bandmaster noticed Arturo, the band stopped playing and started a new tune in his honour. Arturo laughed with pleasure. We left him there, went to the third room and sat under the wall behind a long table. Luciano sat stiffly, his shoulders against the wall, and, silently, began to cry. "Let him," Umberto whispered. It could have been either a wife or a child. And either another man, or death. It must have been something he had lost. Unless he had lost himself. There was no other possibility for that sort of crying. It was old-fashioned. The whole place was old-fashioned. Almost as old-fashioned as the first films with Pola Negri. If Andrea had put a hat on, she could have gone straight to church,—and the first morning mass was due in just a few hours; she had stockings on, a grey skirt, and a grey pullover up to her chin. She pushed a low stool forward, sat on it in front of our table, and quietly and methodically, with her hands only, demonstrated what she could do to an imaginary male member. There was realism in the rhythm of her movements and an open sarcasm at the corners of her lips. And she was being looked at with the greatest respect. Not so—Gracia. Gracia was tolerated. She went along, and with her clenched fist hit each of us, one after another on the shoulder. The third girl, Lucia, said: "She is not a strong woman. She's a cry-baby, she can hit you, but if you hit her, she starts a row and cries for hours. She is not a strong woman. I am a strong woman. I can hit you, and you can hit me, and it's all right. O.K.?"

Without his guitar, which he had left in the car, Arturo looked slightly taller. Maybe because now, without it, he kept his enormous head up, and one saw less of his hairless scalp and more of his smiling face. He came straight to me and said, in French:

"Ecoutez, vous êtes un homme, n'est-ce pas?"

"Yes," I said. "I hope so."

"Alors, moi aussi je suis un homme."

"Yes," I said.

"Et votre ami? Il veut danser avec moi. Dites donc, est-ce qu'il est pédéraste?"

"Nonsense," I said.

"S'il est pédéraste, ça ne me regarde pas; je l'aime bien mais je ne veux pas danser avec lui. Dites-lui que je ne veux pas danser avec lui. Vous me comprenez, je suis un homme, n'est-ce pas?"

"Yes," I said.

"Alors, pourquoi veut-il danser avec moi s'il n'est pas pédéraste?"

"Perhaps because he likes you," I said.

"Il m'aime? Mais non, je ne suis pas sympathique. Il est bien sympathique, lui, si. Je l'aime, mais c'est pas une raison pour danser, n'est-ce pas? Alors pourquoi veut-il danser avec moi s'il n'est pas pédéraste et moi je suis un homme?"

He was almost apologising for being "un homme." And yet he saw the funny side of it all and his black eyes sparkled humorously.

"Pourquoi?" he insisted.

"Perhaps . . ." I started, and thought better of it.

"Oui . . . ?" he asked.

"I don't know," I said. "Maybe you remind him of something that belongs to his past."

Arturo's face changed suddenly. At first it shrank a little for a moment and there was no smile on it. Without a smile it was quite a different face. But almost at once (though slowly, as in a film in which a bud opens before your eyes and develops into a flower) it filled with comprehension.

"Dites donc," he said. "Est-ce qu'il vient de la classe ouvrière?"

I didn't expect that sort of question.

"Well," I said. "Yes, he does."

"Dio mio!" He started rubbing his bald head with the palm of his hand. "Mais comment," he paused for a moment. and then repeated: "Mais comment reussit-il à commencer?"

He put into words what had been puzzling me all the time. He didn't ask: "How did he manage to succeed?" What he asked was: "How did he manage to start?"

Arturo noticed that I had grown somewhat pensive and, to express his sympathy, he held out his hand to shake mine. I appreciated it. But as our palms touched, there was a flash of blinding light bursting in through the door of the middle room and, without a word, we both turned round and rushed in.

The band repeated the same bar three times, and then went on playing. But nobody danced. The slim, black silhouette of Ricardo, cut in two by the red cummerbund which girded his loins, stood there without motion. I had spoken to him before, when he had first come to our table to greet us. Whether he was a Spaniard or not, I didn't know, nor did it matter. In his costume of a torero he looked more Spanish than many Hollywood Spaniards. Yet his Scottish accent was perfect and I didn't know whether he was a male/female whore, or a male/male whore. He was standing there, under the whitewashed wall of the dance-room, proud of his perfect body, motionless and non-committal. But he was not the centre of the stage. At the centre of the stage was a Venetian straw hat, with a red ribbon. It was exactly like the straw hats of a girls' public school in Sussex, and the only strange thing about it was that I saw it on Tom Harris' head.

Silent with cold anger, he stood beside Ricardo, bent forward, one hand on Ricardo's shoulder, the other pointing across the room. There, in the corner, stood a young boy in a dark suit and a bow tie. He was both white with fear and, like a young cock, pushing his bespectacled head forward, ready to attack. In his hands he was holding a flash-light camera and pressing it to his stomach.

When Umberto had come to the dance-room, whether before us or just after us, I hadn't noticed. But he was there now. He walked to the corner where the boy was standing, turned round, and the boy, shut in the triangular space between the two walls and Umberto's shoulders, could do nothing now but breathe and wait.

"The camera, per favore," Umberto said.

The boy pushed the camera from behind, under Umberto's right armpit, and Umberto took hold of it with his left hand. He examined it first, with appreciation, and then, expertly, as if he were a shop assistant demonstrating camerawork to a customer, he released the catch, clicked open the back wall, pulled out a few inches of the film and tore it off. Then he shut the camera carefully, handed it back to the boy, went across the room to where Tom stood watching him, and gave him the bit of film.

The band went on playing.

"Votre ami," said Arturo softly, "il n'aime pas être photographié, n'est-ce pas? Il paraît qu'il est vulnérable," he added.

The photographer tip-toed towards the door and was gone. Tom Harris had taken off his Venetian straw hat and was paying the bill for everybody. With Arturo, I crossed to the front room. The officer of the merchant navy sat there in the same position as before, alone, at the same table. But now, on the bottle of gin in front of him, a gold watch was hanging on a knotted chain, measuring the time he allowed himself ashore. We went to the entrance door and stepped out.

The neon-sign "Zanzi-bar" was glowing red as before, but the sky was no longer black, it was pale blue. We stood at the porch, under the sign, and breathed in the fresh morning air. Luciano came out and joined us. ". . . strike till Monday," he finished a sentence, which he must have begun silently.

One after another, the men were coming out from the joint to greet the rising sun and fill their lungs. We went to the site by the warehouse where the cars had been parked. But then I decided to walk. So did Tom Harris.

It was that early half-hour when the nightwatchman's eyes are already half-closed, and the day-worker's are only half-open.

"Tom," I said.

The sound of his name startled him. But he didn't wait to hear what I wanted.

"I am going away tomorrow," he said, and I was certain he had decided to do so, or perhaps only to say so, just then, at that very moment.

"Tom," I repeated. "Do you know who the boy was?"

"What boy?"

"The boy who tried to take your photograph?"

He didn't answer.

"Was he Bruno's son?" I asked.

He had the most courteous manner of not answering questions. He treated you as if you were talking to yourself and he didn't wish to interfere with your thoughts.

"All right," I said, meaning I don't know what.

The climbing didn't help our conversation. We were too old to talk and climb the stony steps at the same time. When we had finally reached the upper road, I asked him:

"Are you really going away tomorrow?"

"Yes," he said, guardedly.

"Well, then, I suppose I'd better tell you now."

"Tell me what?" he asked.

"Are you going to see Giuseppe?"

"I don't know. Why?"

"Do," I said.

"Why?"

I told him how I had met Bruno at Maria's. He looked pensive but didn't say a word. The church bells started to ring. That peculiar series of sounds in which the original notes are overpowered and drawn in their own harmonics.

"Do you know the boy who tried to photograph you at the 'Zanzi-bar'?" I asked again.

This time he answered me.

"Yes, I do," he said.

"Was it Bruno's son?"

"No."

"Who was he?"

"One of my students," he answered.

"Good Lord!" I said.

"Quite," he said. After a moment, he added: "And that's not all."

"What else?"

"I've lost some papers."

"Stolen?"

"Probably."

"Concerning your work?"

"Concerning my career."

"Well," I said. "Are you going to see Giuseppe?"

"No," he said.

"He will know how to deal with people like Bruno."

"Undoubtedly. But I can defend myself. In my own way."

"What will you do?"

"Nothing till I'm attacked."

"Nonsense," I said. "It is the attack itself that is dangerous. If it comes to a fight later on, I have no doubt that you'll win. But the damage will have been done. Some of the mud will stick."

"And how does it concern you?" he asked.

"That wasn't a very kind remark, you know."

"It wasn't meant to be," he said.

The sun was already sparkling in the blue bay below us. It was certainly worth climbing up to see it. But the hot blood had risen to our cheeks and we felt short of breath.

"Tom," I began. "I came specially to Genoa to warn you . . ."

"You came to warn me?" he interrupted. "I thought you came to see Pamela."

"Well," he added, after a pause, "she is staying at the 'Vittoria.' I don't know if they named the place after our Queen Victoria, or after some other defeated woman."

I spent all Sunday and Sunday night in bed. On Monday morning I took a train to Nervi.

58

Orange trees grew on both sides of the narrow street, oranges fell on the benches but they didn't look edible. A path led to a small gate,—that was the beach entrance to the "Vittoria,"—though the beach was cut off by the railway track hidden behind a mass of anonymous green leaves, and to get to it, or back to the hotel, one had to pass through an underground passage in which the sound of footsteps reverberated and came back from unexpected places at unexpected moments, while an old painter tried to sell you handmade portraits of the male and female members of the family of the never-to-be-forgotten Benito Mussolini.

There were no fewer than four Rolls-Royces among the cars parked in the shade by the drive, and four uniformed chauffeurs playing a game of cards at the edge of the lawn.

"Oh, I hate this place," the lady-receptionist said.

"It's all right," I said, "I shan't be staying long here."

"I wish I could say that," she said.

The view from my window was a view into a hot emptiness. A beautiful, blue, hot emptiness, in which nothing can take its beginning. A bird can cut this emptiness in its flight but it cannot be born anywhere in it. A man can look at it and see images and hear voices, but these images and these voices will be coming to him from the inside of his own skull. The blazing hot emptiness of the sky was void; without the blue brine of the sea beneath, without the black sharpness of the rocky beach, without the shabby yellowish building down there at the edge of the lawn, without the four chauffeurs playing cards in its shade, without the red chaise-longue in the garden—the hot blue void above was barren.

I went down. Perhaps I wouldn't have recognised her if I hadn't known that she was staying at the "Vittoria." But she was unmistakably there; in the garden; in one of those red long-chairs I had seen from my window; a small table by her side and on top of it a few books; two pairs of spectacles and a glass of lemonade.

59

At school she played hockey. Then, and later, she played tennis; she hunted, she swam, and she sailed. She stopped seeing her friends when, for some five years she was married to Tom Harris. Now she was an old lady, white dull hair, wrinkles, brown spots on her hands, and varicose veins on her legs. Yet I recognised her unmistakably and at once.

I took a seat in the long-chair beside her. She was reading *Elle*. I tried to imagine what *I* had been like some thirty years before. She glanced at me, and stopped reading. Then she glanced at me once more, and started reading again. And then the luncheon gong burst out from the French windows of the hotel.

I stood up and went in.

I saw her coming in, but the dining-room was enormous and her table was at the other end of it, and the sight of the menu absorbed my attention. I felt hungry. Maybe that was why I enjoyed the corpses of a sole and two anonymous fishes and a dozen prawns in sauce tartare plus a piccolo bottle of white wine so much that the head waiter came to talk to me and make friends and open the door with a bow when I left.

And now, sitting in the bar of this multi-starred hotel, I poured a spoonful of black coffee over this marine cemetery from which no living cell can escape, and without which no living cell can live, and identified myself with the prawns I had eaten in the same racial way the English identify themselves with Shakespeare, the Italians with Dante, and the French with Descartes.

An ornamental clock above the shelf of bottles seemed to have stopped. But when I next looked at it, its short hand was showing *iv*. What had happened to some two hours? I looked around: there was nothing to tell me where they had disappeared.

/ LETTERS

CARO AMICO,

I am deep in sadness and grief. When you first saw me, I was all in white, except for a little red cross on my cornetta (how do you call it in English?) Today I am all in black. Yes, my dear amico. I have just come back from his funeral, and it has been such a hot day, and the fact that it is to you that I am writing this letter at such a time shows how I feel about you.

Love is God-given, even a misplaced love, and I know that you will understand if I tell that I have never loved any man as really as I loved him.

And now he is dead. I still can't understand it. Why? Why did he do it? He could have lived with the nasty thing for years and years. "Bruno, my darling," I used to tell him, "don't do it, please don't." I bought him a beautiful Old England scarf, it covered the thing completely, and it suited him, and he knew it suited him, and then, all of a sudden, he decided he would be operated on, and that was how he died, under the knife, without regaining consciousness. Oh, my God, why? Why did he want to be operated on? I ask, and ask, but of course I know why. Poor, poor Bruno.

As we were coming back from the ceremony, Silvia embraced me and said "Now try to forget, darling." You know about Silvia, I told you. The only thing I didn't tell you was that she is my sister. I don't know why I didn't tell you that, I really don't know, but well, then, as I said, Silvia embraced me and said "Now try and forget it all, darling Maria," but I don't think that is good advice. No, it isn't. When there is something to grieve over, grief is as vital as joy when there is something to be happy about. I see so many sick people every day, and dead people, and have to talk to their friends and families, and now, suddenly, I am one of those to whom I usually have to talk, and that is what I am telling myself: No, I am not going to escape my grief, I am going to absorb it into my system, to heal my wounds with it.

Silvia couldn't possibly understand this. For her, the world of men and the world of women are two different worlds, run on two different routines. Does she know that he did it for her, because of her? It doesn't make any difference whether she knows or not. She didn't ask him to do it. Within her world, actively, she didn't do anything wrong. And for her, his world is something for which she can't possibly be held responsible: it was not she who established its strange, masculine, incomprehensible ways, and if my poor Bruno, big strong Bruno, who spent forty years of his life making money out of rubber in Malaya, if one day he decides to behave like a child or like a fool, the fact that he does it because he happens to be in love with her and not with some other woman cannot affect her. But that's enough about her.

My dear, dear friend. I don't want to see you now, and it is good that you are away, but it is good also to know that you *are*, and I can write to you, and perhaps ask your advice. Because something has occurred and I am much worried. I haven't yet had time to think rationally about it, but I already know, yes, I am already certain, well, but let me tell you what has happened.

The operation didn't take place in my hospital. Anyway, even if it had, I wouldn't have been there to assist. It is true that in our profession one is trained to be detached and unemotional, yet there are limits which one should respect, unless in an emergency. So you see, I wasn't actually in the theatre, but I was outside, waiting. And praying. Was I praying? I don't remember, but I suppose I was. Where am I? Oh, yes; so I actually didn't see him on the table but I did see him before. I was in his room and stayed with him till they gave him his first injection. Anaesthetic. He looked so big in the white hospital bed, I never thought hospital beds could look so small, he looked like an overgrown, healthy, robust child. "Bruno," I wanted to say, "please, Bruno, don't be a fool. It won't change anything, and you know it," but I didn't. It was too late anyway. The hospital machinery was already working and sucking him slowly into its routine. Besides, I somehow knew that he had no doubt how it would end, and that nothing would have persuaded him now because that was how he wanted it to end, and that was his, the strong man's, way of finishing with it all.

I don't think I cried, but my lower lip trembled and it was such an effort to control the trembling, and as I couldn't control it by an effort of will, I told myself I must do it by using sheer force, by biting my lip. And he noticed it, and he said what lovely teeth I had.

"What lovely white teeth you have, Maria," he said, and sat up.

I thought he was going to kiss me, but he didn't. He slid open the drawer of the little table by his bed, and took a large, thick, manilla envelope out of it.

"I want you to do something for me, Maria," he said.

"Yes, Bruno," I said.

"If I die . . ." he began. But I didn't let him finish.

"What nonsense!" I said. "Of course you will not."

63

"All right," he said, "if I don't die you can give it back to me unopened."

"Good," I said. "I shall give it back to you the first thing tomorrow morning and we shall both have a good laugh together."

"Certainly," he said. "But if I do die, give it to Giambattista."

"To your son?" I asked.

"Yes," he said. "It is my wedding present to him. Do you promise?"

"I promise," I said.

"Good," he said. And I somehow didn't like the way he said it. I couldn't say why, but I didn't like it. "And not a word about it to anybody," he added. "Not a word to Silvia, not a word to Giuseppe!" he said. And I liked that still less.

And then they came to give him his first injection and I wanted to put the envelope into my handbag, but it was too big, so I held it in my hand all the time I was standing outside the operating theatre and till I came back at last and put it in my chest of drawers where it still is.

Oh, Jesus, Jesus, Jesus! Can you still read my handwriting? I feel so shaky, and so . . . all alone in this room, my black hat on the armchair, my black gloves on the floor, my black shoes kicked off wide apart, oh, no, not all alone, he is somewhere here watching me, and his thick envelope is there under the white towels in the chest of drawers, oh my dear friend, I never take tranquillisers, a few drops of valerian or bromide yes, occasionally, but never tranquillisers. I give them to the patients, of course, when I'm told to do so, but I never take them myself, I don't believe in them, I think they change people's personalities and I'm frightened they can make me become somebody else, and I always think I must deal with situations as I may by myself, but how to deal with this present situation I don't know, I don't understand myself, please tell me why, why do I not take the envelope, go to his son, and say simply: "Giambattista, your father asked me to give you this. Here it is. Take it." I don't know why I can't do it, but I cannot. I know that if I did it, I would feel as if I were the blade of a knife held by somebody else's hand.

These are terrible words to say, and he is somewhere here watching me write them down, and what is it actually that has made me feel so suspicious? Just the way he said those few words binding me to keep it secret? And here I am already breaking my promise by writing about it to you, and why to you? I shall tell you in a moment, but it is so hot in this room, I must take off my brassière first, it is black, too, you know, and I must have a drink of water.

Black! I know that black can be very elegant. And exciting, even if in a morbid way, but I am used to being all in white, and being dressed in black makes me feel so old and, oh, dear friend, I can't give Giambattista that envelope without being certain that there is nothing black and horrible in it, but can I be certain without opening it, which, of course, is unthinkable. Is there anybody who could tell me what it contains? I have been asking myself that question from the moment they told me he was dead till now and I think I have found an answer. You can. Yes, you, dear.

You remember the day you left so suddenly? It was Thursday, my day off, not so long ago but it seems ages, but you didn't know my day off was Thursday, and it happened that on my way back home I went to the hospital just for a moment and they told me that somebody had been asking for me, and I guessed it was you, and I was furious, my God, how furious I was, because you had only been staying with me for five days then and were already, as I thought, watching me, spying on me, oh no, Madonna, I wouldn't have it, I was free, I was a professional woman, you might not have known what it meant, here, in Italy, where women are still subdued to men, it costs a lot to become a professional woman, it is like taking vows, it means that you will never marry and have a family in the ordinary way, because an Italian will never have the courage to marry a professional woman who will earn her own money and go out and see other men, no, I told myself, I am free, wives and mothers are not free, nuns are not free, my sister Silvia who is a whore is not free, but I am, and I rushed home in a fury, I don't remember having been so enraged since I was a child, and I took my latch-key and opened the door, and it was like a sudden shower of cold water, the room was empty and your things were gone. I saw your note on the table and I thought I knew what it would say. So I burst out laughing and then I didn't stop laughing and started to cry, I didn't know one could do those two things together, it was loud and ugly, and you see I had known you only for five days then, and yet "Oh, my darling, my darling," I was saying "how could you do such a thing to me? How could you do such a thing to me," I was repeating and repeating, and I do often see people talking aloud to themselves, or to some other people who are not there, and now I was doing the same thing and couldn't help it, it was stronger than me, and then I noticed the empty bottle of Conegliano champagne.

I know only one person who used to drink Conegliano champagne and bring a bottle when he came to visit me. It was Bruno. So I dried my eyes, took your note which was on the table untouched, I took it in my hands and started reading it. It didn't contain what I thought it would, there was nothing in it to show that you were jealous or indiscreet. On the other hand, as you may well remember, it was so short, just a few lines about the urgency and necessity of your going to Genoa. It was its brevity that forced me to do some thinking. I put it back on the table, and only then noticed the ashtray.

I took the ashtray in my hands and walked with it to the window. There weren't any cigarette-ends in it, or ash, it was filled with some bits of glittering metal, bits of broken glass, and a wrist-strap. I recognised it. It was Bruno's. And I was frightened. I was sure that you had been fighting there, in my room, and if it had been your watch, I would have thought that he had killed you; which is silly because why should it depend on whose watch it was, and all the same, if it had been your watch I would have thought that he had forced you to write that note, and then killed you. You know, he was the only man I really loved, but that doesn't mean that I had any illusions, ever.

Half an hour later I was knocking on his door.

"You came to see me today, Bruno," I said.

"I did," he said.

"And what happened?" I asked.

"Nothing," he said.

"Did you have a fight?"

"Nonsense," he said. "We didn't even shake hands."

"And the watch?"

"That was a sort of accident."

"Why has he left, then?"

"Oh, has he?" he said. "I didn't know he had."

"You mean, you left first, and he was all right when you left?"

"Yes," he said. "We drank a bottle of wine, and I went. The rest is none of my business."

"And what *was* your business?" I asked.

"Nothing," he said.

"I *must* know," I insisted. "What were you talking about when you were drinking your champagne and smashing wrist-watches?"

"Well, if you must know, then I will tell you," he said, and waited.

"I must," I said.

"Well then," he said, "we were talking about a wedding present for my son." And he chuckled as if it were a joke.

I also thought it was a joke, but later on, in the hospital, when he handed me that envelope and said "It is a wedding present for my son," I knew that I had already heard those words, and now I'm sure that it was not a joke, and that you must know something about it.

Please, please, dear friend, do answer me, and quickly. Do you know what is in the envelope? If you tell me it contains counterfeit money, I shall give it to Giambattista unhesitatingly. If you tell me it contains the stolen plans of a fortress I shall give it to him. Even if you tell me that you cannot tell me but that it is all right, I shall give it to him, because I have confidence in you. But if you tell me that it hides a black poisonous spider who, as soon as the envelope is open, will creep out and start tormenting people—then I don't know what I shall do; I shall not be able either to fulfil or not to fulfil what I promised him on his death bed.

I am going to the post-office now to send this off and to start waiting for your answer.

Affectionately yours,
MARIA

Maria's second letter:
Milano, May 30, 1963.

CARO AMICO,

Is it possible? Is it true? Of course it is. Oh misery, misery, misery! I spent hours reading and re-reading your long and kind letter, yes, certainly, it all holds together, and it is worse than my worst premonitions were telling me. So what he wants is virtually to charge that poor Signor Harris with a murder which he did not commit, my God, some twenty-five years ago, when I was a little child, and then to put the blame on Giuseppe by showing that he must have been behind it! I think his mind must have been deranged during those long years in Malaya. I think—well, I don't know what I think. I don't know what to do. I don't know why I should have a share in that awful plot. I know, of course, that such awful things do happen in real life, but my life has never been real, not in that sense, no, real life comes to me in ambulances, sometimes with policemen and detectives hanging about, and I wash it, and dress its wounds, and bandage it, but so far I have never been in it, never been responsible for it.

This morning I wanted to change the towels in the bathroom, and went to the chest of drawers to fetch some fresh ones, and simply couldn't force myself to open it, didn't dare look at the envelope that was there underneath. Oh, Bruno, Bruno! Why should you have chosen me to execute your last will? Misery, misery, misery! It's true that I don't quite see why Giuseppe should be spending so much money on that poor Signor Harris, but he could have had some other reasons, not at all sinister. This whole business is much too much involved for me alone, I think I shall go and see dom Antonio. He is my spiritual director. I shall finish this letter after I have seen him.

Venerdì, 31 maggio, 1963.

I have just seen dom Antonio. He received me not in the abbey, as he used to, but in the summer house in the garden. It is very beautiful. Their garden. And the summer house. There was a sort of bottle-green warm shade inside and only a few very thin rays of golden sunlight managed to penetrate the thick foliage around and scratch the air as if it were a bit of stained glass window, well, I don't know how to describe it so that you would feel the happiness of that seclusion, but perhaps it is not necessary. Two heavy armchairs stood there

69

like two thrones carved in wood, and a low thick-legged table between them. On it, a beautiful flask of white wine, and a basket of fruit.

"I thought we should be more comfortable here, in the garden," he said. "It is quite cool in the shade, or is it too hot for you?"

"It's perfect," I said.

He knew at once that I had come not in the ordinary way but with some special purpose.

"Well, relax, my child, and tell me everything from the very beginning," he said.

It took me about an hour to tell him everything from the very beginning, and he listened to me very patiently and kindly.

"You have told me a very strange story, my daughter," he said. "A very strange story indeed."

"You do believe me, father, don't you?" I asked.

"O yes, of course I believe you," he said. "A story doesn't become less true just because it is out of the ordinary."

"What am I to do then, father," I said, hoping he would give me a straight answer, and that the nightmare would be finished. "A dying man asked me to do something for him, and I promised him, and . . ."

"I quite understand," dom Antonio said. "It is a very serious matter. A very serious matter indeed."

And then he said:

"Tell me, my child, that friend of your friend, that Signor Harris, is he a Catholic?"

"Yes," I said at first, without thinking, because in Italy it is natural that people are Catholics, but then I reflected and said: "Well, perhaps not, I don't know, he may be a Protestant, or even, I don't know, there are so many other sects where he comes from, but he is certainly a Christian."

I seemed to have been reading his thoughts, and he mine, and I went on talking, perhaps unnecessarily:

70

"But look, father," I said. "Bruno also was a Catholic, but he didn't practise, either. Giuseppe is a Catholic and he too doesn't practise . . ."

I don't know why I said "either." Why did I take it for granted that Signor Harris doesn't practise his religion, whatever it is? Or did I mean that he should be entitled to at least as much consideration as a non-practising Catholic, like Bruno or Giuseppe? No, I can't say exactly what I meant. And dom Antonio saw it. He held up a finger admonishingly, and said:

"Practising is one thing, and being a Catholic is another. Practising depends on one's will. One can stop practising one day, and then, when the time is ripe, one can start practising again. It is not so well with baptism. Baptism is different. Baptism is an independent physical reality. It is a physical fact. Once one has been baptised, it is for ever. It is indelible."

"Yes, father," I said. "But I understand from my friend (meaning you) that that poor Signor Harris has struggled so much, in his own way, to find his purpose in life, his spiritual purpose in life, and now, suddenly, is being menaced by . . . by that . . ."

He interrupted me:

"I do not question your friend's good intentions. But his concern, undoubtedly a very worthy concern, is with Signor Harris's well-being, even if it is his spiritual well-being; we, however, are not welfare officers, are we?"

"Yet," I said, "we ought to spare people any unnecessary suffering."

"Not all suffering is unnecessary, as you, being a sister of mercy, certainly know."

"Yes, father," I said.

"The way to the Church leads through suffering," he said.

"Yes, father," I said.

"And it should not be barred by us."

71

"No, father," I said.

"Because that sort of suffering is necessary," he said.

"Yes, father," I said.

"And who are we to know which of those two kinds of suffering, necessary and unnecessary, the mysterious envelope will bring to Signor Harris?"

I was silent.

"Listen, child," dom Antonio said. "It is not my duty to judge."

"No, father," I said.

"Now, you tell me," he said. "What is my duty?"

"Your duty, father, is to enlighten me as to what is the right thing to do."

He smiled.

"No," he shook his head. "Not exactly." He looked deep into my eyes, and said: "My duty is to save your soul." And I shivered.

Of course I wanted my soul saved, as everybody does, but it had never occurred to me before that a situation may arise in which something that is necessary for saving one's soul might clash with what one thinks is doing the right thing. The very thought frightened me.

"But, father," I started. He didn't let me go on, and I don't remember now what I wanted to say.

"Would your friend," he asked sharply, (meaning you, of course, my dear), "would he be capable of stealing the envelope from you?"

"O no, father," I said. "I'm sure he wouldn't do that."

"Then," he said, "if he wouldn't steal it for the sake of his friend, how is it that he dares to ask you to steal it by not fulfilling the last wish of a man who is now dead? How dare he ask you to be a judge of envelopes and people?"

"But father," I said, "it is not only the question of Signor Harris . . ."

72

"Hush!" he interrupted me.

"The thing is really aimed at Giuseppe and Silvia."

"Hush!" he said sternly. And only now I noticed that we were not alone. A young monk was standing by the door. As soon as I stopped talking, he entered, bent over dom Antonio's right ear, and whispered something I couldn't hear.

Dom Antonio stood up.

"Excuse me, please," he said, and walked out, followed by the monk.

I was left alone. With a flask of wine I didn't dare touch, in this sort of doll's house, surrounded by green bushes and flowers. I don't know how long I waited. Perhaps half an hour, perhaps three-quarters. When it occurred to me that they might have forgotten me, I stood up in the doorway, wondering what to do. And then I saw another young monk walking along between the flower beds. I coughed quickly, and he noticed me. He stopped and looked at me. His face was pale and calm but I had no doubt that there were traces of tears in his eyes. He held his hands clasped in front of him.

"Could I help you?" he asked.

"Yes," I said. "I am waiting for dom Antonio, and he seems to . . ."

"Dom Antonio," he repeated with astonishment. "Dom Antonio left for Rome with the Archbishop of Milan about half an hour ago," he said.

There was nothing else for me to do there. I went back, first along the pergola to the wall of the abbey, then down a narrow path between the flower beds to the front garden, and finally to the gate. And it was only when I found myself in the centre of the town, at the Piazza della Scala, that I woke up and understood what had happened. Those enormous headlines all around: COLLASSO DEL PAPA. Nelle prime ore di stamane il Pontefice si è aggravato—Nuove emorragie che

73

sono diventate sempre più violente—Al Santo Padre sarebbe
già stata somministrata l'Estrema Unzione.

No, I can't write a word more. I shall finish this letter later.

Sabato, 1 giugno

PRODIGIO! E' ANCORA VIVO! Alle 16 il Papa si è risvegliato e
ha conversato con i cardinali. Stamane aveva detto: "Ho
seguito passo passo la mia morte; mi avvio dolcemente verso
la fine."

Domenica

LA GRANDE ANIMA DEL PAPA IN UN ALTRO GIORNO DI AGONIA.
Mother of God, why must he suffer so much and for so
long? He is the best pope we've ever had, why must he suffer
for so many long days?

Oh, my dear friend, I know that dom Antonio cannot
come back now, and it is so awful because I am waiting for
him to come back, and in my mind these two things have got
mixed together, the saintly agony, and the crime.

Lunedi, 3 giugno

E'MORTO. E'MORTO IL PAPA BUONO.
Il sereno trapasso alle ore 19.49.

No, I can't wait any longer. I am going to see Giuseppe. I
am going to tell him everything.

Affectionately yours,
MARIA

Giuseppe's letter,
Casa Bianca, Faggeto Lario, June 6th, 1963

Dear Sir,

I don't think we have ever met but I did speak to you on the telephone eighteen years ago, on which occasion you were so good as to let me have the address of The Green Man, Paddington, as the place where I was likely to encounter our common friend, Mr Tom Harris.

I take the liberty of writing to you now because I have just seen Maria, who has told me what she knows about recent events. In the circumstances, I am not surprised that she would tend to act melodramatically, I respect her feelings, and I am advising her to do nothing and to leave the problem in my hands. The history of crime and of modern journalism is full of entanglements belonging to that nauseating category, but some effective ways of dealing with them have been known.

I have persuaded Maria that the envelope was meant to be a wedding present and consequently she should feel under no obligation whatsoever to do anything about it before the person's marriage, if ever. To which she willingly agreed.

I intend to handle this case in my own way, which means: privately but openly, in the presence of my legal and other assistants, independent witnesses, and the people concerned.

I do not think, however, that the presence of Mr Tom Harris is indispensable. Neither is yours, Sir. Nevertheless, if you thought it would divert you to accept my invitation, I should be delighted to have this opportunity of meeting you.

I shall inform you of the date and place as soon as the arrangements are made.

Yours truly,
GIUSEPPE C.

/ GIUSEPPE

There were six paragraphs in Giuseppe's letter, and all six began with an "I." It was a good thing to know that the matter was now in his firm hands. He neither panicked nor lingered. No more than a week later he sent me a note confirming the invitation. Enclosed was an order to a travel agency asking them to organise my journey from wherever I happened to be to a place called Faggeto Lario. As I happened to be no more than twenty minutes by boat from it, just across on the opposite side of Lake Como, the carte blanche was rather useless, all the same it showed that Giuseppe was going to give a performance in style.

I had never met him (that brief encounter in the *rapido*, when I didn't even know who he was, didn't count; neither did that short conversation over the telephone when Mrs Holcman forced the receiver into my hand, about which I have already spoken at some length and shall say more later, perhaps). Yet, what I had heard about him sounded most intriguing. Especially, his way of making people's acquaintance. And captivating them. First, it was Tom Harris, in 1938. Then, Mrs Holcman, in 1943. And then Silvia, in 1960. He had the talent of spotting people at the very moment they happened to act out of character. And each time it would start by his giving something for nothing. With Tom Harris, it was some peanuts for his monkey; with Mrs Holcman it was a gramaphone record; with Silvia, it was some flowers he hadn't bought.

It was not in their character to behave as they did. Yet, it happens to all of us, at least once in our lifetime, if not once every year, that we act as if we were different persons, and then it is Giuseppe's business to be there at the precise moment, to penetrate our defences and get hold of our life. Not necessarily to our disadvantage. Tom Harris talked about it as if a kind of destiny had been using Giuseppe to descend upon people's lives. Destiny or not, what Giuseppe saw as he one day, in the late Autumn of 1938, walked into the milk bar in Soho—was a man with a monkey. He immediately withdrew, bought a packet of peanuts from a vendor on the corner of the street, came back and sat at the same table.

"Is it all right if I offer your friend a peanut?" he asked.

It was all right, and ten minutes later Giuseppe knew about Harris's youthful ambition to build a haircutting machine and his more recent preoccupation with mirrors.

"Persevere, my friend, persevere," Giuseppe said. "Hair cutting is of no importance, but there is something in your vision, I tell you. Not about what is outside the skull, the hair, but about what is inside it, the brain. And so it is with your mirrors. A mirror that reflects right-to-right and left-to-left is of *no* importance. You can build such a mirror easily, by putting two mirrors vertically at a right angle, or by taking a flexible mirror and bending it slightly along the middle. What *is* important is symmetry. Justice is not symmetrical, that much we know. Socially, the world is not symmetrical. But is it symmetrical physically? Is it? Kick a ball on its left cheek, it will move to the right; kick it on its right cheek, it will move to the left; so it looks as if the world were symmetrical. But it isn't. Make an experiment: take a coil of wire and push a magnet into it. Immediately some electric current will pass through the wire in one direction, to the left, let's say. Pull the magnet out, and the current will run in the opposite direction, to the right, let's say. Now, why not the other way round? Why doesn't it run to the right when you push, and to the left when you pull? Just as it would be if you looked at it in a mirror?"

It was for the first time in his life (and in 1938 he was about thirty five) that Tom Harris had had a conversation of that sort, a conversation about things that interested him, and not about some fringes but about what was essential, and in language he could understand. It was a pity that he had not met the stranger some time before, when he had been free to give himself wholly to those thoughts. It was too late now. Now he had his monkey, and it would be disloyal to divide his heart between it and some thoughts about coils and magnets. He kissed the monkey between the eyes and went on listening.

In another ten minutes, he learned all, or nearly all, about Giuseppe's work and Giuseppe's troubles.

"You see," Giuseppe said, giving another peanut to the monkey, "your little friend is intelligent. He is almost as intelligent as an average human being. And he is more intelligent than human society. Compare him with a rhinoceros. A rhinoceros is a useless brute. A rhinoceros is a steam-engine, a nineteenth century idea of power. And now look at your little friend's eyes, look at his fingers, observe how he opens the peanut and nibbles it. Do you know how many nerve cells are engaged in that operation? He may be a very old, a very ancient thing, but I tell you, he belongs to the twentieth century, he is the very newest idea of power. And you will see, of course, one day you will see that the big rhinoceros will only make more damage all around. It is the little, minute things that will push the world forward. Such things as those little, minute forces which criss-cross in your little monkey's brain when he nibbles his peanut. Yes, my friend. Do you remember the old radio detector we used to call the 'cat's whiskers'? How much energy, do you think, can pass through them?

Next to nothing. A million times more wouldn't be enough to wind up your wrist-watch. And yet, if you link the right sort of earphones to them, you will hear the fortissimo of Beethoven's Apassionata. Yes, my friend, our future lies in electrons not in elephants. They, the electrons, will do our work. Though, there is one snag there. Listen, do you know why you can't hear what the woman down there, by the cashier, is saying? It isn't because she doesn't speak loudly enough. It is because there is too much noise in the air between her and you. Now, when you amplify an electric signal, you also get noise. An electric noise. It comes from the random motion of electrons which gets amplified too. Do you follow me?"

"Go on," Harris said.

"It is as if you were trying to grow bigger apples, and found that the worms in them had grown bigger still, the size of pigs."

Suddenly, he took a pencil from his pocket, wrote something rapidly for a minute or two, on his paper napkin, and then gave it to Tom Harris. It was a list of books. (The same list of books for which, a few years later, when I visited Harris in prison, he had asked me to apply to the governor, as it had been taken away from him. They were textbooks of physics and chemistry, grammar-school level, but even so not easy to find at that time of the war.)

"Now," he went on, "can you imagine what it would be like if we could get rid of that electric noise? We could amplify input a million times, we could see miles into the darkness, we could use your headgear not for cutting hair but for communicating with the brain, we could build little circuits that would control the flight of aeroplanes,—and I know how to do it."

He stopped suddenly, looked into Tom's eyes, and asked:

"How did it sound?"

"What?"

79

"What I've been saying. Did it sound convincing?"

"Fairly."

"You are sure? Because, you see, I've been rehearsing. I'm going to see some rich bastards, peers of the realm, knights, industrialists, military men, it all depends on *them* now, I have already spent all the money I had, millions, not pounds, lire, on the workshop I have, not far from here, in an attic, in Soho, but the private experimenting is finished, now is the time to start the real work, which needs capital and equipment, they will give it to me, o yes, they will, they know it's business, they aren't stupid, and they are not bad either, the only thing they don't understand is that *all* my lire are gone and I don't have enough small change to wait for their big investments. Anyway, if they don't like me, I can go back to Musso."

"To what?"

"To Mussolini."

"Why don't you? Politics?"

"Yes and no. Something deeper. He likes great things. Big powers. Nothing under megawatts would appeal to him. I like small things. Weak currents. Electron-volts. He is too monumental for me. I like ordinary people."

Five minutes later, Tom Harris showed Giuseppe a cheque he had received the same morning from the executors of Sir Francis's will. It was a cheque for fifty pounds, Sir Francis's legacy.

"Would this be any good to you?" he asked.

Giuseppe looked at the cheque, then at his wrist-watch. It was 2.30 p.m.

"Look," he said, "it is a crossed cheque, I can't cash it myself, you must come with me, quick, before they close the bank."

He gulped down his milk-shake, called the waitress, hailed a taxi, all almost at the same time, and then, in the bank, as they were parting, he said:

"I may be a loser or I may be a winner. If I am a loser, you won't see me again, ever. But if I am a winner, you will hear from me. I don't know when. Maybe in two years' time, maybe in ten, maybe in twenty."

He saw him seven years later, in 1945, the same day that Mrs Holcman pressed the telephone receiver into my hand and practically forced me to tell Giuseppe where he was likely to find Tom Harris.

Many people are as good as Giuseppe. Therefore, if Giuseppe made a lot of money and they haven't, there must have been something going on behind the scenes, there must have been a hidden power somewhere. They looked for it, and found Mrs Holcman. "Well," they would say, taptapping a few lines in the financial columns of *The Times* with the tip of their finger, "it isn't Giuseppe, not really. It's that woman." Which, of course, was nonsense.

At the time Giuseppe got his first government order, Mrs Holcman was still somewhere on the continent learning the Lord's Prayer. And at the time she came over to England, which she managed to do in the fourth year of the war, Giuseppe's company was already happily producing thousands of tiny electronic gadgets for the British army. He was made before he even knew of Mrs Holcman's existence.

It was she herself who told me how she met him. It didn't start with peanuts, it started with a gramophone record. One day, soon after her arrival in London, she felt lonely, and she walked miles from the place where she was billeted to Oxford Street and into the HMV shop to listen to some music. She opened the catalogue and there it was: *Joseph Holcman,* violin. She knew that he was safe in South America; she had two sons, loved both, but saving the other's life was only as important as saving hers; while saving Joseph's was different, because Joseph was not only her son, stupid as he was, stupid and unpleasant, he was also an involuntary carrier of something that was bigger than himself. His ears and fingers happened to be so constructed and assembled that he could play the violin as only one in a hundred million people can. On a slip of paper, she wrote down the number of the record and handed it over the counter. Two minutes later, they gave it to her. There she stood, holding it, the cubicles for the customers who wanted to listen to the records they intended to buy were some twenty paces away, and there she stood, kept standing, and couldn't move.

Giuseppe was about forty then, rather tall, broad shouldered, his hair was still black, except at the temples, where some white hair curled while the black was brushed smoothly back behind the ears. That was, at least, how she described him to me some years later. He walked briskly across the floor and stopped in front of her. It seemed that his reading of human faces never misled him. He knew she had to say something to somebody, so there he was, all ready to lend her his ears. He didn't need to encourage her. She looked at him, and said:

"This is my son's record." And she gave it to him.

He immediately enveloped her with his vivacity. It took him a second to spot the name on the record and start calling her Mrs Holcman (which he pronounced "Holkman"). He said he would love to listen to it with her, and led her to the cubicle: he had plenty to say about the music, and it was both apt and bursting with joy: before she knew what had happened, he had bought two records, one for her, though she had no gramophone to play it on, and one for himself. He asked her to tea in a hotel lounge. A young ATS girl was sitting at the wheel of his car. "Make no mistake, Mrs Holkman, London is a wonderful city," he said as they passed along the walled-up windowless Peter Robinson building at Oxford Circus. As the car turned to the right, to go through Soho, he pointed out to her a Black and White milk bar on the corner. "There," he said, "some five years ago a poor man with a monkey gave me fifty pounds without batting an eyelid. I would give anything to find out where he is now."

At the hotel lounge in the Strand, as she was lifting the teapot, he noticed a long number tattooed on her forearm. "When I was a boy, well, look . . ." he said, pulling up the sleeve of his jacket, "I was romantic enough to let myself be tattooed too,"—and he laughed as he showed her a heart and an anchor and a flower tattooed above his wrist, and she laughed too, and it was the first time in three or four years that she had laughed so lightheartedly.

"I like flowers," she said. "That's what saved my life. I carried a green twig in front of me, and the man said I couldn't be a Jude if at such a time I thought of carrying plants, and they sent me to a camp instead." She didn't say instead of what, but there was no need to be explicit. He thrust forward his jaw, and said:

"Mussolini esercita un gran fascino sulla gioventù. Viva il Duce!" and they had some more tea as the sirens again started sounding the alarm. He asked her what she had been doing yesterday.

"Oh!" she said. "It was very nice yesterday. Yesterday I actually conversed with people. First I said 'Good evening.' Then I said 'Small, black coffee, if you please.' Then I said 'Thank you.' And then I said 'Good night.' And they talked to me too. They answered me. They said: 'Good night, Madam.' It was a pity I was already at the door and couldn't prolong the conversation." And they laughed again.

"Do come to my office tomorrow," Giuseppe said.

The next day she went to his office in the West End, and she remained there, as his private secretary, for eighteen years.

I couldn't stop thinking about Giuseppe. It *was* strange that I didn't know it was he, he and Silvia, when I saw them in the Milan-Venice *rapido*. Was it a parting scene? It must have been. Was I an involuntary witness—perhaps the only man who saw his tears? Didn't they show that he too must have a weak spot somewhere in him, an Achilles' heel, like everybody? How did his mother hold him when she plunged him, as every mother does with her new-born son, into the Styx? Did she hold him by his heel, or by his nose, or by his little penis? What was her way of making him vulnerable?

I knew how he first met Silvia. Maria told me (though she omitted to say that Silvia was her sister). This time it wasn't peanuts, or gramophone records; it was—flowers.

One sunny day in 1960, he was motoring along a busy street in Rome. A man and a woman were standing on the pavement, in front of a flower shop. The man hailed a taxi. He handed the woman some flowers. She got into the taxi, kept the door open for a moment. The man didn't move. She slammed the door and, when the taxi started, threw the flowers onto the pavement. The man didn't move. Giuseppe did. Giuseppe was not somebody who would be put out by the traffic hooting furiously behind him. He stopped his car, picked up the flowers, and put his foot on the accelerator. In a side street he overtook the taxi and halted it. He handed Silvia her flowers and made her move from the taxi into his car. The next evening they were in Milan, at the Scala, listening to Wagner.

He could have bought her a flat, a house, or a villa, but that was not what *he w*anted. He kept her in luxury hotels. He bought her furs and jewelry. They ate in exclusive restaurants. It was enough for her to stop at a shop window and say "Look at that, what a lovely whateveritis" and, whatever it was, he would go in and have it sent to the hotel. If she happened to say "it must be beautiful in Capri now," off to Capri they would go. If she had said "Lago Maggiore," Lago Maggiore it would have been. There was no whim of hers he wouldn't meet. Except one thing: he wouldn't give her any money.

At first she didn't pay much attention to it. She had an open account almost everywhere and money, or rather the absence of if, didn't worry her. On the contrary. At first, she was overwhelmed by the delightful newness of the experience of being served without actually paying a lira. After a while, however, it started to get on her nerves. Especially when Giuseppe was in London, where he lived with his wife and two grown-up children. She could most exquisitely dine by candle light plus soft music where they knew her, but she couldn't go to *a* trattoria and order an ordinary pizza, which she liked. She could have her lingerie sent to her from one recherché place, and her cosmetics from another, but she couldn't go to *a* shop and buy a handkerchief, or to *a* chemist and ask for a packet of tampax. She could book a seat in the theatre, but she had to keep the taxi waiting till the end of the performance, so that she could go back in it to her hotel where the porter would pay the fare. At the beginning she tried to ask him for money. He never said *no*. He would say: I'll be back at six and give it to you. At six o'clock precisely, a pageboy would come with a basket of flowers, or a box of chocolates, or a flask of perfume, and a few lines from Giuseppe who had a sudden, unexpected business appointment. Then he would disappear for a day, or two, or three. In despair, she would sometimes go to Maria and borrow a few coins, just to have them in her handbag. Once, when Maria wanted a pair of shoes, Silvia bought them for her at the best calzolàio with whom she had an account, and then they shared the money Maria had intended to spend. But they both felt awkward about it and didn't repeat the stratagem. She tried to sell some of her own old things, but she would have had to do it discreetly, and it annoyed her, she felt as if she were cheating. At times, she would willingly have sold herself to a passer-by, but she didn't. Instead, she began to have dreams about money. She saw phallic temples built of rouleaus of five hundred lire silver coins. One night she woke

85

up shouting "I want some money! I want some cash!," and she burst into tears. A crise de nerfs. He couldn't pacify it. He called a doctor and took her to a nursing home on the Riviera. But he didn't give her a penny. He told her that he had provided for her, not only in case he died or went bankrupt, but also in case they decided to part. But he didn't tell her *how* he had provided for her, and when she thought about it she shivered with fear, imagining that it would again be some open accounts with big, four or five-starred hotels, restaurants de luxe, maisons de modes, nursing homes, and undertakers. After a couple of years of that life of luxury she was worn out. She was as docile and affectionate as ever, and he loved her, but she was worn out. And she knew that sooner or later she would leave him.

Maria was both cynical and sentimental about it. "He says," she said, "that he doesn't give her any money because Money Spoils Friendship. Perhaps that's what he thinks, but it isn't the real reason. The real reason is that Giuseppe is superstitious. Most scientists are, but Giuseppe is more superstitious than any. When he was a little boy, he was told that men get ruined by spending their money on drink, gambling and women. He never drinks, except with food. He's never played roulette, though he visits casinos. He's never given a penny to any woman he's slept with."

The day I received Giuseppe's invitation to Faggeto Lario, I had a strange dream. I was riding a bicycle and suddenly came across seven dockers who were carrying a big, wooden packing-case. I didn't count them, but I knew that they were seven. I *knew* also, without seeing, that the packing-case contained small arms and that they were carrying it all the way from Genoa to a place called Southampton, which, I was sure, was actually in Malaya. I tried to by-pass them but couldn't. I tried to do so several times, on the left and on the right, but, though I was quick on my bicycle and they were slow, it somehow always ended in their being in front of me, and I knew I would bump into them sooner or later. I did. And, as I did, they dropped the packing-case, its top fell off, and I saw the dead body of Arturo lying peacefully inside it, face upwards, holding the fretted neck of his guitar in his folded hands. But how can this be, I thought in the dream. If Arturo is in the coffin, then Who is the Seventh Docker? I tried to look at their faces, one at a time, but couldn't. I tried to count them, but couldn't. I knew very well they were seven, but couldn't see which was the seventh. All that was happening not on a road but on a smooth surface of water. The water didn't flow, it spread, motionless, between two very high and long hills, one on my left, the other on my right, both thickly covered with bushes from which old trees sprang up and were reflected in the water so strangely that the reflection of the tops of the trees on the left bank seemed to touch the reflection of the tops of the trees on the right.

I seldom remember my dreams, and forgot that one as I usually forget the others. But a few days later, aboard a little steamship, in the middle of the lake which I was crossing on my way to Faggeto Lario, I saw the reflection of both banks, and both green hillsides, in the water, and they were so much like what I had seen in the dream that it came back to me at once in a flash. This recollection somehow changed my mood. That was perhaps why, as soon as I disembarked at Faggeto Lario, it occurred to me that it was not the sort of place from which it is easy to get out.

/ CASA BIANCA

Casa Bianca stood halfway up the bushy hillside, in the middle of a great park in which patches of cultivated garden intermingled with the old, half-abandoned woodland, separated from the rest of this green world by a stony wall, thick and high. It was difficult to find this place, but once there, it would be impossible to leave unnoticed. If you wanted to reach the boat, you had to zigzag your way down the slope, each of your steps observable from the windows; if you wanted to go to your car, or to the bus-stop, you had to zigzag laboriously up the steep pathway, high up to the motor-road terraced out of the hillside; and if you had anything to carry, it would have to be sent first, on a sort of trolley, pushed and pulled on a miniature railway track by a network of screeching wires, wound up and off at the little landing built between two magnificent flowerbeds in front of the house. I looked round and thought that by finding this place for our meeting Giuseppe had overreached himself in stage design. I was wrong. He didn't have to look for this place. It belonged to his mother.

She was a very old lady, but she was a comparatively modern type of old lady. She must have stopped following the changes of fashion sometime in the twenties, and the clothes she was wearing now were perhaps the same she had got used to when Gloria Swanson cut her hair à la garçonne. She must

have been over fifty even then. Now she was very white and
fragile. Yet the odd thing about her was her headgear. That
was neither 1900, when she must have been a young mother
and a widow, nor 1920, nor 1960. It was neither here nor
there. It was a red fez with a blue pom-pom and a short veil,
or fringe, and she seemed to be wearing it all the time, in the
house and in the garden.

"Soyez le bienvenu," she said (in French), and disappeared.

Giuseppe had produced some drinks. I wondered whether
he would recognise me. He didn't. Or, if he did, he didn't
show it. After all, it was I who had seen him in the *rapido*
going to Venice, he had been too much preoccupied with his
own affairs to take any notice of strangers.

"It is good of you to have come," he said, handing me a
glass.

It surprised me that he poured himself a large dose of stiff
whisky. This didn't agree with at least one of what I had been
told were three of his obsessions: no alcohol unless with food,
no betting, and no cash for women.

"Is he here?" I asked.

"Giambattista? Oh, yes. He's already here, in his room,
with his little transistor radio."

"What is he like?"

"Not unlike his father, I suppose. And yet it's
strange . . ."

"What is?"

"I used to understand people as soon as I saw them—"

"I heard something about that," I said.

"Yes, I suppose you did," he said. "And yet, this time, I am
not so sure . . ."

"You are not sure that he is a crook?" I said.

"Oh, no," he waved his hand to dismiss the suggestion.
"What I'm not sure of is how high will be the price he'll
ask."

*

I met Maria later on, in the garden. We went up the steep path leading to some rocks from which a thin stream of water was falling a few feet and disappearing in the silent cushion of moss. There was a bench there, and we sat on it. I was glad she seemed to be as pleased to see me as I was to see her.

"You wrote me two very beautiful letters," I said.

"Do you really think so?"

"Yes, I do."

"Honestly?"

"Of course. Your dialogue with dom Antonio read like a fragment of a novel."

"Oh, no!" she exclaimed. "It really happened exactly as I said. I could never write about something that was not. I am not a lab, you see. I am a clinician."

I *didn't* see, and I said so.

"Oh." She wrinkled her forehead. "It's probably nonsense what I'm going to say, but, you see, clinical doctors first observe patients, then they draw conclusions, make a diagnosis, and then they go *back* to the patients they have observed. With scientists it is different. They also observe first, then they draw conclusions but they don't then go back to the ward; they go to their labs, produce pure cultures of bacteria, use guinea pigs, recreate the essential thing with different material, and prove that the thing is true, or that it is not true. Is not that what novelists do? I couldn't. I can go as far as the diagnosis but then I must always go back to the bedside."

"I do admire you, Maria. All three of you," I said.

"Three?" she asked.

"Yes," I said. "Your body, your mind and you yourself."

"Good," she said. "I like to be appreciated." And she kissed me lightly on the cheek. "You are nice," she said. "And I'm glad, you know, because I feared you might have thought I was making too much fuss about the thing."

"Have you brought it with you?" I asked.

"What?"

"The thing."

"You mean the envelope?"

"What else?"

"Yes, I brought it with me. Of course I brought it with me. It is in my room."

"In the wardrobe?"

"No, in the suitcase."

"Do you still want me to steal it?"

"Did I ever?"

"Yes, you did. Dom Antonio put it into your head, didn't he?"

"Not really. And, anyway, it's up to Giuseppe now."

"Quite so, yes," I agreed. "And still . . . Well, I don't know; but there is one thing that puzzles me: Why so much fuss? If Giuseppe is such a master in dealings with blackmailers, why doesn't he meet the boy somewhere in a billiard room in Milan and strike a bargain with him?"

"You misjudge him," Maria said. "Il biliardo? That wouldn't be his style. Not theatrical enough, you see? And then," a few very thin wrinkles appeared on her forehead, "you forget that, if anybody, then, so far, it is we who are blackmailers, not the boy. Imagine, if the boy came to me now, and said: 'I hear my father left something for me with you; could I have it now, please,' he would be perfectly within his rights, would he not? It is we who want to impose conditions. And that is why Giuseppe would rather not be alone in it, you see? He wants us all to be involved. So that nobody can say afterwards: 'Oh, if I had been there, I wouldn't have let Giuseppe do this or that . . .'"

"Who else will be there?" I asked.

"Everybody," Maria said. "Everybody except your Signor Harris. He would never leave his precious White Jade, or whatever it is, alone in that tower of his, and he can't bring her with him because he knows that Giuseppe hates her. He wanted him to marry an Italian countess, you see?"

"What are you talking about, Maria?" I asked. "Who is that White Jade?"

"His wife, of course," she said.

"What nonsense," I said. "His wife is staying in a hotel at Nervi, and he even didn't go there to see her. He has nothing to do with her any more; he told me that much himself."

She looked at me incredulously.

"Do you mean to say that you don't even know that your friend is married to a sweet Chinese girl, to whom he is all the world? Even Giuseppe admits that."

"No, Maria, that's impossible," I said. "Maybe he lives with her, but he can't possibly be married to her. His wife, Pamela I mean, would never, never give him a divorce."

"Why not? She isn't a Catholic, is she?"

"No, but you see: she was always against it. Not on religious grounds, no, but she thought it was a social disgrace, something that would force her to look upon herself as one of those who cannot be invited to a garden party at Buckingham Palace. I wonder if you see what I mean?"

"No, I don't," Maria said.

"I thought you wouldn't," I said. "But anyway, I'm sure she hasn't divorced him."

"That's too bad," Maria said pensively.

"It looks like it," I said.

And then we started to count up how many we should be to dinner:

"Giuseppe and his mother, Giambattista, you and me. That makes five. Giuseppe's lawyer, and Giuseppe's bodyguard . . ."

"Bodyguard?" I asked.

"Well, he calls him his secretary, but you will see his muscles! Then there is Grazia, Giambattista's fiancée, and dom Antonio . . ."

I didn't say a word; yet she noticed that it surprised me, and she frowned.

"He hasn't come to save my soul," she said. "He's just interested in the story I told him. Not in its future but in its past. Historically."

"Historically?"

"Yes. And I may as well tell you that he has his own sources of information."

"Has he?" I asked.

"Yes, he has," she said.

"How do you know?" I asked.

She looked at me obliquely.

"He asked me whether I knew that Signor Harris was called a Revolutionary Secretary."

"That was Sir Francis's joke," I said.

"Maybe," Maria said. "But he asked me also whether I knew why Sir Francis himself was called a Red Knight."

"That was his theatrical nickname," I said.

"Is that what they were, too—the small arms he was selling instead of bicycles—theatrical pistols?"

"That is precisely the sort of argument Bruno wanted us to swallow."

"Maybe," she said. "But if there is no truth in all this, there is no reason to hide things. Dom Antonio is neither a pig nor a fool, you know?"

I looked at her admiringly.

"Maria," I asked, "do you still believe that this world is as sound as a bell, and if the bell makes awful noises, it's only because some bell-ringers are rotten?"

Earnestly, she nodded.

"And rotten people can be improved," I continued, "therefore there is hope for the world."

She shut her eyes and nodded again.

"Maria," I said. "I want to ask you a question."

"Do," she said.

"Were you not in love with Bruno because you thought that your love would make him less bad?"

She was silent for a moment, then asked:

"Are you saying that to make it easier for me to forget him?"

"No, Maria; I said it to make it easier for you to love other people."

She put her hand on mine, and clasped it. I felt how cold were the tips of her fingers.

"For instance whom?" she asked.

"For instance Dottore Vecchi."

Her hand squeezed mine.

"How did you know he was coming?" she asked.

"I didn't," I said. "I only knew that his day off was also Thursday."

"He loves me," she said.

"And you shouldn't be afraid of falling in love with *young* people, you know."

She looked at one particular flower, yards away, as if she were counting its petals.

"Perhaps you're right," she said, simply.

I stood up, walked to the flower I had thought she was looking at:

"Do you want it?" I asked.

She laughed.

"No," she said, "let it grow."

Then she started to count on her fingers, and exclaimed:

"Oh, we've forgotten Silvia!"

"Silvia?" I asked. "Is Silvia here?"

"Yes, she's here, in her room, I suppose, doing her face. I told you what she's like. She never turns a hair."

"I thought she and Giuseppe had parted."

Maria pushed the heel of her shoe between two pebbles and by twisting her foot to the left and the right tried to make a hole in the ground. I didn't say a word.

94

"So they did, yes, but . . . Well, putting it simply, she told Giuseppe that she was sick of his open accounts and wanted some regular cash; and he let her go. But then he found that he couldn't live without her after all, at least when he was in Italy, and he forced himself to overcome his superstition and gave her some money, and he isn't the same Giuseppe any more."

"How do you mean?"

"He's lost his grip. And he knows it. And now he hates her. I think he hates his mother too, because it was she who put that fear into him, when he was still a little boy, you know, she told him that his father lost all their money on women, drink and betting."

This was unexpected. But after all, it was none of my business.

"Tell me," I asked. "Why does the old lady wear that ridiculous red fez with a blue pom-pom?"

"But don't you think it suits her?" Maria said.

For the first few minutes, the dining-room looked like a railway station. Divided into little groups, they stood here and there, and walked, turned around, made faces, talking, telling stories, asking questions, answering them, laughing, all that against a background of the faint sound of jazz-music which must have been coming from somewhere, but from where? There was an enormous long black table, laid for dinner, but nobody seemed to know where to sit.

"I think I've had the pleasure of meeting you before," Silvia said, "but where was it?"

I couldn't possibly tell her it was in a railway-carriage of a *rapido* going from Milan to Venice.

"Yes, I know your face," I said. "Maria showed me a very beautiful photograph of you."

This, somehow, she seemed to accept as an explanation.

"You are a very old friend of Giuseppe, are you not?"

95

"Well," I said, "actually, this morning was the first time I met him in person, but of course . . ."

She didn't want to listen.

"Do you think he has changed much?" she asked.

And when I managed to utter something unintelligible, she said:

"I am so glad you don't think he has changed."

Dottore Vecchi came across and gazed at me in a mock-professional manner.

"You seem to have recovered all right," he said, and introduced himself.

Then, turning to Silvia, he explained, laughingly:

"At the hospital, we called him the man with a pipe who came from London to get himself knocked down by a tram in Milan."

"Really? How awful!" Silvia said.

"And he didn't let his pipe go . . ." he went on, with a waggish sneer.

"That was because I thought my denture might have cracked, and I was afraid to open my mouth."

He was very pleased. He had already been pleased to see that I was nearly twice his age, and now he was still more pleased to hear about my dentures.

"I don't know about us medicos," he said, "but it cannot be denied that you received the best nursing treatment Italy can afford."

"I quite agree," I said. "And, as you see, I'm perfectly all right now, and fit to go back."

"Back to London?"

"Yes."

He beamed. He thought life was beautiful. He took me by the elbow, and clapped me on the back.

"I hope you like Italy," he said.

"I do," I said. I turned towards the window and looked at

96

the lake below. Then I turned further to the right. "They look nice," I said.

He followed the direction of my eyes, and frowned.

In the far-off corner of the room, alone, as if separated from the rest of the world by some sort of invisible perspex wall, Giambattista and his girl, he in tight white trousers (levis, or jeans,—gênes?) and a black pullover (stoffa inglese), she in tight black trousers (levis, or jeans,—gênes?) and a snow-white pullover (il cashmere, stoffa inglese), wriggled to each other happily undisturbed, their minds and bodies absorbed in the faint jazz-music.

"Scum!" Dottore Vecchi said. "I am ashamed of them."

"Why?" I asked. "They look lovely. You shouldn't."

Dom Antonio had been standing at our side for the last minute or two.

"They don't believe in anything, signore," he said now. "They are pure animals."

"Oh, come now, signore," I said.

"They are worse than those Giovinezza youngsters who at least used to believe in their Duce," he continued with insistence. "They are worse than the communists who, in their misguided hearts are idealists, believing at least in the Anti-Christ of hatred; no, signore, as for them, they believe in nothing. Not even in materialism. Not even in not believing. They are a race apart. And they will cost signore Giuseppe quite a lot of money, you'll see, signore," he added.

"When is he going to talk to them, do you know?" I asked.

"I think," dom Antonio said, "that he will keep this business until after dinner."

Silvia came nearer to us again. She smiled softly, bent a little, and kissed dom Antonio's hand. I walked a few steps back.

"Father," I heard her saying. "Giuseppe has been drinking heavily. He's not used to drinking between meals."

97

I glanced across the room, towards the other corner, where Giuseppe had been standing between his bodyguard secretary and the lawyer. He didn't look a bit drunk.

"Ladies and gentlemen," he said. "Please . . ."

At that moment the heavy, wide door in the middle of the wall opened, and the old lady came in.

A hush fell over the dining-room, and the faint lines of jazz-music, still oozing in from somewhere, served only to emphasize the sudden muteness of the air.

The old lady in her ridiculous red fez sat down at the table, in the middle of its long side.

". . . please, be seated," Giuseppe finished the sentence, and we hurried forward to take our places—haphazardly, as I thought at first.

Now dom Antonio rose to his feet, walked a step or two to where Giambattista and his fiancée were seated, leant forward and clicked off the button of a little transistor radio-set which stood on the table between them. The jazz-music ceased to exist. The old lady didn't move. Dom Antonio returned to his chair, said grace rapidly, and we started to eat—in silence.

The chair opposite the old lady's chair was its faithful replica; carved in black wood, it had a very high back, upholstered in green, which must have been poisonous once upon a time; there was a plate in front of it, on the table, but the chair stood empty between my chair and dom Antonio's. Is somebody late for dinner? As I wondered who it could have been, I noticed a black crêpe ribbon stretched above the seat of the chair.

Obviously it must have belonged to Giuseppe's father, and must have been standing there, empty, for the last sixty years or more. Since 1900? The year King Umberto was assassinated not far from here, at Monza? It must have been standing as now, empty, but dusted every morning, wax-polished on Saturdays and, at least twice a day, the subject of somebody's consciousness of its existence. All that time. All through the reign of Victor Emanuel the Third, the General Strike and the disturbances of 1904, the war with Turkey, the Balkan War, the Great War, the rise of Mussolini, and the Second World War. I looked at Giuseppe. I imagined him as a little boy, hiding under the table, and staring at the sacred chair's black legs. That's how he must have remembered his father. As a black chair. He must have remembered him as a signore who spent money on drink, women, and horses, and was changed into a chair. Garlanded with a black crêpe ribbon.

But how did the old man die? Actually, he wasn't old then. On the contrary, he must have been very young. Did he throw himself into the Lake? Did he shoot himself? Or, perhaps, he was at Monza and got himself trampled by the horses' hooves. I looked across the table at the old lady in her silly red fez. What had *she* been like sixty years ago? Was she like Silvia now, or like Maria? Her face didn't give any indication of what it might have been then. She put her spoon down and turned her head slightly to the right:

"How did you like my garden, Dottore Vecchi?" she asked.

We had already so much accustomed ourselves to eating in silence that the sudden question startled us all.

"Superb!" Dr Vecchi exclaimed, jumping. "Exquisitely superb. That harmonious symbiosis of the natural and the cultivated! And the view!"

"I'm glad to hear you like it," the old lady said. "And now, tell me, Dottore Vecchi, as one who should know: Are these new contraceptive pills I hear about really efficient and really harmless? I'm not asking whether they are sinful, as that is not *your* province."

His answer was stiff and pedantic:

"They seem to be efficient," he said, "and especially suitable for overpopulated, underdeveloped countries and the poorer classes. As to their being harmless, we haven't yet had sufficient time to make sure clinically."

The old lady dismissed him, and turned to Silvia, who was sitting next, at the top of the table.

"Do you use them, Silvia?" she asked.

"No, I don't, signora," Silvia said.

The jewel on the old lady's fez twinkled.

"Did you have a nice journey, Signor Biagi?" She was already addressing the lawyer, who sat next to Silvia.

"Delightful, signora, thank you, delightful."

"Did you come by boat or by car?"

"By car, signora, from Milano. I left it up there on the road. I hope it is safe."

"If your grandfather had had more imagination we could have had a garage up there, on the level of the road."

"My grandfather, signora?!" Signor Biagi asked with astonishment.

"Yes," the old lady said. "You are our family lawyer. Your father was our family lawyer. And your grandfather was our family lawyer. When we sold an upper lot to the newcomers from the South, in 1880, it was your grandfather who drew up the contract and did it so cleverly that now we cannot have access to the road wider than a footpath, unless we fell a few of the old trees, which is of course unthinkable."

"I am desolated to hear that forecasting the future was not one of my grandfather's assets, signora," the lawyer said. "I hope I have inherited some of his virtues without inheriting all his flaws."

"If," she responded, "if, from father to son, we could make the flaws fewer and fewer, the world would become better and better. Well, it does not."

She paused for a brief moment. And then continued:

"My great-great-grandfather was born and lived nearby, in Como. Without him, the world today wouldn't look the way it does. Though, it is true that, sooner or later, some other men would have contrived the same thing. He was Count Alessandro Volta. He discovered the development of electricity in metallic bodies and invented the Voltaic pile. I think Giuseppe might have inherited his talent for electronics from him."

"And . . ." the lawyer tried to draw her out. "And . . ." he repeated. "And what were the Count's flaws?"

But he was already dismissed and forgotten. It must have been one of the rules of her savoir vivre that her duty as hostess was to address everybody once, and she was doing it now, methodically, at her own pace, one person after another, anticlockwise.

I was sitting next to the lawyer, so I knew it was to be my turn. And so it was. Slowly, she veered her head in my direction, but the head didn't stop at once: it made a series of slight, oscillating movements, first horizontally, then vertically, then horizontally again, as if it were adjusting itself for comfort, or precision.

"Would you mind, sir, if I were to ask you to take your napkin in your right hand and wave it above your head?" she said drily.

The request was not only unexpected, it was perplexing. I glanced at Giuseppe who was sitting far away, at the top of the table on my right. The expression on his face beseeched me to do what the eccentric old lady wished me to do.

Trying to look detached, but feeling foolish, I grasped the napkin and waved it.

"That's all right," she said. "Now I know where you are. Merci."

And that was all. I, also, was already dismissed. The red fez turned further to its left. It didn't stay at the empty chair next to me and went straight to dom Antonio.

But dom Antonio was quicker than the old lady; he addressed her first:

"And how is your digestion, dear signora?" he asked. "The

last time I had the pleasure of seeing you, you complained of having eaten something that didn't agree with you."

"My digestion is perfectly all right, dom Antonio. Thank you. I hope yours doesn't cause you any trouble."

And turning to Giambattista and his girl friend Grazia, "I liked the music you were playing when I came in," she said. "What was it?"

"Radio," Grazia said.

"I suppose it was. But did the piece we heard have a name?"

"Yep," said Grazia. "It's called: 'Gimme a Columbus egg for breakfast.' "

"Nope," said Giambattista, "it wasn't. No such thing."

" 'Twas," said Grazia.

" 'Twasn't," said Giambattista. " 'Twas 'You can't be really sad when you're alone, can you?' "

"Yeah, first. But then it was 'Gimme a Columbus egg for breakfast' and the ecclesiastic," Grazia turned to dom Antonio: "You don't mind, do you? . . . switched it off."

"I think the signorina is right," the old lady said. "It must have been 'Gimme a Columbus egg for breakfast.' I liked it."

"Did you?" Giambattista asked.

"Yes, I did."

"Don't believe you."

"Why don't you?"

"Don't know. Born before the war, weren't you?"

"Which war?"

"Couldn't say." Giambattista shrugged his shoulders nonchalantly and switched the transistor radio set on; and then off again.

"That was a bar and a half of Beethoven," the lawyer said.

"Sure," Giambattista agreed. "That's why it's switched off now."

"Don't you like Beethoven?" the old lady asked.

"Nope."

"Why not?"

"Goes back to before the war."

"He was dead before my father was born," the old lady said.

"Yeah. Deaf and dead," Giambattista agreed.

"Please, do tell me," the old lady said. "What does 'Gimme a Columbus egg for breakfast' have that Beethoven has not? Can you tell me that?"

"Sure."

"Well?"

"Grip."

"Doesn't Beethoven have considerable grip?"

"Sure. The wrong sort of grip."

"What sort of grip?"

"A fascist sort of grip," Giambattista said.

"Do you really think so?" the old lady asked.

" 'Mnot interested in thinking about him at all," Giambattista said; and asked "Can one smoke here?"

"Yes, you can," the old lady said.

"Mother . . ." Giuseppe got up from his chair, but the old lady didn't seem to have noticed him. She didn't address his bodyguard secretary either. She turned to Maria, who was sitting next to her:

"It was nice of you, Maria, to bring me those beautiful flowers. They adorn my table, and their fragrance is beautiful. I noticed that you had taken the trouble to remove the thorns. It was very thoughtful of you, and I appreciate it, but it was not necessary."

"It must have been my professional conceit; trying to improve on nature," Maria said.

"How sweet," the old lady said, but her thoughts must already have been somewhere else. She turned back to Giambattista:

"Signor Giambattista," she said. "If I may have your attention for another moment, please. I understand that you are a journalist . . ."

"Am I?"

"Well, recensore? critico d'arte? teatrale?"

" 't's better."

"Anyway, though I haven't as yet had the pleasure of reading anything written by you, I presume that when you write you do use some conventional rules of syntax. On the other hand, when you talk to us here you don't seem to take much trouble to put words into sentences. What I want to ask is: Do you choose that monosyllabic form of expression because you can't be bothered or because you consider it to be a style?"

"Style."

"And you think that sort of style conveys something our ordinary language does not convey?"

"Yeah, it shows the point. Sentences don't show the point."

"And what is the point?"

Giambattista squashed his cigarette in his saucer.

"Wash," he said, "wash, washing basin, huge washing basin, water, water, hot cold, hot cold, hot cold, hot beliefs, cold beliefs, hot ideas, cold ideas, hot saviors, cold saviors, huge stinking washing basin, tip of your finger, two fingers, three, four, five, six, seven, eight, nine, ten! wash off, wash off, truth off, off the hands, down the drain, washwashwashwash, or else, bang! Washwashwash Mrs Macbeth, washwashwashsweet Pilate, or else, what is truth? bang bang bang?"

Giuseppe's bodyguard was standing behind Giambattista's chair. Giuseppe himself was leaning forward over the table and shouting:

"Mother! Listen to me, Mother!"

When at last she had turned towards him, he lowered his voice and said with some equanimity: "Mother, will you excuse us if we leave you now and go to the drawing-room? We have some business to discuss there with Signor Giambattista."

Giuseppe's request sounded so simple that we all were already prepared to get up when the old lady said:

"No. Nobody moves! Sit where you are, please. I have something to tell you."

Giuseppe leaned back in his chair. So did we. The bodyguard secretary went back to his chair and sat down.

The old lady took a tiny sip of wine, just to moisten her lips, and declared:

"The boy is not a crook."

My neighbour, the lawyer, jumped up:

"I wish to make it clear that nobody has ever suggested that he was."

The old lady ignored him. She moved her head a bit to the right and, once more, I noticed those minute, up and down and sideways, oscillating movements . . . When they stopped, the head was directed straight at me.

"*He* is a crook," the old lady said.

The funny thing was that I immediately felt guilty. Now what have I done?—was my first thought. I felt guilty before I felt enraged. Meanwhile, with a sneer, she added:

"The right honourable Sir Mascot!"

What mystified me must have been quite clear to Giuseppe. He was on his feet now, standing by her side, between her and Maria.

"Mother," he said. "You have made a horrible mistake. You must ask the signor his pardon. The signor is *not* Tom Harris."

"You are not Tom Harris?" the old lady asked me.

"No, I am not," I said.

"Then I apologise," she said in a voice in which there was no trace of emotion.

Remembering her liking for round sentences, I took a deep breath and said:

"I accept your apology, signora, but I wish to make it clear that though I am not Tom Harris I consider myself his friend."

This seemed to sting her.

"You consider yourself his friend," she repeated. "You know that he is a parasite living on my son's body, destroying his life, and you . . ."

"I know nothing of the sort, signora," I interrupted her.

"You know that he is a charlatan, who started his academic career with an American GI's papers; you know that he is a bigamist . . ."

"No, I do not know, signora," I said.

"You claim to be his friend, signor, and you seem to know nothing about him. Perhaps you don't know either that he was sent to prison; for four years; because he killed a man; murdered him."

"I know, signora, that a quarter of a century ago he was sent to prison. But he wasn't even accused of committing a murder, or manslaughter. It wasn't because of anything of that sort."

"Because of what then?" she asked.

"Because of a monkey," I said.

". . . of what?" Suddenly her voice became high-pitched and sharp.

". . . a monkey," I repeated. And then I panicked. I had realized that she thought I was deliberately offending her. "He had a monkey," I tried to explain. "That's why he was called 'The Man with the Monkey.' London is a populous and a smoky city, signora. Much like hell. He felt lonely. He *was* lonely. So one day he bought himself a monkey. It became his real friend. He loved it. And the monkey loved him. Neither could live without the other."

106

"Do you mean to say that your friend added the sin of sodomy to his other sins?" dom Antonio asked.

"I don't mean anything of the sort," I said. "And yet, perhaps, that was precisely what one of his neighbours suspected when one evening he knocked on Harris's door to borrow a green penguin."

"To borrow what?" the lawyer asked.

"A book," I said. "A detective story. Would Mr Harris be good enough to lend him a thriller, because he couldn't sleep. And when Harris was looking for a book, the neighbour noticed the monkey. It was sitting on the bed. Sexually aroused. Actually it was in the act of self-fellation, which its anatomy permits it to perform without anybody's help. 'You should give him a wife, poor chap,' the neighbour said. 'You should take him to the zoo, I've heard the zoo people can be asked to arrange a wedding.' The next day Tom Harris took his lovely monkey to the zoo. They looked at it; they said all right; they gave him some papers to sign, and they told him to come back in five days. During those long five days, he became fully aware of his loneliness, and of his love for the monkey. He redecorated his flat, their flat, for its coming back, he made a banner with the words WELCOME HOME (it was later on produced in court as an exhibit, and didn't do him any good), he bought pounds of bananas, nuts, or whatever it is that monkeys find pleasure in eating. On the fifth day he went to the zoo. 'I'm afraid we have some bad news for you, Mr Harris,' the girl secretary said. 'Your monkey is dead.' And the silly girl tried to explain: 'It happens sometimes with monkeys, you know, when they are left alone in the cage, they miss you and they die of a broken heart.' He felt sick with anger. 'Alone?' he asked. 'But didn't he even have his wedding?' 'O no,' the girl said, 'five days of quarantine is the rule; it's regulations.' 'But why didn't you tell me all that before? Why didn't you let me know? I would have come to see him.' The secretary looked at him with a curious, puzzled smile. And he suddenly realised why they hadn't let him know. They hadn't let him know because they didn't think he would have had that sort of feeling. Because to have that sort of feeling about one's monkey befitted a sophisticated Oxford don, or an eccentric dowager, but not a man with a strong cockney accent."

"What is that?" dom Antonio asked.

"What is what? A strong cockney accent? That, dom Antonio, is a sort of phonetic tattoo. Quite indelible. As a matter of fact, it is as indelible as your baptism is. Though it wouldn't make you welcome in the officers' Mess, or at the Club and all that; you know, for your own sake, not to make you feel embarrassed, because if you have that sort of accent, you are not supposed to have certain sorts of feeling, for your monkey for instance. Well, Tom Harris was tattooed with a strong cockney accent, and he knew it. 'You can't hold us responsible, you know; you signed the papers,' the girl secretary said, and ran screaming out of the room. No, he didn't hit her. He didn't even try to hit her. But she must have read something in his eyes and got frightened. Because it was then, at that moment, that one Tom Harris died in him, and another Tom Harris was born. Hic mortuus est Tom Harris the Meek, hic natus est Tom Harris the Rebel. Some men rushed into the office to chuck him out. He slammed the front door so fiercely that the thick glass-pane cracked. It was the first time in his life that he had slammed a door. His old half-asleep self didn't exist any more. He marched boldly down the road as he had never marched before, and the passers-by moved aside to let him pass. And then, in a narrow street, he stopped by a barber's shop. The barber was already outside, locking the door. He refused to open it until he, too, got frightened, and let him in. Tom Harris sat down in the barber's chair and ordered the man to shave him. And such was the strength of his new personality that the barber

meekly complied. After which, Tom Harris left two florins
and two sixpenny coins (that's what he told the jury afterwards) on the marble plate by the wash-basin, and walked
out and started his ten minutes' march through Paddington.
At the end of it, he saw a small crowd on a corner, surrounding a newsvendor. He snatched a copy of the newspaper from
him. It was the first time in his life that he had jumped a
queue. The headline said: war. WAR! For him, it had come
just in time. Everything was so clear and simple now. He'd
go and fight. But the newsvendor was both a pacifist and an
anti-nazi. That combination produced a curiously logical sequence of thoughts in his mind: if the chap wants to go to
war, he isn't a pacifist; and if I, the newsvendor, am an anti-
nazi because I am a pacifist then he, not being a pacifist,
must be a nazi. And the newsvendor rose up against him and
shouted: 'Pay me my penny first, and make your propaganda
afterwards!' Yet, before Tom Harris had time to give him a
penny, a heavy hand had fallen on his shoulder. He didn't
know that the barber had followed him all the time from the
moment he had left the shop until he saw a policeman and
asked him to make an arrest. That was how Tom Harris's
short-lived rebellion came to an end. He was remanded in
custody for further investigation. This showed that he had
assaulted a secretary at the Zoological Gardens, damaged
the office doors, broken into the barber's shop, terrorised
him, escaped without payment (the barber denied having
received any money), stolen a paper from the newsvendor,
caused a public disturbance by trying to incite people on a
public thoroughfare. Finally, his neighbour came forward
to tell the jury what he had seen of the sexual behaviour of
the monkey. That, however, came under the heading of
cruelty to animals. He was found guilty on eight charges.
As it was wartime, to keep up public morale, the judge decided that the eight sentences should be served consecu-
tively, which brought Tom's total prison term up to three

years and eleven months. When he came out, he looked twice as old as when he went in. He grew a beard and stopped caring. He was neither the Meek of Paddington, which he had been taught to be since he was born, nor was he the Rebel of Paddington, which he had tried to be for a couple of hours. At the Green Man, where he would have his lonely pint of beer every night, they now called him the Man with the Monkey, but hardly anybody remembered or knew why. I used to see him at the Green Man occasionally. He was treated there as something that belonged naturally to those shabby surroundings. Like a piece of abandoned furniture. Seeing the grey, old, bearded man, drinking his pint of beer, nobody would stop to think that perhaps he had a past. And even I didn't know that he had a future. Yet it was there where one evening, at 7.30 p.m., Giuseppe found him, and it was from there . . ."

Still talking, I observed the old lady and had the strange impression that her head had started to lean a little to one side. Slowly; so slowly that one couldn't be sure that it was really moving. Like the movements of the minute hand on the face of a clock. If you want to find whether a clock moves, the best way is to notice the position of its minute hand, then shut your eyes, and open them again to see the change. If you look at it without blinking, you just cannot be certain. I shut my eyes and continued:

". . . and it was from there that Giuseppe took him away the same night, and magically, as in a fairy-tale . . ."

I opened my eyes. The old lady's head was definitely a bit further to the left, and still moving steadily. How far can it go like that?, I asked myself. I was glad to see that the high back of her chair had, on the level of her head, a sort of sticking-forward ornamental butt, one on each side. When it touches that, her head must stop, I thought, and I was somehow relieved.

". . . as in a fairy-tale," I repeated, "transferred him into a different soil, under a different sun . . ."

The old lady's head touched the carved ornament, and stopped. But her odd headgear, the red fez with its blue pompom and fringe, continued to move at the same slow, hypnotizing pace, trying to detach itself from the top of her head.

". . . where finally he took root and has been ever since . . ."

The red fez had detached itself from the head, and now it was falling, but it didn't "fall"; it **crashed** on to the floor with a bang.

She was the only person who didn't jump and gasp. Motionless, she sat in her chair without her harness as if she were asleep. Her hair was cropped short. And there was a rectangular bald patch, clean-shaven, and indecently bare.

Maria was standing on the old lady's left side, pressing her fingers into her jugular vein trying to feel its pulse; Dottore Vecchi stood on the other side, trying to open her eyelids, to search for a sign of life in their pupils.

"It's no use," Maria said to him. "She is blind."

Then she straightened up, and added: "She *was*."

/ THE BODYGUARD

A few hours later, I was looking through the window of the drawing-room watching Signor Biagi and dom Antonio as they zigzagged up the slope towards the motor-road where their cars had been parked.

"The Law and the Church decamp," I said to the bodyguard secretary, who was standing beside me.

"I guess so," he said.

His name was Bob Utrillo; he was born in New York and lived wherever Giuseppe happened to be, which meant—in London, mostly. He was tall, big-boned, had enough muscles to move his great body as if it were weightless, and even his voice seemed to be produced with such an absolute lack of effort that whatever he was saying sounded as unimposing as if his words were an incidental by-product, for which his huge frame was neither responsible nor cared. He, too, had been looking at the tiny, far-away figures of the two men, high up on the hillside, and he grinned. Without malice:

"Their time is valuable," he said, "and the boss isn't in the right shape to go on with this crazy business."

"How is he?" I asked.

"He's with Dr Vecchi now. Being given some tranquillisers, I suppose. It's funny, isn't it? Yesterday, he hated the old lady, today he's full of love and remorse. If I were you, I wouldn't try to go near him. He imagines she wouldn't have died if you hadn't talked too much."

"Oh dear . . ." I said.

"Quite so," he said, sympathetically. "Raving mad! Lord, it's so unlike the old Giuseppe, you can't imagine." He threw a quick glance over his shoulder, perhaps to make sure that we were still alone in the room. "Though, on the other hand," he went on, "to tell you the truth, something bloody always happens when he comes south. He was born here but he doesn't fit here. He fits into London. He should have been born there."

Far away, in the middle of the hill-side, the little figures of Signor Biagi and dom Antonio had reached the end of the path where the road was hidden, and vanished behind the old trees. I left the window and sat in the armchair.

"Look here," I said with some determination. "If we could find a drink hereabouts."

"Fair enough," he said. He had crossed the room and from the corner behind the grand piano was now pulling a trolley with a few bottles and glasses.

I was still holding the old lady's headgear in my hands. Bob Utrillo hadn't seemed to mind when, some twenty minutes earlier, I had picked it up from the dining-room floor, where it had lain abandoned. It was an extraordinary contraption. Its weight must have been not much less than two pounds, and the very recollection of the old, blind lady balancing it on her poor head made me shiver. Its top was filled with electronic devices. The jewel under the blue pom-pom was not a jewel at all. It was a lens. It threw a picture of what was in front of it on to a miniature sort of photo-cell-screen inside the fez, and a battery of transistorized gadgetry translated this optical picture into an electrostatic picture straight on to the surface of the bald patch on the old lady's skull. Now I understood why she had asked me to wave my napkin

above my head, and why she made those oscillating movements when she wanted to locate something.

"Did she feel the picture with her sense of touch," I asked
Utrillo, "did she read it with her scalp the way people read
Braille with the fingertips, or was it warmth, or what?"

"I think it was a mild electric irritation. A few hundred
tiny electric shocks tickling the skin where the highlights
were in the picture. And she did learn to use it. She could
even read, letter by letter. It was a real seeing-aid."

"Well," I said, "it couldn't have been *seeing*, not literally."

He observed me for a moment, as if he was making up his
mind whether I was good enough to be told what he was
thinking, or, perhaps, whether what he thought was good
enough to be put into words. He was the third man, of those
whom I had met recently, who couldn't easily go to a shop
and find a suit of ready-made clothes big enough for him.
The first was Bruno, the second—Umberto, the docker, and
he was the third. All three possessed enormous athletic bodies which, though, were endowed with three types of mind
as different as were the tailors who tailored for them. The
rich and tyrannous Bruno, the gentle Umberto who had a
giant's strength but didn't use it like a giant, and—what sort
of mind Bob Utrillo had, I wasn't yet sure.

"Cheers," he said, lifting his glass. Then he took a sip, put
the glass on the trolley, and started in a light-hearted, unas-
suming and yet sort of you-may-take-my-word-for-it-because-I-
have-tried tone of voice: "Imagine," he said, "a man looking
through a window of his second or third storey flat. He has
just noticed a woman passing along the street when a bang
coming from somewhere or other makes him turn his head
and look in another direction. Soon afterwards he is called as
a witness and asked what he has seen. He says he saw a
young, elegant woman walking along the street. They ask
him what sort of shoes she had on. But he didn't notice her

114

shoes. Was she wearing stockings? Sure, she must have been wearing stockings, she looked very smart, but he can't remember their colour. They ask him what colour her coat was. No, he didn't think he actually saw the colour of her coat. What was the colour of her eyes? No, he was too far away to notice the colour of her eyes. Well, was she blond? No, he is sorry, but he will not swear that her hair was, or was not, blond. And so the fact is that he hasn't registered a single visual datum, and yet he knows it was a human being, female, young and elegant. How does he know it? The back of his eye, the retina, is sensitive to light and its colours, but there is not a single rod or cone nerve cell in it that would be sensitive to femininity, or juvenility, or elegance. These notions seem to have been stored in his brain, and roused up in it, not in his eyes, whose role seems to be only instrumental, like that of a switchboard. But, if so, then . . . cannot the picture of an elegant young woman walking along the street be evoked by stimulating the brain not through the eye but in some other way? I may be wrong, but it seems to me that there is something fishy about a philosophy based on observables, such as patches of colour." He didn't look embarrassed. He just laughed, "Ha, ha," as if what he had said was something funny but had nothing to do with him.

I got out of my chair, went across to the grand piano, and put the old lady's red fez on top of it. Some little, loose bits rattled in it when I was doing so.

"Is Giuseppe going to produce more of these?" I asked.

He pouted sceptically.

"Not unless he wants to be knighted," he said.

"Why not?"

"There isn't any money in it."

I somehow didn't expect that sort of answer.

"He doesn't give me the impression of being a man who wouldn't do something that interests him because it doesn't make money."

"No, he doesn't give that impression, does he?" He leaned back in his chair, stretched his legs, and put his feet on the lower shelf of the trolley. His shoes were enormous, and, between the bars of the trolley, they looked like two grown-up and independent animals put into a cage. They were made of some sort of soft, grey, embossed leather, and could have been slippers in disguise. He was giving them a long, speculative look and he must have wiggled his toes because the shoes seemed to be nodding to him. He smiled, looked up at me, and said:

"Why do I not feel disloyal to my boss when I talk about him behind his back to you? How do you do it?"

I gave this serious consideration and decided I didn't know.

"Perhaps it's because I'm a total stranger," I said at last.

"Are you?" he asked.

"Well, am I not?"

"No," he said. "You are a friend of Maria's."

"What is she doing now?" I asked. "Do you know?"

"She must still be with Silvia in the old lady's bedroom. Watching and praying." He tapped the edge of the trolley with the tip of his finger. "Soon this house will be full of people—professionals."

I looked at my watch. I knew that in two hours the last boat would be crossing the lake.

"Do you know which room is hers?" I asked; casually, I thought.

"Whose?"

"Maria's," I said.

"Yes, I do," he said.

But he didn't tell me. He seemed to insist on going back to what he had been saying before.

"And then, you are a friend of that man," he said.

"Meaning Harris?"

116

"Yeah, the man who invented the red fez gadget," he said quietly.

"What?!" I exclaimed.

"You didn't know that, did you?"

No, I didn't. I knew about his haircutting headgear, but I didn't know about the red fez.

"Good Lord," I said. "But if the red fez was his invention, why did the old lady hate him so much?"

Utrillo shrugged his shoulders.

"Who can know all the things that can go on in an old lady's brain?"

He swallowed the rest of his drink, and—(I didn't know whether it was because his mind had jumped a number of steps forward, or because now, when he had already mentioned Harris's name, he wanted to change the subject),—he looked up at me, and asked:

"Have you ever met Giuseppe's wife?"

"I don't think I have," I said.

"Oh," he said. "You should be sorry that you haven't."

This sudden gush of enthusiasm was perhaps slightly comic but I enjoyed observing it.

"What is so peculiar about her?" I asked.

"Well . . ." he said. "She is . . ." He was looking for a word. For a moment I thought he would give a wolf whistle, but perhaps he was considering some American expressions, and decided not to use them . . . ". . . remarkable," he said, finally. "It is an experience to meet her."

Thoughtfully, he refilled our glasses. And then, with a boyish twinkle in his eyes, as if he intended to make some sort of amusing psychological, or sociological, or semantic, experiment on me, he said:

"She won a beauty contest in a seaside resort. You see?"

"Yes, I see . . ." I said slowly.

"No, you don't see." He snapped his fingers. Obviously he

117

was starting a sort of cat-and-mouse game with me. "She was a vicar's daughter," he said. "Does that help you to build a picture in your mind?"

"Yes, in a way," I said. "The fusion of those two elements produces some sort of image."

He was pleased with my answer. It allowed him to display a wry, scornful smile:

"I bet it's all wrong," he said. "You see, her father was not one of those poor clergy. Far from it. Great names, peers of the realm, Eton, Oxford, and what not, on the spear side; banks, big business, industry on the distaff side."

"You are trying to build her identity-kit by knocking me all over the ring."

"Yes," he said, smiling. "And I haven't finished yet."

"Go on," I said.

But his thoughts must have shifted again, or perhaps he had decided to start from another end.

"Shall I tell you the whole story?" he asked.

"Do."

Now, of course, he didn't know where to start. He looked at me somewhat quizzically. "Do you at least know her name?" he asked.

"No, I don't," I said.

"Well," he said, "never mind." He struck a match, then decided not to light his Camel and puffed the flame out. "She believed that Giuseppe had genius, was to be a sort of James Joyce of electronics, and one day, still before they had become officially engaged, she asked her uncle to invite him to dinner. It was at the time when he had already spent all he had on his gadgets, couldn't possibly hope to get any more of his, or the old lady's, lire out of Musso's Italy, was practically penniless, and then, at the last minute, so to speak, met your man with the monkey who gave him fifty quid and disappeared—" He stopped to think, as if casting his mind back to those days.

118

"Did you know him then?" I asked.

He raised his eyebrows. It took him quite a time to understand my question. And then, "Good Lord!" he cried. "At that time I was a junior at St Joseph's school, Brooklyn, New York, wearing short pants and trying to . . ." He burst out laughing and then, almost at once, stifled it. There was death in the house, on the upper floor, just above us.

"Yes, of course," I said. "But listen. I've been wanting to ask this, and I think you can tell me. Fifty pounds may seem very little, or quite a lot. It all depends. But we all know that it wasn't a fortune, even then. What I ask is: How could it do Giuseppe so much good? How could it give him such a spectacular push up the ladder?"

Utrillo grinned, patted my knees, and grinned again.

"You are not by any means naive, sir," he said, trying to be jocular. "On the other hand, you are not very clever, are you?"

"All right, then, enlighten me," I said. "What did he actually do with that fifty pounds? Did he buy fifty electronic valves, or five miles of copper wire, or what?"

Bob Utrillo's eye sparkled with jolly mischief.

"No," he said, and I saw he was going to prolong and enjoy his answer. "No," he repeated. "Giuseppe didn't buy fifty electronic valves. Or five *yards* of copper wire. He bought himself a dinner jacket. And everything that goes with it. The whole outfit. Then he changed one of the remaining crisp, white five-pound notes, put another one in his breast pocket, hired a car, and went to Mr de Marney's country house."

Startled, I couldn't control my voice:

"*Whose* country house?" I asked.

"I told you," he rebuffed me. "The uncle's. His future wife's uncle's."

"You say his name was de Marney?"

"Yeah. What of it?"

"The husband of Lady Celia?"

"I think she was dead at the time. I think he was a widower."

"Of course," I said, "he must have been a widower if it was the time when Giuseppe got fifty pounds from Harris. Harris had inherited it from Sir Francis and Lady Celia died before Sir Francis."

"Did you know her?" Utrillo asked.

"It doesn't matter whether I knew her. Harris did. She and Sir Francis were close friends and, for some time, Harris was as much her secretary as his. They once went to Majorca, all three of them."

He was staring at his ankles crossed on the edge of the trolley.

"Bit of a coincidence, when you come to think of it," he said pensively.

Suddenly, he kicked the trolley away and put his feet on the floor.

"Are you sure that Harris and Giuseppe didn't know each other before? Think about it, now that you know de Marney was Giuseppe's wife's uncle. Are you sure they didn't know each other's faces when they met at the Black and White milk bar?"

"I'm pretty sure of that," I said.

"Then why did Harris give that blasted money to a complete stranger? It wasn't sixpence. It was fifty quid."

"I think the reason was psychological," I said.

"Psychological?" Utrillo repeated. "I'm interested in psychology."

"Well," I said, "fifty pounds was a sum people like Sir Francis would leave to their servants. I rather think that Harris felt offended. I think he wanted to be rid of that gift as soon as he got it."

"Poor chap," he said.

"Well," I said, "don't forget he was practically told he had

killed Sir Francis to inherit it. And that's what the ghost of
Bruno wants us to believe, if not something worse."

He stood up, walked across to the grand piano and opened
it. He looked at the keyboard, then turned his head, looked
at me, just for a second, sharply, and I knew what he wanted
to say. He wanted to say "And how do I know that he didn't
kill him?" But he decided not to ask the question. He looked
again at the keyboard. Then he shut the lid, flipped the red
fez on top of the piano, came back and, heavily, sat down in
his chair again.

"And so Harris and his beloved monkey meet Giuseppe,
who does not know them, and whom they don't know," (he
started, and there was a tinge of sarcasm in his tone of
voice), "and Giuseppe gets his fifty pounds, makes himself
presentable, and drives to Mr de Marney, to dinner. With
some white, crisp cash in the clean, virgin pocket of his new
dinner jacket, he feels quite equal, businesswise. He enjoys
his port and cigar, and tells his host about his project. What
a good investment it will be. And Mr de Marney is extremely nice, and friendly-looking and full of smiles, and
Giuseppe notices of course the sweet smiles; and the miracu-
lous rapidity with which Giuseppe can form a sound judg-
ment of human character tells him that Mr de Marney is
smiling because Mr de Marney is feeling awkward and Mr
de Marney is feeling awkward because he has already decided to say No. So, at once, in midgame, Giuseppe changes
his tactics. 'Well, Sir' (Utrillo imitated Giuseppe's voice),
'what I have told you is true, yet it is an objective truth.
Now, there is a subjective truth to it as well.' 'Tell me
about it,' says Mr de Marney. 'Shall I?' 'Do!' 'Well, imagine, Sir, that you have entered a strange room in which
there is a desk and on the desk there are a great number
of small pieces of paper. On one is written: $5+7=12$; on
another: $1+2=3$; and so on, and so forth. Suddenly, your
eye catches sight of one little scrap of paper on which is

written: 9+6= and then BLANK. Are you not tempted to reach for a pencil and write down 15? Just for the sake of doing so? Well, this is precisely what has happened to me. I don't claim to have made a spectacular discovery, or that nobody else can do the same. But it just so happens that it is I who have come across a BLANK and am feeling a compulsive urge to fill it. I have already done all the preliminary work, using my own pecuniary resources, which, owing to the political situation, currency restrictions mostly, are not unlimited. The parts of the ensemble are there. And they work. Each within its scope. But they are done by using the old sealing-wax and string technique. And they cannot be joined together. To do so, one would have to match them with each other and keep them in balance. And to achieve that, one must first have them built with that technological precision which only the most perfect workmanship can produce. Signor Mussolini would be glad, of course, to supply me with the tools I need. But I still hope that one day I shall find it possible to realise the project in this country.'

"Now the smile has vanished from Mr de Marney's face, he has no more cause to appear friendly and interested, because he *is* now friendly and interested, and Giuseppe knows that the thing has caught on. It has. A few days later the agreement is signed. Giuseppe gets a workshop in one of de Marney's factories, a team of ten people, and carte blanche for one year in which to show the results."

Utrillo stopped for a moment. His usual detachment had evaporated. He wasn't showing any excitement, none at all, yet I knew he was approaching a subject that concerned him.

"Am I boring you?" he asked anxiously.

"No," I said, "go on, please."

"Well," he said, "the twelve months are over, the results *are* what Giuseppe said they would be, the engineering section of the laboratory becomes a full-blown production outfit, it develops rapidly, and then war breaks out, Giuseppe's invention becomes top priority, and the vicar's daughter, who—incidentally—has married Giuseppe in the meantime, gets herself parachuted into France."

"Good Lord," I gasped. "How did that come about?"

"I told you," he said. "I told you she is . . ." He was searching for a word again, and again shrank into himself and used the same epithet as before, ". . . remarkable." But he knew this was not adequate. So he perked up, and tried to explain: "She is a person who doesn't ask anybody for permission to live. She doesn't ask anybody for permission to take part in a beauty contest, or for permission to die. Why she has decided to get herself parachuted I don't know. Perhaps she feels patriotic. Perhaps it's because her mother's family is half-French. Or perhaps because she is married to an Italian, who was to be a genius, but, instead, is busy making fantastic heaps of money producing electronic contraptions for the government. I don't know, and I don't want to discuss her motives. All I know is that one night she jumps into the void, the next morning is hiding in a little village somewhere in France, a liaison officer with the resistance, and then, one day, meets a young French soldier who was told to be a hero and shoots a German from behind the bushes, which makes the Germans take the maire of the commune, and five other men whom she knows, as hostages, and give the village until Sunday, noon, to surrender the culprit. Perhaps the villagers would comply, perhaps not, but anyway they do not know where he is hiding. She is the only one who knows. What she feels on Wednesday, Thursday, Friday and Saturday, I have not the slightest idea. It's beyond my American imagination. What he, the hero, feels, I don't know either. But now the Sunday comes, she hears the church clock strike twelve, and then she hears the shots, one volley after another, and at that moment she gives up, she has had enough. She makes her way to Switzerland, and from there back to England, where she doesn't ask anybody for permission to say what she

123

thinks. And what she thinks is highly unorthodox. She thinks that to kill one uniformed enemy, and let six civilian compatriots pay for it with their lives, is not patriotism but a crime; she thinks that resistance warfare is carried on not to help win the war but to pave the way for politicians lying in wait, ready to seize power as soon as victory is won by the regular army; and she thinks that Pétain is a modern Jeanne d'Arc, or, at least, the first Frenchman who could afford to be proud enough to act as any reasonable Englishman would, giving up the display of his virtues to save the essence of patriotism; that, but for him, Paris would have been a razed Warsaw, and every village of France—a Lidice. This view does not make her popular either with the British or the French. So she withdraws to the country and reads books. Detective stories. In which people make such a fuss as soon as one single insignificant man gets murdered. No medals are pinned to her jumper. And Giuseppe is no longer allowed to enter that part of his own factory which produces some classified bits of the thing which he himself has invented. And so life and war go on, and all that time, somewhere, far away, westward, in a place called New York, lives a boy who attends high school and is too young to enlist, though he's already six foot three inches tall and weighs thirteen stone. His name is Bob Utrillo—no connection with the painter; the painter was born in Paris; my father was born in Torino but became one of the tough boys of New York. And so Bob Utrillo is graduating from high school and thinks America is okay because America is *people*, and he doesn't yet know that in a short while America will also catch the disease and want to be a *nation*, just like any teething African tribe. Yeah, America is still okay and he was born in the right country, though he is not sure that he was born in the right body, he is not sure whether his body is not too big and too strong for the kind of soft thoughts he's having, his body is not expected to produce that sort of thought, unless it is drunk; when it is drunk people forgive it for not being what they expect it to be, so he drinks, moderately, and pretends to be drunk, heavily. And so life goes on, as I've already said, but now the war comes to its end, and a couple of years later he is sent, with a batch of other post-war GIs, to Europe, and, his French being okay, he's plugged into a section of French general staff, to serve as translator, mostly, and is attached to a quite young capitaine, who has a whole spectrum of little ribbons permanently sewn on his breast. Things don't seem too bad, as a matter of fact they aren't bad at all, till one day the whole section is sent to London to discuss with their English counterpart something that anyway has already been decided by the politicians, and, to make everybody feel nice, there is a reception, black tie and decorations sort of thing, all very correct, le capitaine is a smart talker and is enjoying himself when one of the black ties approaches and introduces him to a nice-looking couple. The guy is middle-aged, she's much younger and strikingly beautiful. Le capitaine recognises her, but she has already recognised him, and now she turns round and, without a word, walks away. Le capitaine loses his sang froid, jumps on Giuseppe, tells him his wife is a fasciste, une Pétainiste, who should have had her head shaved, and when Giuseppe tells him to shut up, he challenges him to a duel. Upon which the young American boy, who is one foot taller and three or more stone heavier than le capitaine, lifts the latter bodily off the parquet floor and carries him out and down the marble staircase. What le capitaine is shouting in the process is highly insulting to the U.S. flag, nation, and culture, thanks to which Bob Utrillo isn't even reprimanded by his superiors, he's just released from the post and, subsequently, on Giuseppe's personal request, discharged from the service, to become Guiseppe's secretary and bodyguard, to nurse him and protect him, which is what he has now been doing for more than ten years, and will go on doing as gladly as ever, even if Giuseppe was not her husband but her poodle."

There was absolutely nothing I could say. He couldn't possibly *want* me to say anything. That was a moment when pipes are useful. I filled mine and lit it up. Then I emptied my glass and, when he reached for the bottle, I said "No, no more, please." When we stood up and I had to lift my head to look at him, I felt small and frail and odd; but strangely enough I didn't feel old.

"It's on the second floor, next to the lavatory," Utrillo said.

His tone of voice was again, as at the beginning, light and unconcerned.

"What is?"

"Maria's room. I thought you asked me where it was."

"So I did, thanks," I said.

I looked at my watch. I didn't have much time now. But he stopped me with a gesture.

"Before you go," he said, "perhaps I'd better tell you that the boy carries a penknife. In the pocket of his jeans."

"Giambattista?"

"Yeah."

"A penknife?" I repeated.

"Well, it's sharp enough, by whatever name you call it. You press your thumb, release the spring, and four and a half inches of steel flicks out."

"I'm sure he's never used it," I said.

"Sure he hasn't." Utrillo shrugged his shoulders. "There aren't many who have the chance of using a toy like that for the second time. But there can always be a first time."

I thought he was exaggerating.

"Bruno might have been right in saying that as a journalist

the boy hasn't any news sense, but I don't think he would try to create news."

"Yeah," he said. "Sure."

I shut the door behind me, crossed the passage, and walked softly up the stairs. Maria, I hoped, was still with Silvia in the dead lady's bedroom, and Giuseppe in his, with Dr Vecchi. Both rooms, I knew, were on the first floor. I stopped for a moment and heard no sound. Slowly, I walked up to the second floor. Very lightly, with my finger-nail, I knocked on the door next to the lavatory. There was no answer. I turned the knob; the door wasn't locked. I opened it; the room was empty. I went in and bolted the door behind me. I noticed the suitcase at once: on the chair between the bed and the window. The little key was hanging on a bit of string attached to the handle. It took me a second to open the suitcase. It wasn't like Maria not to have unpacked as soon as she had arrived. But it was her suitcase, I recognised the smell before I saw the things. I found the envelope at once and took it out. A large heavy thick manilla envelope. It was too big to fit into my pocket. I unbuttoned my shirt and put it in, next to the skin. I hoped it wouldn't give me a psychosomatic rash.

It was nice to be safely back downstairs.

"Hallo, children," I said, entering the room.

They looked up at me, not knowing what to expect.

"How is the old lady?" Giambattista asked.

They didn't know she was dead. Nobody had told them. They thought she had fainted.

"Come on, let's get out of here," I said. "I'm staying at a hotel on the other side of the lake; we can arrange something there for tonight, and tomorrow we shall see . . ."

Their eyes brightened.

127

"There is nobody here we need say goodbye to," I said, and we went out, closing the door behind us, and started zigzagging our way down to the jetty.

It was a dark night, and when we were in the middle of the lake, the dark patches of land, the one we had left and the one we were going to, felt as far away as if we were in the middle of the ocean.

/ THE ENVELOPE

"Oh, don't be a fool," I said.

"He isn't a fool. It is his philosophy that tells him not to get involved with *you* people," Grazia said.

I turned from her to Giambattista, and asked:

"Why did you accept Giuseppe's invitation, then? Why did you come?"

"Why shouldn't I?" he said.

"All right," I said, "but don't you want to know *why* he invited you?"

"He asked me to come, and I came, and that's that. I don't want to know why he invited me. I'm not interested."

I started unbuttoning my shirt and, while they were watching me not knowing whether I was doing it to scratch myself or what, I drew out the manilla envelope and showed it to them. It was warm, and there were two greasy patches on it.

His reaction to objects appeared to be different from his reaction to words. His eyes narrowed and focused on the envelope.

"Before he was wheeled off to the operating room," I said, "your father asked Maria to give you this envelope—if he died."

Giambattista's right hand moved forward an inch, but he

might not have been aware of it. He was still maintaining the same air of contemptuous indifference.

"Well, he did die, didn't he?" he said with forced harshness.

"Yes," I said.

"What was she waiting for, then?"

"You mustn't blame Maria," I said. "She had reasons for thinking that there was something in the envelope which would make her an accessary to what she disapproved of. It troubled her conscience. She didn't know what to do, so she asked Giuseppe, and Giuseppe decided to make you an offer."

"An offer?"

"Yes."

"An offer!" Giambattista exclaimed in a tone of voice the meaning of which wasn't quite clear to me.

I let it pass, and went on:

"He wanted to offer you a hundred thousand lire for the right to look at what's in the envelope as soon as you opened it. With the stipulation that you would accept five hundred thousand lire more for any item he may wish to possess if he thinks it might have been stolen, or may incriminate other people."

"Who are those other people?" he asked.

"I'll tell you in a moment," I said.

"And what if Giam wouldn't agree to accept his offer?" Grazia said.

"Yes." Giambattista repeated: "And what if I wouldn't accept, what then?"

"Then, I suppose, he would have asked dom Antonio to appeal to your Christian soul, to tell you that your transistor will not make you happy about your life, to ask you to curb the intellectual pride that drives you to moral compromise, to advise you to establish your relationship with God by establishing your relationship with individuals, which you could best do by accepting Giuseppe's offer."

"And supposing the Grace of God didn't touch me?" he asked.

"In that case," I said, "Signor Biagi, the lawyer, would have put the envelope into another envelope, still bigger, which he would have sealed, according to the rules of his profession, and taken to the Commissioner of Oaths, or the judge, or the police, whatever the exact legal procedure is, whom he would then have told about his suspicions and asked to open it officially. Which wouldn't have benefited anybody."

He shrugged his shoulders:

"It wouldn't have hurt *me*," he said.

"Giuseppe thought it would," I said.

"How could it have?"

"Well," I said. "First, you would have had no claim on the six hundred thousand lire he was offering you. And next . . ."

But he interrupted me. Throwing his hands about, he started to shout:

"Giuseppe is a silly ass. I am inheriting all Bruno's fortune, every bloody lira of it, and he thinks he can tempt me with his stinking six hundred thousand!"

"Well, yes," I agreed, "I suppose he didn't think about that. But there would still have been the other thing he thought you wouldn't like."

"What other thing?"

"Well, suppose the envelope did in fact contain some legally doubtful documents; once it was in official hands, you would not have the chance of getting hold of them any more quickly than other journalists—to make your scoop."

His eyes opened widely.

"To make my scoop?!" he repeated with childish amazement.

"Oh dear," I said, "that's what the whole mess is about, didn't you realise that?"

"Didn't I realise what?" he asked, aggressively, but as if he wanted to hide his bewilderment.

Grazia butted in:

"Excuse me," she said, "dov'e il gabinetto?"

"If you open the door, you'll find it just opposite," I said. But she didn't move.

"No, no," she said. "I only wanted to know."

"Well?" Giam insisted.

"Well," I said, "do you remember the article you published not so long ago, on some twenty cases of rusty small arms sent to Malaya, and 200 bicycles stuck in Southampton?"

He blushed.

"It was . . . It was Bruno, my father . . ." he stammered. His face was green and he was shaking a good deal. "I never wanted to be that sort of journalist. It was he . . . don't you understand that I had to do it? I had to! I had to!" His face twitched hysterically between laughter and crying.

Grazia put her hand on his shoulder:

"Don't you want to go to the gabinetto, Giam?" she asked with concern.

He ignored her.

"I know you despise Bruno . . ." he went on, talking to me.

"I don't," I said.

"Yes, you do. But he was my father and he despised me. He thought I was a sissy. He would never understand that I didn't *want* to be a . . . , even a Walter Lippmann. It meant so much to him. He had lived for forty years in Malaya, you know? I simply couldn't disappoint him."

"Were you born in Malaya?"

"No," he said. "My mother wouldn't go there for anything in the world. She played the harp at La Scala. She didn't have to, he used to send her plenty of money, anyway till a few years ago, but she *wanted* to play the harp, she couldn't play the harp in Malaya, could she? So he used to come home every two years, for a month or two. I haven't seen him more than *ten times* in my whole life."

"And why did he stop sending her money?" I asked.

"Oh, stop questioning him," Grazia said.

"I'm sorry," I said.

"It's all right," he said drily. "She left him. She went to Hollywood. She is in Hollywood now."

"Playing the harp?" I asked.

"No. She makes hats. She's a *modista*."

Suddenly, his face changed. It was no longer the face of a boy. It was the face of a grown-up man.

"Let's see the envelope," he said curtly.

And yet, while I was handing it to him, he hesitated. His emotions swung like a pendulum.

"*You* open it," he said.

"No, Giam," I said. "*You* must take it and open it."

The envelope was made of thick, strong manilla paper, and as he half-heartedly attempted to tear it, with fingers that were starting to tremble, it slipped and fell on the floor.

"Try a knife," I said.

His hand moved to his pocket and stopped halfway.

We regarded each other steadily for one queer moment, and of course I knew that he knew that I knew what sort of knife he was carrying in the pocket of his jeans.

"Perhaps this will do . . ." Grazia said. She had opened her handbag, and now produced a long nail-file.

He took it from her, jabbed it into the corner of the envelope and slit the edge.

The first thing he drew out was a letter. He read it slowly and then passed it to Grazia. She scanned the page rapidly, turned it, seemed to be just glancing at the other side, but I was sure she hadn't missed a word; then she gave it to me.

It was Bruno's letter to his son. It said exactly what we thought it would. His handwriting was clear and even, and I

133

wondered how his large and sinewy hand, in which an ordinary pen couldn't feel bigger than a toothpick, had managed to produce such orderly lines. It was his style that gave him away. If he had used his spoken voice, shown his big, strong, convincing face, he would probably have succeeded in giving the impression that he had put himself to all that trouble solely for Giam's sake, to help him find his feet. But the written word had betrayed him. There was too much insistence in his trying to show that the real villain was Giuseppe. "Don't forget to stress, my dear son," he wrote, "that though Harris delivered the blow, Giuseppe was behind it, and has been paying him large sums of money for the last eighteen years." But it was obvious that it was not even Giuseppe who was the ultimate target Bruno had wanted to reach. The ultimate target was Silvia. He knew he would die, and he wanted to be remembered by her. As he couldn't achieve that by making her happy, he wanted to force her to remember him by making her curse him for having annoyed Giuseppe. What was it that made him want to be remembered by Silvia, and not somebody else, Maria for instance, Maria who had bought him the Old England scarf to cover the thing on his neck? No, it had to be Silvia, the same Silvia, who, funnily enough, had been the first to say, when he died, "Now try and forget it all, darling Maria." It was in her, Silvia's mind, that he wanted to survive his death. Silvia, a beautiful animal, born with the whore's knowledge of life which is the knowledge that one is mortal, that everything that groweth on the earth is mortal, and that therefore nothing, absolutely nothing, can be of greater eternity than the functioning of her own living cells.

I gave the letter back to Giam. He folded it and put it into his pocket.

The thick manilla paper envelope was still there, in his lap. He had a funny sort of face when he started to take things out of it. About sixty items, all neatly numbered and indexed. Press-cuttings, mostly from English newspapers, 1939; xerographic prints of birth-certificates and two marriage licences, one made in London, one in Genoa; a photostat of a page in the day-book of a firm called TRICYCLE Ltd; the testimony of a nurse to Lady Celia de Marney; a dozen photographs of Tom Harris, with and without his beard, among them his prison photograph; a photograph of the matriculation papers of an American college made out in the name of one Harry Thomas; a post-mortem photograph of Sir Francis; of an oleander tree standing on a balcony; and of a strange-looking couple, captioned: *"Baron Dr Reinach von Reinacherhof & Helen (see item 12)"*; some letters, two feet of micro-film, and three exercise books, filled with very close handwriting, presumably that of Tom Harris.

Giam looked at it all with hostile indifference.

"It stinks," he said.

For a moment, I thought he was going to demonstrate what he had said by pinching his nose, but it wasn't that. His finger and thumb dipped into the mass of papers and drew out a picture-postcard. His eye brightened.

"Have a look at that!" he exclaimed.

The picture-postcard was addressed to a Baron Dr Reinach von Reinacherhof and sent from Majorca, in 1933 or 1935, according to the poorly stamped postmark. It read:

> *"Our vivisecting Shakespeare hasn't spoiled the colour of the sea. It is as blue as it must have been when Chopin stayed here with that awful woman. We have shanghaied our revolutionary secretary aboard this island, made him read Hamlet aloud, and think his comments quite useful for our theory of faces. Francis asks me to send you his greetings with mine. Celia."*

"Do you see what I see?" Giam asked, excitedly.

I paused to think.

"I see that there was, after all, a connection between Sir Francis and the baron," I said.

He looked at me with complete incomprehension.

"Look at the postage stamp," he said patiently, as if to a child.

I looked at it but saw nothing.

"Look at the green sign and the price. It's a discovery copy. Hell! It's printed upside down, don't you see, it's unique; it's worth millions."

He snatched the picture-postcard away from me, tore it neatly in four, took the quarter with the postage stamp, and gingerly put it in his wallet.

"I'll take this," he said, "and you may have the rest. All the rest," he added, pushing the pile of papers with the tip of his shoe.

A moment later, he bent down, gathered all the papers together, put them back into the manilla envelope, and handed it to me.

"That's the bargain," he said. "And now, let's talk about something else."

/ DEPARTURE

When I awoke next morning I didn't know where I was. That didn't frighten me. I never wake up all at once. In the army, your body wakes first, to the din of the reveille, your mind—later on, perhaps as late as after breakfast, and you yourself nobody cares when, perhaps only when you have been discharged, down here, or up in heaven. When you go on leave, the sequence is radically and rebelliously reversed, and that reverse sequence has stayed with me for the last twenty years: *I* wake first, my mind—later on, and my body is the last to follow. Modern philosophers, who have already proved by perhaps too great a variety of means that the distinction between mind and body is illusory, may be sneering at this moment at my having enlarged the number of terms to three instead of reducing it to one. Their contempt is fully justified. Yet there remains the fact that I wouldn't know how to describe the process of my waking up if I were forbidden the use of all three terms: *I*, my mind and my body.

As my mind still wasn't telling me where I was and when, I decided to wake up my eyes and tried to stare in front of me, into the grey, dawning space. There was in it a white patch and a black patch, and a black patch and a white patch, which I wasn't able to identify and name. I saw them but I didn't know what they were. With no help from my mind, I simply didn't know what they were. Half disconcerted, half amused, I could do nothing but wait till my mind consented to give me some bearings, some co-ordinates, to which I could relate what I was seeing. Finally, and I don't know whether it was a question of seconds or minutes, my mind gave up its dumb stubbornness, and all of a sudden, without any further ado, it told me that it was the morning of the next day, and that I was in my own room, the enormous hotel-room on Lake Como. As soon as I had been told that, my eyes recognised without difficulty the diffused shades of greyness as the far-away wall, the expanse above me as the ceiling, the two rectangular shapes on the right as blinded windows, and those on the left as two doors and a wardrobe. The black and white patches in front of me were a black pullover and white jeans, and white pullover and black jeans, hanging on the backs of four chairs. Where had they come from? That I didn't know yet. Cautiously I moved my feet, then bent my knees. What they felt confirmed the hypothesis which I had already been considering myself: that my body was covered with a blanket, and that I was lying in a bed.

I didn't see the bed itself because it was under me, and I was looking up at the grey expanse of the ceiling above, but I remembered it. It was an enormous, heavy, six-foot-by-six-foot, square bed. I remembered it well. And what I needed now was a message from outside, a few more sense-data. To get them, I woke up my left hand and pushed it a little away from me. It moved an inch or two and grasped something, which I knew was the edge of the bed. I sat up, turned my head to the right and looked down, and as I tried to co-ordinate what my eyes were perceiving with what my mind had kept in its memory, I understood the meaning of that soft murmuring sound which had been trying to get itself noticed by my ears for some time now. Giam's head was on the pillow in the middle of the bed, Grazia's—on the other side. Both were asleep, and breathing peacefully. All that might have lasted a very short, or a very long, time, as measured by clocks. I don't know. But I *was* fully awake now, all three of me—I, my mind and my body. I left all six of them, their two inconceivable "I"s, two dreaming minds, and two sleeping bodies, where they were, and got up.

Beautiful clean shower. I was fiddling with the taps. The hot and the cold. Turning the left one just a little to the right and the right one just a little to the left, simultaneously; and then the other way round. Making the streaming water just a little too cold, and then just a little too hot, and *da capo* again and again. I wished it would last for ever. The pleasure of it. I didn't see why it shouldn't. Lovely clean streams of artificial rain, cool like a mountain spring, and then warm like a jungle, but without its mosquitoes, and its serpents, and its Eves. Why did I say: Eves? All of a sudden the thousands of falling drops lost their momentum and stopped short, suspended in mid-air. I turned the taps off. The drops fell and disappeared. Now I remembered the dream I had had that night. I was standing on the brink of a gorge, wide as a valley. Its walls were yellow, sun-coloured sand, with a few shrubs and bits of roots here and there, steep walls, falling headlong down, where a narrow stream was flowing bluishly from somewhere far away on the left to somewhere far away on the right. On the other side of the stream, walking along its edge, was a she I knew, but whether it was Pamela, or Grazia, or Maria, I wasn't sure. I tried to climb down and it was very easy for the first few feet, but then—no, it couldn't be done; I knew it couldn't be done from that point, so I stopped and climbed back to the edge, walked a few steps farther to the left, and tried again from there, but it was the same as before—dead easy to begin with, and then an almost vertical face of yellow, loose sand; and at that moment I noticed him, down below on the other side of the stream, and who he was I didn't know, but I saw him approaching her, who didn't stop walking along the stream, on its other side, and now they were walking together, and I thought There must be some ordinary way of crossing the gorge, and getting to the other side of the stream, and I climbed back again to the edge, and thought Why not ask the attendant? And I saw the attendant approaching, in his dark-blue uniform with a red stripe, a whistle and a railwayman's watch hanging from his patch-pocket, and I asked him, and he told me to follow him, which I did, along the sunny edge of the gorge first, and then through the gloomy damp hall of a huge railway station, and then into the station square, with its taxi-ranks, lorries and a few human silhouettes, and I took from my pocket a coin, wondering Will that be enough? Or will that be too much? I didn't know what currency it was. Will it carry me across? It was a silvery, small nickel; I thought it was called Obol, but what was stamped on it was: five ore, and it couldn't possibly *be* five ore as it was one obol, and I gave it to him, and he was very pleased, so I thought It will be all right, and we went on, through the narrow streets of a small town, away from the gorge, in the opposite direction, and I thought They must have built a flyover at the other end of the town, that's why we are going away from the gorge, and then I stopped and said Look here, I left my winter overcoat there, and he asked Where?, and I said Somewhere by the gorge, and he said Go back and fetch it, I'll wait for you here; and it was warm and I didn't need my winter overcoat but I knew it would lead to some complications if I didn't fetch it, so I went, in spite of the fact that I also knew that I should not find my way either to the gorge or back to the attendant, and I kept walking through some grey narrow streets and yards and passages, and then I saw that the only way left open for me went through the back door of a fish-butcher's shop, and it wasn't the fishmonger's, it was the fish-butcher's, and as I went in I saw them behind me, without turning my head I *saw* them behind me: two enormous fish-butchers, standing side by side behind the marble slab. Their aprons had some green blood stains, the knives in their hands had grey, triangular steel-blades, and their eyes were cataract-white, with a blue tinge showing through, and they were motionless and colossal like Gog and Magog, and I wondered why they hadn't killed me while I was passing them, and I felt the smell of the sea, and there was plenty of fish around me, and when I crossed through, through the shop, to the front door, and went out, I knew I would not go back to the attendant because they were not going to let me pass, as soon as they, with their blind eyes, saw me approaching them from the front, they would not let me pass, and when I left the fish-butcher's shop, I found myself in the market-place, which was empty; it was a large, square market-place, with rows of small houses along all four sides and no indication that could show me where to turn to go to the sun-yellow gorge, and as I stood in the very centre of the empty market-place, it occurred to me that there was no philosopher there to teach me, and that I was not a philosopher to teach anybody anything, and that anyway there was not a single soul there to teach, and no way out, back or forward, and that it must have been the wrong day, and therefore time to wake up, and so I dreamt that I woke up and found myself naked and embraced by some naked warm arms, and clinging to a naked and warm human body, and the rest of it was pure sex. An undisguised sexual orgy. Well, one isn't responsible for one's dreams. And yet I felt disconcerted. Because it was tactless of me to have invited them to stay, to share my room and my bed with me, and then to dream such a dream as the latter part of mine. Hastily, I dressed and went down.

First, I telephoned Maria, across the lake, and told her how the problem had solved itself to the satisfaction of everybody and asked her to dismiss the thought of the envelope from her mind, at once and forever.

Next, I tried to telephone Harris, at Genoa. Not without

some apprehension. Because I knew somehow with what sort of—to me inexplicable—indifference he would receive my account of what was actually the business of saving his skin and not mine. And so I was glad when a sweet young female voice said:

"I'm afraid my husband is not in; could I take a message?"

I asked her to tell him that everything was fine, generally, and that I was going to write to him from London.

It was at that moment that I decided to go back to London at once. I put the receiver down, went to see the manager, explained how my guests had missed the boat the previous night, asked him to prepare the bill, ordered a large breakfast for three, and returned to my room.

They were still asleep. I started putting things into my suitcase. The brown manilla envelope was already in it. I took out from the envelope one of the three exercise books, opened it at page one, and read:

"My name is Tom Bradlaugh Harris . . ."

I closed the exercise book and put it back.

"It's funny," I said to myself. "I didn't know his second name was Bradlaugh!"

Then I went to the windows, threw the blinds up, and let the sun come in.

PART TWO

When, for some obscure reason, you happen to look at a map of the Eastern half of the earth and notice a little dot called London, you are bound to think it lies on the sea. And yet, if you live in London, it will take you at least an hour and an half (and half as much to the station and from the station) to get to the nearest point from which you can see the sea—here, where I am now, sitting at a little table, in front of the solitary window of my room, on the first floor of this seaside hotel, and looking at the ocean of grey waves under the grey sky. Everything is grey. A hundred variations of greyness.

I couldn't tell what time of the year it is. Is it a very cold summer, or a mild winter? The five minutes of sunshine yesterday morning, when a ray of sun hit a seagull in its flight and made it illuminate the whole seascape—was it the spring sun? And the gale that followed: was it an autumn gale?

Well, this is an inter-pause, an intermission, a half-break. Why was I so rash? If I hadn't acted so rashly I would not have needed to leave London again, to find myself here, in this seaside hotel, sitting in an armchair at a small table under the window, looking at the grey sea, and trying to identify myself with Tom Harris.

Would I understand him better if I put his mask on my face? I shut my eyes to chuckle at the picture—it was pretty funny. And yet that was, in a way, what I was trying to do on Friday (I left London yesterday and today is Sunday), when I went to Bell Street to see Harry Brown, the Chinese waiter —he is a very old ex-waiter now—who lives in Tom's flat again. I say "again" because he did live there once before, with his little daughter, long ages ago, during the blitz, when Tom was, as they say, "inside." I didn't ask him about her, but I asked him about the monkey, and then he mentioned the child.

"Yes," he said, "the monkey,—I came with my little daughter to see once; old time ago; before the war; when Harris said: we,—live on the floor; the monkey,—lives everywhere between the floor and the ceiling; monkey,—three-dimensional; we,—two-dimensional. My little daughter,— she remembers his saying it. A little microscope,—he gave her as Christmas present."

There were distinct commas and dashes after each noun with which he started his sentences.

"Did you ever think," I asked him, "that one day Harris would start a new life again and work with real microscopes?"

"I never think," Brown said. After a moment, he added: "Peoplewise." And then he said: "No impossible thing,— can exist. Therefore, everything,—possible." He added again: "Peoplewise," and offered me a cup of fragrant green tea.

I looked round. Things seemed to be the same, more or less, as they had been before, when Tom Harris lived here. Except for a papier mâché mask on top of the television set (the television set was something new here as well, of course). It was the mask of a white man. And, as I looked at it, a crazy thought came to my mind; more than a thought, a crazy conviction; that he, Brown, used to put it on his face every time he went down into the street to make friends.

I praised his tea and got up. At that moment my eyes

146

found themselves on the level of the shelf hanging opposite, between the windows. He looked at me enquiringly, and I had to say something. So I put my finger on the spines of a few exercise books lying flat on the shelf under some boxes and asked:

"Did they belong to Harris?"

He smiled, very, very politely.

"No," he said. "They,—they are my little daughter's old school-exercises. Keeping them, 'cause the time she was a little schoolgirl,—they remind me of."

At that I said goodbye and left.

Bell Street hadn't changed much since after that time after the war, yet there was already in it that readiness to feel that at any moment now it may disappear completely. The Salvation Army building, with its HELP OTHERS IN NEED Self Denial Appeal, was still there, but on the other side of the road, on the corner of Penfold Street, the white-tiled wall of a newly built school was already ushering in the future.

I went into the Green Man, on the corner of Edgware Road, and asked for a tankard of ale. They used to have pewter tankards, but now they only had glass. And a Tzigane potpourri from a loudspeaker. And red and gold wallpaper. Quite fresh.

"Do you remember the old man with the monkey who used to drink his beer here every night some eighteen years ago?" I asked the barman.

"A man with a monkey?" he repeated.

"Well," I said, "at that time he didn't have a monkey any more, but that's what he used to be called: the Man with the Monkey."

"Nope," he said. "What about him?"

"Nothing," I said. "I just thought you might have remembered him."

"Well, I don't," he said, and turned away from me.

I happened to be born with an intelligent face. Tom Harris was born with a stupid face. I can sit for an hour in a state of stupor, not a trace of thought in my blank mind, and my culture-conditioned brethren will still think that I'm diving somewhere deep, or scheming something clever, and they will keep their distance, alerted and mistrusting. He, with his face, may be thinking feverishly, or be in an agony of despair, and they will not notice him any more than a piece of not very valuable wooden furniture, which they can knock about with nonchalance, or touch to avert misfortune. The very presence of our respective faces changes the world around them, and that is why the people he knew are not the same people when I meet them. It was there, at the Green Man, that I realised how futile my empirical efforts were bound to be. I couldn't see things as he had, the same beer must have tasted differently in his mouth, the same four corners of his room must have looked different to him, the same stinking staircase must have creaked differently under his feet. Physical realities were of no help to me; on the contrary, by striking me otherwise than they had struck him, they made it more difficult for me to imagine what the world round him was like, and I was quite certain now that if I left the whole naive realism of it altogether I would find my task much easier. This is how it happened that I left London (so soon after having come back from Italy),—and am now sitting in this arm-chair, in front of the window, and looking at the indifferent and non-committal grey waves.

For a life-time—or two—or twenty—philosophers, social reformers, saviours, writers, economists, artists, will be producing beautiful verities composed of words, and succeed in changing nothing. And then—one day—anywhere—somebody produces a fact: a penicillin, a plastic, a pill, a pile, a peace-bomb, or just a new way of making a profit,—and the whole way of life changes overnight, though it will take a generation to notice the change, to admit its existence, and to invent verbal excuses for having broken the unbreakable: tradition.

Perhaps to put words together in some sort of way is not precisely what I set up to do here. Perhaps what I really think is that I have discovered (well, re-discovered) a fact. A fact about human beings. Perhaps what I'm trying to do here is to demonstrate it. It may well be that instead of writing so much for so long, one could have squeezed the essence of it into an epigram . . . ? Brown tried to do it for me when he was fighting with words to express the idea that there is no sense in classifying a person as something or other, and giving up all hope, or fear, as the case might be, that "peoplewise," as he said, everything is possible. And this is precisely what I mean. An epigram, however, even as crisp and brilliant as any of La Rochefoucauld's, will still be merely an opinion. And I'm not interested in opinions. Even in my own. What I'm interested in is the truth. And truth without facts is empty and brittle. That's why what concerns me here is to represent the facts. A few days ago, I had over 100 pages of facts in my hands. And . . . Alas!

"Registered, please," I said to the clerk at the post-office. And as soon as I was given the receipt, I regretted it. I knew I would regret it. But it was too late now. The three exercise books were already on their way back to Tom Harris.

Why did I do it? It would have been so easy to copy them now,—if only I hadn't been so rash! Why didn't I, at least, read them before sending them back? Was it decency, or what? Well, yes, I knew the first sentence:

"My name is Tom Bradlaugh Harris . . ."
then, yes, I admit, I *looked* through the exercise books, let's say, just as one looks through a book in a book-shop, turning an odd page here and there, and then quite automatically (thoughtlessly?), I made the parcel and took it to the post-office. All three exercise books, filled with his handwriting.

149

The three exercise books in a thick manilla envelope, which I had taken from Maria's suitcase and brought with me to London.

And so now I sit here, at this small table under the window, look at the grey waves of the sea, and try to reconstruct the three exercise books which I haven't read.

FIRST ATTEMPT AT RECONSTRUCTION

My name is Tom Bradlaugh Harris. I am over sixty, and I hate the first forty years of my life.

They call me here *il professore,* and they do so because they like to be seen in the company of important people. And a professor, here, is a sort of "your grace," which he has never been on either side of the Thames.

I do remember, when I was a barber, the boss, after having shorn the heads of some particularly long-haired customers, used to say to them:

"Now you look like a gentleman, sir."

To which, once, one of them said:

"And what did I look like before?"

"Before?" the boss said, "before you looked like a professor, sir."

"But I *am* a professor," the man said.

I hoped he would come again and I would clip his hair, and talk to him, but he never did.

As I've said, they like to boost their egos here by calling me *il professore.* Though I am not a professor. I am what may be called a junior assistant lecturer at the university of Genoa. People who do not know that some twenty years ago I was an old, bearded man with no education to speak of, may and do wonder how it is that at my advanced age I still have a junior post and receive a junior's salary. But that is perfectly all right, I have other sources of income, and no complaints of any sort. On the contrary. I am perfectly satisfied with what I have achieved, and wish things would only continue as they are at present.

I love Genoa and its blue bay, which I can observe from the twenty-first and a half floor of the skyscraper in which I live. I love White Jade. And I like my work.

In the last five years I have published three short papers in a scientific journal, and an article in a philosophical magazine. The papers were routine contributions, and their main merit consisted in their brevity. Yet, they seem to have originated a new line of approach which is now being followed by two research laboratories, one in Switzerland and one in India. I am glad this is so, because their technical equipment is much more advanced than what I have here at my disposal, and also because the scientists who are in charge there are much more competent than I am. My advantage lay in my having been new to the subject, knowing less of what had already been done by others, and therefore (thanks to my ignorance rather than courage), more free (or, if you wish, less prejudiced) to try an unorthodox way of looking at the problem.

Putting it simply, it occurred to me that in some cases the stimulus needed to cause an unconditioned reflex is much lower than that which it is necessary to apply to cause a conditioned reflex. In other words, we could say that an animal (a butterfly, for instance) can react to an outer stimulus which is so weak that he is not *aware* of its existence.

That interpretation of behaviour creates a philosophical problem. I have written about it in a book which is going to be published soon, here in Genoa. Though the language I have used is non-technical, I have tried not to go into the world of phantasy, anyway not beyond the limits allowed by scientific discipline. Alas, my publisher's publicity man tells me that the book will be an enormous success. I have

153

thought about the things that made him think so, and I see he is right. The book will be a success; unfortunately it will be a success for the wrong reason. There is in the book an observation that Perfectness of Chromosomal Ordering can be checked by applying aesthetic criteria. There is also a reversed speculation that Aesthetic Criteria may be the result of chromosomal ordering. This involves the problem of randomness versus ordering. And leads to an idea which will make hasty people say that there exist instants when empirical methods fail, and that at least some scientific problems can be solved philosophically. This is what the mystics, metaphysicians, and the church are waiting for. They will take what was originally my intellectual honesty as the basis for their irresponsible hullabaloo, and that will end my scientific reputation, modest as it is.

It is not quite clear to me why I sat down to write all this. Unless it is the habit, or discipline, acquired during the last two decades. I have learned that no thoughts, no researches, no results, are of any value if they are not translated into words, or symbols, or figures, put in black on white paper. Because it is easier to scrutinize and check the consistency of a set of signs than that of the events to which they refer. Does this apply to one's own life?

Pamela's arrival at Nervi (of all places!) here, nearby, and just now (after thirty years!) is, of course, pure coincidence. Do I hate her? Do I hate the boys? I've had a glimpse of them. One is a barrister. The other is a naval officer. No, I don't think I hate them. There exist feelings which you can choose. And some others which you cannot—they are in you, whether you want them to be in you or not. This is the sort of feeling with which I love White Jade. And the view of the blue bay. And the three steps carved in stone at the entrance to the laboratory, I love them, I love to put my feet on them, and I would be sorry if the labs had to move somewhere else. These are the feelings I couldn't choose, I just have them.

My feelings for Pamela and the boys I could choose. And I have chosen not to have any.

Now, I remember, once upon a time, in my (so to speak) first life, I was interested in the problem of symmetry (parity was a word I didn't know then). How naively, but with what perseverance, I set about it, frightening poor Brown to death. And not knowing, and not being able to discover by myself (which fact I now admit with shame), that it was enough to bend a mirror a little, and make it slightly concave, or to take two mirrors at right angles to each other, to . . . Why did I need Giuseppe to tell me that?

[I stopped here. No, this was no good. No good at all. I'm going to cross these pages out. What was it that made me so blind? Insensitive. Out of tune. Thoughtless. This was *not* how Tom Harris would have written. Besides (and how could I have forgotten it?), he didn't write his exercise books now, in 1963, in Genoa; he wrote them no less than eighteen years ago, in London, in his flat in Bell Street. That much is quite certain.

For a long time I looked at the grey waves, impudent and noisy at the coast, but getting thin and anonymous as the eye followed them towards the horizon, where they changed imperceptibly into the sky of the same grey colour.

And then I tried again:]

SECOND ATTEMPT AT RECONSTRUCTION

My name is Tom Bradlaugh Harris. I am just back from prison, an old man, made—as all old men are—of many layers, each going back to its own winter and summer, but all in the present together, and a young man comes, offers him a glass of beer, and says: "Are you enjoying yourself?" and the old man consults the layers, to make sure what "enjoying yourself" is, and he sees that in each layer it is a different thing, and none of the things are dead, and all are present together, like the rings in a tree-trunk, together, under the bark, which is smooth and white if the tree is a birch-tree, and mossy if the tree is an old oak stump, and one can't do away with any layer, because if one does away with a single one, the tree will become a hollow tree, and if one does away with them all, there will be no tree, because a tree-trunk *is* its many layers, and so is an old man,—and before I have made up my mind what to answer, the young man is gone. And so I finish my draught at the Green Man, silently and alone, wipe my grey whiskers, and go, home, what used to be *home*, not far away, in Bell Street, but was it ever? Let's say then—the little flat, I climb the stairs to my little flat, open the door, switch the light on, sit down at the table, under the window on the right, open the exercise book I bought myself a week ago, stare at the top line,—till tonight I hadn't written more than the top line, well, two lines: *My name is Tom Brad-*

laugh Harris. I am just back from prison, an old man . . .
—An old man! Indeed! It's only now that it strikes me, all of a sudden, that I am not much over forty years old,—and hate every year of it.

When my father was young, younger than I am now, he must have been much impressed by Mr Charles Bradlaugh, who had made the status of unbelievers something officially recognisable, and so he (father) insisted that "Bradlaugh" be my second name, and that was all he (father) did for my spiritual upbringing.

Not that I blame him. No. I don't blame anybody or anything. Not even myself. Why should I? Why should a Greek slave blame himself? What? Some of the slaves were philosophers? Yes, father, I know. And some cockney boys have been knighted? Yes, I know, father. And thank you very much, father, but as for me, I happened to be a dull little boy, and I cannot blame a dull boy for being dull, can I? I can despise him, I can loathe him, and I think I do, but I cannot blame him, can I? Or can't I?

"Could I be the King and have seven wives if I killed a widowed queen's kiddies?" I asked once,

and my father said: "Not likely,"

and I said: "Why?"

and my father said: "Because your father is an honest working man."

I don't remember now exactly whether he said: An honest man, or An honest working man, or just A working man, but it was clear to me anyway that to be a king or a duke was out of the question, and it was taken for granted that the bottom of the class was too dull to produce an admiral, or a general, or a prime minister, and it occurred to nobody that some dull boys become quite bright grown-ups, and that some dull grown-ups were once quite bright boys, and the only thing I heard in connection with the purpose of my existence was that I must be good enough to be employed by other people,

and if I tried to learn sums and spelling I would be employed
by richer people, and if not then I could only be employed by
poorer people, which was all right as well because some
poorer people who were employed by the richer ones must
also have somebody to employ, but, nevertheless, to be employed by richer people was an honour, and to be employed by
poorer wasn't so much, and it all depended on me, I was free
to choose, if I tried to play soccer *properly* and get some education, I could become a man who drives his governor in a
Rolls-Royce to a club in St James's Street, or to a country
house, or perhaps to Buckingham Palace, and if I didn't then
I would have to be pleased with unloading garbage from a
lorry, unless I sank still deeper and made my living by stealing, which all sounded to me not convincing, not convincing
at all. My uncle, for instance, my mother's brother, could
hardly read or write, nevertheless he was rich and becoming
richer and richer; he could tell you 7 per cent of twelve
pounds five shillings and twopence in two seconds out of his
head, though he would never have managed to do the thing
with a pencil on a bit of paper, and it was he who used to give
me pocket money most of the time, not my father, who read
public-library books, and so I didn't think that education was
so important for making one's living, and I wanted to stay at
the bottom of the class with the other dull boys, because dull
boys are not easy to rule, and I was not to be ruled by anybody, so that was the best way, because, so long as you are
dull, they don't know how to get at you, they shrug their
shoulders and say: "Leave him alone, he's thick-headed,"
and that way you get your bit of freedom, and I might not
have known all this in words, but I felt it all right, and I
didn't budge to move up from the bottom of the class, and so
I left school, far behind the others, good for nothing, there
wasn't even a prize book for me, and not knowing how to
look a man straight in the face, but my uncle said: "A man
has to eat his own life from his own plate," and I thought I

understood his meaning, and for a year or two I didn't open a book or glance at a newspaper, not to be tempted by the carrots in other people's bills of fare but to live on my own fish and chips, and now I as I am now think how strange that lad was, I mean, I as I was when I was a lad, and on the other hand perhaps no more strange than other lads were or are, very strange indeed, because it is only now, when it is too late, that I see clearly that the purpose of our existence is to find the purpose of our existence, which may sound a little confusing at first, but is not, not really, though it is difficult to explain, and anyway now it is too late, and then it was too difficult to understand for a boy who was sent by his uncle on an errand to Covent Garden and when coming back along Charing Cross Road pinched a book from a bookshop.

[This is not Tom Harris speaking. This is me: I am looking at the sea-waves again, but with hostility this time, hostility that I can't help, as if it were all their fault. Let me tell myself the truth. Nothing else is good enough. What I have just written either doesn't sound like the Tom Harris I knew, or when it does—and there are passages, especially towards the end, so much like him that I can't believe it was I who wrote them,—it doesn't sound like a person from whom the present Tom Harris could possibly have developed. And yet I know that in reality it was so. I can't stand the sight of those boring grey waves any more. They jar on my *eyes*. Neither the view of the sea nor the visit to Bell Street has helped me. I must cross out all these pages and try again. I must shut my eyes to the trivia of the world around me and imagine I am a sort of a piano that can attune itself. I must go to bed and shut my eyes. Shut them. Not just let the lids of my eyes drop, but shut them forcibly, so that I could see him, as he was then, pale and unshaven at first,—then his beard grew longer, as he was drinking his beer every night at the Green Man till closing time and then coming back and writing,—but how was it that he started to write, what was the idea?

161

No, I must do better than that, he's just back from prison, back in his old flat, Brown and Brown's little daughter lived there when he was "inside," but they left the very day he came back, and so he sits there now, alone, he has already been to the kitchen, his half-kitchen, half-bathroom, there was a packet of tea there, and a loaf, and some bacon and butter left for him by Brown, he had a nice twitch, tic, of a smile when he saw it, but now he is in the room, sitting at the table, alone, he smells the air, these are quite different smells from those he felt for four years, his nose isn't used to them, it gets wet, he sniffs, and then he hears footsteps, on the staircase, he is all attention now, somebody knocks on the door, he takes a deep breath, "Come in!" he says, and the door opens. It is Brown's little schoolgirl.

"May I come in, Mr Harris?" she says.

"Sure," he says, "nice to see you here, White Jade."

And she comes in and says: "It's that I forgot my exercise books, Mr Harris, I'm sorry I burst in like that, There they are, do you mind?"

And she goes to the shelf between the two windows and takes the three exercise books in green covers; and then she turns to him and says: "Dad said you were to tell me if you needed something, Mr Harris. Did you find everything all right?"

"Tell him everything is fine. Nice of him to have asked."

"So that's all, Mr Harris, and sorry for the interruption."

"That's all right, White Jade."

"So now I'll say goodbye."

"Goodbye, White Jade."

And now she's gone, and he stands in the middle of the room, he's alone, in prison he was never alone, in prison one can never be alone, one is always with people one doesn't want to be with; it is only in London that one can be alone, really alone; he stands in the middle of the room and the room feels empty, it feels more empty than it did before and he knows that something is missing in it now, he feels that there is a bit of fresh void somewhere, with his finger he touches the shelf hanging between the two windows, there is no speck of dust on it, they had spring-cleaned the room before leaving, he goes to the door and tries it, it opens, he doesn't lock it behind him, he goes down, the wooden steps creak, to Bell Street, towards Edgware Road, turns to the left, walks slowly, patiently, till he comes to Strakers' stationery shop, "Have you got any exercise books?" he says, he doesn't know what sort, he doesn't mind, so long as they have green covers, some have green covers and he buys three, and the Green Man is already open, so he goes in and asks for a tankard of draught, and the barman who has served him now comes back to him and says: "I reckon I know you?"

And he says: "Sure you do."

And the barman knits his brows and says: "Didn't you use to come here before the war, chum?"

And he says: "Sure I did."

"With a little monkey."

"Yes," he says.

"And what happened to it?" the barman asks.

And he doesn't answer.

So the barman says: "I'm sorry," and he goes to his other customers.

And Tom Harris finishes his beer and goes out, and back to his room, and it is dark now, so he switches the light on, and switches it off at once, goes to the windows and pulls the blackout down, now he goes back slowly in the darkness and he knows, but he isn't quite sure that he knows, that he remembers how high the switch by the door is, but his hand does remember, and he switches the light on and goes to the shelf between the windows and puts on it the three green-covered exercise books he has just bought and he feels the room is a bit less empty now, and then he goes to the kitchen which is dark, and he looks out of a little window there, and there are roofs and roofs and roofs, some a shade lighter, and some a shade darker than the sky above them, and now he is back in the room, takes one of the three exercise books and puts it on the table. He has opened it. He looks at the first blank page. Stares at it for a long time. It is white, and void, and he doesn't know what to do with it, so he writes on top:

My name is Tom Bradlaugh Harris.

Now he gets up and takes off his shoes. He has come back now, he looks at what he has written as if the page were a mirror, and he shrugs his shoulders. And now he picks up the pen again, and starts, without haste—

It was many years ago, and this will be the first time I have mentioned it, even to myself. And I am quite sure that if I had]

THIRD ATTEMPT AT
RECONSTRUCTION

* PAMELA

My name is Tom Bradlaugh Harris.

It was many years ago, and this will be the first time I have mentioned it, even to myself. And I am quite sure that if I had been caught then and taken to the magistrate and perhaps called a thief, a thief I would have become, because a thief is a person who steals, and if I had been told that I was a thief, I would have made stealing the purpose of my life. And my blood boils when I hear of some youngsters being dragged before the magistrate, sometimes by their own parents, and then told that they are thieves, which is a rude thing to say to a boy, a tactless thing, and especially if he actually had pinched something or other, it hurts his self-respect, and once one's self-respect is gone, everything becomes an enemy, and before he was brought to court, the boy might not have known who he was, and he was free to become anything, but the moment he was called a thief, he was ready to take to stealing professionally, that's to say, if they had convinced him he was a thief, and if he was not convinced that he was a thief, and yet was called one, then he must have felt terrible hatred and contempt towards the magistrate and the police and the rest of the world, and all that because a tactless word was pronounced, and also an untrue word, because one drop of water does not make rain rain, and, as Aristotle says, "A man is not necessarily a thief because he has stolen something or an adulterer because he has committed adultery, or a brigand because of some act of brigandage." And then, there is a difference between stealing and pinching. And the other thing is that when they do it among themselves, boys, it is stealing, but they are hardly ever caught, but when they steal from grown-ups it is not stealing, it is difficult to explain but it is something which sooner or later they must do, and if they don't it is still worse, because it grows bigger and bigger in them, and I wouldn't be surprised if some historians found that Hitler had never pinched a postage stamp from anybody when he was a boy, because stealing from grown-ups is like fishing from a strange ocean, I mean, from an incomprehensible ocean, it is something boys must do to reassert themselves, if you get my meaning; and it is something very private, like going to the toilet, and in that sense, to catch a boy stealing and tell him that he is a thief is indecent, I mean obscene, as if you were to open the door of a public lavatory unexpectedly and show him jumping up from his seat to the whole world, terrible, and things like that happen, and are even done by educated men, and that is why I am grateful to Providence that I was not caught pinching the book, and if Mr Bookseller of Charing Cross Road knew how much good the book had done me I'm sure he wouldn't mind my having taken it, because in this world in which it is not possible to do good in one place without wronging someone in another, we should also, contrariwise, not be too mean and churlish about doing wrong things such as taking someone's unguarded dinghy to help a man drowning in the river, or pinching one man's roll of bread when another one is dying of hunger, unless we prefer to be saintly prigs rather than full-blooded men, which doesn't mean escaping consequences, but pinching a dinghy or a roll comes first, and filling in forms after, because life is full of contradictions and it is often better to do a thing that is wrong and then pay for it, than wash your hands of it and do nothing. This is clear to a full-grown man, but not to a boy who is just learning about the world by experience and who is finding it more complicated than the patterns they showed him at school or at church, and the book wouldn't have done me so much good if I had bought it, or if somebody had given it to me, it wouldn't have become so much my own as it did, it wouldn't have had what picture theatres call "magnetic fascination." For the first time in my life I at last had something that was mine and nobody else's, it was my friend, and you cannot buy a friend, I had literally, I mean physically, wrenched him out of the strange world, quite a foreign world, I had come across in the Charing Cross Road, when coming back on my errand from Covent Garden to Harrow Road. To me that strange foreign world was like an Africa, not as Africa is today, but as it was for our grandfathers, and they were not used to buying what they discovered in Africa, white ivory or black men and women, though now I come to think about it they did *sell* them, and it never occurred to me to sell my friend, I mean the book I discovered in the Charing Cross Africa and carried off as my booty, I kept it under my mattress, and came back to it whenever I could, and when I couldn't I was happy that it was there waiting for me till I could lock the door behind me and take it out to read it, and it was called A Short Encyclopaedia, it had twelve hundred pages, but it was called A Short Encyclopaedia, and I wondered what a long encyclopaedia must be like if the short encyclopaedia had twelve hundred pages, and it wasn't like any book I had ever seen at school, it neither bullied you nor treated you like a sissy, it didn't tell you what you ought and what you ought not to do, it just told you what was known about things, take it or leave it, it didn't even try to tell you which of the things were more and which less important, no segregation between upper class and lower class, rich and poor, old and young, masculine and feminine, everything was arranged, so to speak, democratically, in al-

phabetical order, you could open the book at the word you
wanted, read the description, and then look up the words
that were used in the description, and then those that were
used to tell you what the words meant which were used to
describe those that told you about the first description, and
so on, till you came back to the words you had already
learnt by heart, and as the title page of the book claimed
that all words, except rude ones, were explained there, it
seemed that if one learnt all the words with their descrip-
tions, what I mean is definitions, one would have learnt
everything that was learnable about the world, and so I
thought it would be simpler to read the book from the first
page, and so I did, and when I was half way through the
letter A I left the greengrocery and became an apprentice to a
gentlemen's hairdresser, and at the beginning of the letter E I
was already a hairdresser myself, and I think my conversations of that adolescent time must have contained a big ag-
glomeration of adornments beginning with the letters A, B, C
or D, and I wonder if any of my argentiferous customers ever
apprehended this bizarre, coruscant dysuria, and I don't say I
didn't like being a talkative barber, in a way I did, it was
better than anything else I could think of at the time, in my
opinion a hairdressing saloon where you meet all sorts of people is a much better place for a young man than a factory,
which develops in him what I would call social agoraphobia,
or, otherwise, working man's claustrophilia, which makes
him afraid of people living in another street, or those living a
different life, or those who pronounce words differently, and
results in what I would call a worker's narrow-gauged chau-
vinism, which consists in his being proud of his being ignorant of everything that is different from what he knows, and
this a hairdressing establishment doesn't do to you, and I
would probably still have been in the profession if I hadn't
invented that haircutting machine.

I worked on it for eighteen months, almost all my nights

and my earnings I spent on it, that's to say not the whole model but half of it, the right hand half, which wouldn't have made much difference because the left hand half would have been exactly the same, only reversed, as in a mirror, so it was sufficient to build half of it because if one half worked satisfactorily then the whole would too, the secret of it was that you put it against your hair, that's to say I mean literally against the hair, it was a sort of helmet made of combs, steel combs, they were easily adjustable and once one had adjusted it to one's head and according to the style of haircut one wanted, it could be dialled to the same number and used again and again without bother, and trim to precisely the same style, all you had to do was comb the helmet on to your head from behind, which made all the hair stretch between the teeth, and all the hair left out, I mean the ends of the hair that stuck out the helmet, were automatically singed off, by a red-hot electric wire that made one upward movement along the helmet like a burning scythe.

I tried it on myself first, it worked all right, but it was only the right hand side, so when I went to the shop next morning I asked my colleague to trim the left hand side, and he wondered what had happened to my hair, and I took great pains not to give away my secret, but another boy who was an electrical engineer and had helped me with some of the electrical side of the model knew about it, and then I tried it on some of the other chaps as well, and the news spread in the profession, and one evening four barbers came to my lodgings, they had razors in their waistcoats and they didn't even need to ask me where the machine was, it was there in the corner, and two of them held me on the bed and I was gnashing my teeth and biting my lips, while the other two smashed the model into pieces, into pulp, and the next day I was given the sack. After that I tried five other saloons in different parts of London but in none of them did I stay longer than a fortnight, they always found me out, and then I was given the sack and told to keep away from the profession or something worse would happen to me, and they called me a blackleg and said that the machine would have finished the hairdressing trade and that I wanted millions of hairdressers to be jobless and their wives to be walking the streets and their kids hungry, which all sounded much graver at the time than it would have now, and they told me that if I tried to make another model and patent it, or sell the idea to a manufacturer, that would be the end of me, and the position was that they were clever boys and they thought I was a clever boy too, but I was a dull boy and so it had never occurred to me that I could have built more than one machine or that I could have sold the rights, and it may be that I would have come to thinking about it later, but as it was I was just interested in making it work, as it was, I understand, with the Chinese who invented a steamboat some 2,000 years ago, but were not interested in building another, and a clock and many other inventions, just one of each, and the strange thing is that not knowing then about the Chinese inventions, what I was thinking of at the time was of going to China, only I didn't know how to arrange it, but I liked the Chinese people I met and they were mostly working in their restaurants in Soho, very nice people, not like the Christians at all, their religion was more like my Short Encyclopaedia than like the Bible, only it was not about words but about consciousness, and suffering, and life, but it didn't bully them into doing anything, and if they did something, right or wrong, it was their own doing, not as it is with the Christians who always have God on their side, and can always find a saying that suits them; one day it is "love your neighbour as yourself," or "turn the other cheek," and the next day it is "I came not to send peace, but a sword," which is both confusing and convenient, it makes it easier for you to do things in passion or in need, right or wrong, and not feel so very responsible for what you do, and at that time I thought that

171

what the Jehovah's Witnesses were saying was correct, only that they were proud of what was a rather sad thing: I thought that the English, and perhaps Christians in general, were the revolutionary Jews who had revolted against their king and his constitutional government, and that those whom we call Jews now were the Conservatives and Liberals who were chucked out of their country like the French émigrés, and Jesus was a kind of Trotsky who wasn't satisfied with making brotherhood in Russia alone, and wanted to spread it all round the world like the popes tried to do from Rome till we protested and said we wanted to have our own Christianity in one country, which was all quite unlike what the Chinese people were, who invented gunpowder but used it for making fireworks, but they were far away, on the other side of Russia, and perhaps it was Lenin not Trotsky, I don't think I had heard of Stalin then, and Lenin being bald or almost, I wondered whether the Russians would mind my making the haircutting machine, as I didn't think that the barbers were right that it would cause unemployment, because, I thought, if people buy the machines then there will be less need for hairdressers, correct, but on the other hand, there will be more need for men in the factories building the machines, so the barbers were wrong, though, after a thought, I liked that idea still less, because I didn't like the idea of switching men from hairdressing to the factories, which would be a cruel thing to do, as I knew very well by then, because, after I had been chucked out of the fifth establishment, I found a job in a works in Stepney, which was agony. In my opinion the whole place is quite unsuitable both for dull and for very bright boys, only normally bright boys can withstand it, normally bright boys who are clever at everything they do, and don't care about the purpose of their existence; otherwise, if you are not a normally bright boy, you just become bored stiff, they bring you some bits of metal, and you bend a bit of wire, and solder on a bit of tin, and tie a bit of string round it, and glue on a bit of label, and they take the thing out and bring some other bits of metal, and a bit of tin, and a bit of string, and a bit of a label, which are precisely like the first ones, which is not the case with hairdressing where no two heads are quite the same, but as the way back to hairdressing was barred for me by then, I thought the second best would be to try to become a waiter, and I left the Stepney factory, and I thought a Chinese restaurant would be a nice place to work in, and I remember I was reading about the "Elgin Marbles" in the Encyclopaedia the day I decided to escape from Stepney, and it was soon afterwards that I got married.

The barristers who used to come to one of the hairdressing saloons I was working in liked me to talk to them but were very difficult to tell anything to because they were all deaf except to the answers to their questions, and as it is only possible to ask questions about things one had already heard of, it was clear that they could never learn the things they had never heard of, and their world must be full of blank patches, even if they don't know that it is so, and that is what education does to some people, it shrinks the world for them and they swallow it and don't know that the whole world is bigger than the shrunk bite they have eaten and they get bald, as bald as an egg, because they only listen to the answers to the questions they ask, and when I tried to tell a barrister who used to come to the saloon:

"Your hair is getting thin on the left side, sir, would you like me to make the parting on the right,"

he asked: "Which side does the Prince of Wales have his parting?"

"On the left," I said.

"Are you a Republican?" he asked.

"I shouldn't think so," I said.

"A freemason, then?"

"No, sir," I said.

"Then why do you say the right hand side and show me the left hand side?"

So I said: "You are seeing it in the mirror, sir. I was showing you the right hand side but you saw it in the mirror as the left hand side."

"Can one make a mirror that doesn't reverse the picture?" he asked.

"I don't know, sir," I said.

"And why do mirrors reverse from left to right and not upside down?" he asked, and we both forgot about his getting bald, and that question stuck in me somehow and I didn't think any more about the haircutting machine but about mirrors.

I left hairdressing for waiting, but the question was still there, all the time gnawing in my mind: Why do mirrors reverse from left to right and not upside down, why do they? That's what I was thinking about when I noticed her at the table in the Chinese restaurant I worked in, not at my table, I mean not at one of the tables I was serving, but at one I had to pass by, and she had a dirty neck and was a real lady, that's what the Chinks had told me, they could always tell a real gentlewoman by her dirty neck, a real gentlewoman takes her bath twice a day, they said, she soaks in the water up to her neck reading books and drinking gin, then she cleans her face from the tip of her nose to the back of her ears, and so her neck stays dirty, unless she has come straight from the hairdresser's. It was strange I hadn't heard about that at the hairdressing saloons I had worked in, but as a matter of fact they were all really barber's shops, and the barbers were Englishmen, and you heard more about horses there than about women, and she looked like a gentlewoman all right, sitting stiffly on her chair and carrying the food up to her mouth instead of bending down towards her sweet-and-sour or meeting the fork half-way, and I don't know why I noticed her more than the other customers, perhaps because she was sitting alone at the table, which is rather unusual in a Chinese restaurant, or it may be that I didn't notice her more than I did the others, only remembered her better because of what happened afterwards, which was as follows: she paid her bill but didn't leave the table, and about a quarter of an hour later Jack the Cyder came in. I don't know why he was called Jack the Cyder, perhaps he was first called Jack the Spider, because he looked like one, he had only one arm, and nevertheless with his empty sleeve flapping about him and his overcoat just thrown over his shoulders, he looked as if he had twice as many arms and legs as a normal human being, and he went straight to her and sat down, and they obviously had an appointment there, and we all knew of course who Jack the Cyder was, so I watched them and saw her take a pound note out of her bag and give it to him, and a pound note was quite a lot of money at that time, and he gave her an envelope, and she put it into her bag, after which he was gone and she powdered her nose and got up to go, and I asked the Chinaman to take over my tables for a moment and I put on my raincoat over my dress-coat, we used to serve in tails in that place, and I went out and followed her for a bit till we found ourselves in a dark street where I could talk to her, and so I approached her from behind and said: "Excuse me, Madam,"

she didn't turn her head, neither did she slow down nor quicken her step,

so I said: "Didn't you leave your gloves in the restaurant, Madam?"

so she stopped, turned round and asked me: "What gloves?"

which was silly, because I didn't have any to show her and

she had hers on her hands, but as she was now facing me I could talk to her, so I said: "I want to buy the envelope you have in your bag."

"What do you mean?" she exclaimed.

"Look," I said, "you paid a pound for it," and I took a pound note from my pocket and showed it to her. "Here is a pound. I want to buy it from you."

"You're crazy," she said, "please go away. Or shall I shout for help?"

She kept cool and what she said she said as if she were discussing a timetable at Cook's.

"No," I said, "with that envelope in your bag you are not in a position to call the police. And, altogether, what is it all about? I am not robbing you. I want to buy it. And you are not at all keen on it. On the contrary, you are a bit scared. And what you would really like is to get rid of it. So what is all the fuss about?" And I gently opened the bag she was holding, slipped in my one-pound note and took the envelope out.

She didn't say a word when I clicked the bag closed.

"Well, that's all," I said, and went a few steps towards the gutter, and dropped the envelope between the iron bars of a drain.

"There now, Madam," I said, "I must go back to my Chinks. No hard feelings, I hope," and I turned to go, but now she called me back.

"Wait a moment," she said, and when I stopped and looked at her she asked: "Why did you do it?"

Now I didn't know why I had done it, and I answered honestly: "I don't know," and I saw that it was the wrong answer, because I could see somehow in her face that she thought it was because I was in love with her or something of the kind, which at the time was certainly not so, and on the whole it seems to me that we don't do things because of something or other, but we just do them and look for a reason afterwards, and there are always many reasons to choose from, so we pick one up, but what it is that makes us pick one up rather than another I don't know, and what makes us actually do things is not reason at all, but mood, and thank Heaven for our having moods. Sometimes I think God took an anatomical machine and made it moody and it became human, and for moods there is no reason, sunspots may be more the sources of them, I think, than anything we may find in our bodies, as they are now or as they were when we were babies, so when she asked me: "Why did you do it?" I shouldn't have answered: "I don't know," what I should have answered was: "Because of my mood," because in the mood I was then I would have done the same thing for the ugliest bitch in the world, and another day in another mood I wouldn't have bothered to move my little toe for Betty Compton herself, if you remember who she was, the beautiful blonde who used to hunt lions and elephants in Africa, in the motion picture theatre my uncle, the grocer, sent me to on Saturdays when I was a dull boy. Very exciting it was, with the pianist's stick banging the top of the piano bang! bang! whenever there was some shooting on the screen, so that was what I thought, about sunspots and about moods, but she probably knew better, and six months later we got married, and as a matter of fact I didn't know actually why she married me, I mean, I didn't understand why she did, all the same I didn't say no.

She was a good wife, not that she had much cooking to do, lunches and dinners I used to eat at the restaurant, so it was only breakfast and tea that we had together, she sitting there on a round pink pouffe, and serving me with tea, tea-first-milk-afterwards fashion, and passing the sugar to me as if transferring it into another world. And that's what I thought then, that there are many worlds in the world, something like different department stores, and what I wanted to do was not to sit in one but to know all the department stores of

that odd business we were born into, and before that I
thought that the main department stores were nations,
churches, races, till it occurred to me one day that there was
more understanding between Mr Baldwin and Mr Lenin,
and between the Archbishop of Canterbury and the Pope,
and between an employment agent I knew and a slave-trader
in the Middle East, than between any of them and myself.
On the other hand I understood much better my Chinese
fellow waiters who had come here from the other side of the
world than I understood my wife, who was born less than 30
miles south-east from Bell Street. I knew when they would
laugh or cry or be angry or be happy, but I never knew that
much about her, because she never laughed and never cried
and was never angry, and I don't know whether she was
happy or not, and so I came to think that instead of going to
China to see the other side of the world, it might be a good
idea to go to Kent instead, and I hinted that we should visit
the place she came from, but she said I wouldn't like her
family, and that wasn't what she meant, what she really
meant, I only now know, because later on I met that kind of
people, but then I didn't know anything about them, and
that was also why I wanted to go to her place in Kent, because I wanted to find out what about her was she, and what
was her, so to speak, class. Did she pick her teeth because she
liked it, or because her people had the habit? Or such a thing
as going stark naked around the room at bed-time, was it peculiar to her, or was it what all her folk did? I had never
before conversed with a "lady," so I had nothing to compare
her with, not knowing the latitude, as the sailors would say,
and if she thought, as she did, that she rebelled against her
latitude, it wasn't exactly so, because she rebelled within it
and not away from it. She was a rebel among her own people,
but she never cut off her roots; it was I who rebelled from my
latitude, left it, because I didn't accept it, I didn't like my
being fixed to one latitude, whatever it was, Bell Street or not

Bell Street, I wanted to cross all the latitudes and longitudes all round the world, and it seemed that it would be easier to go to China to study the Mandarins than to go to Kent to see my wife's people, which she didn't want me to do because she didn't want me to be humiliated.

And I didn't like her being sure that it was *I* who risked being humiliated, and it was all rather mean for my taste, though, as a matter of fact, I didn't care; nevertheless that doesn't mean that I wasn't hurt, it is not the same thing, not to care, and not to be hurt; you may be above caring about something and nevertheless your feelings may be hurt, and that is why the man who humiliates you doesn't need to be a very important person, not at all, he may be an innocent ass, and it may hurt just the same, that is what I think, and that is what the whole African and Asiatic latitude knew, and the white Sahibs and the Tzar did not know, and having been a dull boy at school I knew everything about humiliation, and should have been made a Governor somewhere in the colonies if the Colonial Secretary, Mr Churchill, had known how to run the Empire, but it was her father who was one, I mean my wife's, in Africa, and my father wasn't very happy about my marrying her. "If one doesn't want a wife to stay where she belongs," he said, "one should marry a girl who is climbing up, not one who is climbing down," and he thought that a girl that climbs down must be either rotten, or stupid, or a Socialist, and as she didn't look at all Socialist, he thought she was rotten or stupid, and so did the rest of my family, and they pulled her leg and I didn't like it, so I saw them less and less, and then not at all. She wasn't aware that they had pulled her leg; it would never have occurred to her that people on her so to speak latitude might have their legs pulled from below. No, that would have just made nonsense —one of those things that are not possible; and so she sat there on the pink pouffe, lovely to look at, handing me another cup, and I knew that she would rather, supposing someone pressed her to put a drop of cod-liver oil into my tea, she would rather be killed, hanged, drawn, quartered, than do it, but on the other hand, I knew that if somebody else put arsenic into my cup she wouldn't do more than tell me: "Look out, darling, there is some poison in your tea," and if I said: "Nonsense!" or something of the kind, she would go on sitting with poise on the pink pouffe, looking pained, but she wouldn't lift her arm, she would sit silently and watch me make her a widow. Not that she would like to be a widow, no, she would not, and I was reading the letter i at the time in my Encyclopaedia, and I read that Islam meant surrender to the will of God, and peace, and facing things with fatalism, and she was Church of England all right, but there was a fatalism and apathy in her, and I thought if all her family is like that maybe that was why they made her father a Governor in Africa, that's to say, to suit the Muslims there, and as to my Short Encyclopaedia, I still had it with me and read it, though when I looked for a word I did it in front of her, but when I read it properly then I did it in the toilet, because I couldn't tell her that I knew one doesn't *read* an Encyclopaedia, page by page from beginning to end, but that's what she would have thought I didn't know, and she wouldn't have known whether to tell me about it or not, not to hurt my feelings, so I thought I had better read it properly where she didn't see me, and so she thought I had a poor digestion, and as I was a waiter, she thought that all waiters had poor digestions, and she had a theory that it was because they dealt so much with food without eating it.

She had studied philosophy at the university when she was a girl, I don't remember whether it was Cambridge or Oxford, one of those two, but when I asked her why the mirror reverses from right to left and not from top to bottom, she said: "Oh, does it? Never thought about it," and I should have said that was a philosophical question, but she wouldn't have lifted her little finger to solve it, no, she would sit there on the pink pouffe she brought with her as her dowry, watching me as I drank arsenic in my tea, so to speak, which seemed to me then not to be natural, as I didn't know very much about life yet, and I myself, I think, wouldn't have been like that at all, I would have smashed the teacup, even if I had had to kick her or to break her arm, though perhaps it was not the same thing, because as a matter of fact she didn't mind being hurt, physically, I mean, I wouldn't say she liked it, but she needed it in a way, I wouldn't say psychologically, I would say physiologically, and I should say we too often insult people nowadays by taxing them with psychological reasons which may all be due to the fact that more and more men have nothing real to fight for and think their own precious soul is more important than the lives of other people, and carry it, this soul, in their cat baskets embedded in cotton wool, which is psychological, I agree, but due to conditions of life, which is physiological, like her wanting to be hurt physically was physiological too, and not psychological, it was meant to wake up her nerves, and not to sweeten her remorse, as she hadn't any. And that, I think, was why she couldn't feel properly about war and about colonial people and about the depression, because all the boys in her family had passed through those schools for leaders where they undernourish them, freeze them stiff in winter, and don't allow them to be alone for a moment, and flog them on Saturdays, so whenever she heard of some people being cold or hungry, yes, of course she disapproved of it, but she did so half-heartedly, because at the same time she knew that her father and her cousins when they were boys had also been hungry and cold, and it had done them good. And when she heard of some rough stuff, naturally she knew it was a shame and a pity that things like that had to be done to some people who are unruly, still the thought tingled somewhere in her mind that there was some pleasure in being hurt, and it *was* a philosophical question, the one about the mirrors, surely it was, why they reverse from right to left and don't reverse upside down.

"It is a physical question," she said,

but I said: "No, surely it's a philosophical question,"

so she said: "It may be a physiological question,"

but I said: "Surely not, it's a philosophical question,"

so she said: "Perhaps it is a psychological question,"

but I said: "No, it is a philosophical question, surely," and I knew what I was talking about,

and she said: "After all, I am not sure whether it is not a philological question";

and here I wasn't sure of her meaning but I repeated: "It *is* a philosophical question,"

and I was sure it was, and I wondered how it could have come about that this girl who had studied philosophy at the best university in the world still couldn't answer an essential philosophical question, and I thought it was a devastating question; if there were an answer to it, it should have been the first thing to be taught at the universities, and if there wasn't any answer, then how could mankind go on living without trying to find it, as it was more important than the religious questions, because it was apparent that a mirror was something quite different from, for instance, my haircutting machine. A haircutting machine didn't know what it was doing, you could put it back to front on to your head and it would still try to singe your hair, it couldn't distinguish between front and back, any more than a football for that matter—kick it to the left and it will go the left, kick it upwards and up it goes; of its own accord, it cannot distinguish between the right and left here and the up and down there, while the mirror can do so, of its own accord, as if there were an intelligence in it. Surely it distinguishes the right and left from the up and down if it reverses the one and leaves the other as it is, and it was silly and unbelievable, because there were ten million people in London, and nobody cared why mirrors reverse from right to left and do not upside down. And two years after we were married a baby came. She wanted it, and a year later another one, both boys, lovely to look at, and healthy, and I couldn't say she wasn't a good mother, she loved them and kissed them, though I must say she would have done the same if they had been little monkeys, or crippled, exactly the same, and it was nice of her that she would have been the same to them even if they had been cripples, but they were not cripples, they were lovely to look at and healthy boys, and why should lovely to look at and healthy boys be kissed the same way as cripples would be, hygienically, and now, when the kids came, I mean, I knew that I should never go to China, she was what is called "of independent means," only the means were not big enough, she had less monthly from her stockbroker than I had from my Chinks, only she didn't need to work for it, but even so I couldn't leave her and the kids and go to China, or anywhere else, no, but all the same it was not because of that that I started feeling less sure of myself, I didn't know where it came from, and I didn't know what the feeling was exactly, but it felt as if some poison had entered my blood, not that I had noticed anything new of any kind, either in bed or out of it, but all the same it got me somehow or other, a kind of thought that what I knew of her couldn't possibly be the whole person, that there must be something hidden behind what I saw, and what about Jack the Cyder? I had never mentioned the name to her, but she did once, it happened when she was pregnant with the older boy. "You know what I liked about the way you handled the Jack the Cyder affair?" she said suddenly. "It was that you behaved like a gentleman. You acted without preaching." And that was all she ever said about it, but was that all there was? How could I know? And when I was at work, a fear started to come to me, just like that, without warning, a fear that the door would open and she would come in with some gentlemen who acted without preaching and she would sit at my table and ask to be served, which was a crazy idea, quite impossible, though in a way I knew it was possible, because she thought that to be a waiter was just a job like any other job, therefore it would be beneath her dignity to avoid that particular place just because her husband worked there; on the contrary, if she came in boldly, it would straighten all the crookedness if anybody thought there was any, so in that way it was possible. Still, I knew after all that she wasn't that stupid, so it was impossible, but all that meant that I didn't understand her character, and if I didn't understand her character, then I couldn't be sure of anything, for instance, what was she actually doing while I was at work? And a suspicion would grow in me, as ugly as a red lobster on a plate, till I would jump out in the middle of work, take a taxi and rush from Soho to Bell Street, climb the stairs, open the door, and see her quietly feeding the child, or sewing, or reading a French novel, and if it was the French novel, she would put it down and say: "Quelque chose ne va pas, Chéri?" though I didn't know any French at all, and the few words I can say I learnt not from her but later on, and so I would go back to work, ashamed of myself, and yet at other times it would happen that I came home happily and gaily, knowing she would be there, waiting for me, and I would climb the stairs, unlock the door and say: "Hello!" and find she wasn't there, the two kids left alone in the room, and I would wait an hour or longer, and then when she finally came back I would ask: "Where have you been?"

and she would say: "In town,"

and I would say: "What about the kids?"

and she would say: "I left just before you came, they haven't been alone for long,"

and I would say: "Did you see anybody?"

and she would ignore it, because it was beneath my dignity

to ask such a question, so the best thing was to pretend that it hadn't been asked at all, and so the red lobster was there again on the plate, complete with huge pincers, long moustaches and pin-point black cooked eyes, though it must be said that the Chinese didn't serve it whole, except occasionally, the usual way was to break it in pieces and mix it with other stuff, that was their philosophy, that nothing is entirely what it is, that everything is a mixture, and I would be carrying six plates at a time towards the customers, and would have to stop half-way so as not to drop the whole damn thing on the floor, that's to say because my hands had started to tremble all of a sudden, and I was only 25 then, or so, which seemed to be a strange thing to happen to a 25-year-old, strong man, and another strange thing did happen, though not to my hands but to my ears, and it must be said that a waiter's ears get to be as well-trained as his hands, they don't dare to get pink or to prickle, and they have to have a hole behind their eardrums so that the customer's impertinences can go out as soon as they come in, otherwise you couldn't work in a restaurant, you would boil in your own blood, and besides, you wouldn't remember the orders, many bright boys would have found it difficult, so the hole behind the eardrum is a basic essential for the job, and what happened was that it had got stuck, and my ear began to notice the conversations at the tables, which was bound to be a disaster, because the proper relation between the customer and the waiter is that the waiter is a portion of transparent air for the customer and the customer is a piece of furniture to the waiter, and once this relationship is changed, efficiency and peace are gone, because once you get those bits of their talk inside you, you can't help thinking: "What you have just said about politics, sir, shows that you are a stupid ass; that may not be your own opinion of yourself, but that only aggravates your stupidity, and the fact that you consider yourself a gentleman cannot excuse your vulgar ignorance any more

185

than the fact of your companion's talking like a lady can con-
ceal the fact that she thinks like a whore, so don't look so
haughty, because you have some boiled rice stuck in the little
brush you carry under your nose, and now I'm going to give
the lady a fork that stinks of fish," and they may not notice
that the fork stinks of fish, but they notice the smell of
your thoughts all right, and you feel their feelings, and they
look for an excuse to call the manager and make a row, or
to ask to be served by a Chinese waiter whose face is more
difficult for them to read, so you try to control yourself, because you can't afford to have more than one complaint a
week, and it makes you angry, and you wait till you see a
timid girl who looks as if she belongs to the Fabian Society,
or a couple who wouldn't have the courage to call the manager, and you throw the plates on *their* table with a bang, and
you tap your fingers to hurry their making up their minds,
and you hate yourself for being like that, and your tips
shrink, and your nerves go to pieces, even if you are 25, as I
was then, and I thought of leaving the profession altogether,
though it wasn't easy to find a job at that time, what with the
unemployment and all the rest, and one day Mr Li Chu
called me upstairs to his office and said: "By now surely you
must have put together some economics, eh? Make a break,
eh? For a fortnight, eh? Take your lady and the kids to the
seaside, eh? And come back your old self, eh? Good idea, eh?"

It did strike me as a good idea, and why I hadn't thought
of it myself was that taking a holiday wasn't a habit then in
the part of the world I came from, my father never left his
job for a day unless there was a strike or lockout, and my
mother, if she ever took the train to the country, it was to see
her family, for a wedding or a funeral, or to take me to that
place for children, so the idea just hadn't occurred to me.
Yes, I had thought about going to China, but I never thought
of a holiday in a resort, and my wife, she had been all over the

country, and abroad, to France and Italy and Spain, that's to say when she was a girl, but all the five years we had been married she hadn't mentioned anything like that, so I said: "Thank you, Mr Li," and I rushed home and she was preparing tea and I waited till she sat down on the pink pouffe, and before I had time to open my mouth she said: "I want to tell you something."

"So do I," I said gaily.

"What is it?" she asked.

"Oh, you tell me first," I said.

"No," she said.

"Yes," I said.

"No," she said.

"But you said it first," I said, "it isn't fair."

"No," she screamed, and her legs got stiff, and I didn't like it when her legs got stiff, it usually happened when I wanted to take her to the movies and she didn't want to go, or when I had to go out and she wanted me to stay with her, and I don't say that she wanted her legs to be stiff on such occasions, no, she neither wanted them to be stiff nor didn't, they just became stiff on their own accord, it's like your arm going up on its own to protect your face when you have to defend yourself, you neither think of lifting it nor not lifting it, and there it goes. It's different if you are a boxer, then you study the technique and then you do think about how to lift it properly, and so I didn't like it when her legs got stiff, they were pretty legs and I had to massage them, though I didn't think there was anything wrong with them in particular, still there was one small blue button sticking out of the vein, which she got when pregnant with the younger kid, so I said: "All right, my news is that we are going to pack our chattels and go for a holiday."

"If you want to," she said.

"Don't you?" I asked.

187

"Yes, I do," she said.

"You don't sound as if you do," I said, "and you don't have to if you don't want to."

"Of course I do," she said, and she stood up and turned round on tiptoes, and it was a bright, hot summer all that fortnight, and we shot Baldwin on his pipe at the amusement park, we took a boat to the Rock of Death and listened to what happened on it 1,000 years ago, we had a swim now and then, we lay for hours on the beach and danced in the ballroom in the evening, and it looked as if we were having lots of fun, all four of us, and it must be said, however, that it isn't as simple as that, because it sometimes happens that things seem grey and eventless when they are taking place, but there is some hidden brightness in them, and when the time has passed it is the brightness that you remember. On the other hand, it may be that everything seems lightness and gaiety and fun, and you think you are enjoying every minute of what is going on, and yet an invisible shadow is hanging somewhere above you, and when the whole thing is past it is the shadow that you remember, and so we went back to Bell Street, and when the kids had been put to bed she sat on the pink pouffe and the shadow was already there, and I sat in the chair and lit a small cigar. I had taken to smoking small cigars at that time, because as you couldn't smoke at all on the job, I found that one small cigar at night after work was the best you could do to stop your craving for tobacco, and she said: "I want to have a talk with you,"

and I said: "Yes,"

and she said: "You know that I was in love with somebody before we married?"

"I guessed as much," I said.

"And he was in love with me," she said.

"What went wrong, then?" I asked.

"He had a wife," she said. "And two children."

"I see," I said.

She narrowed her nostrils like a rabbit, my cigar annoyed her. I tried to hold it behind my back, and hoped that that way the smoke wouldn't go in her direction.

"I have met him again," she said.

"When?" I asked.

"It doesn't matter," she said.

"You mean recently?" I said.

"Yes," she said.

"I see," I said, but I didn't see anything at all, I felt again like the dull boy I had been at school, to whom things are being explained too quickly, much more quickly than he can grasp them.

"He says he still loves me," she said.

"He does, does he?" I said.

"Yes, and he's free now," she said.

"What happened to his wife?" I asked.

"She's in a madhouse," she said.

"She can't have been very happy with him," I said.

"No," she said, "and neither was he with her."

"Would you?" I said.

"Would I what?" she asked.

"Nothing," I said, and I was wondering what was going on with the cigar hidden behind my back, when it would start burning my fingers. I took a little puff and hid the cigar again.

"I think I would," she said.

"You would what?" I asked.

"I am sure," she said.

"Does he know you're married?" I asked.

"Of course he does," she said.

"And that you have kids?"

"Oh, that's all right," she said, "he has two of his own."

"You've already told me that," I said.

"So I have," she said.

"Yes," I said.

"You don't need to hide your cigar," she said, "as a matter of fact I like it."

"That's news to me," I said.

"No," she said, "I've told you before that I like it."

"You've told me nothing," I said.

"I've told you everything," she said. "As a matter of fact I am telling you now, only you don't want to listen."

"I do," I said. "What are you telling me?"

"I've already told you," she said.

"Poor man," I said. "First he couldn't marry you because he was married, and now he can't because you are. You shouldn't encourage him, you know, if you don't want to go and live with him."

"But I do," she said.

"Oh," I said, "that makes it different."

It was funny but the face I knew to be her face was never like the face I saw when I looked at her. That was so now, but I couldn't tell why.

"Do you mind?" she asked politely, in the same voice that she used to ask: "Do you mind?" when she was going to open a book and read instead of switching off the bedside light; and I didn't know whether I minded or not, and she said: "If you do mind, I won't go, and I shall never reproach you for not having let me go. I don't want to make anybody un-happy, darling, so it's up to you now," she said, and I got up and asked her not to do anything silly before I came back, and I left. I crossed Edgware Road and went to a cinema, not so much to have somewhere to sit as to look at the picture because I don't think when my mind is not occupied with something else; I must give it something to do if I want it to leave me alone with my thoughts, otherwise it starts med-dling with them till I don't know where I am and what I am to do, and so I looked at the picture and let my mind be busy with it, and during that time I was free to be face to face with my problem, and when the end came I left the cinema

190

and I knew that I knew the answer, though I didn't know yet
what it was, and when climbing up the staircase I told myself: if I force her to stay, there will be three unhappy people,
the gent, she and myself, and the kids won't be happy either;
if I let her go, there will only be one person, namely myself;
how I would be unhappy I didn't exactly know, but I knew
there was a way in which I would be very much so, and so I
opened the door and there she was, sitting as before on the
pink pouffe, her legs straight and stiff, she must have been
like that all the time, and I suddenly saw that if I were to say
No, I don't want you to go, she would remain like that for
ever, and I felt in me a certain slight spiteful pleasure at the
thought. I shut the door behind me and I said: "When do
you want to go?"

and she said: "Tomorrow,"

and I said: "That's all right,"

and she got up, threw her arms around my shoulders and
kissed me, we didn't kiss very often, it seemed that we made
love more often than we kissed, and now she kissed me on
the mouth and said: "Thank you, darling," and her face
changed, it was now more like the face I knew was her face
when I didn't look at her, and it was already late, so I took
some pillows and blankets and was going to spread them on
the floor, and she asked: "What are you doing?"

and I said: "Making a bed,"

and she said: "How sweet!" and she laughed, and then she
said: "Don't be ridiculous," and she took the blankets away
from me, and she went to the bathroom, and I heard the
familiar noises, and I wondered, as I often did, is it peculiar
to her class or to herself only that she keeps the bathroom
crystal clean, like a dentist's surgery, and the room like a pig-
sty? And I was taking my shoes off when she opened the door
and came in, naked, as she used to, and then I went to the
bathroom, and I think that it was then one of no more than a
dozen bathrooms in the whole of Bell Street, and when I

191

came out she was already in bed making room for me beside her, and it was as if it were not our last but our first night, a kind of reversed honeymoon of passion, we made love and then we cried, and then we made love and cried at the same time, we shouted and hated and loved and fought each other all through that hot and moist summer night, and when I woke up late in the morning, she was there busying herself around the room, calm mistress of herself, she must have been out already, I guessed, telephoning from a street call box. "Twelve thirty-five from Charing Cross Station," she said. It was strange how little there was to do, mostly because her suitcases were still packed and she was taking them as we brought them from the holiday, and how it happened that none of my things seemed to be in her suitcases I don't know, and when the time came she handed me a piece of paper with an address on it and said: "You may come and see the children any time you want. Here is the telephone number. It's better to 'phone first."

And though I hadn't given it a thought before, the decision came to me as of its own accord.

"No," I said, "it's over. I shall never go and see them."

"Oh!" she said, and she was vexed, everything that was not as she had planned was below her standard, and I went to fetch a taxi, I wanted to go with them to Charing Cross Station, but there was no room for me among the suitcases and kids, so I stood there at the taxi door and then, not exactly myself, but my mind, the one that had worked at the film the night before, made me say:

"Promise that if you get a word from me you will come and see me, or will let me see you, whatever happens; I shan't do it more than once, and I don't know when, perhaps in ten years' time, perhaps in fifty. But you must promise me that."

"All right," she said and she looked half-sympathetic and half-annoyed at my making such a fuss about something so simple and natural; after all, ours was one of the millions of partings that were taking place all the time all over the world. "I do promise," she said, and the taxi drove off, and I went back home, and I threw myself on the bed and pushed a corner of a pillow into my mouth and bit it, and the house was full of her smells, they stood like pillars in certain places in the room, and one had to learn how to walk around and not bump into them, and then I found her old pyjamas and I stuffed them with all the old rugs and things that had ever belonged to her, and I made a dummy and put it on the bed, and I sat at the table and opened a French book that she had left behind, and looked for such words as *précipice, existence, on, as,* which were spelt the same as in English whether they meant the same thing or not, and I stayed in the room for three days till there was not a scrap of anything eatable left, and I thought of going to a pub, but I always felt afraid of drinking when I felt worried or miserable, I could drink a lot when I was cheerful and fine, but not otherwise, so I didn't go to the pub, I bought some food, and I went to Mr Ready's shop and bought three mirrors, ordinary looking-glass mirrors, and then I went back and cooked myself some thing or other to eat, and decided to think how to make a mirror that wouldn't reverse from left to right, and it was a difficult thing to think about, rather complicated and confused, it needed some studying to be done first, that's why I bought the mirrors, and I looked into one and saw that it was not accurate to say that mirrors reverse from left to right, not at all, they don't, what I mean is that if you hold a razor in your right hand, the hand with the razor will appear in front of the hand with the razor, and the other one will appear in front of the other one, and not vice versa, which shows that the mirror reverses neither the sides nor the top and bottom, but what it does reverse is the back and the front; what is behind appears to be in front of you in the mirror, so it struck me that perhaps she was right when she said it was a philological question, the question about reversing from left to

right, because if you put your mirror facing south and call
your left hand your "west hand," and your right hand your
"east hand," there will be nothing to be puzzled about, the
picture of the west hand shows opposite the west hand and
the picture of the east hand shows opposite the east hand, so
after all it looked like a philological question, because when I
called my hands left and right, the mirror did reverse them,
and when I called them west and east, it did not; and yet, all
the same, when I shaved the next morning, the picture of my
east hand appeared to the east, and it held the razor all right,
but nevertheless it looked more like my west hand, and the
picture of my west hand, although it held no razor, looked
more like my east hand, though it was on the west side all
right, and so I cursed the barrister who was getting bald and
put the whole idea into my head, because if the mirror makes
my west hand look like my east hand and vice versa, why
doesn't it make my feet look like my head and my head like
my feet? Why, indeed? I asked myself, and it was a difficult
question to answer, because it didn't depend on philology,
and it didn't depend on geography, because when I tried to
lie down in front of the mirror the picture of my upper hand
still looked like my hand below, and vice versa, and yet the
picture of my head refused to look like my feet, and vice
versa, so I stood in front of the mirror again and thought:
would it be an anatomical question after all? Is it something
in the way heads, hands, feet are built that makes the difference? Because there is a difference between the head and the
feet, it strikes the eye, but there is also a difference between
your two hands; if there weren't any you couldn't say which
was which and you can, wherever they are, and so, I said to
myself, there must be a difference such that the difference
between the hands must be differently different from the
difference between the feet and the head, and to prove that I
took off one shoe and put it on my head, and the picture of
my shoe on my head looked exactly like the real shoe on my

foot, while the picture of the shoe on my foot looked exactly like the real shoe on my head, so I watched myself in the mirror, and at that moment there was a knock at the door and Harry Brown came in and saw me standing in front of the mirror with one shoe on my foot and one on my head, and he was called Harry Brown but he was a Chinaman of course, and when I looked at his face I saw that he would have given a pound note not to have come, so I said: "Hallo, Brown, this is a nice surprise," to put him at his ease, and I took the shoe off my head and threw it behind me, which was southwards, and it struck me that the picture of the shoe in the mirror fell northwards, so I said: "Did you notice? It reverses from south to north."

And he would have been very pale if he hadn't been so yellow, and he said: "Yes,"

and I said: "Nice weather, the warmest summer for twelve years,"

and he said: "Hot,"

and I said: "How are you, Brown, how are things going in the restaurant?"

and he said: "I'm fine. We,—just wondered what,—the hell was the matter with you, work,—you didn't come to, and a word,—you didn't send."

He was looking at the shoe that I had thrown from my head on to the floor.

I took it and put it on my foot.

"O," I said, "some family troubles," and I knew that he thought I was crazy, so I thought I mustn't tell him I wasn't because that's what all mad people do, and if he leaves here thinking I'm mad, they will never take me back and I'll lose my job. Not that I was thinking about going back; I neither was nor wasn't, but the mirror and the shoe business had to be explained to him, so I said: "I am making a new kind of mirror."

"Yes," he said, but he didn't look at me, he was sitting at

the table where I had put him and looking at the corner where the bed was, and the tip of his tongue was showing between his lips, and in the bed under the blanket there was still that silly dummy I had made.

so I thought, blimey, poor Harry Brown thinks there is a body hidden there and it gives him the creeps, so I took the dummy from under the blankets, trying to reshape it, as I did so, into a bundle, and I said: "My wife has gone, you know, I shall have to take these things to the laundry."

And I took the thing to the bathroom and left it there, dirty linen with no body inside, and then I said: "Are you in a hurry?"

and he said: "No, that's to say . . ."

so I interrupted him: "Good," I said, "then you can help me with the mirrors. Take your pad and a pencil (waiters always have pads) and jot down what I tell you."

And I put the second mirror on the chair so that it rested against the east wall and made a right angle with the first mirror, and the third mirror I put on the floor, and I said: "Harry Brown, take notes please."

And then I said: "Write down:

FACING THE NORTH MIRROR
The North Mirror:
West against west, east against east,
top against top, bottom against bottom,
South reversed northwards
Left looks like right.

The East Mirror:
North pointing north, south pointing south,
top against top, bottom against bottom,
West reversed eastwards,
Left looks like right.

The Bottom Mirror:
North pointing north, south pointing south,
West against west, east against east,

top reversed downwards,
Left looks like right.

The North Mirror as seen in the East Mirror:
East pointing west, west pointing east,
top against top, bottom against bottom,
South reversed northwards,
Left looks like left; right looks like right.

The North Mirror as seen in the Bottom Mirror:
West pointing west, east pointing east,
North pointing south, south pointing north,
top reversed downwards,
Left looks like left; right looks like right.

The East Mirror as seen in the North Mirror:
West pointing east, east pointing west,
top against top, bottom against bottom,
North reversed southwards,
Left looks like left; right looks like right.

The East Mirror as seen in the Bottom Mirror:
West pointing east, east pointing west,
top as top, bottom as bottom,
South pointing south,
Left looks like left; right looks like right.

The Bottom Mirror as seen in the North Mirror:
West against west, east against east,
North reversed southwards,
top reversed downwards,
Left looks like left; right looks like right.

The Bottom Mirror as seen in the South Mirror:
West pointing east, east pointing west,
South pointing south, north pointing north,
Top reversed downwards,
Left looks like left; right looks like right."

At that point I noticed that with one mirror one of the three directions was reversed, and the left always looked like the right, while with two mirrors, two directions were reversed, but the left always looked like the left and the right like the right, so I thought, what about three mirrors, and I tried to put my head in such a position that looking into the bottom mirror I would see the south one reflecting the north mirror with the picture of myself in it, and I said: "Go on, Brown. West points south, east points north. Got it? South points . . ."

when suddenly he said in a high voice: "That razor,—put it down, will you?"

and I was in fact holding a razor in my right hand, but that was because I had been shaving before and had then picked it up again just to see better which my east hand was, as it was becoming more and more complicated to find it out in the mirrors, confusing. And when I heard his voice, I instantly saw in the mirrors the four barbers with razors in their hands, the four barbers who had come to smash my haircutting machine, and I put the razor down and turned to Harry and said: "What's the matter?"

and he said: "Nothing,"

and I said: "Look Brown, I don't know, it could be that your people have already invented a mirror that doesn't reverse, it could be that they did it 2,000 years ago, but *we* haven't invented such a mirror, and I am going to do it. Right?"

"Mirrors,—it's not safe to play with too many," he answered.

So far as I knew it could have been a Chinese proverb, but it made me think that the whole business looked different in the eyes of a so-to-speak outsider, I mean, in the eyes of another person, not the one that looks at himself in the mirror, so I felt that I must see how the thing looked in the eyes of that other person, and I put the pink pouffe in front of the north mirror and got him to sit on it, and then I pushed the chair with the other mirror on it behind his back, and what I saw at once was that I could now see what he couldn't see, namely, that when I looked in the mirror behind his back so as to see in it the north mirror which he was facing, I could see him there as he really was, looking northwards, and top to top, bottom to bottom, left hand looking left and pointing west, right hand looking right and pointing east, just as if he were sitting behind his own self, so I said: "I say, Harry Brown, I've got it! The picture is O.K. behind you, only you cannot see it because you haven't got an eye at the back of your head. If I could bore a hole at the back of your head and fix an eye there, I would make you see your face in a mirror that doesn't reverse," at which he jumped up and said: "Did you have any breakfast this morning?"

That's exactly what he said, and at the moment I saw that he had said it to show that he wasn't interested, but I answered quietly that I didn't remember, which was the honest truth, and he said: "I'll make you a cup of tea," and moved into the kitchen, and the kitchen was practically the bathroom because the bath was in the kitchen, my wife had had it put there, and there was only a kind of partition, or rather, a curtain, and I thought that it all depended on him whether they took me back at the restaurant or not, it all depended on what he told Mr Li about me, and I thought: "If he asks me now when I'm coming back, then it's O.K., but if he doesn't, then it's not worth trying," and I said: "I'll make the tea," and we both went into the kitchen, and he had had no chance to examine the bundle that was half behind the curtain, and I said: "My wife has taken the kids to the country,"

and he said: "Yes?"

and I didn't say any more,

and then we had tea in the room,

and then he said: "You,—do you know that you look ill?"

and I said: "Do I? I feel fine,"

and he said: "If I were you I would go and see a doctor,"

and then he left, and he didn't ask when I was coming back, and what he said about my looking ill had made me think of something, which was that I had been feeling some inconvenience for the last few days, though I shouldn't like to describe the details of it, and when I went to bed that night I took a mirror and a torch under the blankets, and the next morning I popped into the Gentlemen's, read one of the addresses that were printed on the wall, and then took a bus, as it was a long way to go, and the name of the doctor in the hospital was, I remember, Dr Freebody.

"You've got it all right," he said, and I was lucky that it wasn't *the* thing, only the lesser evil, because I had made a resolution when I was going there in the bus that if it proved to be *the* thing then I should find out how long it would be till my nose started falling off, and then I would divide that time in two and, when the half way moment came,—I should kill myself. People nowadays don't understand these things, I notice, with all their penicillin and sulpha drugs, it is as if original sin itself has been done away with by the medical profession, which I dare say does change that part of life in more than one way, better than social reforms did, and so Dr Freebody said: "When did you contract it?"

and I said: "I don't know,"

so he said: "Of course you don't," and he lit a cigarette in a cigarette holder, which I remember because I saw it many times afterwards and because its end was in the form of a little human skull with a hole to stick your cigarette in, and he asked: "When did you notice the symptoms?"

and I said: "Three days ago,"

and he said: "When did you last have intercourse?"

and I said: "A week ago,"

and he asked: "Are you married?"

and I said: "Yes,"

and he said: "When did you last have extramarital intercourse?"

200

and I said: "About six months ago,"

and he said: "Are you sure?"

and I said: "Yes," and I asked: "You don't think I could have got it then?"

"I am not a preacher," he said, "to me this illness is like any other."

"That's how I feel about it," I said.

"Good," he said. "I should like to see your wife. Could you ask her to come?"

"No," I said.

"Why not?"

"Because we have separated."

"When?" he asked.

"A week ago," I said.

He took off his glasses and covered his mouth with the back of his hand. I thought he was going to yawn. But he didn't.

"Any children?" he asked.

"Yes," I said. "Two boys."

"How old?"

"Two and one."

"You must be careful with children," he said, "wash your hands. I'll give you something to clean their eyes with."

"But they are with their mother," I said.

Now he did yawn. If we had been on an equal footing he would certainly have excused himself, he would have said he hadn't slept the night before because he had been at a party, or because he had been on duty at the hospital, but we were not on an equal footing so he said nothing though I must say it wasn't socially that we were not on an equal footing, no, it was something else, even if I didn't see then what it was, but it was a kind of me being in his hands, and not the other way round, I mean his having the right to go into my private affairs and me not knowing a single thing about him, that was what it was, and my trousers were still unbuttoned, and he put another cigarette into the little human skull, and said: "Has your wife had any symptoms?"

"Not that I would know of," I said.

"Ask her to come and see me," he said.

"No," I said, "I can't."

So he put his glasses back on his nose and said: "But you will go and see the children, sooner or later, won't you?"

"No," I said, "that's all over. I don't want to see them again."

Now he yawned without covering his mouth. "It's none of my business," he said, "but I would feel safer if I knew that your wife knew all about it."

"Tell her," I said, and I took out the note with the telephone number and gave it to him, and I didn't think he would do it, or, at least, not in front of me, but he just took the receiver up, and it was a trunk call, so I wondered whether I should pay him for the call or not, or perhaps I should pay the hospital, or perhaps it didn't matter, and I somehow felt grateful, I didn't remember when I had last felt grateful, perhaps I had had nothing to be grateful for, perhaps I had never felt grateful? And it was a nice feeling, feeling grateful, I mean, I liked it, I looked at him holding the receiver and giving orders to the switchboard girl, and I felt warm, I felt safe, I was in his hands and he was doing something for me. I buttoned up my trousers, and if he had been in danger I would at that moment have done all the things that are done in wild western films to save him. It wasn't of course all that personal, no, later on, and I was still to see him several times, I found that he just didn't remember me, and when I came in he had to look me up in his medical files, but I didn't know that then. Yet if I had known I would have admired him still more, because what I admired in him was not exactly that he was kind to me, but that he was kind to a stranger, that he was doing something he didn't necessarily have to do, and that in such a matter-of-fact way, and I thought, my God, what wouldn't I have given to be a doctor, and at that moment he said: "This is Dr Freebody speaking," and he asked to speak to my wife, and I didn't hear what was said at the other end, but he said: "No, she doesn't know me," and then there was a silence, and he covered the mouthpiece with his hand and asked me: "Is your wife working there?" but before I had had time to shrug my shoulders, she was already on the phone, and he repeated his name and the name of the hospital and said he had just seen me, and there was a squeak on the phone, and he said quickly: "No, you misunderstand me. There has been no accident, and he is perfectly all right. Yes, he came to consult me, and I find that as the children are with you it would be advisable if you could come and see me. No, I'm afraid I couldn't explain it over the telephone but I will give instructions that you shall be let in without waiting, wherever your prefer, either at the hospital, tomorrow morning, or at my consulting rooms in the afternoon." He put the receiver down, looked at me in the puzzled way, and asked: "Who is your wife?" but he didn't wait for an answer. "Please," he said, "don't come near this place tomorrow, I don't want to have any scenes," and then he turned around on his chair, shouted towards the door: "Next please," and he covered his mouth with the back of his hand again, and when I was back in the street I felt as if I were almost glad I was ill. "Good old Dr Freebody," I said to myself aloud. "Pity he's such an ugly man"—because his face was all wrong in all the details. When he held his fancy cigarette holder in the right corner of his mouth, it was right under the tip of his nose, but when he moved it to the left corner it was miles away from it, and altogether he looked like the crookedest crook I had ever seen, which was in a gangster film at the cinema, the night my wife told me she wanted to leave, which crook was not only clever, but also spiteful and mean, and if it hadn't been for the young man who was skiing and risked his life for her, the girl would have been condemned to the electric chair by the jury, and now my thoughts became so confused that I had to stop in the middle of the street, because it was a difficult question, though I didn't know yet what the question was, and I asked myself, could it be that Dr Freebody too is a crook? And a suspicion began to worm its way into my mind, and I remember there was a tree there, in a hole in the pavement, and some rusty bars enclosed it very tightly, and I stood there and grasped one of the bars, and I can still feel its roughness in my hand and, I don't know why, something like the taste of iron in my mouth, and somebody asked: "Are you all right?"

and I said: "Sure, I'm fine,"

and to myself I said: "You bloody bastard, you saw the man (I meant Dr Freebody, not the passer-by) and he was kind to you and you felt nice about him, and now, just because he has the sort of face cinema people think crooks have, are you going to think he's a crook? And what kind of a face do you think you have?" I asked myself, and though I had been looking so much into mirrors those last few days, I couldn't exactly remember what kind of a face I had, actually, and the most I could see, I mean in my mind, was a snapshot I had of myself when I was a schoolboy, and it was funny that I couldn't remember my own face, but I could the photograph, and in it there was that dull boy with his mouth half-open, as it was before they took out my tonsils, and gaping at something or other, you couldn't tell what, and it struck me, I mean then, in the street, that it was perhaps because of my face that they had put me at the bottom of the class, and altogether thought I was an idiot, because I have seen many people who look one thing and are something else, and now I knew that I wasn't interested in haircutting machines or mirrors any more, I was interested in faces instead. I mean, I wanted to find out how it was that we said what a nice face was and what an ugly one was first, and only then found out about the people. I meant, how was it that we had feelings about faces before we had feelings about the people; it seemed to me all wrong.

I left the tree to a dog that wanted to pee there, and I went on and thought I would divide the whole population into two groups: those who are good and wise to the left and those who are bad and stupid to the right, leaving the good and stupid and the bad and wise aside for the moment, and then I would see what kind of faces those on the left had, and would call them beautiful, and those on the right I would call ugly, and in that fashion I would find out what was worth calling beautiful and what was not, and I would teach schoolchildren that kind of beauty, and ask artists to think about it, and I went along the street and looked hard into people's faces, straight into their eyes, and they surely thought I was a foreigner, because Englishmen don't like looking into people's eyes, nor to have their own looked into, one would rather show oneself naked than be trespassed on in that way, I mean through the eyes, it's even forbidden in the Army to look straight into people's eyes, and that is because it gives you the creeps, and that's a fact, because so long as you don't look into a man's eyes he isn't so very real to you, is he? You know that he is there, that he exists, but it is not the same, just as knowing that South Africa is in the southern hemisphere is not the same as being a miner down the pit in the copper belt; what I mean is that when you look at a customer's moustache or at his parting you may not be quite sure whether he really exists or not, I mean whether he exists when you don't see him, that's to say till he comes back to the shop, but if you look into a man's eyes, which Englishmen never do, then you have no doubt that he exists, and it is a philosophical question, and this time I was pretty sure of it, and I asked myself whether, since Englishmen don't stare into men's eyes and foreigners do, whether English philosophy has to be different from foreign ones, and this took me to the same old question, which is rather confusing and difficult, I mean the one of there being two true truths about the world, the hungry man's truth and the cozy truth, very confusing, because if the world is one, how can there be two philosophies, one philosophy of those who look into a man's eyes and another of those who look at his parting, because, as I've just said, if you look into a man's eyes you have no doubt that he exists, the creeps it gives you tells you that. Why, I should say, you are more sure of his existence than of your own, and I should put it this way: he is, therefore I think; surely—for how could I think about him if he were not? That would be a dream, wouldn't it? Which I could put this way: he isn't, therefore I dream; and as people are less, I mean exist less, when you look at their parting than they do when you look into their eyes, then the world must be more dreamy for those who, like Englishmen, don't look into people's eyes, than it is for foreigners who do, and so I went along and stared into people's eyes, and they certainly thought I was a foreigner, and that's how I met my brother who'd just stepped out from around the corner, and he was five years younger and a sailor, well at least that's what he was trying to be, and I said: "What are you doing here?"

and he said: "I've been on leave, I'm just going back now," and he jerked the kitbag he was carrying on to his shoulder,

and I said: "You've been on leave and you didn't come and see me?"

"Well," he said, and the skin around his eyes somehow tightened when he looked at the sky, as if he had lost something there, while his thumb was rubbing first his left cheek and then his ear, "Well," he repeated, "they said you had turned your back on the family and I wouldn't be wanted."

"John!" I said, "that's ridiculous!" and even before I had said that I knew it was the wrong word to say, it was my wife's word, not my family's, she used to say: "That's ridiculous," I should have said: "That's daft," but it was too late,

206

and it is daft and ridiculous that words divide people instead of putting them together, as they should, but there is nothing better at dividing people than words, and that's why any Chink can chin-wag with any English bloke more easily than I can, because they can't place each other, that's why, they don't know enough words to see how rich the other is or what class he belongs to, and so I said: "I'll come with you, John, and see you to the station," and the bus had just come, and I saw a tall old man with a gold-topped cane waving for a taxi, but the taxi didn't stop, and we got on the bus, and the old man too, and we sat on the top deck, and the old man in front of us, and I wondered what his face might be like, because I hadn't seen it, only his white hair, and I said to John: "How are things going?"

and he said: "Lousy!"

"What's the matter?" I asked.

and he shrugged his shoulders and said: "Don't like the stinking Chincha dung-boat." He gave me a cigarette and: "If you want to know," he said, "I don't like the water. Too much of it makes me sick,"

and that sounded strange because we think that if there is somewhere any number of people that like their jobs it is sailors, and perhaps firemen, we expect them to like what they do because, we think, why should they choose to be sailors or firemen otherwise? And I knew why John chose to be a sailor, it was because he was fair-haired and had blue eyes and everybody was always telling him: "Johnny's a born sailor," and so I said to him: "John, it's because of your looks,"

and he said: "What are you talking about?"

and I said: "It's because your looks stood for something you were not, see? We all suffer," I said, "because our bloody looks stand for things we aren't. It's clear, isn't it? You had a sailor's mug, so you went to sea. I had a stupid one, so they pushed me down to the bottom of the class; they don't look to see what you are, only what you look like, the same as they do with lions, they put one on the King's arms, because of its looks, and they would rather not think that a lion is the first to show its teeth to the Christian and its tail to the gladiator, because, silly as it is, your eyes, your hair, your pock-marks, tell people more things about you than what you say with your tongue, only what they tell them is more likely than not a pack of lies, because when you talk you choose your words, but when you show yourself to people you don't choose your red hair, or your squinting eyes, and how can the thing you haven't chosen tell them anything true about you? And the same applies to women, I don't know why we think some girls are pretty, and some aren't. No pretty sweetheart knows so much about love as an ugly rejected one, so I don't know why we shouldn't think her crow's feet or her double chin beautiful," I said, and I wouldn't be repeating in such detail all I told him if it hadn't come to be so important later on, and when I say important, I mean important for my whole life, and I said: "What I want to find out is Why some faces stand for beauty or, as the case may be, for crookedness, or for courage, or for meanness, because people are not at all like the faces they wear, so if the faces are not like the people, how did it come about that we call faces what they are not? Do you see?" I asked.

"Ah," he said.

So I said: "It's only that before I start finding out, I have to make up my mind what kind of question it is, whether it is a philosophical question or a psychological or historical or . . ."

But John stopped me.

"Who's going to pay you for that?" he asked, and as I didn't anwer, he added: "Your wife?"

And so I said: "Seems rather foolish to be unpleasant, John. Don't let's be——, my stinking Chinky eatery stinks as much as your stinking dung-boat, and I work there as hard as you do. Right? And what I'm telling you about faces isn't a job, it's an idea."

And so he scratched his head, and there were a heart and an anchor and a rose tattooed on his forearm, and he said: "You know, brother," he said, "if you're worrying about yourself, I'd better tell you that you are just what your mug looks like, and no mistake. And I know what I'm talking about because I knew a mug like that, only it wasn't faces he put his mind on but tits, and we had to leave him in the first port which was Port Said in a strait-jacket, so don't tell me I didn't warn you." And we climbed down the stairs of the bus and I wanted to see him to the station which was across the road, but he jerked his kitbag on to his shoulder and then he got his revenge: "Don't be——," he said, and grinned, "re-diculous is the word," and off he went across the road to the station, leaving me at the bus stop, and if I had turned to the right my life would have been different, by which I mean that it would have been more as it had been before, but I happened to look to the left, at the bus, and it was already some distance from the stop, and I saw the old gent who had been sitting in front of me on the top deck, and he was stand-ing on the platform and fighting with the conductor, and it looked as if he wanted to stop the bus, and the conductor wasn't going to let him, and I thought the white-haired gent was signaling to me with his stick, unless he wanted to hit the conductor with its gold knob. You couldn't hear a word, of course, and I started walking in the same direction, and the bus stopped of its own accord at the traffic lights, and the gent jumped out, and at that moment a car edged forward on the near side and my eyes shut for a split second, and when I looked again the gent was already on the pavement walking towards me.

** THE RED KNIGHT'S FOLLY

 ask your pardon, sir," he said in a high-pitched voice, "if you find my addressing you in this fashion presumptuous. But I thought you would like me to tell you that your question is no doubt an historical question."

"What question?" I asked.

"Now, sir," he said, "I have already apologised for accosting you in the street, and I must do the same for having listened to your conversation. Hearing it was unavoidable, as I was sitting in front of you, but actually listening to it was the result of its being so full of interest."

"That's all right," I said, "the top of a bus is a public place."

"Quite," he said, "and so is the street," and he asked me to accept his invitation to a nearby place where we could talk quietly, and though at first I had thought he was potty, I wasn't so sure about it now, because potty people don't invite you as a rule, they rather expect you to invite them, and the nearby place he invited me to was one with a commissionaire in blue and gold sticking out his medaled chest, and he welcomed the old gent with a: "Did you see the rainbow, Sir Francis? It was beautiful," and I thought he must be an Italian to have spotted a rainbow in London, and when we were sitting at the table, Sir Francis Pewter-Smith, because that's who the old gent was, said: "In my opinion, yours is an historical question,"

and I thought he was not unlike my wife's father whom I hadn't ever seen except in a photograph taken in Africa, and I said: "Do you mean that something happened in history that made people see some faces as beautiful and others as ugly?"

"I do," he said,

and I wondered whether the head waiter was wondering who I was, I always have to think about something else when I am thinking about something, and I asked: "What is it?"

and he said: "Literature and art,"

and that was a difficult subject for me, I should say an impossible subject for me, because about spondees and complementary colors I knew something, it's true, but about actual literature and art I knew nothing. All the same I had to say something, so I repeated: "Are you saying that literature and art made people see some faces as beautiful and others as ugly?"

and he said: "I am, sir,"

and I felt not quite at my ease, and less so as I was wondering whether I should call him "sir," as he did me, or perhaps Sir Francis, as the head waiter addressed him, and I said: "But there must have been a reason, sir, why literature and art picked out one type of face to praise and not another."

And he said: "Quite so." And he didn't add "sir," which made me wonder whether he had stopped calling me sir because I had started calling him that, and I thought, well, here we are, back at the beginning, all my wife's silly stuff again, how the hell do you win a battle with a knight across a bottle of wine, because it was a bottle of wine that he had ordered and we were drinking, and he took another sip and said: "You may think I am being cynical, but . . ."

but here I interrupted him, I too took a sip of wine, and as I remembered the definition I said: "When you say cynical, do you mean that I will think that you condemn ease, wealth and the enjoyments of life, or that you deny and sneer at the sincerity or goodness of human motives and actions?"

"My dear sir," he answered, and he seemed to be no more impressed by that round quotation from my Encyclopaedia than he had been by what I had been saying out of my own head, "I am too old to be interested in sneering. I am interested in truth. And if you will allow me, I shall go back to our subject. You asked why literature and art pick out one type of face and not another. Literature and art are writers and artists, sir, and writers and artists—I am talking about the old days—used to find it more profitable to praise the chief of their tribe, or their prince, than to flatter a slave. Now, there is a type of human being that has the impulse to manage men, and naturally that type supplied more chiefs and princes than any other. Therefore, the praising of princes was at the same time the praising of that particular type of human being. Furthermore, who among that type had more chance of becoming a successful prince? Obviously, those who didn't hesitate to plot, cheat, rob, plunder and murder; and that is how the reflections in their faces of those aptitudes became implicit in the notion of beauty that we now entertain, the result being that we consider Socrates ugly, and Siegfried beautiful."

Talking seemed very easy to him, and it was, after all, my own thought about faces that was coming back to me through him, but I didn't quite recognise it when put in that educated fashion, I mean, it now seemed that there was more in it than I had thought, and I was somehow frightened and confused, and lonely, and when that thought about faces was in me, it had been a kind of warm thought, and now when it came back to me so well expressed, it appeared so cold and strained and daft, and why I hadn't said "daft" to my brother instead of "ridiculous" I don't know, but I hadn't, and now I drank my wine, though Dr Freebody had said that the first thing to do was to keep off alcohol, and I found that it would make me sick to enter into that thought about faces any further, but Sir Francis of course didn't see it, of course he couldn't see it, he was a mental steam-roller and he didn't see that I badly needed to go the lavatory. "It is your own thought that I am developing," he said, and all that was going much too quickly for me, I would have needed a year to develop such a thought, and it is not that I didn't understand what he was saying, I did, but that's what is peculiar when you have no education, I mean that you can't be sure whether you have understood *all* of what was there to be understood or not, and he said: "The Romantic revolution was . . ." And while I was trying to sort out in my mind what was Roman, and what was Romanesque, and what was Romantic, he went on: "Was the greatest swindle of all," and while I was trying to guess whether he was talking of Cromwell, or Robespierre, or Lenin, he went on: "Would you agree that they were not looking for a real shepherdess to praise? They were looking for a shepherdess who happened to look like what they thought the ideal princess should look like, called her beautiful, painted a picture of her, called the picture beautiful, and sent the picture to a museum and the model to a brothel to provide men with the illusion of having slept with the aristocracy, just as today they pick up a barmaid who happens to look like a whore and send her to Hollywood to play a princess."

He picked a flower from a little bunch in the centre of the table, I don't know anything about flowers, don't recognise them by their names, in any case it was blue and as big as a sixpence, and he sniffed at it and said: "Would it be agreeable to you if we went to see Lady Celia?"

"Did you say *Lady* Celia?" I asked,
and he said: "I did,"

213

so I said: "If you don't mind I would rather not,"
and he said: "May I ask for your reasons,"
and I said: "Well, it is a little embarrassing, and you may
think I am prejudiced, but the fact is that I don't like mixing
with the aristocracy."

"Quite," he said, "neither do I."

"You don't notice," I said, "when they become too familiar with you, and then climb up on to your head."

"Precisely," he said. "Though when you meet her you will
agree with me that Lady Celia is different."

"Who is she?" I asked.

"Lady Celia is the wife of Mr de Marney."

Now, at that time everybody knew who Mr de Marney
was, the name spelt money, and everybody knew that, and I
asked Sir Francis to excuse me and I went to the lavatory,
and it smelt very posh, the place there, and I pressed my
forehead to some cool white tiles and gave back all the wine I
had drunk, and I don't know whether it was because Dr Freebody had said I shouldn't drink because of the illness or because I hadn't eaten anything the whole day, not because I
couldn't afford it but because it had just happened so, because
things like that do happen sometimes and it isn't exactly because you forget, sometimes you neither forget nor remember, and anyway how can you be sure that everything must be
because of something; it may be that some things happen
without any cause, and I said to myself, right there on the
spot: "You can't deny it, my boy, the world is a strange place
to live in, right here, in these toilets, between those posh cool
white tiles, nevertheless a strange place, nothing rough, no
shooting, no Betty Compton, no tigers, no Lindberghs, just
the cool white tiles and nevertheless a strange place, confusing, you grope your way as if through a wood, there is no
wood in the Harrow Road or in Bell Street, and nevertheless it is like groping one's way through a wood, a wood of
white glazed trees, cool and silent and sweating," and I

washed my face in the basin, and there was another door leading to the backyard, and I was tempted to put my best foot forward into the backyard and escape into the street, but then I thought: "And what if they misplace their silver salver, or if Sir Francis has lost his gold watch, the first thing to pop into their minds would be that I'd stolen it, that's certain, 2 plus 2 four," so I drank some water from the tap, the way boys do, it's easy to show how, difficult to describe, maybe there are more things which are difficult to describe or cannot be talked about at all, but could be shown if one tried, the purpose of one's existence, for example; anyway, you hold your hands palms downwards, then you so to speak dovetail the fingers of the left hand with the fingers of the right one so that the tips of the fingers of the right hand find themselves under the left palm, and the tips of the fingers of the left hand under the right palm, as far as they can go, and then you bend both hands a little at the joints at the roots of the fingers, and you will find there, between the knuckles, a kind of trough, the near end of which you put to your mouth and the other one under the tap, which is very simple when you are actually doing it, and so I drank some water in that fashion and then I thought: "Why do I make all that fuss about going to Lady Celia's, after all, she can't eat me, can she? and, after all, yes, my wife has left me all right, but should that be enough to make a man a posh ladies' hater? And, after all, isn't it true that what they call 'common' people are no angels, either, that the barbers smashed my haircutting machine, and Harry Brown acted stupidly about the mirrors, and my own brother John sneered at my 'faces,' and is it not true that in the whole of London it was after all only my upper class wife, and the middle class Dr Freebody, and now the aristocratic Sir Francis, with whom I could have just a little understanding? So just don't be nervous," I told myself, "it's just because you shut yourself in your room for a week, and forgot to eat properly, and don't feel comfortable in other ways, too," and I pulled myself together and went back to the room, and on our table there was now a dish of hot buttered toast, and all that was somehow the wrong way round, because when we come in, it was tea time and they shouldn't have given us wine, and now it was nearly dinner time and they shouldn't have given us tea, though there wasn't any tea, only buttered toast, and Sir Francis said: "I shall relish that, won't you?" and he put one piece on my plate and one on his, and I ate mine and it was good, and warm, but he didn't even try to eat his, just nibbled at it, and I thought that if I had been there alone they would have expected me to buy some caviar, but to Sir Francis they were glad to serve a penny bit of bread, though to me it was better than caviar, my stomach felt nice and warm now, and Sir Francis said: "Would it be too bold to ask whether you are engaged in any work now?"

"No," I said, "not at the moment."

"Strong black coffee?" he asked. "I should like some strong black coffee," he added, and then he put the little blue flower I didn't know the name of back into the vase and said: "I should be very glad if you could consider becoming my secretary for a special purpose,"

and when I heard these words my hands fell on to my knees, which after all was the right place to hold them, which waiters usually forget when they are themselves sitting at a table, and I thought: "Maybe he is potty after all, and will ask me to pay the bill, which would be a disaster," and I decided to cut it short, I mean the whole awkward situation. What does he think I am?, I thought, and I said: "Look here, Sir Francis, I don't know any shorthand. If you showed me a page of shorthand and a page of Arabic, I wouldn't know which was which. And I have never seen a typewriting machine from a lesser distance than the length of my arm twice. And the last time I had a pencil in my hand was to write bills in a Chinese restaurant where I worked. I don't even remember when I last wrote a letter, it is such a long time ago. So the best thing will be if we just skip it, if you don't mind,"

and he said: "I feel precisely the same about writing letters. I hate writing letters. I usually dictate them to Tony and he gives them to Florence who types them."

"Who is Tony?" I asked.

"Tony," he said, "is my private secretary, and Bernard Spike is my business secretary; you will meet them in due time, they do all the writing that is to be done, you don't need to worry."

Now, was it all real? If you only *see* something, it is not necessarily real; because it may be for instance a picture, and then the picture is real and not the thing; and if you only *hear* something, it may be a gramophone record and not the person who sings; and likewise if you only notice a smell, or touch something, or dance—it doesn't necessarily have to be real; but if you see and hear and smell and touch and take part in a situation all at the same time, then that's real because that's exactly what is called real; you shut your eyes and there is still something to hear or to touch; you go away but there is still something to expect when you come back; and so that's what is called real, and I couldn't come to any other conclusion than that Sir Francis was real, at least what is called real, that's to say, not like the roast beef and plum pudding you see in your dreams when you go to bed hungry, but like the one you see when you eat it, and so I said: "You have a private secretary and a business secretary, what kind of secretary can you possibly need now?"

but instead of answering me he said: "We shall discuss it later if you don't mind; now I would suggest that we go to Lady Celia."

And the commissionaire got us a taxi, and Lady Celia was almost as old as he was, which meant she must have been at least ten years older than her husband, Mr de Marney,

and the police were all wrong when they subsequently
thought that Sir Francis had gone with a Spanish dancer,
Esterhase, or Esmeralda, or Esperanta, to Minorca for a fortnight, that was all nonsense and they just picked it up in the
pubs of Fleet Street, because Sir Francis neither knew any
Spanish dancers nor had been to Minorca, and the story I'm
sure sprang from another one, told by his sister, who complained that he was ruining their country estate by spending
money on the international language Esperanto, which again
was not as it was at all, and perhaps what his son said was
nearer the truth, when he said: "All this trouble comes from
his mixing with the mob." That's what he said, but what
actually happened was that Sir Francis went to Majorca, and
not to Minorca, and not with any Spanish dancers but with
myself and Lady Celia, and three volumes by William Shakespeare, I mean three copies of the same volume, one for each
of us, though I never saw Lady Celia open it. "The idea is
crystal clear," she said and left it to us, while she herself
played Chopin's "Raindrop Prelude" on the grand piano, because Chopin composed it in Majorca when he was there
with Mrs Sand, and so she, I mean Lady Celia, went on
playing the "Raindrop Prelude" there, while Sir Francis and I
were reading *Hamlet*, which I had never read before, and my
business was to think how different from what people think
the characters in the play can look and still be able to say the
things they say and do the things they do. I mean, I had to
read the play again and again and tell Sir Francis what I, with
my kind of experience of life, would expect them to look like,
and my first thought was that the villains who are not recognised as such on the stage should not be recognised as such
by the audience, which means that they should look innocent and honest, but it was not as simple as that, because, as
Sir Francis said, we were not going to assume that there were
honest faces and dishonest ones, and when I said they should
look honest I should have said they should look what people

think looks honest, and we would show them exactly that what they think is not necessarily true, though it didn't mean that the contrary of what they think is true, no, that would be too simple, what we were up to, he said, was the truth, and what was a contradiction of truth was a contradiction of beauty, and we were to teach them to see beauty in the thrill of truth, which is often what is now called ugly, but sometimes is what is already called beautiful, so we were to be very honest and scientific in studying the looks of those characters in the play by William Shakespeare, and the whole thing was more complicated than one thought at the very first moment, though not so very much so. "I feel as if we have brought barrels of gunpowder with us," said Lady Celia when, back from Majorca, we arrived at Victoria Station, and the very next day Sir Francis got in touch with some theatrical people, and a fortnight later he booked a West End theatre for the next season. He knew, of course, that as an outsider he would have to pay two, three, four times more for anything he wanted, still it must be said that the things he wanted were fairly unusual, and he was prepared to pay for them, especially as Lady Celia wanted to cover the expenses after he had spent the first ten thousand.

"I respect your desire to patronise the arts, Sir Francis," said his lawyer—because I was now expected to accompany Sir Francis everywhere, whether I was needed or not,—and it was clear to me that he, I mean the lawyer, thought it was a baronetcy, or whatever it is that comes above a knighthood, or a ribbon of something or other, that Sir Francis was aiming at, and he, I mean the lawyer, looked at me most of the time, and I didn't like his looking at me, I didn't like it at all, and he said: "Business with artists, well . . . One seems to know where one is when one starts, but one can never be certain where one will be led to. Queen Victoria said 'Beware of artists. They are dangerous because they cut through all the layers of society, and find themselves at home everywhere.' Your difficulty, Sir Francis, is that you're too wealthy to be contented with giving them five-pound loans or gifts, yet not wealthy enough to endow a foundation on a national scale."

"Hmm . . ." was Sir Francis's reply.

And I saw he just didn't care to explain that it was a question not of the arts or artists, but of a social revolution, because it was then that the term came to his mind for the first time: "Isn't your first name Tom?" he asked, and of course he knew my first name was Tom,

and I said: "Yes, it is,"

and he said: "Will it be agreeable to you if I address you by your Christian name?"

I'm not up to quoting him verbatim, I mean: word for word, but almost, and up to then he had still slid in a "sir" when talking to me, or said "my secretary," or my surname when talking about me, and so I said: "Yes, that's all right. After all, I call you by your Christian name, Sir Francis,"

and so he said: "Do you remember, Tom, the first night we met I told you that I had a private secretary and a business secretary, and you asked me what my new secretary was to be?"

"Yes," I said. "I did. But you didn't answer."

"I can answer now," he said.

"Well?" I said,

and he said: "You are a Revolutionary Secretary."

That's what he said, and he waited for the effect, just like a child who says that he's found a firework and asks you for a box of matches, and I must say I didn't like it, it somehow didn't go with his white hair and his manner, "How do you mean?" I said, "a revolutionary secretary?"

and he said: "Look, Tom, you realise that what we are aiming at is a social revolution, don't you?" and he waited for my answer,

and I must say I was taken aback, because I thought it

wasn't the proper time to make jokes like that then—, because nowadays it is different, I mean: Nowadays young people don't understand these things, maybe they understand
some other things we don't, because I don't say they don't
feel (I would say:) loyal at all; maybe they do, only to something else *we* don't understand; because if the purpose of our
existence is to find the purpose of our existence, as I've already said I thought it was, then with all these nowadays
atoms, and Bevan, Minister of Health, of course you have to
go a different way to find it, because nowadays, I mean now,
when I'm writing this, a young man from Bell Street or anywhere else will be able to say that just before *he* married
there was full employment, but just before *I* married there
was a general strike, and then the Russians began their five-
year plan, and at the time my wife left me Hitler's party entered the Reichstag, and Spain became a republic, and Mac-
Donald was chucked out of the Labour Party, and De Valera
became a prime minister, and that's why I was taken aback
when Sir Francis said that what we were doing with the faces
was a social revolution, and I thought he was a crackpot after
all, and I said: "How is that going to solve the unemployment problem, Sir Francis?"

And when I asked the question something about him
twitched with impatience, and I had never before noticed
any signs of impatience in him, and I didn't know what precisely it was now, something in the way he carried his shoulders, perhaps, and he said: "I am not particularly interested
in that problem at present,"

and I said: "But I am,"

and it would be too difficult to explain why I was, and for a
second I read in his face that he thought I was hopeless and
to be given up, but in the next second he must have changed
his mind, one could always see how he discussed things with
himself before saying anything aloud, so now, for a change,
there was a sort of kind smile in his eyes, and he said:

"Well, Tom, what could you tell me of what was going on in the world some fifty years ago? Let's say in the 1800's? Are you very excited by the events that occurred when I was your present age, let's say in 1885? You are not. But I was, and still am. And you may take it for granted that in fifty years' time, when you are my present age, you'll also feel more excited by what's going on now than by the new problems, whatever they will be. Perspective, my dear. And thus I do not see why I should take it from you that present-day events are of greater importance than any other events, past or future, why should they be? Just because you happen to be young man now?"

"Well," I said, "one can't do anything about what happened fifty years ago, but surely one can try to do something about what's going on now."

"You mean a Social Revolution?" he asked.

I had somehow never had confidence in big words, so I said: "If you want to call it that."

"And a Social Revolution is exactly what we are trying to make," he said, and he pushed forward his lower jaw which was very small, hardly a jaw at all.

So, obstinately, I said again:"How is it going to solve the unemployment problem, Sir Francis?"

and I saw that he thought that I thought that he was a crank, which in a way I did, I wasn't quite sure, but all the same I thought his calling me a revolutionary secretary was just a little too much for my taste anyway,

and he said: "I am not interested in revolting against symptoms, such as unemployment, government, war. I'm too old to be interested in surface revolutions, in which man overthrows a government, wins a war, gets rid of unemployment, and then goes on along the old path, choosing his leaders as before, according to the age of their bodies, the features of their faces, the gestures of their arms, the oratory of their larynxes, the clothes they wear . . ." He stopped abruptly and repeated the word "clothes," and then he got up hurriedly and said: "Yes, *clothes*, let's go,"

and we went to a bookshop where he asked for Plato, but they didn't stock it, the girl suggested Professor Joad, but Sir Francis thanked her politely and we went to another one but it was already closing time, and Sir Francis asked me to ring up Lady Celia: did she think there was any Plato in her husband's library? She didn't know, she would ask him, hallo? De Marney thought he should have Jowett's edition in the country, he could have it sent to London; it was very kind of him, but no, thank you, that was where Sir Francis's own Plato had been all the time, in the country, not here; I came out of the telephone box and looked up at the sky, where thousands of starlings circled above Nelson's column. "Is it really impossible to find a book at six p.m. in London?" asked Sir Francis, and that reminded me of the time when I myself had wondered: "Is there really nobody to ask why mirrors reverse from right to left and don't upside down?" and a pretty long time seemed to have passed since then, and Sir Francis again said: "Let's go."

And he was a quick walker, and we crossed Trafalgar Square, passed a crowd surrounding Irving's statue with a man in a sack underneath, I mean there was a real man in a sack throwing off his chains, and we went along Charing Cross Road and then turned left into Soho, and there were women there, as usual, old and young ones, on high heels, on the corners and under the lamp-posts, behind the Packards and Fords and Austins parked along the curb, and he said he wasn't certain whether he would recognise the house, though he didn't say what house, but it was there all right, opposite a restaurant and a pub, and the front door was open, and there was a yellow hand-written poster pinned to the wall by the staircase, and so we went up to the first floor, but there were many doors on both sides of a long corridor, and he knocked on one and turned the handle.

"I am sorry to bother you," he said, "but would it be possible for me to see Father Thompson?"

and out of the dark room a man came, "That's all right," he said, I mean the man who had come out of the dark room, "Father Thompson is on the next floor." And leaning on the banister he bent his head backwards as if he were going to gargle, and shouted: "Father Thompson! A visitor!" and as there was no answer, he added: "It's the third door on the left. Do you think you'll find it, or shall I come with you?" but we thought we'd find it all right, and we climbed up to the second floor, and Father Thompson was sitting at his desk at the window, an evening paper in front of him under a table lamp with a green glass shade, and he turned in his chair and got up.

"Hallo," he said, "nice to see you again," and he didn't look surprised at all, though I understood they hadn't seen each other for more than ten years, and Father Thompson said: "It isn't actually cold, but just a little; let me put the fire on, and do sit down, please," and he offered us his armchair and a stool and went and sat on the bed.

And Sir Francis said: "I thought you might have some volumes of Plato. He was a kind of Catholic, pre-Christian saint, wasn't he?"

and Father Thompson went to the bookshelf and asked: "Greek or English?"

"English," said Sir Francis.

and Father Thompson jerked the books out of the shelf, brought them to the table, and said: "I think I'll leave you now; you can take any of these books with you."

And it was very strange and sudden. I mean it was strange because it was so sudden, and when we were left alone, I mean Sir Francis and I, Sir Francis started to go through the books looking for what he wanted, and then he stopped at a page and said: "I would like to dictate a few passages to you, if you don't mind," and he gave me Father Thompson's pen

224

and his notebook, and it was the first time that I had been asked to take dictation, and I remembered my wife once saying that Plato was not fashionable among English philosophers any more, and not knowing what she was talking about, I made a fool of myself and said: "Nonsense, philosophy cannot be fashionable or not fashionable, it can only be true or not true," and she said: "Let's go to the pictures," and we went to the pictures, and afterwards I looked in my encyclopaedia but there was nothing about Plato, there was only "Platonic," and I didn't see exactly what she meant. And when Sir Francis asked me to take the dictation, I felt uneasy and I said: "If you show me the page I will copy it," but he said: "I want to change a word here and there and leave out some lines, so it would be preferable to dictate it," and he started to read what he wanted, very slowly, I admit, and I don't remember the actual words now, but it *was* about clothes, it was about the Greek God Zeus, who got angry because the judges were making bad judgments, and he said he had had enough of it, he said the judgments were bad because the persons who were judged had their clothes on. And, he said, there were many persons who had evil souls but they were dressed in beautiful bodies, or in wealth, or rank, and witnesses were impressed by that kind of dress and came forward and testified on behalf of those people that they had lived honestly, which was not always so. And the same with the judges. Because the judges too had their clothes on when judging. And by their clothes, he meant their eyes and ears and their whole bodies which didn't let their souls see, so to speak, the souls of the judged ones. So he decided that both the judges and the judged would be stripped of their bodies and one naked soul would see the other naked soul. And so the naked judge would inspect the naked soul quite impartially, not knowing whose the soul was; perhaps it belonged to the King of Persia, never mind, if the soul was bad the judge would only know that he had got hold of a villain. And

225

the other way round. And before I had finished writing down the dictation, a thin yellow fog had started to creep into the room and it smelt of sulphur, the fog, I mean, and it was at about that time that the daughter of a Danish high official went mad, tried to kill herself, and was sent by her family to a London nursing home.

Now, Lady Celia's grandmother was Danish, because, strange as it may sound, we bombarded Copenhagen in 1807 without caring to declare war first, and one of the English officers who took part in this bombardment married a young Danish widow and brought her with her little daughter to England, which little daughter was Lady Celia's grandmother, while the little daughter's younger brother, who had been left with the family of his deceased father in Aalborg, was the grandfather of the Danish high official whose daughter had gone mad, and it was now intimated to Lady Celia by the Danish part of her family that Lady Celia might visit her in the London nursing home where she had been sent, and so one day we went there together, Lady Celia, Sir Francis, and myself, and saw the girl in that private madhouse where she was permitted to play tennis every morning but only given spoons to eat her meals with, and her name was Ingelburge, which means I forget what, and she was very tall and heavy, and even if what she was saying was nice and polite, her voice was loud and harsh and somehow obstinate, and her hair was black and cut short and curled, and her face was exactly like a horse's, and the second time we went to the so-called nursing home we took Thelma Springfield (who was to play Ophelia) with us to show her the mad girl Ingelburge, and then we took Mr Collis (who was to play the King) to Manchester to show him a baronet who had poisoned his brother and we took Harold Grimes to the Old Bailey to show him a boy who was going to be hanged for shooting his mother's co-respondent, and that boy had narrow, wet eyes sunk in a swollen round face, and practically no neck at all, so I

226

couldn't help thinking: how will they manage to put the rope under his chin, and I looked at the jury, one after another, and wondered which of them would be clever enough to put the rope round something the boy hadn't got, though of course I knew it wasn't their job to do that actually, and the boy's hands were very red and his legs were bent like a jockey's, and when studying those legs, Harold Grimes turned to Lady Celia and Sir Francis and asked: "Are you both sure that I really need to have bent legs like that to play Hamlet?"

to which Sir Francis replied, rather too high-handedly, I thought: "Is the nobility of the Prince in the straightness of his lower limbs?"

"Well, it's you who are paying the piper," said Harold, and it was an offensive remark but they had to swallow it, and Lady Celia said that it was much easier to find participation than co-operation, and there were many things now that they just had to swallow, they had been nicknamed Mrs Krupskaia and Mr Trotsky, and in the wings the whole thing was called The Red Knight's Folly, and such was what they call the power of money that nobody was quite sure that the thing might not end by being a big hit after all.

It didn't.

The first night was a disaster, and Lady Celia held Sir Francis's hand in hers most of the time, and specially when people couldn't stand Hamlet's bent legs or the long, horsy face of Ophelia, and laughed, and Betty Immergut came to our box and said: "Well, it's all over. They won't laugh any more,"

and Sir Francis asked: "How do you mean?"

and Betty Immergut said: "Well, it's all over, isn't it?"

and now Lady Celia asked: "How do you mean?"

and Betty Immergut said: "Well, we pack up, don't we?"

and Sir Francis put his hands behind his back like policemen do when they want to make it quite impossible for you to say that they have hit you, and he said: "We do nothing of the kind."

"Of course not, Betty," said Lady Celia.

Betty Immergut had not been with us from the very beginning, because at first Sir Francis had engaged a man called Douglas McCoulough, whom I thought I had once seen in the Chinese restaurant I worked in, and he had a golden bow tie round his neck, and five bracelets on his wrists, though he had only one wrist-watch, and he called Lady Celia "Darling Krupskaia," and Sir Francis he called "Honey Trotsky," and he had looked very excited about the Red Knight's Folly, yet it soon came out that he had an idea of his own as well, and his idea was to play the play in diplomatic uniforms, so when Sir Francis saw that Douglas McCoulough wanted to force his uniforms on us, he decided to break his contract, and I was sorry for Douglas McCoulough, because his idea might have been silly, as it probably was, though I was not the one to judge that, but I knew that once one has an idea one wants to do something about it, and also that one's own idea always seems more worth trying than another person's, so, clearly, it must have seemed to him that we were doing Sir Francis's idea, and not his, only because Sir Francis had money, which in a way was so, and somehow or other I didn't like the look of my idea fed on Sir Francis's money, because it had been, in a way, my idea, as Sir Francis said it had, but I didn't feel it to be so any more, because what I was interested in was why we think some faces beautiful, etc., and some ugly, etc., and even if that was an historical question, as Sir Francis had said it was, I would rather have gone on working at the Chinese restaurant and thought about the idea slowly, in my spare time. And still at the very beginning, even before we went to Marjorca, I had told him that I had had some other ideas, more straightforward ones, in case he wanted one to do something about, and he asked: "What, for instance?" and I told him about the haircutting machine, but he said he wasn't interested, so I told him about the mirror that doesn't reverse, but he said he was interested in faces and nothing else, and so I knew how Douglas McCoulough must have felt about it and I was sorry for him when he put Sir Francis's cheque into his pocket and said: "You know, Honey Trotsky, I could kill you," and he had tears in his eyes, as this, I understood, was his only chance of producing a play in a West End theatre, and three people heard him say that and became busy lighting cigarettes, and Douglas McCoulough was replaced by Betty Immergut who wasn't actually a producer but had a casting agency, and she was just under forty, always in a black tailor-made costume, which was the wrong thing for her to wear, because a tailor-made costume is all right when it is thinnest where the belt is, I mean the belt to the skirt, and that was where my wife was very thin, and she looked very pretty in one, but that wasn't the thinnest place in Betty Immergut who had started to grow a belly which was now cut in two by the belt, though she always had a fresh white flower in her lapel and looked very smart, and so Lady Celia said: "Of course not, Betty," meaning that we were not going to pack up, and then she said: "Betty dear, we really don't mind their laughing, so much. I think it was defensive laughter, and so to that extent we have succeeded," and Betty Immergut took Lady Celia by the hand and said: "*You* don't mind. You only think about what *you* mind or do not mind. Doesn't it occur to you to go backstage and see what's going on there; whether *they* mind?"

But we didn't go backstage. We went for a walk along the Embankment, and I stayed with them, that's to say with Sir Francis and Lady Celia, because Betty we had left in the theatre, and I thought we would talk about what to do now, but we didn't, there was a full moon that night, but we were on the wrong side of the river to see its reflection in the water, and Sir Francis had no car, he didn't want to be bothered with cars and chauffeurs, he preferred to call a taxi or go by bus, or he would just walk, because he was a good walker and could go on walking for hours, and Lady Celia used to take two small steps to each one of his, and felt out of breath, so I thought she should have taken three steps to his two, which would have been easy for her as she was a piano player, but she didn't, and nobody said a word about the theatre, and so when I saw, on the Embankment, that they were not going to talk about the theatre, I left them there, under the full moon, and went home, and when I went to see him the next morning as usual, he was in bed, eating his breakfast, and there was a pile of newspapers on the floor, and he had already looked through them all, and there was not a single line about the day before's first night, and so he tucked a hot water bottle under his right shoulder and took two aspirins in a glass of hot wine, not because of the newspapers but because of his lumbago, and that night Lady Celia didn't go to the theatre because of the Polish sugar because, as Lady Celia explained, the Poles put up the price of their sugar so that their peasants wouldn't be able to buy it, and they sold it to England at half price to feed our pigs, because they, I mean the Poles, needed our currency, but as we could now feed our pigs cheaply on that Polish sugar which they made from beetroot, our imports of their bacon decreased, which didn't please them at all, and so Mr de Marney decided that he would import their bacon if they agreed to be paid with the cane sugar that he would import for them from Jamaica, and to make the scheme work he had to go to a reception at the Polish Embassy which was held that night, and he always had to have Lady Celia by his side on all official occasions, very likely it was then that he saw Lady Celia most, on official occasions I mean; anyway, that was the reason why Sir Francis went to the theatre alone that night, and by alone I mean with me, of course, and we got there rather late, because of Sir Francis's lumbago, in the middle of the second act, and we sat in the foyer and listened, listened not to the

stage, of course, but to the house, and it sounded quite different from the first night, it sounded friendly, and I thought,
now if it had changed, if everything was all right, I would
leave Sir Francis, not because I didn't like him, I did, but I
didn't feel at my ease, somehow, and Sir Francis offered me a
cigar and we smoked our cigars in the foyer and listened to
the house, and I wondered how it had been, after all, did my
wife like the smell of cigars or didn't she?, and we hadn't
heard any laughter, and after the second act there was quite
an amount of clapping, and so we went to our box, and Sir
Francis put his legs on another chair, because of his lumbago,
and then the curtain went up, but I didn't see the stage, because when the lights started to fade out I had happened to
glance round and there, in the front row of the dress-circle, I
saw my wife, and from that moment on it was impossible for
me to take my eyes off her and off Dr Freebody who was sitting beside her, in evening dress with a white tie, and her arms
were naked and her hair was piled so high that the people
sitting behind her would have complained if they had had
any sense, and I wondered how it had happened that she was
carrying on with Dr Freebody, because I hadn't seen Dr
Freebody for several months, as he had told me that I was
completely cured, and a long time before, when I had asked
him whether he had seen my wife, he had said: "Your children are all right, everything has been arranged satisfactorily," and I hadn't asked him any more questions, because
first, he wasn't the man to ask questions of, and second, I
didn't want to show that I cared, so now I had no clue whatsoever, and as it didn't look as if they were just casually together, on the contrary they looked like a couple, and I wondered, if she had now switched over to Dr Freebody, what
the position of my kids was: whether Dr Freebody was being
a father to them, or the other gent, whom I had never seen in
my life, at least so far as I knew; and then I felt Sir Francis's
hand on my shoulder, and he said: "Bastards," and I had

231

never heard him say such a strong word either before or after, and his hand felt so heavy, though it was a very frail white hand with long fingers, and he said: "You haven't looked at the stage once," and the hand turned me towards the stage, and at that moment Rosencrantz said: "*We shall, my lord*," and both he and Guildenstern made their exit, so I had only seen them for a few seconds and couldn't believe that what I had seen was true, because we had been working on Rosencrantz and Guildenstern for a long time, Rosencrantz being modelled on a young Scotland Yard inspector and Guildenstern on a secret service agent; both had been fair-headed and sprightly and had that open look which made you feel that you would trust them, and that was what Rosencrantz and Guildenstern had been like during the rehearsals and on the first night on Friday; but what I had just seen on the stage was quite different, completely different, their eyes were both sly and piercing under their black eyebrows, their noses were crooked, mouths twisted, spines bent and (except for the spine) they looked exactly like Dr Freebody, and now I saw why Sir Francis had said: "Bastards." They had betrayed him, Rosencrantz and Guildenstern had betrayed him, and Ophelia, who had completely repainted herself and wasn't like Ingelburge of the private loony bin any more, had betrayed him, and so had Hamlet, he hadn't done much, Hamlet, he had just removed the pads from his stockings and thus made his legs look straight again, while our Hamlet's legs were meant to be crooked, after all it was in a sense those pads that had cost Sir Francis £10,000, and he had just simply removed them, and Sir Francis got up and left the box, and I was frightened that he might do something silly and I followed him, and the doorman was standing at the stage door and instead of moving aside and letting us in, he produced an envelope from his pocket and gave it to Sir Francis, and Sir Francis opened it and read the letter, and then we left the theatre, went to the pub round the corner and had

some brandy, and at a quarter past ten we went back to the
theatre and Sir Francis made a row, and the Queen said that
it was a success and she would have thought he would have
been thankful for their having saved the play, but Hamlet
didn't say a word, and Betty held Ophelia in her arms and
kissed the tears off her eyes which were covered with anti-
macassar, I mean with mascara, and Sir Francis said, very
well, he would sue them for breaking their contracts, and the
King's Ghost said Sir Francis was welcome to shoot at them
with one of his automatics if he wanted to, which was a
rather nasty thing to say, and who but Sir Francis would
know how to deal with people and broken contracts, because
he was a business man first of all, and what the King's Ghost
said was nasty because the TRICYCLE & Co Ltd manufactured
not only carrier tricycles and invalid chairs but also small
arms, and Sir Francis *was* the TRICYCLE, and as I see it now
there was more there than met the eye, I mean my eye, I
don't mean in the TRICycle, I mean in the theatre, I mean
both, which was strange because there I was, in the centre of
it, and as I see it now, I see that I didn't see nine-tenths of
it, and the tenth I did see was probably not at all important,
because what was important for me was not important for
them, and what was important for them was not important
for me, and I could only see in them what was important for
me, and they could only see in me what was important for
them, and there was a thick glass wall in between, and I
think Sir Francis was that thick glass wall.

On the other hand, if you had removed that thick glass
wall, I mean Sir Francis, there would not have been any room
there for me at all, they would have said: "Who are you,
and what are you doing here?" and the doorman would
have looked at me wondering where he had seen that face
before, and he would have asked: "What do you want?
This is not the entrance for the public," because I was nothing but Sir Francis's shadow there, and people don't like

233

shadows without the substance of the body, even in theatres, and there was not a single person there with whom I had exchanged two words in my, so to speak, private capacity, except perhaps the barmaid, which was strange as well, because, as I see it now, it may be that she just didn't want to be seen with me, I mean with Sir Francis's shadow, because everybody was spooning all the time in all the backstage corners, but she insisted on going out, and not to the place she lived in, and not to my place in Bell Street, never, and so it had to be Hyde Park in the dark, and anyway it only happened twice, and it was long after Dr Freebody had said that I was all right, and I thought: "What is the matter? Had I let my wife show off? No, I hadn't; had I ever let her impress me by her higher education or by that silly upper class stuff? No, I hadn't. Well, then, how was it that I let Honey Trotsky, I mean Sir Francis, lead me by the nose?" And I discussed the question honestly with myself and came to the conclusion that it was money that had done it, because, after all, to be his revolutionary secretary was an easier and better-paid job than the job of a waiter or a labourer or a hairdresser; perhaps it wouldn't have been so for anybody else, but it was for me, and so, after all, it was money and not the idea, I mean my idea about faces, no, not at all, on the contrary, that idea about faces I wanted for myself, because I liked to have things I could think over quietly and with no hurry, and it had grown instead into something too big for my mouth, I just knew I couldn't bite it, and it was exactly as if a child had wanted a kitten and been given a fully grown tiger, all inclusive, the cage, the attendants, and even some ice cream, and it's much more impressive than a kitten, I mean a real tiger is, except for one important thing—you just can't cuddle a tiger, and that's how it was in that theatre, there was nothing there to cuddle, even the barmaid who had a Russian name, I mean Christian name, because her surname was, well, never mind, and it was only her Christian name that was Vladimira, you couldn't cuddle her, not really, and our outings to Hyde Park didn't really count, neither for her nor for me, and I wondered whether Dr Freebody had examined my wife when she first went to visit him, or whether he hadn't, and when I spotted him there in the dress circle he hadn't looked to me half as ugly as I had remembered him, he had a good figure after all, and when Sir Francis made that row and said he would sue the actors and I told myself Well, it's all over now, I felt somehow free, as if I were re-born and could start life again from a beautiful nothing, and how wrong I was I didn't know then, because it wasn't all over at all, I should say the trouble hadn't even begun, I mean for me, but I couldn't have known it then, and the next day was Sunday, and I didn't go to see Sir Francis at all, I stayed in bed all day, I mean I got up and cooked myself a nice breakfast and went back to bed again, I cooked myself eggs and bacon and Batchelor's beans, they say they contain phosphates and are good for the brain, and I went back to bed again, as I have already mentioned, and there was no hurry, plenty of time and peace, and I told myself The theatre is over, now I can start some quiet thinking about faces, because with Sir Francis at my heels, I mean with me at his heels, I hadn't done any thinking at all, because it was taken for granted that the question about faces was an historical question, and if it was an historical question, then it was taken for granted that what Sir Francis was doing was the right thing to do and no more thinking was called for, which as from now would no longer be the case, and I felt cosy, I stretched my legs under the blankets, lit a cigarette, put my elbows up and my hands under my head, on the pillow, and I looked at the ceiling and thought: If it isn't an historical question then surely it must be a philosophical question, be-cause if you look at a number of faces which are, geometri-cally speaking, no more like each other than they are like any other faces, and nevertheless they are all beautiful to you,

while those others are not, then they must have something in
common, I mean something that makes them look beautiful
to you, and that something is surely not seeable, because if it
were seeable you couldn't have said they were no more like
each other than they were like any other faces, and that's
exactly what has just been said, and neither could that something be sniffable at, or heard, or touched, and as all questions about such somethings that cannot be seen, or heard, or
touched, or sniffed at, and yet can be talked about, are philosophical questions, then ours was a philosophical question as
well, and first of all, and so I went on looking at the ceiling,
and felt warm and happy, nobody to kick my shins in the
bed, nobody to make noises in the bathroom, and I went on
thinking: Suppose there were sixteen faces in a house, and I
thought eight of them beautiful and eight ugly, and put the
beautiful eight into the first floor flat and the ugly eight into
the ground floor flat, a funny idea, but let's suppose it, and
let's suppose that a chap from some other part of the world, a
Mongolian, or a sort of somebody like that, well, let's suppose he comes and says: "There are sixteen faces in that
house, but they are all mixed up, eight of them I think are
beautiful, but the other eight are ugly. I want to separate the
beautiful ones from the ugly ones." And he goes to the first
floor flat and puts the four faces he thinks beautiful into the
bedroom, and the four he thinks ugly into the drawing-room,
and then he goes down to the ground floor and puts the four
faces he thinks beautiful into the ground floor bedroom, and
the four he thinks ugly into the drawing-room, and he clasps
his hands and says: "Now, thanks to me, all the beautiful
faces are in the two bedrooms and all the ugly ones are in the
two drawing-rooms!" And at that I shrug my shoulders and
say: "Nonsense, Mr Mongolian. All the beautiful faces are
on the first floor, and all the ugly ones are on the ground
floor," to which he's bound to say: "Not all, my dear fellow,
only four. Four beautiful faces are on the first floor and four

ugly ones are on the ground floor, and if you want to find *all* the beautiful faces you must look into both bedrooms, and if you want to find *all* the ugly ones you must look into both the drawing-rooms," to which I will say: "Not all, Mr Mongolian, only four; only four beautiful faces are in the bedroom, namely in the first floor bedroom, and only four ugly faces are in the drawing-room, namely in the ground floor drawing-room." And so we would go on talking pleasantly in some lovely surroundings, sitting on deck-chairs, for instance, agreeing that four faces are beautiful, four ugly, and disagreeing about the other eight, and then I would finish my soft drink, drop the straw on to the warm sand, and I would say: "Now I want to separate the honest-looking faces from the dishonest ones," and I would go back to the house, on the first floor first, and I would choose four honest faces, which would be one beautiful bedroom face, and one ugly bedroom face, and one beautiful drawing-room face, and one ugly drawing-room face, and I'd push them towards the south walls, overlooking the beach and the sea, and the dishonest ones I would push towards the north walls, overlooking the mountains, their snowy peaks deep in the clouds, and then I would go to the ground floor flat and do exactly the same, and then Mr Mongolian would say that he would now separate the honest-looking faces from the dishonest ones, and he would go to the house too, and in each room, whether bedroom or drawing-room on the first floor or on the ground floor, he would push one of my south faces westwards and another one eastwards, and the same with my north faces, one westwards and the other eastwards, and then he would say: "Now all the faces by the east walls are honest and those by the west walls are dishonest," and I would say: "Nonsense, stranger, only those faces by the east wall which are at the same time by the south wall are honest, those that are by the north wall are dishonest; and only those faces by the west wall which are at the same time by the north wall are dis-

honest, those that are by the south wall are honest!" And so
we would go on discussing the thing very pleasantly, perhaps
some seagulls would fly over our heads, that's to say if we are
still on the beach, in our deck-chairs, drinking our soft drinks
and perhaps drawing the plan of the house with our toes in
the sand, because there were sixteen faces in the house and
the house had two floors, and two rooms on each floor,
which would make it four, and four corners in each room,
which would make it sixteen, and the faces had been pushed
by myself and the Mongolian so that we now found there
was one face in each corner, but there were only two faces we
both thought the same about: one was in the south-east
corner of the first floor bedroom, and we both thought it
was honest and beautiful, and the other was in the north-
west corner of the ground floor drawing-room, and we
both thought it was ugly and dishonest; on the other
fourteen faces we just couldn't agree: if it seemed beautiful
and honest for one of us it had to be either beautiful
but dishonest or ugly but honest, or ugly and dishonest for
the other, and so on, and so I said, I mean I would have said:
"It is strange, very strange, Mr Mongolian, very strange indeed." And he would say: "Why so, Tom, my friend?" And I
would say: "I can understand that we aren't of the same
mind about which face is beautiful and which is ugly because
their looking beautiful or ugly depends on our eyes, and yours
may be different from mine. But what I can't understand is
why we aren't of the same mind about which face is honest,
and which dishonest. Their honesty does depend on them,
and not on us, doesn't it? So if you call dishonest the same
face I call honest, maybe what you think is honest is not the
same as what I think it is," and this is what I would have
said. And he would give me a look with his slanting eyes and
ask: "What do you mean by honest?" "Putting it shortly," I
would say, "I would say it's not to make a nuisance of oneself," and he would say: "I would say the same," so I would

say: "But if we agree what honest is, then why don't we say the same when we look at the same face?" And he would wave his hands and say quickly: "Wait a minute, wait a minute! What you see when you look at a face is not what it is but what it looks like. An ugly face may look beautiful and a dishonest face may look honest. And the other way round. Like with actors in the theatre . . ." "Don't talk to me about the theatre," I would cut him short, and he would say: "All right, don't get excited," but I wouldn't get excited. No. It was so nice to lie the whole day in bed and talk about faces to him, I mean to myself, that I wouldn't spoil it now by getting excited, no.

I looked around, not at the sea and the sky and the seagulls, but at the ceiling and the walls of my room in Bell Street, and I got up, shaved, dressed and went out. I would have liked to go to the Metropolitan, just across Edgware Road, that was an honest theatre, I thought, because the actors there didn't pretend to be something else, I mean they didn't really pretend that they were not actors, if you see what I mean, but it was Sunday and of course the Metropolitan was closed, and the churches were closed, not that I was a church-goer, not at all, it had perhaps been ten years since I had last been in a church, but what I thought of was finding myself somewhere where it wouldn't be like it was every day, and that's exactly what it is so difficult to do on a Sunday evening, much more difficult than on a weekday, and so I went to a pub and had a glass of bitter, and then picked up a girl in Praed Street, she was a waitress from Lyon's, adding to her budget in the evenings, and then I came back home, feeling free and happy, and I slept soundly till the morning, and when I woke up I still felt nice, planning how to break the news to Sir Francis, and it was only in the bus that the Mongolian in me woke up all of a sudden and said: "But look here, my friend, if the same faces seem beautiful and dishonest in the south of England and ugly but honest in Mongolia, then surely it isn't a philosophical question but a geographical one." And now I knew that I hadn't got away from Sir Francis, just wasted my Sunday with fancy thoughts, because if the question was geographical, then its roots were historical not philosophical, and that's exactly what Sir Francis thought, and so I had gone round back to the beginning and was again well in his hands, and I got off the bus and walked one bus stop back and went to the library, because my mind works slowly and it was only now that I had taken in what I had once overheard, and it was almost a year before, when Sir Francis was engaging Douglas McCoulough. Douglas Mc-Coulough had said: "I have read your book, Sir Francis," and Sir Francis had seemed not to hear it, and he never mentioned to me that he had written a book, and so I went to the library and looked in the catalogue drawers, and there it was, on a card: *Pewter-Smith, Sir Francis: Historical Development of Facial Expressions in Man, Its social causes and significance,* xxv–284 pp. *Philosophical and Psychological Series, London,* 1902; and I must say that that little card almost killed me; to think that he had written a book on faces even before I had had time to be born, twenty-five plus two hundred and eighty-four pages, and there was a rubber stamp on it *Issued on application,* so I didn't ask for it, and if it wasn't a philosophical question but an historical question then the truth was not with me but with Sir Francis, and you cannot rebel against the truth, you can only rebel for the truth, at least that's what I think, and I felt like a dog must when he tucks his tail between his legs and goes to see his master, and I took the bus again and went to see Sir Francis, and he was still in bed though it was already half past ten, and he said: "Good morning," and handed me a packet of letters, and they contained nine doctor's certificates, from Hamlet, Ophelia, Gertrude, Claudius, Rosencrantz and Guildenstern, one of the grave-diggers and two understudies, all saying the same thing: *"unable to take part for at least a week because of acute laryngitis."*

"We must push that tree a little farther off," Sir Francis said, as a score of pigeons were fighting for a place on the oleander tree behind the window, and I should have said that it was a tree in a huge wooden bucket which stood on the balcony, because the room was on the third floor, and so the pigeons were almost right above his head, because his bed was under the window, and it must be said that the balcony went all round the building, which was a block of flats, with a restaurant on the ground floor, not that Sir Francis couldn't afford a house of his own, it was the same as with the car, he thought it was a bother and he didn't want one, he preferred taxis, and he preferred to live in a flatlet, he had three in different parts of London, so that wherever he was he was near his home, and a hundred times I had wanted to push the oleander tree farther along the balcony, and something had always happened to stop me, and so it was now, too.

"Let me push it now," I said,

but he said: "No, we'll do it some other time," and he jumped out of bed as if he were a young man and asked me to 'phone up Harry, his business secretary, and went to the bathroom, and I had to shout to the bathroom and into the 'phone questions and answers, all about the winding-up of the Red Knight's Folly, and then we went down and stopped a taxi, and he said, not to me, but to the taxi-man:

"What would you say to going to Richmond Park?"

and the taxi-man said: "A very nice idea, sir,"

and then we stopped the cab by a baker's shop and Sir Francis bought a loaf of bread, and then the taxi smelt of warm dough, and we entered the park through Richmond Gate and a small herd of deer was walking slowly along the edge of the road, and Sir Francis took the loaf out of the taxi,

241

tore off small bits and fed the deer, and at half past one we drove to a pub to lunch, we two and the taxi-man, and we had beer, Windsor soup, roast mutton with mint sauce, bread-and-butter pudding, and tea, and Sir Francis knew everything about ball bearings, and the taxi-man was interested, and at half past three we were back in town, and he decided to walk from Sloane Square, so he paid the taxi off there, and as we were near Lady Celia's house we saw that Mr de Marney's car was just leaving, and I saw a smile on Sir Francis's face, and I never knew whether Mr de Marney never had tea at home because Sir Francis always came at tea time, or whether Sir Francis used to come at tea time because Mr de Marney was never at home then, however I could easily go on living without knowing that, and it was now four o'clock exactly, and before we touched the knocker the front door opened and all the servants including the cook were in the hall, and the butler said that they had been trying to get hold of Sir Francis since the morning, and that the doctor was with Lady Celia in her bedroom, and so we went upstairs quickly, and Sir Francis said: "Hello, Celia, darling," and she was there, in her four-poster bed, breathing, but her head didn't move, and I wasn't sure whether she slightly lifted the fingers of her right hand or not, I looked but I just couldn't say, and her head had not moved, that I knew definitely, and Sir Francis turned to the doctor and said: "My name is Pewter-Smith. I am a friend of the family."

and the doctor asked: "Are you a relation of John Pewter-Smith?"

and Sir Francis said he was John's father,

and the doctor said: "I am glad you have come, Sir Francis. I am not satisfied that Mr de Marney has grasped how serious Lady Celia's condition is. Perhaps you'll find a way of conveying to him that she . . ." but Sir Francis didn't let him finish his sentence, he took him by the elbow and pushed him into the dressing room and shut the door behind us.

"How can you, man!" he said. "As if she couldn't hear you!"

"I'm afraid she couldn't," the doctor said.

And it was now a quarter past four: fifteen minutes before, Sir Francis had been smiling as Mr de Marney's car left; a few hours before, he had been feeding the deer in Richmond Park, and I thought the whole set-up was crazy, too silly for words, strange, and Sir Francis looked straight into the doctor's eyes and asked: "What are you trying to say?"

The doctor didn't answer and rang the bell, and the butler must have been waiting behind the door because he came in that very second and the doctor said: "Could we have some brandy?" but he didn't need to say that because the tray was in the butler's hands and the brandy on it, but I noticed that there were only two glasses, and then the doctor said: "It depends on what you mean when you say 'to hear,' Sir Francis. In a sense the patient's hearing is unimpaired, but spoken language is unintelligible to her. I am afraid she is word-deaf,"

and Sir Francis said: "How do you know?"

and the doctor said that Sir Percy Brown had seen Lady Celia twice, and what he, the doctor, was telling Sir Francis was his, Sir Percy's, opinion, as well as his, the doctor's—audito-physic dysphasia, and articulatory motor dysphasia had followed—and I couldn't get all those words but I understood the position all right, and thought if Lady Celia was a piece of timber, then why not just give her morphia and nicely send the body to the crematorium? But, on the other hand, if there was a chance of there still being a bit of her soul in her, then why risk hurting her?

And Sir Francis's thoughts must have been running on the

same lines, because he turned to the doctor and said: "How do you know it is a hæmorrhage of the mid-cerebral artery and not of its smaller branches?" And then he said something strange, the whole set-up was strange, and I felt pretty sick in my stomach and needed a drop of brandy, but there were only two glasses on the tray, and what he said was: "And even if she is word-deaf, must that imply that she cannot understand the meaning of what is being said? Does it not happen that we understand the meaning of a poem, though the words are unintelligible?"

"Modern poetry?" the doctor asked.

"Either very modern, or very old," Sir Francis said, and then he said: "Now I will ask you a practical question. Can you guarantee that she is word-deaf to English and to other languages, French, Italian, Esperanto, which she has learnt at different times in her life, can you guarantee that she is deaf to the mood and to the rhythm?"

"I can guarantee nothing," the doctor said,

and Sir Francis came back to the bedroom, and pronounced very loudly and distinctly: "Celia darling," and in the doctor's eyes he was of course making a fool of himself, but it seemed he didn't mind that. "Celia darling," he repeated slowly, "the doctor says you must have a good rest and you will be better soon. I will come again tomorrow and have tea with you."

The nurse who was unpacking her suitcase had her back turned to Sir Francis, but I saw her face, and I didn't like it, it was neither a nice face nor an ugly one, neither honest nor dishonest, it was a disapproving face and I didn't like it, and after that Monday, every afternoon at four o'clock, day after day for the next six months, he, Sir Francis, sat beside Lady Celia's bed, a cup of tea on his knee, and he talked, and at the beginning I thought that in a fortnight he'd become potty, but it took six months and he didn't, and the moment he arrived the nurse would disappear and leave us alone with the patient till the clock struck five, but I knew she was in the next room drinking her tea and disapproving, and from that Monday on our whole way of life was changed, every morning he went off to his TRICycle office, and I was free till one o'clock, except for buying some papers and books for him, and then we had lunch in town, a walk in Kensington Gardens, and then, from four to five, he was talking lies and poems to Lady Celia, and the rest of the day we were thinking what to tell her the next afternoon, though the lie he'd told her the first Tuesday was not thought out beforehand, it just happened, I think, "Do you know, Celia," he said, "do you know that our *Hamlet* is doing fairly well, after all?"

That was what he said, and that was how it started, and he repeated it in French and Italian and Esperanto, and I think he said it because, a long time before, it had been agreed between him and Lady Celia that they would both cover the *Hamlet* expenses, he would provide the first £10,000, after which she would invest up to the same sum, and Lady Celia knew that his share had already gone and that it was now her turn to sign the cheques, and Sir Francis must have thought that if there was still a thinking something in her brain, that something might be worrying about her not being able to pay. "Monday night," he went on lying, "was quite a success. And there is an article in today's *Times*. You see the significance of that, don't you? It shows they are beginning to understand that what we are aiming at is something more than a theatrical event."

And he repeated it again in French, Italian, and Esperanto, and the lie signed us on for a strange cruise in which we wouldn't sight land for a long time, but the Red Knight's Folly had become a part of his and Lady Celia's life and, in the circumstances, the lie of its success had to go on, and that's how it went on and on, lies, then French, Italian, and Esperanto, and a poem, and the next day new lies all over again, and my job was now to read *The Times* every morning

245

and make suggestions, and this was rather a hard sort of job, and confusing, because my mind was slow, but my memory was good, and once I had taken something in, a new word or a way of putting something into words, it stayed there, I mean in my mind, for years, and it was rather confusing because my mind was now stuffed with words from Shakespeare and words from *The Times*, and when I tried to think in words, I couldn't understand myself somtimes, and so I had to think without words, and that is more difficult; thinking in words is easier, because when you think in words and have finished, it's all done, but when you think without words you only then, I mean when you've finished thinking, have to start looking for words to tell you what you have been thinking about, which means much more strain and work, but that couldn't be helped, and I would cut out an article from *The Times*, and give it to Sir Francis, and he would read it, cross out a word here and there, or, still better, change the main word into another; that was his main trick, he could change a word like "fish" into a word like "revolutionary," and the whole article would still make sense, even more so, I should say, especially for the purpose, and so at four o'clock we would go to Lady Celia's and he would say: "Now I shall read you what *The Times*'s editorial says about us," and he would open the paper and read something like: "*Great, epoch-making truths are neither invented nor discovered. They are the happy formulations of ideas which already exist, ripe in people's minds,*" and before going further he would translate it into French, Italian, and Esperanto, and then he would read in English again: "*The trend has always been towards the classifying of human beings according to the masks they wear and away from a straightforward appreciation of faces,*" and the same in French, Italian, and Esperanto. "*The frenzy of interpretation, by attributing to a human face some purpose deriving from the mask, makes the world look most unreal,*" and the same in French, Italian, and Esperanto. *"Yet the word 'masks' seems too antiquated for modern usage, and the truth about them needs to be reformulated in a more contemporary idiom,"* and the same in French, Italian, and Esperanto. *"Hamlet, if the news reaches him across the Styx, must have been delighted to read yesterday that the new production of the play caused the Philosophical Society to adopt a formula which, they hope, will enable them to clarify many of the misunderstandings which are now worrying humanity,"* and the same in French, Italian, and Esperanto. *"Says the Society's President: 'The Society's hopes are that the idea of us being symbols for what we are not, for that is how it has been formulated by what is becoming known as the Red Knight's Folly, will cut across the philosophical, political and all other divisions that quarter humanity,'"* and the same in French, Italian, and Esperanto. *"For there comes a time when one can no longer see reality through the geometry of symbols. The time comes when masks have been worn for so long that it is forgotten who is acting whom, and the comedy stops being funny. Then a peep beneath the mask is called for,"* and then the same in French, in Italian, and Esperanto. And then a bit of a poem, that kind of poem which you feel that you understand when you just listen to it, but you don't understand when you *want* to understand it and try to think; and the next day the same thing all over again, only it wasn't the Philosophical Society, but the Liberal Party and the Society of Friends, and then it was the House of Commons, and the French Parliament, and the League of Nations, the whole world was changing from one day to another, and we never met Mr de Marney there, I don't say that he never was there, I say he never was there between four o'clock and five o'clock, and one day it was Stalin writing to Hitler: *"For a few million of our contemporaries I am the symbol of a good little father. For some other millions, I am the symbol of a rather bad uncle. In reality I am neither. How could I, with my ambitions, not be disturbed by the conclusion that I have been loved and hated for what I am not?"* and the same in French, Italian, and Esperanto, and a bit of a poem, and the next day it was the converted Hitler answering the transformed Stalin: *"My Dear Brother, A real man will not be satisfied so long as he sees any discrepancy between himself and his symbolic factotum, whether the latter makes him a success among his brethren, or a failure,"* and the same in French, in Italian, and in Esperanto, and a bit of a poem, and so on and so on, day after day, between four o'clock and five o'clock. The Theory of Faces became triumphant. Hollywood film producers were visiting workhouses to find the new-style film stars. Eros in Piccadilly Circus was taken down and a bronze of an old gentleman with white hair and a walking stick with a gold knob was put up, though how you could see the white hair and a gold knob on a bronze statue I didn't know, and then a delegation of Americans presented a bunch of flowers to that whore with a wooden leg who used to walk along Lisle Street, and the same in French, Italian, and Esperanto, and a bit of a poem, and I suddenly got frightened, it was as if somebody's fingers had gripped me by the throat all of a sudden, only it wasn't fingers, I mean it was a thought, and the thought was: "And what if she does hear, and does understand? What then? And what if she now wakes up and says: 'Why do you invent so many lies? Why do you torture me?'" and I was, as they say, seized with panic, I got up and looked into her eyes, but there was nothing to be seen in them except the reflection of the curtains, and so I went to the next room and asked the nurse to come in, and she came in, touched Lady Celia under the chin, and then walked out to the telephone, and I followed her, and as she walked along the hall she said: "You have experimented her to death all right."

"How do you mean?" I asked, and she didn't bother to answer, but before she took the receiver off she turned her head and said:

"Couldn't you have left him alone with her for a moment so that he could have had a chance to tell her that he loved her? Perhaps she would have understood that."

And before I had taken in what the nurse said, she was already talking on the phone, and what she had said to me went right into my heart, like a thorn, and I didn't know whether I was stupid or lonely, that is a question I haven't solved till the present moment, it has been going on and on in me from the time when I was put at the bottom of the class till this present moment, and I have never found an answer to it; was I stupid or lonely? Maybe I was both, though that isn't a proper answer, not in the sense I mean it, and when that thorn went right into my heart, I knew I *could* forget it together with the other thorns that had blistered it, but I also knew that if something happened they would give me pain all the same, those forgotten thorns, and I thought that what had made me so stupid, or lonely, I didn't know which, was perhaps the fact that I had a good memory but not for thorns, I never knew where they were, and I thought it would be a good idea to take my heart out of my body and into my hands and examine it closely and make a map of all the thorns on a piece of paper, so that I could always have it in front of my eyes and see where I was gong, because so far I only knew that in my dealings with my own people I got cramps in my stomach, and in my dealings with the upper classes I got thorns in my heart, which was all silly, I mean, to *think* that way was, but there was so much hatred in her eyes when she turned her head towards me and said what she said, the nurse, I mean, though later on I told myself: "Look here, wasn't the bitch by any chance so angry because you didn't give her a chance to be alone with Sir Francis, and not because you didn't leave him alone with Lady Celia?" And I

249

didn't know whether it was true or not, anyway in the evening of the day Lady Celia was burnt to ashes, Sir Francis had a long talk with Mr de Marney in Mr de Marney's study, and the next morning I went to an employment agency to put my name down, and it wasn't as simple as I had thought it would be, because a hairdresser I had been I didn't even remember when, and a waiter I had ceased to be some years before, and what I had been doing during those years was difficult to tell them, and you can't *not* tell them because if you don't tell them they think you have spent that time in prison, so it was difficult, especially as I didn't know exactly what kind of work I was looking for, so I gave Sir Francis's name as my employer, but what I was really worrying about that morning was that he would go crazy, I just thought he might go on with his newspaper monkey business, and I waited till four o'clock, but he seemed all right, he didn't say a word that might remind one of those tea-time hours set aside for lies, and the only change in him that I thought I noticed in the days that followed was that he had somehow become more greedy, both about food and money, by which I mean that now when he ate he concentrated on food, and when he talked business he looked as if he were counting threepenny bits, and sometimes I would ask myself where all those threepenny bits were coming from, I meant: where all those small arms were being sent to, because invalid chairs were not for export, at least I didn't think so, and I could of course have asked him to give me a job in TRICycle, but that was exactly what I didn't want to do, I mean, I neither wanted to ask him nor to get it, and then one day we took a taxi and went to see his lawyer, and I carried his attaché case from the taxi to the lawyer's room, which was on the first floor, and so I had the attaché case in my hands for some three minutes, or five, no more, and Sir Francis was with me all that time, except for one minute, because first we went together from the taxi straight into the house, but his bladder for the last few months had not been too good, so when we were on the first floor he went to the lavatory for a moment, and I don't think he was there longer than one minute, because what was wrong with his bladder was that he had the feeling every half hour, not that he had to, so I was alone with the pigskin attaché case for no longer than a minute, in the hall of the first floor, and the attaché case had two locks and three leather straps clasped and fastened, and then Sir Francis was back and we went in to the lawyer's room, and Sir Francis took the attaché case from me and sat in the armchair on the other side of the lawyer's desk, and I sat ten yards away in the corner at a round table and I started to read some American magazines piled up there on my table, and I neither looked nor listened, but as I was in the room I was just aware that Sir Francis had taken a paper from his attaché case and handed it to the lawyer, and the lawyer asked him to sign it, and there had to be somebody to witness his signature, so I expected they would ask me, as I had done it before on many occasions for Sir Francis, but they didn't, and two girl typists came from the other room and they must have signed it, and it was all right with me, as I neither knew nor cared what it was all about, I was reading something about Charlie Chaplin in a magazine, an old copy, something about his first talkie which he didn't want to do for some years, and then I heard Sir Francis saying: "My sister has swindled me,"

and the lawyer said: "You realise that she is likely to tell their Lordships about how you have spent certain sums of money during the last two years or so?"

Well, that's all I heard, and then we left, our taxi was still waiting for us in the street, and we went to see Sir Francis's son.

"As you know, John," Sir Francis said, "your aunt has swindled me."

"Will you have a drink?" John asked.

251

"The position is," said Sir Francis, "that if I sue her she's likely to ask the court to declare me incapable of managing my affairs."

"We have already talked it over a number of times," said John.

"We have and we haven't," Sir Francis said. "The position is that their Lordships are bound to think one's crazy if one spends a lot of money as one likes. Unless it is on women."

"Quite," said John.

"Well," Sir Francis said, "I'm glad you agree. Because that's where you come in, my boy."

"I?" asked John.

"Yes, you," Sir Francis said. "Let's suppose that I die to-day. And that your aunt also dies today. What happens? You inherit from her what she has swindled from me, and you inherit from me what I have in TRIcycle. Now, if I sue her and win the case, before we die, the sum she swindled you will inherit from me, but as for TRIcycle, it will not amount to much, you know, a few invalid chairs, and that will be all."

"Why?" asked John.

"Because if I sue your aunt," Sir Francis said, "she's bound to mention Lady Celia, and if poor Celia's name appears in the papers, de Marney moves his little finger and TRIcycle is gone. He told me as much himself. Over the brandy the night of the funeral."

"Well," John said, "but can he do it?"

"Of course he can," Sir Francis said.

"How?" John asked.

"How?" Sir Francis repeated. "How? He has in his hairy hand every military attaché in every embassy of every blasted country that doesn't know how to make a bit of iron with a hole in it. That's how."

To which John didn't answer at once, only his eyebrows were moving up and down as if they were rowing his thoughts through some troubled waters, and then they stopped moving, and he said:

"You want me to pay you for not suing your sister, is that what's in your mind?" and when Sir Francis didn't answer, John said: "If you need some money, father, why don't you come straight out and say so? Why do you make up this fantastic story?"

"I do not need money. I have it," Sir Francis cut him short. "And I want that swindled money back, not because I need it but because I like order."

All that talk, well, I don't know, it was new to me, I mean I had never heard Sir Francis talking like that before, and it occurred to me that the old man was gaga, like old men often are, especially about money, and when that thought occurred to me I must have blushed, or I don't know what, and John saw it and he pointed at me with his chin and said coldbloodedly: "I'm sorry, father, but must that man always follow you wherever you go?"

That's what he said, or some words to that effect, and he waited for an answer, coolly, and I got up and moved towards the door, my heart in my stomach, because he was quite right, though it wasn't my fault, and he didn't need to say it the way he did, and I hated his fat fingers and the gold chain on his belly, he was not at all like Sir Francis, nobody would have said he was Sir Francis's son, and when I reached the door Sir Francis was already running after me, and we left the house together, and when we were in the taxi, it was the same taxi all the time, it was the same taxi-man who had taken us to Richmond Park some eight months before, and so when we were in it, I said: "I want to tell you something, Sir Francis."

But he said: "No, please don't, I'm sorry about the way he behaved, I don't know why I call him my son."

And I said: "It wasn't *that* I wanted to tell you. What I wanted to tell you was that I'm looking for a job."

And he said: "Let's have some food now, and we'll talk it over."

And so we went to his block of flats, there was a restaurant on the ground floor, and the food was good but there wasn't much of it and it was very expensive, and Sir Francis said: "Yes, I quite agree, you must think about your future," and he didn't ask any more questions, and after we had had coffee he said: "I shall be delighted if you come to see me whenever you wish to," or words to that effect, and what I had told him was that I was *looking* for a job, not that I'd *got* one, but he took it the way he did, so it became a kind of farewell party, not very gay, not gay at all, I should say, I should say an unexpected farewell, and rather sad, and when he moved towards the lift, I said: "And what about those pigeons, Sir Francis? I'll come with you now and push that oleander tree farther down, as I've been meaning to for the last two years,"

and we took the lift and the liftman landed us on the third floor, it was just opposite Sir Francis's door, and Sir Francis hung up his hat, put aside his walking stick, and then, fully dressed, he lay down on his bed, which wasn't his habit, and I went out on to that balcony that ran all round the building and I pushed the wooden barrel with the oleander tree farther away, some three windows farther, and then I came back, and I can't be sure whether I shut the balcony door behind me or not, but I don't see why I shouldn't have, and Sir Francis took a detective story in a yellow cover from his table and started to read it, and I said: "Goodbye, Sir Francis,"

and he said: "Goodbye, Tom,"

and that's how I left him, lying fully dressed on his bed, the detective story in his hand, and that's how the maid from the restaurant who came in at half past eight with his morning tea found him dead.

* * * HELEN

What was the matter? The matter was that the world neither took me with it nor left me alone. If you see what I mean. A boy goes along the street and there is a pebble on the pavement. What does the boy do? Does he take it with him? Does he leave it alone? No, he kicks it. Then he walks towards it, kicks it again, and keeps kicking it as he walks till the pebble jumps aside and disappears from the path. And that's that. Because a pebble has no business to be in the street. Its place is on the seacoast, where it can be washed smooth by the sea and warmed by the sun, or in the country, where it can be caught by a horse's hoof, but not in the street, whether it is Bell Street or any other street, and this has something to do with the situation I find myself in now, I mean after Sir Francis's death, but how could I possibly tell all that to the police? How could they possibly understand? No, the thing took place ages ago, because, yes, I have already mentioned that it wasn't the custom in our family to go on holidays, and that was true, I mean, in general, though, as I said, ages ago, when I was thirteen or so, I was on board a flagship going to Gallipoli to free 10,000 (or was it 100,000) British Tommies bottled up in Kut-el-Amara by the Turks who joined the Germans, and the policeman didn't know of course that I was the admiral of the fleet and he himself was a pasha of three horse-tails, how could he? He

knew only what he saw, and what he saw in the dim light of
the evening was a dull boy hanging on behind a cart and pulling a face at him; and though it was for the first time in his
thirteen years life that the boy dared imagine himself a hero,
God smote him then and there because of his presumption,
guns went off, "put out the lights!," "Zeppelins about!,"
shrapnel from the guns fell on the cart, the horses bolted,
and the boy, I mean I as I was then, bumped down just at
the very moment when at the nearby street a motor-omnibus
was blown to bits, after which an ambulance carrying a pregnant woman took me to a hospital where they kept me for
more than a fortnight, quite unnecessarily, because there was
nothing much wrong with me, though during the first days it
seemed to be rather to the contrary, very much to the contrary, and they called my mother and told her I would be a
hunchback, either hunchbacked or dead, to which my
mother said: "O Jesus, I will do anything if You will save
him," and she meant it, but, mind you, she didn't say she
would do anything to save me, no, her bargain with the Al-
mighty was of a different nature. He was to save me first and
my mother was to pay Him for it afterwards. And that's how
it was in the end. Because when she came the next time, I
mean a week or so later, and insisted on seeing the old doctor, she said: "How is his spine, doctor?"

and he said: "What about his spine?"

and she said: "Will he be a hunchback?"

and he said: "Good heavens, woman, are you mad? There
is nothing wrong with his spine, there is nothing wrong with
his bones; it was just a concussion, you know, and . . ."

But neither did he finish his sentence nor did she listen to
him any more. Of course, she thought, the whole thing was
the result of her bargain with God. Well now, as for me, I
noticed one day, it was *before* my mother came the second
time but *after* that hunchback alarm, well, they came to my

256

bed, asked me my name again to be quite sure, took all the cards that were there, temperature card, treatment card and what not, and changed the number on them; where there had been a 3 they changed it to an 8, so that instead of some such number as 19,383, I was now number 19,883, which mistake must have caused a lot of confusion, and under the circumstances did amount to something like a little miracle, for my mother, at least, to whom they told nothing about it; on the contrary, when she came next to take me home with her, the young doctor tried to look grave, and I think that even then I saw the comic side of the whole business. Perhaps even more than I do now. "Your boy is quite all right, so far as his injuries from the accident are concerned. But are you aware that there are some spots on his lungs—oh, it's nothing now, they have healed themselves, nevertheless, you know, and besides there is his, well, never mind, I'll write it down on his card, and if I were his parent I wouldn't leave it to chance. You are not very poor, madam?" he asked suddenly, and whatever my father's income my mother obviously had to object.

"What makes you think we are?" she hissed at him.

"Splendid!" he said. "If I were you I would send him to the country for a month. He needs to recuperate. Prophylactically, you know."

"Is it very dangerous?" she asked.

"What?"

"Phophilaccy, the thing you said," she said.

"No," he said, "but I shouldn't send him to a cousin who happens to live in the country, he must go to a proper place for children where he can have injections of arsenic and strychnine . . ."

"Oh no!" my mother protested, "not arsenic, not strychnine!"

He looked at her slightly bewildered, which was very funny, though it doesn't seem so funny to me now, less and

257

less of the things that have really happened seem funny to me now, and he said: "Iron, you know, it will produce more blood in him,"

and he gave my mother a printed card with the address of the place he recommended, and she thought, well, if God had accepted her offer and changed my hunchbackedness into "prophilaccy" for the price of sending me to that place, then sent I must be, and she went not to my father but to my uncle, the greengrocer, and showed him the address of the place, and my uncle said: "Take him there, sister, and ask them to send their bills to me," which was very typical of my uncle who, as I said, could calculate complicated figures in his head as easily as if he were eating raspberries from a plate, but couldn't do two plus two if he saw it written on paper. And there was another thing typical of my uncle which I only found out about by chance, when I was already there, in that place for children, when one day a van came and delivered some boxes of food; cereals and margarine, and some tins, though tins at that time were not so many as they are now, not so popular, I mean; anyway, I knew the boxes had been sent by my uncle because of the labels, because although he started as a greengrocer, he had a grocery as well on the same premises, and he had special labels printed for himself, I mean for his grocery, labels with a drawing of a woman sitting in a hammock, printed in green ink, and these green labels were stuck on to the parcels, so I knew that my uncle had arranged to pay for my board there in kind, instead of in hard cash, which must have been convenient to both sides, anyway, that's what I thought when I saw those parcels with their green labels arriving at that place, which was a very nice place, in the middle of a large garden, which they called a park, which was in the middle of a nice wood. And the place was run by an old doctor and his wife; there was a young doctor there as well, their son, in a smart uniform, but he only came for week-ends, and there were about thirty children, I mean babies and children, and the oldest child was nine, and I was thirteen, so when I heard that, that the oldest child was nine, I decided I wouldn't stay there, and I was just going to tell my mother that I wouldn't stay there and would go back with her when the door opened and Miss Helen came in, and the moment I saw her I decided I would stay there, and the same evening I went for a walk with her into the wood, and I kissed her and she kissed me. And the same the next evening, and they were not childish kisses, they were of a very serious nature, and I am sure there are many grown up people in the world who have never in their lives kissed like that.

She said that she was seventeen, but I said that I was fourteen and I was thirteen, so she might as well have been sixteen, but she was not a child, she was a young woman, and she worked there as a nurse, not a medical nurse but a kind of governess to take care of the younger children, and so day after day I walked around, doing nothing, speaking to nobody, and particularly not to any of the kids, waiting till they went to bed and left her free, and then disappearing with her in the park or in the wood. I don't know what we talked about, I can't recollect a single sentence, and I can't imagine now what it could have been, though I am sure it was neither about her family nor about mine, neither about the past nor about the future, neither about the world around us nor about what was in the inside of ourselves, which, arithmetically speaking, would leave us with only the immediate present, the present that was within the reach of our arms, for the subject of our conversations, but I can't recollect a word of it, nor can I imagine what kind of a word it might have been. Her mother was a postmistress, I only discovered that because one Sunday she came by train to visit Helen, she was very unlike her daughter, she was small, squat, and everything about her was grey, her round hat with a silk ribbon, her tailor-made suit, and her face. Her face was taciturn, sad-

dened, and to me the few hours she came for looked rather
like an investigation than a visit. She cast suspicious glances
at the young doctor, he had beautiful and such very *clean*
white hands, and was there as usual for the week-end with his
parents, but of course she didn't take any notice of me; in her
eyes I was a child and didn't count, and when we at last saw
her to the station, as we were walking along the road through
the wood, she actually warned Helen not to let the young
doctor in his smart uniform come too near her, though even
then she looked as if her real thoughts were very far away,
somewhere perhaps where she had come from, and what I
thought was that in my family nobody had such a grieved
face as hers. But when the train left and we were walking
home, I just don't remember whether Helen said that her
mother had come to collect her (Helen's) wages or whether
she didn't; whether she did or whether it is just my imagination I can't be sure, and it is of no importance, it was a very
hot summer and the nights were beautiful, and nothing else
was of any importance, and one day I went to the nearby
town to a hairdresser and had my hair cut and my hands
manicured; it was the first and last time in my life that I had
my hands manicured, I mean by a professional manicurist,
even later on when I was a barber myself and could have had
it done on the premises, no, that was the first and last time,
and I don't remember whether she noticed it or not, and another day I walked five miles to a place where one could hire
horses, and I hired a horse pretending to the man that riding
was nothing new to me, and I rode back along the road and
through the wood and into the park, and round the flower bed
that was in the middle of the garden in front of the house,
and when I saw that she had noticed me I rode back, I didn't
dismount, it was a very apathetic but very tall grey horse, and
I wasn't sure that I wouldn't have some difficulty in mount-
ing it again properly, so I rode around the flower bed and then
back to the place where I had hired the horse, and the mani-

cure and the horse had swallowed up all my pocket money so I hadn't any left to buy her any flowers or a box of chocolates, not that she expected any, no—the young doctor had tried to give her a tiny wrist-watch, a silver wrist-watch, and she had flung it back at him, and in the evening we went for a walk again, and we lay down on the ground and kissed and pressed ourselves against each other, our hands always on each other's shoulders, but our tongues deep in the other's mouth, and our legs brushing against each other and kicking and jumping as if we were walking on stepping stones across a stream. In the middle of that night I got out of my bed and opened the door. On my left there were three or four little beds in which some of the youngest children were sleeping soundly; on my right there was her bed. I sat on it. And then I slipped under the blankets. I was wearing a nightshirt and so was she. Half asleep, she put her arms round my neck, but then she behaved in a way I couldn't understand, she defended herself, and she was very strong, but at the same time she wouldn't let me go, she would press me towards her with one hand, and push me off her with the other at the same time; it was most inconsistent, most unlike her usual self, and of course I was rather puzzled, especially when she began to shiver as if she were very ill, I thought that perhaps she had the grippe, that's what 'flu was called there in those days, because she was all in flames and breathing so heavily that she sounded as if she were groaning, more and more loudly, in the middle of the night, in that house full of sleeping people and children, and when I tried to embrace her and console her, she pushed me out of her bed, though still holding my head in her hands and pressing it to her throat which was hot and throbbing and sounded so strange and insane that I didn't know what to do, until she calmed down and let me go, and I was glad it ended like that because all the time I was wondering what to do so as not to make her pregnant and I didn't know exactly, and I went back to my room and slept soundly till morning, and I didn't remember anything about it when I woke up, I mean I didn't think about it at all, till after tea, when I found myself alone with her again, in the porch, where she was mending some linen or something, and I said: "Did you mind?"

and she knew what I was referring to, and she said: "No, I was grateful,"

which word sounded embarrassing to me, and I asked: "Then why didn't you let me stay?"

and she said: "That I can't tell you,"

which was something new between us, because so far there had been nothing we couldn't tell each other, not because we were so free or familiar, but because we never talked about things that were not talkable-about between us, and so I said: "Why can't you?"

and she said: "There is something, you know, that only women know, and no man knows about it, because no woman would ever tell him such a thing," but this sounded too far-fetched to me.

"Do you mean to say that in millions and millions of years no woman has ever mentioned it, not even to her doctor?"

"Yes," she said, "even doctors don't know about it."

Well, this I couldn't believe, the young doctor, the son, perhaps—perhaps he didn't know, but the old doctor, the director, his wife would have told him, perhaps in her sleep, but she would, they always looked so confidential, so to speak, when they were together, like a couple of pigeons, and then what about hospitals, and post mortems, no, it couldn't have been possible.

"Do tell me," I asked.

"No, I can't," she said.

"Is it something that all women have?" I asked.

"Yes," she said, "every month," and she blushed, and I blushed, and we didn't pursue the subject, but of course I knew what she was talking about, more or less, though I

262

didn't know and wondered what it had to do with her not letting me stay in her bed, but at that age thoughts come and thoughts go, and in five minutes, or even in one minute, one is already somewhere else, though I must say that since that day our evenings in the wood were much gentler than they had been before, and I never ventured to go to her room again, and we both knew that my time there was coming to its end, which was something quite natural and known from the beginning, and when I left I wrote to her and she wrote to me, though I couldn't possibly tell now what we wrote about. They weren't very long letters and we didn't write them very frequently, once every few months, or even once every six months or more, and she wrote from various addresses, and at times she would disappear without leaving any address at all, which was all right as well, in a sense, and that's how it was that many years later, when I was already a hairdresser and inventing my machine, I didn't have her address at the time but, I don't know why, I made some enquiries at her old address and found her new one, it was a WC2 address, and one day I went there to see her.

If somebody asked me, and I don't necessarily mean a Scotland Yard detective, I mean just what I say, somebody, if somebody asked me if I was in love with her I wouldn't know what to answer, because when I think about it I don't think I know what love is. I mean, love as you see it in films, or in Shakespeare, for instance, like a millionaire being in love with a poor girl, or an employee in love with the millionaire's typist, that kind of thing is, so to speak, beyond my comprehension, I don't think I could feel like the King felt about his brother's wife, and what he felt must have been love, mustn't it?, though so far as Hamlet himself felt about girls, or Charlie Chaplin, for instance, I don't know whether it is called love or not, and if you can't answer that question then I can't answer yours, because, for instance, my feeling towards my wife was what it was, and my feeling towards Helen

263

was what it was, and your calling these feelings love, or not love, is of no interest to me, because it is of no interest to me whether you find something in common between these things I'm talking about and those things in films or in Shakespeare, or not, and I would say that it is as if there were some chemicals hanging all around a person, somehow, and sometimes it happens that the chemicals that are around a person, and the chemicals that are around you, somehow fit, and you, I mean both you and the person, are bound together, in a way, which is not necessarily how things are with people in films, or in Shakespeare, where you always see some other considerations at work, and so there, those other considerations may be the cause of what they call "love"; the King's crown, for instance, or psychology, instead of chemicals, which chemicals are perhaps not chemicals but geometrical solids, one person being one kind of geometrical solid and another person another kind, and the difference may be quite big, but even so it may be that if they happen to be standing in some particular way, one wall of one geometrical solid may happen to fit one wall of the other, even if as a whole they are quite different geometrical solids, and that's how it was with Helen and me, we were two very different geometrical solids, but if turned the right way and pushed on to the right plane, there was one wall here and one wall there that fitted each other, though what the wall was I couldn't say, except that it was there all the time, like your kidneys are in you all the time, whether you think about them or not, whether they hurt you or they don't, and it was a good feeling to feel that there was somewhere in the world a so to speak wall that fitted yours, I don't mean your kidneys, I mean your wall, I mean one wall of the geometrical solid that is you, and so, when the barbers came to my room and smashed my haircutting machine, I made some enquiries and found her address, which, as I said, was in WC2, and one night I went there to see her, and I don't mean that by saying "to see her" I mean I wanted to talk to her, no; and when I said "to see her," I didn't actually mean to see her, I mean visually, either; no, it's difficult to explain, it is very difficult to explain it precisely. Perhaps I went there just to go there, what I mean is that perhaps I went there because I had to go there and not necessarily because I wanted to be there, anyway, it was a very dark and rainy night, and the flat was supposed to be a ground floor flat with its front door opening on to a courtyard, but the yard was in darkness and the windows on the ground floor looked black too, in spite of which I knocked on the door, and, when it opened, the first thing I thought was that the electricity in the flat must have been cut off because the only source of light was an old-fashioned paraffin lamp standing on a table, and the light it gave was yellow and smelly, I mean the light was yellow and the air was smelly, and wet, and standing there, by the side of her own shadow, was a very tall and very thin woman and, though the light looked yellow, everything about her was grey; her face was grey and her tailor-made suit was grey. Unlike the postmistress, I mean Helen's mother, this woman wasn't wearing a hat with a silk ribbon, but her hair too was grey, by which I don't mean it was white, her hair was blond but it looked grey, and when I asked about Helen the woman said: "I am her sister," and she said it in such a way as if what she said was: "I am cross-eyed, sir," or: "I am pockmarked, if you don't mind."

She looked like a school-teacher, and everything she said was half grief and half annoyance. And half . . . or should I say a third? or a fifth? to be precise. A fifth of grief, a fifth of annoyance, a fifth of bitterness, a fifth of suspicion and a fifth of jealousy, but whether they were exactly one fifth I don't know, nor what they were fifths of, nor what the whole was that they were fifths of, you know how to apply your arithmetic to adding up the customer's bill and that's the end of it; nobody has told you, and you don't know, whether it makes sense to apply fractions to things that have no length, no weight, but only duration, like love, for instance—you can give your love to five hundred or a thousand persons, like the loaf of bread Jesus gave to the people He liked, and each will receive your full love; on the other hand, to some other person, you can give only one twelfth of your love, no more, you just can't do it otherwise, and it doesn't mean that you have hidden the remaining eleven twelfths somewhere, no, but perhaps, as I said before, perhaps what you call love has nothing to do with what I am talking about, perhaps for you it is a different kind of sadness from that I have in mind, anyhow, what she said was: "If I were you I wouldn't try to see her,"

and I asked: "Why?"

and she shrugged her shoulders,

and I asked: "When will she come back?"

and she said: "Nobody knows,"

and I asked: "Can I leave a message?"

and she said: "If you like,"

and I asked: "Where is she now?"

and she said: "Not far away, at a corner,"

and I wanted to ask which corner, but somehow felt that would be a tactless question, because I thought about what a wet and chilly night it was, and so I left a message and went, and I walked round the block and through some neighbouring streets, and for a moment I thought well now, if I see her I can pay her and go to bed with her, which was a crazy thought, coming from nowhere, and altogether going to bed wasn't the purpose of my visit, though the thought, well, the thought was certainly there at the back of my mind, but anyway, firstly the thought was only momentary, and secondly she wasn't at any of the corners I turned, and so, though it wasn't Saturday which, when I was in the hairdressing business, used to be the working man's day for getting rid of his surplus glandular secretion so that it wouldn't climb up to his brain and affect it, I picked up a professional in Soho and

afterwards went home to the debris of my haircutting machine and turned on the wireless, put the earphones on, and
they announced what they called the Goldberg variations, a
Jewish name, Goldberg, but it was composed by Bach which
is a German name, and it was played on a harpsichord which
is a kind of piano where the strings are plucked by some sort
of mechanism instead of struck, and if you have ever seen a
dragon-fly through a magnifying glass, as I have, its wings and
its head and its eyes and its alimentary canal, such fine bits of
precision engineering, when you look at them through the
magnifying glass, then you too, listening to those variations,
would think that you were seeing God the Creator Himself
sitting in the skies, a watchmaker's eyepiece in His eye, and
embroidering out of sounds one tiny and complicated bit of a
dragon-fly after another, "That's what the Goldberg variations are," I thought, till I went to sleep and woke up in the
morning shouting: "I don't want to be a slave! I don't want
to be a slave!"

I remember the words exactly because I heard myself
shouting them, and before I woke up I had a dream, and in
that dream there was a house, and in that house on the top
floor there was a harpsichord and a lady was playing it and a
gentleman was sitting beside her and listening, from time to
time nodding his head in appreciation, and on the first floor
there was a kind of roundabout with armchairs in which
some people were sitting and reading newspapers, no, not exactly newspapers, I mean they were magazines, *The Strand
Magazine*, *The Sphere*, and the sort you usually find in a
hairdresser's saloon, but on the ground floor there was a huge
cage with a half-naked Negro, and there was some sort of
machinery so constructed that whatever the Negro did in the
cage, his movement turned the roundabout on the first floor,
it wasn't necessary to tell him to work, whatever he tried to
do *was* work; if he tried to sit down, his pressing the chair
down made the roundabout turn; if he stood up, his stretch-

267

ing his limbs made it turn; his walking made it turn; his fists hitting the iron bars of his cage made the roundabout turn; he couldn't revolt, his revolting would make it turn and turn and turn round and round, and I think it was my appreciation of that horrible situation in which I saw him that made me wake up screaming from that dream which, I think, was an expression of my social consciousness and not of my sexual subconsciousness, though I must say that my social consciousness, likewise my arithmetic, is not based on any solid knowledge that you have when you are properly educated in economics and politics, but rather on my haphazard observations and experiences. This, however, has nothing to do with Helen.

In spite of the years that had passed we had no difficulty in recognising each other; it was about a year or more after my seeing her sister, we just went straight towards each other and kissed each other politely on the cheek, and there we were, sitting in a posh tea-room, and everybody there was looking at her, men and women alike, and some men would have whistled if it had been a less posh place, that tea-room, I mean, and her very presence there made people around somewhat conscious that there was an elegant woman there in the centre of the room, so to speak, because as a matter of fact we were sitting in the corner by the window and not in the centre, and I perhaps wouldn't have noticed how expensively she was dressed, but she pointed it out to me—her lizard skin high-heeled shoes, the same lizard skin belt and handbag, and even a bit of the same skin, or is it leather?, on her hat, and she was obviously built for making love, every inch of her nerves, and every square inch of her skin, and every cubic inch of her body was built for that purpose and, when looking at her, one knew immediately, without thinking, that she could do nothing else, not really, and that nothing else would ever really interest her, and though I said before that I hadn't remembered, nor could imagine, a word of what we used to talk about in that children's nursing home, yet now, suddenly, something has just unwrapped in my memory, and I can see her as she was then in the park, showing me her bare foot and explaining to me how the thin, pencil-thin, she said, Achilles tendon at the back of her foot, above her heel, and her second toe a trifle longer than her big toe, and the powerful muscle curving, like an upside-down beer bottle, upwards towards her knee, made a beautiful leg, and I didn't say anything to the contrary then, because that was exactly what her leg was like, but that was exactly what anatomically speaking my leg was like too, and I couldn't understand why those particular geometrical details should be accepted for what makes a leg beautiful, and I couldn't understand it because, I thought, one couldn't *choose* the leg one has, and therefore what she said could *not* be true, because *why* should beauty depend on something that doesn't depend on you?, something that doesn't depend on you can be no more beautiful or ugly than it can be good or evil, I thought, and to think otherwise was nonsense, I thought, and I now think that what I thought then about girls' legs was the same that I thought later about faces, which fact would show that my idea about faces was older than Sir Francis's, though it is true that Sir Francis wrote a book about it, and wrote it even before the first war, but I hadn't read his book so I couldn't have known about it, and all the same it was a rather sad and strange thing, I mean what happened a bit later, I mean: in connection with faces, which I will tell you in a moment, because there, in that tea-room, she asked me to come and visit her in a place she went to for her summer holidays, and the next Sunday I went there by train, and by boat, because it was on one of the Channel Islands, either Jersey or Guernsey, I don't remember which, and there was a villa in which she had a room and I remember we sat in her room, she sat at her dressing table, which was under the window, and I sat beside her, or rather beside the table, and she was in her dressing gown and brushing her hair in front of the mirror which was a part of the dressing table, and we talked, though what we talked about I don't remember, and there were various combs and brushes and creams on top of the dressing table, and it was an exceptionally hot day, they said it was the hottest day for 48 years or so, a very hot and stuffy day, and the room was so to speak boiling hot because there were no curtains at the windows, and white patches of sun were burning all over the room, and as I sat there beside the dressing table I took one of the tubes from it between my two fingers, and the tube was unscrewed and melting hot, and though I didn't press it, not really, some two inches of the white cream it contained suddenly jerked out on to the top of the dressing table, and at the same moment her face changed into something I'd never seen before, and that something I'd never seen before lasted no longer than a fraction of a second, perhaps not long enough to take a snapshot of it, it just kept like that for a fraction of a second and then returned to what it had always been, but during that fraction of a second I saw something I had never seen before, and as I saw it, everything I had ever felt about her disappeared, dissolved, was no more, it was as if she had suddenly vanished and another woman had taken her place at the dressing table, and I felt ashamed, I thought I was some sort of a lower animal, not only dull, uneducated, and boring, but also unfaithful and unreliable, and as all this took place in me without my wanting it to take place in me, I thought I was something abnormal, because I thought that what was taking place in me was a fact of injustice, I mean a fact of injustice and not an act of injustice, and if a fact of injustice can take place in somebody without him wanting it to, then it is surely something abnormal, and a fact of injustice it was because everybody can feel annoyed, or angry, or even mean, for a fraction of a second as she had, and it shouldn't make so much difference to other people, but that's how it was, she sat there as before but was now some-body completely alien to me, and when a little while later she asked me if I would marry her, I said no, I didn't actually say "no," I thought if I said "no" she would think I was say-ing "no" because she was a kept woman, so I said I was al-ready engaged, and that was how I married my future wife, because when I said I was engaged, I felt I was engaged, and as I felt I was engaged, it followed that I should become en-gaged, and what a fraction of a second of the expression on someone's face can do to a human being cannot be shown in the theatre, no; in the cinema, perhaps, but Sir Francis was not interested in the cinema, the cinema was too vulgar for him, Lady Celia would have nothing to do with film people, unless it would bring her some money; poor Lady Celia, she couldn't have been very happy with her Mr de Marney, and I didn't see her again, I mean I didn't see Helen again until the time of that theatrical disaster; of course she had nothing to do with it, but it was when I saw my wife with Dr Free-body in the dress circle, it was then that I went to see her again, I mean to see Helen again, at that time she lived not very far from the theatre and not very far from Sir Francis, in Cadogan Square, in a rich house, she had a large room there and though it was two o'clock in the afternoon she was in bed, and what I noticed first was that she spoke twice, I mean once and a half, approximately, as fast as she had used to, and she told me everything, I mean many things, about her travels, though I couldn't follow what she was saying, I couldn't follow very accurately because of the speed, and also because of the very many foreign names, of people and of places, which she recited one after the other, inserting some French words or expressions between them, such as "Oh là là, do you not feel the draught, Monsieur?!" which sounded very silly though excitingly exotic to my ear, and she showed me hundreds of snapshots taken in many countries, and there was one among them showing a man on a horse and herself, in a bathing suit, beside him, which photograph was taken, she said, at the Court of Prince Sankishko or something, somewhere in Eastern Poland or somewhere, where she had been with a party, so she said, and the name of the man was Baron Dr R. von Reinacherhof, and when I tried to kiss her she turned her head away, which was all right, I thought, because kissing was her profession, and I came as a friend, so kissing would be out of place between us, but when I was leaving she jumped out of bed, and she wasn't wearing pyjamas, she was wearing a thin, long, transparent night-dress, and she stood in her night-dress at the door, facing me, and she uncovered her left breast, took it in both her hands as if it were a large fruit, and pointing it at my face—strictly speaking, towards my eyes: "Look!" she said, "look at it well," and she forced me to look at it for a long time, which could have been almost one minute or so, repeating again and again: "Look at it, look at it well," and then she let it disappear under the lace and she said: "Now I know that you will never forget me," and that's how it is, and I think that if I were shown five hundred breasts now, I would still recognise hers at once and without hesitation, and I think that what I said about legs and faces applies to breasts too, I mean that their shape is independent of the character of the person, and if it weren't for the painters and sculptors who have glorified for one reason or another one shape of breast and not another, our feelings about them would have been quite different, and so different girls would have become American film stars, which is silly; I mean it is silly that your becoming a star depends on the shape of your breast, or your leg, or your face, and it is silly because if a standard-type star discovers something for you, tells you something you didn't know about the girl she enacts, you find it difficult to apply the truth you have learnt to a real girl who may have different proportions and so, in my opinion, the whole effort of making a film or producing a play is lost, except that it brings you money, which was not the case when Whatshername played Ophelia to a Hamlet who had crooked legs, which cost Sir Francis ten thousand pounds, and more, as poor Lady Celia died before she had had time to pay what was over, but as Sir Francis died too, then what does it matter after all, who else is there in the whole world to think about it at all, except myself who, after all, didn't count, didn't count at all, except for those vital hours, the four vital hours they were so interested in, and how could they possibly understand what I was really doing during those four vital hours if I didn't tell them the story about Helen, which I didn't, because how could I tell them the story about her if I knew they could neither understand it, nor have the patience to listen to it, the police, I mean.

At that time I spent very little on food. Fish and chips, a pint of beer, a sandwich, was all I needed. And as during my association with Sir Francis I had to dress properly and differently on different occasions, I had quite a number of suits and shirts in my wardrobe and they could last me for a long time. The real expense was the rent, which was higher now, because of the bathroom, I mean the bath tub in the kitchen, because as my wife installed the bath tub in the kitchen, even though she paid for it herself, they decided that the value of the flat was now higher and increased the rent, I say *they*, but you don't even know who they are, which is unnatural, so to speak, machine-like, because you live in a house and don't even know whom it belongs to, you pay for the right to live there, and you don't know where your money goes, to a poor chemist's widow, or to a company, or to a whoever he may be who owns houses, it is just none of your business to know, your business is to go every three months to the estate agent round the corner and pay, and if you are hard up he gives you seven days of what he calls "grace," which is the same word some waiters addressed Sir Francis with, though he was not "your grace," he was, well, as if it did matter, to some people it does matter, to Sir Francis and myself it didn't, and as a matter of fact, Bell Street, where I live, does not belong to Paddington, though I think I said it did before. It belongs to Marylebone, though to me it is much more like Paddington Green, which is on the other side of Edgware Road, than like some of the streets in Marylebone, though on the other hand there are other streets in Paddington, somewhere near Bayswater, let's say, which have more in common with some of the streets in Marylebone, somewhere near Regent's Park, let's say, than they have with let's say Harrow Road, which is in Paddington all right, and this makes me think that all this is a matter of perspective, because if you are far away, the difference between Paddington and Marylebone seems to you even less than the difference between Chile and Peru, that's to say if you live on this side of the Ocean; on the other hand, if you are very near, I mean really very near, in Bell Street itself, then the difference disappears too, because then you see that parts of Marylebone and of Peru have more in common with some parts of Paddington and of Chile than with other parts of Marylebone and of Peru, and so it is only from the middle view, I mean a middle class view, that the differences look real, whether they are differences between the boroughs or between countries, and that may be why, when a war or something like a war occurs, they always explain it from that middle class distance, the distance from which you can see the differences between Chile and Peru and between Marylebone and Paddington, and they, I mean the government and the press, have to do so, because neither from the far-away nor from the close-to distance can those things be explained, I mean things like a war, for instance, and so when I heard somebody knocking on my door the next morning, and as a matter of fact it was already noon, and I woke up, I was puzzled to see the estate agency's manager himself coming in, it was puzzling firstly because such a thing as his climbing my staircase in Bell Street personally had never happened before, and secondly because my rent was fully paid, so I just looked at him puzzled when he said: "I'm sorry, but you know what house-surveyors are, I'm sure. Our surveyor is worried that there might be dry rot in the house, and these two gentlemen are here to inspect it. I hope you will give them any facilities they may need," and before I had time to say "It's all right," he had disappeared, all smiles, and two well-built men in blue serge suits that were bulging with muscles came in, produced screwdrivers, or rather, bodkins, out of their pockets, and though they were only two the place all at once seemed to be full of people.

Now, the way I'm made, if I want to say something nasty to you and you in the meantime offer me a cigarette, I just find it impossible to say the nasty thing I intended to, you can offer me a hundred pounds and it will make no difference, but if you offer me a cigarette, that's different, I suppose it is the same as with the red Indians and their peace pipes, and so when at the very moment that I was going to say: "Look, where do you think you are?" one of them offered me a cigarette, I said: "That's very kind of you," and offered him a light, and I'm sure my hand was pretty steady, which, as I see it now, must have been a surprise to him, and he said: "You're not working today?"

and I said: "No," and then I said: "I think I'd better dress, if you don't mind,"

and he said: "That's a very good idea,"

and then I said to the other man: "Look here, you don't think you'll find dry rot in the fireplace, do you?"

and he said: "You never know, you know!" good-humouredly,

and I thought they were two fat cats and I was a mouse, and then one of them looked through the window, and a minute later there were some steps on the staircase and a uniformed cop came in, and now I felt there were three fat cats in the room and I was the mouse, and he said they wanted me at the police station to help them.

"What about?" I asked, but he said he didn't know.

"Wait a moment," I said, "till these two gentlemen go."

"Don't worry about us," they said, "we'll leave the key with the estate agent."

"They're all right, you can leave them here," the policeman said, and added: "Hurry up,"

and though nobody lifted a little finger, there were forces around me that pushed me out of the room, and I wondered how it was, if none of them had lifted a little finger then it shouldn't have mattered how heavily built they were, and nevertheless it did matter; if they had been lightweight chicks I could have imagined myself sitting or standing there and saying: "Clear out," and going to the station on my own conditions, but as they were heavily built, bulging with muscles, it was just unthinkable, and so, without being touched by their little fingers, I was pushed, so to speak, invisibly downstairs, to the car, and driven to the police station.

"You must be thirsty," the man said, moving a tray with a glass and a decanter across the table towards me.

I didn't feel thirsty, not really, but to oblige him I picked up the decanter with my right hand, poured some water into the glass, then I took the glass in my left hand, drank some water and replaced the glass on the tray. Immediately after I had done so a young man who was standing in the corner walked up to the table quickly, took the tray and disappeared with it through the door on the right.

"I understand you didn't go to work today," the man behind the table said.

"No," I said.

"Why not?"

"Because I've given up my job."

"When?"

"Last night. Why?"

"Never mind why. Where did you work?"

"I worked for Sir Francis Pewter-Smith."

"As what?"

"That's difficult to say."

"Why should it be difficult?"

"Well, Sir Francis called me his secretary."

"Do you know shorthand?"

"No."

"Can you type?"

"Not really."

"What kind of secretary were you, then?"

"Sir Francis called me his revolutionary secretary. But that was a joke."

"A revolutionary secretary?"

"As a joke, I said," I said.

"Have you ever been abroad?"

"No," I said.

"Are you quite sure you've never been abroad?"

"Quite," I said, and felt not at all at my ease.

"Haven't you ever been to Minorca?"

"Oh," I said. "Yes. And no. I've been to Majorca. Not to Minorca."

"You said you'd never been abroad."

"Yes," I said, "I don't know why, but I completely forgot."

"Have you ever been to Lisbon?"

"No."

"To Morocco?"

"No."

"To Cairo?"

"I told you, I've never been abroad."

"But you were in Majorca, weren't you?"

"Well, I forgot."

"You might have forgotten that you were in Kuala Lumpur."

"Well I haven't and I wasn't."

"Do you know any foreigners?"

"No, not really."

"I mean, either foreigners who live in this country, or British subjects who live abroad."

"No."

"Where did you work before you were engaged by Sir Francis?"

"In a restaurant."

"Is that where you met Sir Francis?"

"No."

"What restaurant was it?"

"A Chinese restaurant in Soho."

"You mean a restaurant run by Chinamen?"

"Yes."

"Aren't Chinamen foreigners?"

"I suppose they are."

"And didn't you say you don't know any foreigners?"

"I suppose I did."

"Look here, we're asking you to help us . . ."

"Why?"

"I'll tell you why, but try to answer the questions correctly, please, to the best of your knowledge."

"That's what I am doing," I said.

"All right then. Let me see. Where did you say you met Sir Francis first?"

"Some years ago. To be exact . . ."

"I am asking *where* you met him first?"

"Oh," I said. "In a very posh place, a kind of club called *Ninetynine*."

"Were you working there?"

"No."

278

"You don't mean to say you belonged to it?"

"No, Sir Francis took me there, and it was the first and last time that I saw it."

"Didn't you say that it was there you met Sir Francis for the *first* time? How could he take you there before you had met him?"

"Well, I met in the street and he took me there."

"So you met him first in the street, and not in the club."

"Well, it was almost the same. We met in the street and he took me to the club."

"Why? How did you pick him up?"

"I didn't pick him up. It was he who approached me."

"Was it?"

"Yes."

"Why?"

"Because of what he overheard of what I was saying to my brother on top of the bus."

"You mean Sir Francis was on top of a bus with you?"

"Yes, sitting in front of us."

"So you met him first on top of a bus, and not in the street or in the club."

"Well in a way, yes."

"In a way, yes?"

"Yes."

"Who is your brother?"

"A sailor."

"Do you know the name of the ship he was serving on at the time?"

"No."

"Are you a homosexual?"

"Certainly not."

"Do you possess any small arms? Pistols, for instance?"

"No, I don't."

"Any spare parts? Any blueprints?"

"No, why should I?"

"Well, you were called Sir Francis's revolutionary secretary, were you not?"

"I told you, it was a joke. And it concerned the theatre."

"The theatre?"

"Yes."

"Did you know a man called Douglas McCoulough?"

"Yes," I said, "he is a theatrical producer. He was to have produced *Hamlet* for Sir Francis, but Sir Francis finally decided against him."

"Is *he* a homosexual?" he asked. He had to repeat his question twice. I suddenly recollected what Douglas had said when he received his last pay check from "Honey."

"How can I know?" I said at last.

"Was Sir Francis a homosexual?"

"Nonsense," I said. And then I said: "Why did you say *was*? Has anything happened to Sir Francis?"

"Are you an actor?" he asked.

"Of course not," I said. "But what's going on? You must tell me."

"Haven't you read the newspapers?" he asked.

"I haven't had time to buy one," I said.

"There is one sticking out of your pocket," he said, "take it out and read it."

I looked at my pocket and, as he said, there was a newspaper sticking out of it, though how it came to be there I had not the slightest idea. I took it out, and it was the first edition of an evening paper, I mean a paper that is called an evening paper, though its first edition appears before noon, and there it was, on the front page: "Death of a Knight," the chambermaid came in with his early morning tea and screamed. He was fully dressed on his bed, and it was his death-bed.

I put the paper on the table, and looked at him, not knowing how to begin.

280

"Well, you may go now," he said, to my surprise, but when I had already reached the door, he stopped me: "Wait a minute," he said, "would you mind telling me what you were doing last night, between ten p.m. and two a.m. approximately?"

I was quite sure that as he asked me that question he was making up his mind which method of investigation to employ: to bully me, or to boil me soft, and, well, I knew that on the whole the difference was not of much importance, I mean, not of any very great importance, and, after all, except for one or two things, nothing is of very great importance, just as nothing at all, I mean nothing, without any exceptions, is of no importance at all, and if I preferred to be dealt with softly it wasn't because I thought there was any real difference between one way and another, but because my mind was slow, and if your mind is slow and you're being bullied into talking, it is as if you were playing football on the slope of a hill against a team that is spread out higher up; not that it was so important, no, but it is tiring and somehow strikes one as being unfair, even if not important, so I felt grateful when I saw that he had chosen the soft way, even if I knew that my feeling grateful was to his advantage, but I think he too preferred to play it softly, which I think, wouldn't be the case today, because things about the police have changed very much, I think that today they would prefer to bully you, even where it is not to their advantage, because today they don't respect themselves as they used to in those days; in those days, yes, a London policeman had self-respect, and as he had self-respect he didn't have to feel so anxious about whether you respected him or not, and as he didn't seem so anxious about it you respected him still more, and as he saw you respected him, he felt his self-respect was real, and so he didn't feel any special need to bully you, and I think that that is not so today, I think that today he respects himself less, and as he respects himself less he wants you to respect him more,

and to be more respected he insists on there being two different laws, one law for you, and another law for him, which
means that if you are killed your killer can escape the rope,
but if he, the policeman, is killed, *his* killer is bound to
hang, which is silly because dealing with killers is *his* profession and not yours, and accidents among his profession
are not more frequent than among other professions, such
as firemen, for instance, or miners, and neither firemen nor
miners ask for a special law for themselves, and they, I mean
policemen, do, and the more they ask for that special treatment, the less you respect them, and the less you respect
them the more they feel the need to bully you, which is all, I
think, the result of architecture, I mean, of the way houses
are built, because if you think about the past, you will find
that houses were built either in caves, or on the ground, or on
pillars; when you wanted a shelter from mammoths, or, let
me say, bombs, you hid in a cave, or in a tube station; when
you needed a shelter from single animals of the same size as
you, or a shelter from your own neighbour, you built four
walls on the ground around you; but when you wanted to
keep a crowd at a distance, I mean a mass, whether a mass of
smaller beasts, or of sand, or of water, you knew a cave was
no good because the mass of whatever it was would flood it,
and you knew that four walls on the ground were no good
because the mass would wash them away, you knew that
whenever it was a question of a mass you could not defend
yourself by defending yourself, you could only defend yourself by avoiding it, the mass, I mean, you had to build your
house high up on stakes and let the mass go by harmlessly under the floor; and, to my mind, that is precisely what some
years ago the architects, or the chemist's widow, or whoever it
is who gives the architects their orders, forgot to see; horses
died out, a stinking mass of motor cars flooded the streets,
but the architects didn't take any notice of it and went on
building their four walls on the ground instead of going back

to the old tradition of building houses on stakes, I mean reinforced-concrete pillars, and letting the wild animals, or a muddy river, or a rolling mass of motor cars pass underneath, and the result of it today is that motor cars have to squeeze into narrow streams running between houses, and it is the police who do all the squeezing, and so all along those lines where those squeezed streams are creeping, the country becomes a kind of police-state, and when a man has got used to being a policeman-in-a-police-state when he is standing on the crown of the road, he will retain something of it when he actually steps off the carriage-way and on to the footpath, and one just can't help it, neither he nor you nor I can help it, he starts by bullying drivers, then he bullies pedestrians, and then he ends up by bullying people sitting on their buttocks on benches in the police station, and that is why I said that today he would prefer to bully me because of faulty architecture, but at the time I'm talking about, he wouldn't have, unless it were necessary, and so I said: "I was walking,"

and he asked: "Where?"

and I said: "Here and there,"

and he asked whether anybody had seen me,

and I said I didn't know,

and then the man who had taken the decanter and the glass came back again and put a piece of paper in front of the man behind the table, and the man behind the table looked at the paper and said: "Why did you go back to Sir Francis's apartment?"

and I said: "I didn't go back,"

and he said: "Yes, you did. And we know it," and he produced a sheet of paper, not the one that was now in front of him, another one which he took out of a folder, and he passed it to me and asked: "Do you know any of these people?"

Six names were typed on the list, all unknown to me, but beside one of them, a Baron Dr R. von Reinacherhof, there was Helen's name pencilled in brackets (which surprised me, as I had thought that Helen still lived in that rich house at Cadogan Square). I was glad it was written in pencil because that fact somewhat excused me from taking it into consideration.

"I don't," I said,

in answer to which he nodded his head sadly.

"We already know," he said, "that you forget things easily. I will therefore try and help you. These are the names of the people whose flats open on to the same balcony as Sir Francis's. Last night, did you go through any of these apartments, with or without the consent of the owner, on to the balcony?"

"No," I said. "Why should I?" I said, and what I was thinking was that Helen must have been a few doors from Sir Francis when I was making a fool of myself walking round Cadogan Square, where I had thought she lived still,—and who the hell was Baron von Reinacherhof anyway, the name sounded familiar but who was he, a gamekeeper? I didn't know why I thought about a gamekeeper, but: "Anyway," I said, "if I had wanted to go on to the balcony I could have gone straight from Sir Francis's bedroom."

"Not after you had left it by the front door," he said.

"How do you know I went on to the balcony *after* I left him?" I asked,

and he played fair: "Did you go there before?" he asked,

"Yes," I said, and I told him about the oleander tree and the pigeons, and when I had more or less finished, a uniformed man, who had been sitting all the time silently in the corner, said to the man behind the table, not to me:

"With your permission, sir," he said, "oleander trees don't grow in this country."

"Of course they do," I said. "There is one growing in a wooden tub on Sir Francis's balcony, isn't there?"

"It is quite impossible to grow them here outside green-houses, sir," he said, not taking any notice of me.

"Of course it is possible," I said. "It was Lady Celia's Italian maid who brought a seedling here with her from a convent garden in Udine. She potted it and at first she kept it in the house. And when it was five foot tall she gave it to Sir Francis, I mean Lady Celia gave it to Sir Francis, and he let it stand on the balcony and it was quite happy there, and it is a white oleander, into the bargain."

"White oleanders don't exist, sir," said the policeman.

"Of course they do!" I said.

"No, they don't," he said.

"All right, Anderson, you may go and take a cutting of that oleander," said the man behind the table.

Then he turned to me:

"There is one thing about last night that you must remember," he said.

"Yes?" I said.

"The rain," he said.

"Oh yes," I said. "I was soaked through and went home."

"Where were you when it started to rain?"

"Piccadilly Circus," I said.

"Well," he said, "you can see for yourself. It started to rain at three o'clock exactly. If you left Sir Francis at ten thirty, there are four and a half hours you cannot properly account for; I give you half an hour for walking from Sir Francis's to Piccadilly. What were you doing in the remaining four hours?"

It was the same silly question again. I shrugged my shoulders. How could they understand what I was doing during the four vital hours if I didn't tell them the story about Helen, whose name was written in pencil in their own files, beside the name of Baron Dr Reinach von Reinacherhof, and how could I tell them the story if I knew they couldn't un-

285

derstand it, nor would have the patience to listen to it, though to me the whole thing seemed quite natural, because, if you just think about it, when I left Sir Francis that night as he was, fully dressed on his bed, reading a detective story, and when I climbed down all those stairs, knowing that that was the end of my being employed by, or let's say associated with him, what would you expect me to do? Where do you think I should have gone, the night still being beautiful at that time, and my room in Bell Street cold and empty, and my wife away in the country, or with Dr Freebody, perhaps?, and my children wherever she had left them, and my family, I mean where I come from, strangers, less than acquaint-ances, and the cinemas already playing "God save the King," and the public houses already shouting, "Time, gentlemen, please!," well, not being properly educated, or what they call a gentleman of independent means who can afford to be unusual, and my address being Bell Street, could I possibly have told them that during the four vital night hours I was walking round Cadogan Square *for sentimental reasons?*

"I was walking," I said, and he struck the table with his fist.

And the next thing I remembered was a poster in the shop window across the road, and it was a poster of the same West End theatre where Sir Francis's *Hamlet* was put on, and it said "The Importance of Being Earnest," because, for some reason or other, they didn't arrest me there and then, though I was pretty sure they would, I mean when he struck the table with his fist; perhaps they thought I wouldn't know *how* to bolt, I don't know, anyway, for some reason or other they did let me go, they said "May we have a specimen of your signature," and I said "if you want to," so they put a sheet of paper and a pen in front of me, and I asked "what shall I write?" and one of them said "I suggest you write: 'This is a specimen of my signature'—and write your name as you usually do, and the date, and then sign it," and so I did, and it seemed funny to put your signature twice, so I added quotation marks to the first signature and then the thing looked more logical, and they let me go, though I didn't expect they would, because when he struck the table with his fist, I thought "Well, this means that I'll never go to China," which was just a thought, I mean: of no great importance, and if I were what they could call a gentleman they would have thought it was my upper class composure that accounted for my coolness under such unequable circumstances, but as I was definitely not what they would call an upper class gentleman, they surely thought it was my Bell Street lack of imagination, in which they were right, in a way, because when he struck the table it was as if he had struck my imagination, it got agitated but only a little, not enough to picture the danger I found myself in, and so the only thought I had at the time was "well so what, so I will not go to China, and if I don't go to China, I don't go to China, and that's all one can say about it," and that was all my imagination could produce to scare me, it would go just that far and no farther, and the title of the play, I mean the importance of being earnest, was familiar to my ear because Betty Immergut used to say on many occasions, "Surely, you underestimate the importance of being earnest,"—but I had never seen it written, and only now, when I looked at the poster, I saw that it was really Earnest and not Ernest and that it was by Oscar O'Flahertie Wilde and not by George Bernard Shaw, as I somehow thought it had been, which was no surprise because I had seen one play by one and one by the other and they'd got somehow mixed up in my mind, because of what they had in common, I suppose, which was that both were like some loaves of bread or pastry with some bits of glass in them, and when you tried to bite them, the crumb proved to be just coloured cotton-wool, while the bits of glass had changed into some salt crystals that were badly needed by your bones, and it is so because, I mean my having mixed Oscar O'Flahertie Wilde with George Bernard Shaw is so, because when I see two new things, the first thing I see is what they have in common, what the Goldberg variations have in common with the way a dragon-fly's wing is built, and the barber's mirrors with the way the world is built, but this is what everybody knows and it is of no importance, no importance at all, let them bang the tops of their tables with their fists as much as they wanted to, it was of no importance, no importance whatsoever, and if they had sent two cops to follow me, the two cops must have thought I wanted to see in the mirror if I was being followed or not, because it was Mr Ready's shop, just behind the printer's shop where Queen Victoria's portrait made of 173,000 words (so it said) was displayed, but the shop where the poster of the Importance of being Earnest was hanging was Mr Ready's shop, and there were flat mirrors and curved mirrors, blue mirrors and green mirrors and yellow mirrors in the window, and my faces in the mirrors looked like nothing on earth, and it didn't really matter whether they followed me or not, so far as I was concerned, it was of no importance whatsoever, I didn't even bother to remember all their tricky questions: if I had been guilty maybe I would have, but I wasn't; and I should say now that it must be easier, in a way, if you *are* guilty, because if you *are* guilty you know the mark they are aiming at, and you can defend the pit of your stomach, so to speak, which is not so if you are innocent, because you've been taught since you were a child that whoever is not guilty need not fear, because truth will prevail, and so if you are not guilty you think: the more you say, the sooner it will prevail, I mean the truth, and it is not like that at all, because the whole thing is a sort of battle, a battle between you and the man who's got the technique, the special education in things that gives him the knowledge about striking the top of the table with his fist at the right moment, and so if you are innocent you think let him see the truth, and you lay down your cards, and you think: now he'll see what *you* see and'll let you go, but he doesn't, he goes on having you on toast and pecking your answers to his tricky questions out of you, especially if you happen to be the last person who has seen the victim alive; and have just been dismissed from his service; and cannot account for your movements for the four vital hours following his death, unless you admit that years ago you were in love with a girl whose name is pencilled beside the name of a baron something von something who lives next door to the scene of the crime;—and, anyway, why should they believe you rather than the victim's own sister, and his son, and the lawyer who drew up his will, who would all testify that you had first bewitched the crazy old man and then sponged on him for as long as you could? Yes, why should they believe *you*? Because of your innocent face? But didn't your own theory of faces, and Sir Francis's theory of faces, say that a face may show one thing and the person behind the face may be something else? So what did I want? To betray my own theory by expecting them to believe *me* because my face looked honest, assuming that it did look honest in their eyes? It looked like nothing on earth in Mr Ready's mirrors, and I didn't even know the name of the barrister who had made me think of a mirror that doesn't reverse from left to right, but even if I had known his name and if he had lived in the house I was just passing by, I wouldn't have stopped for a second; I would not have changed my direction because the direction in which I was walking was of no importance, and nothing was anymore more important than no importance. Why, of course! if a mad lorry driver had charged the pavement in Seymour Street, I would have jumped out of his way, I mean my body would have jumped out of his way. Still, I knew that it was of no importance. There would be no beauty in it, no goodness and no truth, if I got run over, but there was no beauty, no goodness, no truth in my walking along Seymour Street either. Just an event of no importance. And why I mention these three words I don't actually even know, beautiful is an ugly word, the sound of it is ugly; good is a bad word, it lets you forget that nothing can be good unless it is good *for* somebody or something; and true is a wrong word, it doesn't tell you what it is about, it is an endless word; and they are like the three mirrors, these three words, the three mirrors which I bought at Mr Ready's shop a long time ago, when my wife left me, and made an experiment with, to find out why mirrors reverse your picture from left to right and don't reverse it upside down, and so I thought now, as I walked along Seymour Street, of doing the same with the three words, I mean the same thing as with the three mirrors, to make it clear what the world looks like when you see its picture in the word "beauty" and in the word "good" and in the word "truth"; and what it looks like when its picture as shown by the word "beauty" is reflected again in the word "good"; and its picture as shown by the word "truth" is reflected again in the word "beauty"; and its picture as shown by the word "goodness" and reflected by the word "beauty" is seen in the word "truth"; and its picture as shown by the word "truth" and reflected by the word "goodness" is seen in the word "beautiful"; but I didn't have my uncle's memory for figures, and Harry Brown, who once helped me to take notes about the three mirrors, wasn't there with his pad and pencil, I was all alone walking along Seymour Street, and if the lorry driver had gone mad now and run me over, it would have been of no importance, of no importance whatsoever. Some other people, yes, perhaps; I mean if he had knocked down some other people walking along Seymour Street, it would not have been the same. Because they were part of a whole. They were all part of a whole. I mean of London. I mean they were making London. They were London. What was in their minds, in their bowels, in their ambitions, shimmered and grew together and was London. London was explainable bit by bit by their single, particular lives. It was not so with me. I was not London but London was me. It lay on my shoulders, it was attached to my feet. I was explainable in the heavy language of the weight of its wholeness. And its rope was there round my neck, as I walked along Seymour Street, on my way to Charing Cross Station, from which each hour a train went to C.

Nobody saw the rope, and it didn't matter that nobody saw it. Neither did I see the neckties, and the strings of pearls, and the fingers and thumbs tightening round their necks. And it was all right and of no importance. A boy on a bicycle crossed the road; a sparrow, frightened, winged away; and a huge round brown ball of horse-manure remained on the pavement. This was something seldom found on the London asphalts. Either a brewery-van, or a mounted policeman, or the Pearly King and Queen of London must have passed through here. And it was the only thing that was a work of Nature. When a horse lifts its tail, and the black roundness turns inside-out and produces a warm round ball that still radiates the smell of the fields and of the sun, and then the pink flesh returns in and the black muscle shuts with precision, the Londoner slams the door of his car and hurries away. But it is of no importance. The sparrow went back to the brown ball, but this was of no importance either. Because at that time everything was of no importance whatsoever, but it was of no importance whatsoever not because nothing was of any importance, but because there must have been somewhere something so important that nothing else was of any importance any more. If you die of hunger, you die because you haven't had enough of what's necessary, and not because you haven't had enough of what's important. But what do you die of, please tell me, when you die because you haven't had enough of what is of importance?

A NOTE ABOUT THE AUTHOR

Stefan Themerson was born in 1910 in Plock on the Vistula ("a small, historic 12th century town in Poland with countless schools, churches and cemeteries"). During the 1914–1918 war he moved with his parents to Russia, where his father ("a doctor, *homme de lettres* and typical 19th century medical idealist") served as a captain in the Tsar's army. After the Revolution, Themerson returned to Poland, and in 1928 he went to Warsaw to study physics, then architecture, but deserted both to devote himself to writing and filmmaking. In 1938 he moved to Paris and on the outbreak of the Second World War volunteered for service in the Polish army in France. After the Polish debacle, he escaped to England, where he re-enlisted in the exiled Polish army there. Until his death in 1988, Themerson made his home in London, where he published a number of philosophical fantasies, composed music, and contributed articles on aesthetics and philosophy to scholarly journals.

LANNAN SELECTIONS

The Lannan Foundation, located in Santa Fe, New Mexico, is a family foundation whose funding focuses on special cultural projects and ideas which promote and protect cultural freedom, diversity, and creativity.

The literary aspect of Lannan's cultural program supports the creation and presentation of exceptional English-language literature and develops a wider audience for poetry, fiction, and nonfiction.

Since 1990, the Lannan Foundation has supported Dalkey Archive Press projects in a variety of ways, including monetary support for authors, audience development programs, and direct funding for the publication of the Press's books.

In the year 2000, the Lannan Selections Series was established to promote both organizations' commitment to the highest expressions of literary creativity. The Foundation supports the publication of this series of books each year, and works closely with the Press to ensure that these books will reach as many readers as possible and achieve a permanent place in literature. Authors whose works have been published as Lannan Selections include Ishmael Reed, Stanley Elkin, Ann Quin, Nicholas Mosley, William Eastlake, and David Antin, among others.

SELECTED DALKEY ARCHIVE PAPERBACKS

PIERRE ALBERT-BIROT, *Grabinoulor*.
YUZ ALESHKOVSKY, *Kangaroo*.
FELIPE ALFAU, *Chromos*.
  Locos.
  Sentimental Songs.
IVAN ÂNGELO, *The Celebration*.
  The Tower of Glass.
ALAN ANSEN, *Contact Highs: Selected Poems 1957-1987*.
DAVID ANTIN, *Talking*.
DJUNA BARNES, *Ladies Almanack*.
  Ryder.
JOHN BARTH, *LETTERS*.
  Sabbatical.
SVETISLAV BASARA, *Chinese Letter*.
ANDREI BITOV, *Pushkin House*.
LOUIS PAUL BOON, *Chapel Road*.
ROGER BOYLAN, *Killoyle*.
IGNÁCIO DE LOYOLA BRANDÃO, *Zero*.
CHRISTINE BROOKE-ROSE, *Amalgamemnon*.
BRIGID BROPHY, *In Transit*.
MEREDITH BROSNAN, *Mr. Dynamite*.
GERALD L. BRUNS,
  Modern Poetry and the Idea of Language.
GABRIELLE BURTON, *Heartbreak Hotel*.
MICHEL BUTOR, *Degrees*.
  Mobile.
  Portrait of the Artist as a Young Ape.
G. CABRERA INFANTE, *Three Trapped Tigers*.
JULIETA CAMPOS, *The Fear of Losing Eurydice*.
ANNE CARSON, *Eros the Bittersweet*.
CAMILO JOSÉ CELA, *The Family of Pascual Duarte*.
  The Hive.
LOUIS-FERDINAND CÉLINE, *Castle to Castle*.
  London Bridge.
  North.
  Rigadoon.
HUGO CHARTERIS, *The Tide Is Right*.
JEROME CHARYN, *The Tar Baby*.
MARC CHOLODENKO, *Mordechai Schamz*.
EMILY HOLMES COLEMAN, *The Shutter of Snow*.
ROBERT COOVER, *A Night at the Movies*.
STANLEY CRAWFORD, *Some Instructions to My Wife*.
ROBERT CREELEY, *Collected Prose*.
RENÉ CREVEL, *Putting My Foot in It*.
RALPH CUSACK, *Cadenza*.
SUSAN DAITCH, *L.C.*
  Storytown.
NIGEL DENNIS, *Cards of Identity*.
PETER DIMOCK,
  A Short Rhetoric for Leaving the Family.
ARIEL DORFMAN, *Konfidenz*.
COLEMAN DOWELL, *The Houses of Children*.
  Island People.
  Too Much Flesh and Jabez.
RIKKI DUCORNET, *The Complete Butcher's Tales*.
  The Fountains of Neptune.
  The Jade Cabinet.
  Phosphor in Dreamland.
  The Stain.
WILLIAM EASTLAKE, *The Bamboo Bed*.
  Castle Keep.
  Lyric of the Circle Heart.
JEAN ECHENOZ, *Chopin's Move*.
STANLEY ELKIN, *A Bad Man*.
  Boswell: A Modern Comedy.
  Criers and Kibitzers, Kibitzers and Criers.
  The Dick Gibson Show.
  The Franchiser.
  George Mills.

  The Living End.
  The MacGuffin.
  The Magic Kingdom.
  Mrs. Ted Bliss.
  The Rabbi of Lud.
  Van Gogh's Room at Arles.
ANNIE ERNAUX, *Cleaned Out*.
LAUREN FAIRBANKS, *Muzzle Thyself*.
  Sister Carrie.
LESLIE A. FIEDLER,
  Love and Death in the American Novel.
FORD MADOX FORD, *The March of Literature*.
CARLOS FUENTES, *Terra Nostra*.
  Where the Air Is Clear.
JANICE GALLOWAY, *Foreign Parts*.
  The Trick Is to Keep Breathing.
WILLIAM H. GASS, *The Tunnel*.
  Willie Masters' Lonesome Wife.
ETIENNE GILSON, *The Arts of the Beautiful*.
  Forms and Substances in the Arts.
C. S. GISCOMBE, *Giscome Road*.
  Here.
DOUGLAS GLOVER, *Bad News of the Heart*.
KAREN ELIZABETH GORDON, *The Red Shoes*.
GEORGI GOSPODINOV, *Natural Novel*.
PATRICK GRAINVILLE, *The Cave of Heaven*.
HENRY GREEN, *Blindness*.
  Concluding.
  Doting.
  Nothing.
JIŘÍ GRUŠA, *The Questionnaire*.
JOHN HAWKES, *Whistlejacket*.
AIDAN HIGGINS, *A Bestiary*.
  Flotsam and Jetsam.
  Langrishe, Go Down.
ALDOUS HUXLEY, *Antic Hay*.
  Crome Yellow.
  Point Counter Point.
  Those Barren Leaves.
  Time Must Have a Stop.
MIKHAIL IOSSEL AND JEFF PARKER, EDS., *Amerika: Contemporary Russians View the United States*.
GERT JONKE, *Geometric Regional Novel*.
JACQUES JOUET, *Mountain R.*
HUGH KENNER, *Flaubert, Joyce and Beckett: The Stoic Comedians*.
DANILO KIŠ, *Garden, Ashes*.
  A Tomb for Boris Davidovich.
TADEUSZ KONWICKI, *A Minor Apocalypse*.
  The Polish Complex.
ELAINE KRAF, *The Princess of 72nd Street*.
JIM KRUSOE, *Iceland*.
EWA KURYLUK, *Century 21*.
VIOLETTE LEDUC, *La Bâtarde*.
DEBORAH LEVY, *Billy and Girl*.
  Pillow Talk in Europe and Other Places.
JOSÉ LEZAMA LIMA, *Paradiso*.
OSMAN LINS, *Avalovara*.
  The Queen of the Prisons of Greece.
ALF MAC LOCHLAINN, *The Corpus in the Library*.
  Out of Focus.
RON LOEWINSOHN, *Magnetic Field(s)*.
D. KEITH MANO, *Take Five*.
BEN MARCUS, *The Age of Wire and String*.
WALLACE MARKFIELD, *Teitlebaum's Window*.
  To an Early Grave.
DAVID MARKSON, *Reader's Block*.
  Springer's Progress.
  Wittgenstein's Mistress.

FOR A FULL LIST OF PUBLICATIONS, VISIT:
www.dalkeyarchive.com

SELECTED DALKEY ARCHIVE PAPERBACKS

FOR A FULL LIST OF PUBLICATIONS, VISIT:
www.dalkeyarchive.com